"Cut one card—  my gold against ̶̶

Gulden flung the ch

"No, damn you! No!" cried Kells in a fury.

In the corner beautiful Joan Randle cowered in fear and shame.

Suddenly, with a motion of his hand, Kells signified agreement.

"Don't," whispered Joan.

"Cut!" cried Gulden.

Kells's shaking hand crept toward the card. Then swiftly he held it high for all to see. It was the king of hearts. "Beat that!" he snarled.

THE BORDER LEGION
was originally published by
Harper and Row, Publishers, Inc.

Books by Zane Grey

Published by POCKET BOOKS

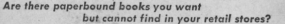

THE
BORDER
LEGION

Zane Grey

PUBLISHED BY POCKET BOOKS · NEW YORK

THE BORDER LEGION

Harper & Row edition published 1916

POCKET BOOK edition published March, 1957

12th printing.....................October, 1975

L

This POCKET BOOK edition includes every word contained in the original, higher-priced edition. It is printed from brand-new plates made from completely reset, clear, easy-to-read type. POCKET BOOK editions are published by POCKET BOOKS, a division of Simon & Schuster, Inc., 630 Fifth Avenue, New York, N.Y. 10020. Trademarks registered in the United States and other countries.

THE
BORDER
LEGION

1

◈

JOAN RANDLE reined in her horse on the crest of the cedar ridge, and with remorse and dread beginning to knock at her heart she gazed before her at the wild and looming mountain range.

"Jim wasn't fooling me," she said. "He meant it. He's going straight for the border. . . . Oh, why did I taunt him!"

It was indeed a wild place, that southern border of Idaho, and that year was to see the ushering in of the wildest time probably ever known in the West. The rush for gold had peopled California with a horde of lawless men of every kind and class. And the vigilantes and then the rich strikes in Idaho had caused a reflux of that dark tide of humanity. Strange tales of blood and gold drifted into the camps, and prospectors and hunters met with many unknown men.

Joan had quarreled with Jim Cleve, and she was bitterly regretting it. Joan was twenty years old, tall, strong, dark. She had been born in Missouri, where her father had been well-to-do and prominent, until, like many another man of his day, he had impeded the passage of a bullet. Then Joan had become the protégée of an uncle who had responded to the call of gold; and the latter part of her life had been spent in the wilds.

She had followed Jim's trail for miles out toward the range. And now she dismounted to see if his tracks were as fresh as she had believed. He had left the little village camp about sunrise. Someone had seen him riding away and had told Joan. Then he had tarried on the way, for it was now midday. Joan pondered. She had become used to his idle threats and disgusted with his vacillations. That had been the trouble—Jim was amiable, lovable, but since meeting Joan he had not exhibited any strength of character. Joan stood beside her horse and looked away toward the dark mountains. She was daring, resourceful, used to horses and trails and taking care of herself; and she did not need anyone to tell her that she had gone far enough. It had been her hope to come up with Jim. Always he had been repentant. But this time was different. She recalled his lean, pale face—so pale that freckles she did not know he had showed through—and his eyes, usually so soft and mild, had glinted like steel. Yes, it had been a bitter, reckless face. What had she said to him? She tried to recall it.

The night before at twilight Joan had waited for him. She had given him precedence over the few other young men of the village, a fact she resentfully believed he did not appreciate. Jim was unsatisfactory in every way except in the way he cared for her. And that also—for he cared too much.

When Joan thought how Jim loved her, all the details of that night became vivid. She sat alone under the sprucetrees near the cabin. The shadows thickened, and then lightened under a rising moon. She heard the low hum of insects, a distant laugh of some woman of the village, and the murmur of the brook. Jim was later than usual. Very likely, as her uncle had hinted, Jim had tarried at the saloon that had lately disrupted the peace of the village. The village was growing, and Joan did not like the change. There were too many strangers, rough, loud-voiced, drinking men. Once it had been a pleasure to go to the village store; now it was an ordeal. Somehow Jim had seemed to be unfavorably influenced by these new conditions. Still, he had never amounted to much. Her resentment, or some feeling she had, was reaching a climax. She got up from her seat. She would not wait any longer for him, and when she did see him it would be to tell him a few blunt facts.

Just then there was a slight rustle behind her. Before she could turn someone seized her in powerful arms. She was bent backward in a bearish embrace, so that she could neither struggle nor cry out. A dark face loomed over hers—came closer. Swift kisses closed her eyes, burned her cheeks, and ended passionately on her lips. They had some strange power over her. Then she was released.

Joan staggered back, frightened, outraged. She was so dazed she did not recognize the man, if indeed she knew him. But a laugh betrayed him. It was Jim.

"You thought I had no nerve," he said. "What do you think of that?"

Suddenly Joan was blindly furious. She could have killed him. She had never given him any right, never made him any promise, never let him believe she cared. And he had dared—! The hot blood boiled in her cheeks. She was furious with him, but intolerably so with herself, because somehow those kisses she had resented gave her unknown pain and shame. They had sent a shock through all her being. She thought she hated him.

"You—you—" she broke out. "Jim Cleve, that ends you with me!"

"Reckon I never had a beginning with you," he replied, bitterly. "It was worth a good deal . . . I'm not sorry. . . .By Heaven—I've—kissed you!"

3

He breathed heavily. She could see how pale he had grown in the shadowy moonlight. She sensed a difference in him—a cool, reckless defiance.

"You'll be sorry," she said. "I'll have nothing to do with you any more."

"All right. But I'm not, and I won't be sorry."

She wondered whether he had fallen under the influence of drink. Jim had never cared for liquor, which virtue was about the only one he possessed. Remembering his kisses, she knew he had not been drinking. There was a strangeness about him, though, that she could not fathom. Had he guessed his kisses would have that power? If he dared again—! She trembled, and it was not only rage. But she would teach him a lesson.

"Joan, I kissed you because I can't be a hangdog any longer," he said. "I love you and I'm no good without you. You must care a little for me. Let's marry . . . I'll—"

"Never!" she replied, like flint. "You're no good at all."

"But I am," he protested, with passion. "I used to do things. But since—since I've met you I've lost my nerve. I'm crazy for you. You let the other men run after you. Some of them aren't fit to—to— Oh, I'm sick all the time! Now it's longing and then it's jealousy. Give me a chance, Joan."

"Why?" she queried, coldly. "Why should I? You're shiftless. You won't work. When you do find a little gold you squander it. You have nothing but a gun. You can't do anything but shoot."

"Maybe that'll come in handy," he said, lightly.

"Jim Cleve, you haven't it in you even to be *bad*," she went on, stingingly.

At that he made a violent gesture. Then he loomed over her. "Joan Randle, do you mean that?" he asked.

"I surely do," she responded. At last she had struck fire from him. The fact was interesting. It lessened her anger.

"Then I'm so low, so worthless, so spineless that I can't even be bad?"

"Yes, you are."

"That's what you think of me—after I've ruined myself for love of you?"

4

She laughed tauntingly. How strange and hot a glee she felt in hurting him!

"By God, I'll show you!" he cried, hoarsely.

"What will you do, Jim?" she asked, mockingly.

"I'll shake this camp. I'll rustle for the border. I'll get in with Kells and Gulden. . . . You'll hear of me, Joan Randle!"

These were names of strange, unknown, and wild men of a growing and terrible legion on the border. Out there, somewhere, lived desperados, robbers, road-agents, murderers. More and more rumor had brought tidings of them into the once quiet village. Joan felt a slight cold sinking sensation at her heart. But this was only a magnificent threat of Jim's. He could not do such a thing. She would never let him, even if he could. But after the incomprehensible manner of woman, she did not tell him that.

"Bah! You haven't the nerve!" she retorted, with another mocking laugh.

Haggard and fierce, he glared down at her a moment, and then without another word he strode away. Joan was amazed, and a little sick, a little uncertain: still she did not call him back.

And now at noon of the next day she had tracked him miles toward the mountains. It was a broad trail he had taken, one used by prospectors and hunters. There was no danger of her getting lost. What risk she ran was of meeting some of these border ruffians that had of late been frequent visitors in the village. Presently she mounted again and rode down the ridge. She would go a mile or so farther.

Behind every rock and cedar she expected to find Jim. Surely he had only threatened her. But she had taunted him in a way no man could stand, and if there were any strength of character in him he would show it now. Her remorse and dread increased. After all, he was only a boy—only a couple of years older than she was. Under stress of feeling he might go to any extreme. Had she misjudged him? If she had not, she had at least been brutal. But he had dared to kiss her! Every time she thought of that a tingling, a confusion, a hot shame went over her. And at length Joan marveled to

5

find that out of the affront to her pride, and the quarrel, and the fact of his going and of her following, and especially out of this increasing remorseful dread, there had flourished up a strange and reluctant respect for Jim Cleve.

She climbed another ridge and halted again. This time she saw a horse and rider down in the green. Her heart leaped. It must be Jim returning. After all, then, he had only threatened. She felt relieved and glad, yet vaguely sorry. She had been right in her conviction.

She had not watched long, however, before she saw that this was not the horse Jim usually rode. She took the precaution then to hide behind some bushes, and watched from there. When the horseman approached closer she discerned that instead of Jim it was Harvey Roberts, a man of the village and a good friend of her uncle's. Therefore she rode out of her covert and hailed him. It was a significant thing that at the sound of her voice Roberts started suddenly and reached for his gun. Then he recognized her.

"Hello, Joan!" he exclaimed, turning her way. "Reckon you give me a scare. You ain't alone way out here?"

"Yes. I was trailing Jim when I saw you," she replied. "Thought you were Jim."

"Trailin' Jim! What's up?"

"We quarreled. He swore he was going to the devil. Over on the border! I was mad and told him to go. . . . But I'm sorry now—and have been trying to catch up with him."

"Ahuh! . . . So that's Jim's trail. I sure was wonderin'. Joan, it turns off a few miles back an' takes the trail for the border. I know. I've been in there."

Joan glanced up sharply at Roberts. His scarred and grizzled face seemed grave and he avoided her gaze.

"You don't believe—Jim'll really go?" she asked, hurriedly.

"Reckon I do, Joan," he replied, after a pause. "Jim is just fool enough. He had been gettin' recklessler lately. An', Joan, the times ain't provocatin' a young feller to be good. Jim had a bad fight the other night. He about half killed young Bradley. But I reckon you know."

"I've heard nothing," she replied. "Tell me. Why did they fight?"

6

"Report was that Bradley talked oncomplementary about you."

Joan experienced a sweet, warm rush of blood—another new and strange emotion. She did not like Bradley. He had been persistent and offensive.

"Why didn't Jim tell me?" she queried, half to herself.

"Reckon he wasn't proud of the shape he left Bradley in," replied Roberts, with a laugh. "Come on, Joan, an' make back tracks for home."

Joan was silent a moment while she looked over the undulating green ridges toward the great gray and black walls. Something stirred deep within her. Her father in his youth had been an adventurer. She felt the thrill and the call of her blood. And she had been unjust to a man who loved her.

"I'm going after him," she said.

Roberts did not show any surprise. He looked at the position of the sun. "Reckon we might overtake him an' get home before sundown," he said, laconically, as he turned his horse. "We'll make a short cut across here a few miles, an' strike his trail. Can't miss it."

Then he set off at a brisk trot and Joan fell in behind. She had a busy mind, and it was a sign of her preoccupation that she forgot to thank Roberts. Presently they struck into a valley, a narrow depression between the foothills and the ridges, and here they made faster time. The valley appeared miles long. Toward the middle of it Roberts called out to Joan, and, looking down, she saw they had come up with Jim's trail. Here Roberts put his mount to a canter, and at that gait they trailed Jim out of the valley and up a slope which appeared to be a pass into the mountains. Time flew by for Joan, because she was always peering ahead in the hope and expectation of seeing Jim off in the distance. But she had no glimpse of him. Now and then Roberts would glance around at the westering sun. The afternoon had far advanced. Joan began to worry about home. She had been so sure of coming up with Jim and returning early in the day that she had left no word as to her intentions. Probably by this time somebody was out looking for her.

The country grew rougher, rock-strewn, covered with cedars and patches of pine. Deer crashed out of the thickets and grouse whirred up from under the horses. The warmth of the summer afternoon chilled.

"Reckon we'd better give it up," called Roberts back to her.

"No—no. Go on," replied Joan.

And they urged their horses faster. Finally they reached the summit of the slope. From that height they saw down into a round, shallow valley, which led on, like all the deceptive reaches, to the ranges. There was water down there. It glinted like red ribbon in the sunlight. Not a living thing was in sight. Joan grew more discouraged. It seemed there was scarcely any hope of overtaking Jim that day. His trail led off round to the left and grew difficult to follow. Finally, to make matters worse, Roberts's horse slipped in a rocky wash and lamed himself. He did not want to go on, and, when urged, could hardly walk.

Roberts got off to examine the injury. "Wal, he didn't break his leg," he said, which was his manner of telling how bad the injury was. "Joan, I reckon there'll be some worryin' back home tonight. For your horse can't carry double an' I can't walk."

Joan dismounted. There was water in the wash, and she helped Roberts bathe the sprained and swelling joint. In the interest and sympathy of the moment she forgot her own trouble.

"Reckon we'll have to make camp right here," said Roberts, looking around. "Lucky I've a pack on that saddle. I can make you comfortable. But we'd better be careful about a fire an' not have one after dark."

"There's no help for it," replied Joan. "Tomorrow we'll go on after Jim. He can't be far ahead now." She was glad that it was impossible to return home until the next day.

Roberts took the pack off his horse, and then the saddle. And he was bending over in the act of loosening the cinches of Joan's saddle when suddenly he straightened up with a jerk.

"What's that?"

Joan heard soft, dull thumps on the turf and then the sharp crack of an unshod hoof upon stone. Wheeling, she saw three horsemen. They were just across the wash and coming toward her. One rider pointed in her direction. Silhouetted against the red of the sunset they made dark and sinister figures. Joan glanced apprehensively at Roberts. He was staring with a look of recognition in his eyes. Under his breath he muttered a curse. And although Joan was not certain, she believed that his face had shaded gray.

The three horsemen halted on the rim of the wash. One of them was leading a mule that carried a pack and a deer carcass. Joan had seen many riders apparently just like these, but none had ever so subtly and powerfully affected her.

"Howdy," greeted one of the men.

And then Joan was positive that the face of Roberts had turned ashen gray.

2

◈

"It ain't you—*Kells?*"

Roberts's query was a confirmation of his own recognition. And the other's laugh was an answer, if one were needed.

The three horsemen crossed the wash and again halted, leisurely, as if time was no object. They were all young, under thirty. The two who had not spoken were roughgarbed, coarse-featured, and resembled in general a dozen men

Joan saw every day. Kells was of a different stamp. Until he looked at her he reminded her of someone she had known back in Missouri; after he looked at her she was aware, in a curious, sickening way, that no such person as he had ever before seen her. He was pale, gray-eyed, intelligent, amiable. He appeared to be a man who had been a gentleman. But there was something strange, intangible, immense about him. Was that the effect of his presence or of his name? Kells! It was only a word to Joan. But it carried a nameless and terrible suggestion. During the last year many dark tales had gone from camp to camp in Idaho—some too strange, too horrible for credence—and with every rumor the fame of Kells had grown, and also a fearful certainty of the rapid growth of a legion of evil men out on the border. But no one in the village or from any of the camps ever admitted having seen this Kells. Had fear kept them silent? Joan was amazed that Roberts evidently knew this man.

Kells dismounted and offered his hand. Roberts took it and shook it constrainedly.

"Where did we meet last?" asked Kells.

"Reckon it was out of Fresno," replied Roberts, and it was evident that he tried to hide the effect of a memory.

Then Kells touched his hat to Joan, giving her the fleetest kind of a glance. "Rather off the track aren't you?" he asked Roberts.

"Reckon we are," replied Roberts, and he began to lose some of his restraint. His voice sounded clearer and did not halt. "Been trailin' Miss Randle's favorite hoss. He's lost. An' we got farther 'n we had any idee. Then my hoss went lame. 'Fraid we can't start home to-night."

"Where are you from?"

"Hoadley. Bill Hoadley's town, back thirty miles or so."

"Well, Roberts, if you've no objection we'll camp here with you," continued Kells. "We've got some fresh meat."

With that he addressed a word to his comrades, and they repaired to a cedar-tree near-by, where they began to unsaddle and unpack.

Then Roberts, bending nearer Joan, as if intent on his own pack, began to whisper, hoarsely: "That's Jack Kells, the California road-agent. He's a gun fighter—a hell-bent

11

rattlesnake. When I saw him last he had a rope round his neck an' was bein' led away to be hanged. I heerd afterward he was rescued by pals. Joan, if the idee comes into his head he'll kill me. I don't know what to do. For God's sake think of somethin'! . . . Use your woman's wits! . . . We couldn't be in a wuss fix!"

Joan felt rather unsteady on her feet, so that it was a relief to sit down. She was cold and sick inwardly, almost stunned. Some great peril menaced her. Men like Roberts did not talk that way without cause. She was brave; she was not unused to danger. But this must be a different kind, compared with which all she had experienced was but insignificant. She could not grasp Roberts's intimation. Why should he be killed? They had no gold, no valuables. Even their horses were nothing to inspire robbery. It must be that there was peril to Roberts and to her because she was a girl, caught out in the wilds, easy prey for beasts of evil men. She had heard of such things happening. Still, she could not believe it possible for her. Roberts could protect her. Then this amiable, well-spoken Kells, he was no Western rough—he spoke like an educated man; surely he would not harm her. So her mind revolved round fears, conjectures, possibilities; she could not find her wits. She could not think how to meet the situation, even had she divined what the situation was to be.

While she sat there in the shade of a cedar the men busied themselves with camp duties. None of them appeared to pay any attention to Joan. They talked while they worked, as any other group of campers might have talked, and jested and laughed. Kells made a fire, and carried water, then broke cedar boughs for later camp-fire use; one of the strangers whom they called Bill hobbled the horses; the other unrolled the pack, spread a tarpaulin, and emptied the greasy sacks; Roberts made biscuit dough for the oven.

The sun sank red and a ruddy twilight fell. It soon passed. Darkness had about set in when Roberts came over to Joan, carrying bread, coffee, and venison.

"Here's your supper, Joan," he called, quite loud and cheerily, and then he whispered: "Mebbe it ain't so bad.

They-all seem friendly. But I'm scared, Joan. If you jest wasn't so dam' handsome, or if only he hadn't seen you!"

"Can't we slip off in the dark?" she whispered in return.

"We might try. But it'd be no use if they mean bad. I can't make up my mind yet what's comin' off. It's all right for you to pretend you're bashful. But don't lose your nerve."

Then he returned to the camp-fire. Joan was hungry. She ate and drank what had been given her, and that helped her to realize reality. And although dread abided with her, she grew curious. Almost she imagined she was fascinated by her predicament. She had always been an emotional girl of strong will and self-restraint. She had always longed for she knew not what—perhaps freedom. Certain places had haunted her. She had felt that something should have happened to her there. Yet nothing ever had happened. Certain books had obsessed her, even when a child, and often to her mother's dismay; for these books had been of wild places and life on the sea, adventure, and bloodshed. It had always been said of her that she should have been a boy.

Night settled down black. A pale, narrow cloud, marked by a train of stars, extended across the dense blue sky. The wind moaned in the cedars and roared in the replenished camp-fire. Sparks flew away into the shadows. And on the puffs of smoke that blew toward her came the sweet, pungent odor of burning cedar. Coyotes barked off under the brush, and from away on the ridge drifted the dismal defiance of a wolf.

Camp-life was no new thing to Joan. She had crossed the plains in a wagon-train, that more than once had known the long-drawn yell of hostile Indians. She had prospected and hunted in the mountains with her uncle, weeks at a time. But never before this night had the wildness, the loneliness, been so vivid to her.

Roberts was on his knees, scouring his oven with wet sand. His big, shaggy head nodded in the firelight. He seemed pondering and thick and slow. There was a burden upon him. The man Bill and his companion lay back against stones and conversed low. Kells stood up in the light of the blaze. He had a pipe at which he took long pulls and then sent up clouds of smoke. There was nothing imposing in his

13

build or striking in his face, at that distance; but it took no second look to see here was a man remarkably out of the ordinary. Some kind of power and intensity emanated from him. From time to time he appeared to glance in Joan's direction; still, she could not be sure, for his eyes were but shadows. He had cast aside his coat. He wore a vest open all the way, and a checked soft shirt, with a black tie hanging untidily. A broad belt swung below his hip and in the holster was a heavy gun. That was a strange place to carry a gun, Joan thought. It looked awkward to her. When he walked it might swing round and bump against his leg. And he certainly would have to put it some other place when he rode.

"Say, have you got a blanket for that girl?" asked Kells, removing his pipe from his lips to address Roberts.

"I got saddle-blankets," responded Roberts. "You see, we didn't expect to be caught out."

"I'll let you have one," said Kells, walking away from the fire. "It will be cold." He returned with a blanket, which he threw to Roberts.

"Much obliged," muttered Roberts.

"I'll bunk by the fire," went on the other, and with that he sat down and appeared to become absorbed in thought.

Roberts brought the borrowed blanket and several saddle-blankets over to where Joan was, and laying them down he began to kick and scrape stones and brush aside.

"Pretty rocky place, this here is," he said. "Reckon you'll sleep some, though."

Then he began arranging the blankets into a bed. Presently Joan felt a tug at her riding-skirt. She looked down.

"I'll be right by you," he whispered, with his big hand to his mouth, "an' I ain't a-goin' to sleep none."

Whereupon he returned to the camp-fire. Presently Joan, not because she was tired or sleepy, but because she wanted to act naturally, lay down on the bed and pulled a blanket up over her. There was no more talking among the men. Once she heard the jingle of spurs and the rustle of cedar brush. By and by Roberts came back to her, dragging his saddle, and lay down near her. Joan raised up a little to see Kells motionless and absorbed by the fire. He had a strained and tense position. She sank back softly and looked up at

14

the cold bright stars. What was going to happen to her? Something terrible! The very night shadows, the silence, the presence of strange men, all told her. And a shudder that was a thrill ran over and over her.

She would lie awake. It would be impossible to sleep. And suddenly into her full mind flashed an idea to slip away in the darkness, find her horse, and so escape from any possible menace. This plan occupied her thoughts for a long while. If she had not been used to Western ways she would have tried just that thing. But she rejected it. She was not sure that she could slip away, or find her horse, or elude pursuit, and certainly not sure of her way home. It would be best to stay with Roberts.

When that was settled her mind ceased to race. She grew languid and sleepy. The warmth of the blankets stole over her. She had no idea of sleeping, yet she found sleep more and more difficult to resist. Time that must have been hours passed. The fire died down and then brightened; the shadows darkened and then lightened. Someone now and then got up to throw on wood. The thump of hobbled hoofs sounded out in the darkness. The wind was still and the coyotes were gone. She could no longer open her eyes. They seemed glued shut. And then gradually all sense of the night and the wild, of the drowsy warmth, faded.

When she awoke the air was nipping cold. Her eyes snapped open clear and bright. The tips of the cedars were ruddy in the sunrise. A camp-fire crackled. Blue smoke curled upward. Joan sat up with a rush of memory. Roberts and Kells were bustling round the fire. The man Bill was carrying water. The other fellow had brought in the horses and was taking off the hobbles. No one, apparently, paid any attention to Joan. She got up and smoothed out her tangled hair, which she always wore in a braid down her back when she rode. She had slept, then, and in her boots! That was the first time she had ever done that. When she went down to the brook to bathe her face and wash her hands, the men still, apparently, took no notice of her. She began to hope that Roberts had exaggerated their danger. Her horse was rather skittish and did not care for strange hands. He broke away from the bunch. Joan went after him, even lost sight of camp. Presently, after she caught him, she led him back to camp and tied him up. And then she was so far emboldened as to approach the fire and to greet the men.

"Good morning," she said, brightly.

Kells had his back turned at the moment. He did not move or speak or give any sign he had heard. The man Bill stared boldly at her, but without a word. Roberts returned her greeting, and as she glanced quickly at him, drawn by his voice, he turned away. But she had seen that his face was dark, haggard, worn.

Joan's cheer and hope sustained a sudden and violent check. There was something wrong in this group, and she could not guess what it was. She seemed to have a queer, dragging weight at her limbs. She was glad to move over to a stone and sink down upon it. Roberts brought her breakfast, but he did not speak or look at her. His hands shook. And this frightened Joan. What was going to happen? Roberts went back to the camp-fire. Joan had to force herself to eat. There was one thing of which she was sure—that she would need all the strength and fortitude she could summon.

Joan became aware, presently, that Kells was conversing with Roberts, but too low for her to hear what was said. She saw Roberts make a gesture of fierce protest. About the other man there was an air cool, persuading, dominant. He ceased speaking, as if the incident were closed. Roberts hurried and blundered through his task with his pack and went for his horse. The animal limped slightly, but evidently was not in bad shape. Roberts saddled him, tied on the pack. Then he saddled Joan's horse. That done, he squared around with the front of a man who had to face something he dreaded.

"Come on, Joan. We're ready," he called. His voice was loud, but not natural.

Joan started to cross to him when Kells strode between them. She might not have been there, for all the sign this ominous man gave of her presence. He confronted Roberts in the middle of the camp-circle, and halted, perhaps a rod distant.

"Roberts, get on your horse and clear out," he said.

Roberts dropped his halter and straightened up. It was a

16

bolder action than any he had heretofore given. Perhaps the mask was off now; he was wholly sure of what he had only feared; subterfuge and blindness were in vain; and now he could be a man. Some change worked in his face—a blanching, a setting.

"No, I won't go without the girl," he said.

"But you can't take her!"

Joan vibrated to a sudden start. So this was what was going to happen. Her heart almost stood still. Breathless and quivering, she watched these two men, about whom now all was strangely magnified.

"Reckon I'll go along with you, then," replied Roberts.

"Your company's not wanted."

"Wal, I'll go anyway."

This was only play at words, Joan thought. She divined in Roberts a cold and grim acceptance of something he had expected. And the voice of Kells—what did that convey? Still the man seemed slow, easy, kind, amiable.

"Haven't you got any sense, Roberts?" he asked.

Roberts made no reply to that.

"Go on home. Say nothing or anything—whatever you like," continued Kells. "You did me a favor once over in California. I like to remember favors. Use your head now. Hit the trail."

"Not without her. I'll fight first," declared Roberts, and his hands began to twitch and jerk.

Joan did not miss the wonderful intentness of the pale-gray eyes that watched Roberts—his face, his glance, his hands.

"What good will it do to fight?" asked Kells. He laughed coolly. "That won't help her. . . . You ought to know what you'll get."

"Kells—I'll die before I leave that girl in your clutches," flashed Roberts. "An' I ain't a-goin' to stand here an' argue with you. Let her come—or—"

"You don't strike me as a fool," interrupted Kells. His voice was suave, smooth, persuasive, cool. What strength—what certainty appeared behind it! "It's not my habit to argue with fools. Take the chance I offer you. Hit

17

the trail. Life is precious, man! . . . You've no chance *here*. And what's one girl more or less to you?"

"Kells, I may be a fool, but I'm a man," passionately rejoined Roberts. "Why, you're somethin' inhuman! I knew that out in the gold-fields. But to think you can stand there—an' talk sweet an' pleasant—with no idee of manhood! . . . Let her come now—or—or I'm a-goin' for my gun!"

"Roberts, haven't you a wife—children?"

"Yes, I have," shouted Roberts, huskily. "An' that wife would disown me if I left Joan Randle to you. An' I've got a grown girl. Mebbe some day she might need a man to stand between her an' such as you, Jack Kells!"

All Roberts' pathos and passion had no effect, unless to bring out by contrast the singular and ruthless nature of Jack Kells.

"Will you hit the trail?"

"No!" thundered Roberts.

Until then Joan Randle had been fascinated, held by the swift interchange between her friend and enemy. But now she had a convulsion of fear. She had seen men fight, but never to the death. Roberts crouched like a wolf at bay. There was a madness upon him. He shook like a rippling leaf. Suddenly his shoulder lurched—his arm swung.

Joan wheeled away in horror, shutting her eyes, covering her ears, running blindly. Then upon her muffled hearing burst the boom of a gun.

3

❖

JOAN ran on, stumbling over rocks and brush, with a darkness before her eyes, the terror in her soul. She was out in the cedars when someone grasped her from behind. She felt the hands as the coils of a snake. Then she was ready to faint, but she must not faint. She struggled away, stood free. It was the man Bill who had caught her. He said something that was unintelligible. She reached for the snag of a dead cedar and, leaning there, fought her weakness, that cold

19

black horror which seemed a physical thing in her mind, her blood, her muscles.

When she recovered enough for the thickness to leave her sight she saw Kells coming, leading her horse and his own. At sight of him a strange, swift heat shot through her. Then she was confounded with the thought of Roberts.

"Ro—Roberts?" she faltered.

Kells gave her a piercing glance. "Miss Randle, I had to take the fight out of your friend," he said.

"You—you— Is he—dead?"

"I just crippled his gun arm. If I hadn't he would have hurt somebody. He'll ride back to Hoadley and tell your folks about it. So they'll know you're safe."

"Safe!" she whispered.

"That's what I said, Miss Randle. If you're going to ride out into the border—if it's possible to be safe out there you'll be so with me."

"But I want to go home. Oh, please let me go!"

"I couldn't think of it."

"Then—what will you—do with me?"

Again that gray glance pierced her. His eyes were clear, flawless, like crystal, without coldness, warmth, expression. "I'll get a barrel of gold out of you."

"How?" she asked, wonderingly.

"I'll hold you for ransom. Sooner or later those prospectors over there are going to strike gold. Strike it rich! I know that. I've got to make a living some way."

Kells was tightening the cinch on her saddle while he spoke. His voice, his manner, the amiable smile on his intelligent face, they all appeared to come from sincerity. But for those strange eyes Joan would have wholly believed him. As it was, a half doubt troubled her. She remembered the character Roberts had given this man. Still, she was recovering her nerve. It had been the certainty of disaster to Roberts that had made her weaken. As he was only slightly wounded and free to ride home safely, she had not the horror of his death upon her. Indeed, she was now so immensely uplifted that she faced the situation unflinchingly.

"Bill," called Kells to the man standing there with a grin

on his coarse red face, "you go back and help Halloway pack. Then take my trail."

Bill nodded, and was walking away when Kells called after him: "And say, Bill, don't say anything to Roberts. He's easily riled."

"Haw! Haw! Haw!" laughed Bill.

His harsh laughter somehow rang jarringly in Joan's ears. But she was used to violent men who expressed mirth over mirthless jokes.

"Get up, Miss Randle," said Kells as he mounted. "We've a long ride. You'll need all your strength. So I advise you to come quietly with me and not try to get away. It won't be any use trying."

Joan climbed into her saddle and rode after him. Once she looked back in hope of seeing Roberts, of waving a hand to him. She saw his horse standing saddled, and she saw Bill struggling under a pack, but there was no sign of Roberts. Then more cedars intervened and the camp site was lost to view. When she glanced ahead her first thought was to take in the points of Kells's horse. She had been used to horses all her life. Kells rode a big rangy bay—a horse that appeared to snort speed and endurance. Her pony could never run away from that big brute. Still Joan had the temper to make an attempt to escape, if a favorable way presented.

The morning was rosy, clear, cool; there was a sweet, dry tang in the air; white-tailed deer bounded out of the open spaces; and the gray-domed, glistening mountains, with their bold, black-fringed slopes, overshadowed the close foot-hills.

Joan was a victim to swift vagaries of thought and conflicting emotions. She was riding away with a freebooter, a road-agent, to be held for ransom. The fact was scarcely credible. She could not shake the dread of nameless peril. She tried not to recall Roberts's words, yet they haunted her. If she had not been so handsome, he had said! Joan knew she possessed good looks, but they had never caused her any particular concern. That Kells had let that influence him—as Roberts had imagined—was more than absurd. Kells had scarcely looked at her. It was gold such men wanted. She wondered what her ransom would be, where

21

her uncle would get it, and if there really was a likelihood of that rich strike. Then she remembered her mother, who had died when she was a little girl, and a strange, sweet sadness abided with her. It passed. She saw her uncle—that great, robust, hearty, splendid old man, with his laugh and his kindness, and his love for her, and his everlasting unquenchable belief that soon he would make a rich gold-strike. What a roar and a stampede he would raise at her loss! The village camp might be divided on that score, she thought, because the few young women in that little settlement hated her, and the young men would have more peace without her. Suddenly her thought shifted to Jim Cleve, the cause of her present misfortune. She had forgotten Jim. In the interval somehow he had grown. Sweet to remember how he had fought for her and kept it secret! After all, she had misjudged him. She had hated him because she liked him. Maybe she did more! That gave her a shock. She recalled his kisses and then flamed all over. If she did not hate him she ought to. He had been so useless; he ran after her so; he was the laughing-stock of the village; his actions made her other admirers and friends believe she cared for him, was playing fast-and-loose with him. Still, there was a difference now. He had terribly transgressed. He had frightened her with threats of dire ruin to himself. And because of that she had trailed him, to fall herself upon a hazardous experience. Where was Jim Cleve now? Like a flash then occurred to her the singular possibility. Jim had ridden for the border with the avowed and desperate intention of finding Kells and Gulden and the bad men of that trackless region. He would do what he had sworn he would. And here she was, the cause of it all, a captive of this notorious Kells! She was being led into that wild border country. Somewhere out there Kells and Jim Cleve would meet. Jim would find her in Kells's hands. Then there would be hell, Joan thought. The possibility, the certainty, seemed to strike deep into her, reviving that dread and terror. Yet she thrilled again; a ripple that was not all cold coursed through her. Something had a birth in her then, and the part of it she understood was that she welcomed the adventure with a throbbing heart, yet

22

looked with awe and shame and distrust at this new, strange side of her nature.

And while her mind was thus thronged the morning hours passed swiftly, the miles of foot-hills were climbed and descended. A green gap of cañon, wild and yellow-walled, yawned before her, opening into the mountain.

Kells halted on the grassy bank of a shallow brook. "Get down. We'll noon here and rest the horses," he said to Joan. "I can't say that you're anything but game. We've done perhaps twenty-five miles this morning."

The mouth of this cañon was a wild, green-flowered, beautiful place. There were willows and alders and aspens along the brook. The green bench was like a grassy meadow. Joan caught a glimpse of a brown object, a deer or bear, stealing away through spruce-trees on the slope. She dismounted, aware now that her legs ached and it was comfortable to stretch them. Looking backward across the valley toward the last foot-hill, she saw the other men, with horses and packs, coming. She had a habit of close observation, and she thought that either the men with the packs had now one more horse than she remembered, or else she had not seen the extra one. Her attention shifted then. She watched Kells unsaddle the horses. He was wiry, muscular, quick with his hands. The big, blue-cylindered gun swung in front of him. That gun had a queer kind of attraction for her. The curved black butt made her think of a sharp grip of hand upon it. Kells did not hobble the horses. He slapped his bay on the haunch and drove him down toward the brook. Joan's pony followed. They drank, cracked the stones, climbed the other bank, and began to roll in the grass. Then the other men with the packs trotted up. Joan was glad. She had not thought of it before, but now she felt she would rather not be alone with Kells. She remarked then that there was no extra horse in the bunch. It seemed strange, her thinking that, and she imagined she was not clear-headed.

"Throw the packs, Bill," said Kells.

Another fire was kindled and preparations made toward a noonday meal. Bill and Halloway appeared loquacious, and inclined to steal glances at Joan when Kells could not

23

notice. Halloway whistled a Dixie tune. Then Bill took advantage of the absence of Kells, who went down to the brook, and he began to leer at Joan and make bold eyes at her. Joan appeared not to notice him, and thereafter averted her gaze. The men chuckled.

"She's the proud hussy! But she ain't foolin' me. I've knowed a heap of wimmen." Whereupon Halloway guffawed, and between them, in lower tones, they exchanged mysterious remarks. Kells returned with a bucket of water.

"What's got into you men?" he queried.

Both of them looked around, blusteringily innocent.

"Reckon it's the same that's ailin' you," replied Bill. He showed that among wild, unhampered men how little could inflame and change.

"Boss, it's the onaccustomed company," added Halloway, with a conciliatory smile. "Bill sort of warms up. He jest can't help it. An' seein' what a thunderin' crab he always is, why I'm glad an' welcome."

Kells vouchsafed no reply to this and, turning away, continued his tasks. Joan had a close look at his eyes and again she was startled. They were not like eyes, but just gray spaces, opaque openings, with nothing visible behind, yet with something terrible there.

The preparations for the meal went on, somewhat constrainedly on the part of Bill and Halloway, and presently were ended. Then the men attended to it with appetites born of the open and of action. Joan sat apart from them on the bank of the brook, and after she had appeased her own hunger she rested, leaning back in the shade of an alderbush. A sailing shadow crossed near her, and, looking up, she saw an eagle flying above the ramparts of the cañon. Then she had a drowsy spell, but she succumbed to it only to the extent of closing her eyes. Time dragged on. She would rather have been in the saddle. These men were leisurely, and Kells was provokingly slow. They had nothing to do with time but waste it. She tried to combat the desire for hurry, for action; she could not gain anything by worry. Nevertheless, resignation would not come to her and her hope began to flag. Something portended evil—something hung in the balance.

The snort and tramp of horses roused her, and upon sitting up she saw the men about to pack and saddle again. Kells had spoken to her only twice so far that day. She was grateful for his silence, but could not understand it. He seemed to have a preoccupied air that somehow did not fit the amiableness of his face. He looked gentle, good-natured; he was soft-spoken; he gave an impression of kindness. But Joan began to realize that he was not what he seemed. He had something on his mind. It was not conscience, nor a burden: it might be a projection, a plan, an absorbing scheme, a something that gained food with thought. Joan wondered doubtfully if it were the ransom of gold he expected to get.

Presently, when all was about in readiness for a fresh start, she rose to her feet. Kells's bay was not tractable at the moment. Bill held out Joan's bridle to her and their hands touched. The contact was an accident, but it resulted in Bill's grasping back at her hand. She jerked it away, scarcely comprehending. Then all under the brown of his face she saw creep a dark, ruddy tide. He reached for her then—put his hand on her breast. It was an instinctive animal action. He meant nothing. She divined that he could not help it. She had lived with rough men long enough to know he had no motive—no thought at all. But at the profanation of such a touch she shrank back, uttering a cry.

At her elbow she heard a quick step and a sharp-drawn breath or hiss.

"Aw, Jack!" cried Bill.

Then Kells, in lithe and savage swiftness, came between them. He swung his gun, hitting Bill full in the face. The man fell, limp and heavy, and he lay there, with a bloody gash across his brow. Kells stood over him a moment, slowly lowering the gun. Joan feared he meant to shoot.

"Oh, don't—don't!" she cried. "He—he didn't hurt me."

Kells pushed her back. When he touched her she seemed to feel the shock of an electric current. His face had not changed, but his eyes were terrible. On the background of gray were strange, leaping red flecks.

25

"Take your horse," he ordered. "No. Walk across the brook. There's a trail. Go up the cañon. I'll come presently. Don't run and don't hide. It'll be the worse for you if you do. Hurry!"

Joan obeyed. She flashed past the open-jawed Halloway and, running down to the brook, stepped across from stone to stone. She found the trail and hurriedly followed it. She did not look back. It never occurred to her to hide, to try to get away. She only obeyed, conscious of some force that dominated her. Once she heard loud voices, then the shrill neigh of a horse. The trail swung under the left wall of the cañon and ran along the noisy brook. She thought she heard shots and was startled, but she could not be sure. She stopped to listen. Only the babble of swift water and the sough of wind in the spruces greeted her ears. She went on, beginning to collect her thoughts, to conjecture on the significance of Kells's behavior.

But had that been the spring of his motive? She doubted it—she doubted all about him, save that subtle essence of violence, of ruthless force and intensity, of terrible capacity, which hung round him.

A halloo caused her to stop and turn. Two pack-horses were jogging up the trail. Kells was driving them and leading her pony. Nothing could be seen of the other men. Kells rapidly overhauled her, and she had to get out of the trail to let the pack-animals pass. He threw her bridle to her.

"Get up," he said.

She complied. And then she bravely faced him. "Where are—the other men?"

"We parted company," he replied, curtly.

"Why?" she persisted.

"Well, if you're anxious to know, it was because you were winning their—regard—too much to suit me."

"Winning their regard!" Joan exclaimed, blankly.

Here those gray, piercing eyes went through her, then swiftly shifted. She was quick to divine from that the inference in his words—he suspected her of flirting with those ruffians, perhaps to escape him through them. That had only been his suspicion—groundless after his swift glance at her. Perhaps unconsciousness of his meaning, a simulated innocence and ignorance might serve her with this strange man. She resolved to try it, to use all her woman's intuition and wit and cunning. Here was an educated man who was a criminal—an outcast. Deep within him might be memories of a different life. They might be stirred. Joan decided in that swift instant that, if she could understand him, learn his real intentions toward her, she could cope with him.

"Bill and his pard were thinking too much of—of the ransom I'm after," went on Kells, with a short laugh. "Come on now. Ride close to me."

Joan turned into the trail with his laugh ringing in her ears. Did she only imagine a mockery in it? Was there any reason to believe a word this man said? She appeared as helpless to see through him as she was in her predicament.

They had entered a cañon, such as was typical of that mountain range, and the winding trail which ran beneath the yellow walls was one unused to travel. Joan could not make out any old tracks, except those of deer and cougar. The crashing of wild animals into the chaparral, and the scarcely frightened flight of rabbits and grouse attested to the wildness of the place. They passed an old tumbledown log cabin, once used, no doubt, by prospectors and hunters. Here the trail ended. Yet Kells kept on up the cañon. And for all Joan could tell the walls grew only the higher and the timber heavier and the space wilder.

At a turn, when the second pack-horse, that appeared unused to his task, came fully into Joan's sight, she was struck with his resemblance to some horse with which she was familiar. It was scarcely an impression which she might have received from seeing Kells's horse or Bill's or any one's a few times. Therefore she watched this animal, studying his gait and behavior. It did not take long for her to discover that he was not a pack-horse. He resented that burden. He did not know how to swing it. This made her deeply thoughtful and she watched closer than ever. All at once there dawned on her the fact that the resemblance here was to Roberts's horse. She caught her breath and felt again that cold gnawing of fear within her. Then she closed her eyes the better to remember significant points about Roberts's sorrel—a white left front foot, an old diamond brand, a ragged forelock, and an unusual marking, a light bar across his face. When Joan had recalled these, she felt so certain that she would find them on this pack-horse that she was afraid to open her eyes. She forced herself to look, and it seemed that in one glance she saw three of them. Still she clung to hope. Then the horse, picking his way, partially turning toward her, disclosed the bar across his face.

Joan recognized it. Roberts was not on his way home. Kells had lied. Kells had killed him. How plain and fearful the proof! It verified Roberts's gloomy prophecy. Joan suddenly grew sick and dizzy. She reeled in her saddle. It was only by dint of the last effort of strength and self-control that she kept her seat. She fought the horror as if it were a beast. Hanging over the pommel, with shut eyes, letting her pony find the way, she sustained this shock of discovery and did not let it utterly overwhelm her. And as she conquered the sickening weakness her mind quickened to the changed aspect of her situation. She understood Kells and the appalling nature of her peril. She did not know how she understood him now, but doubt had utterly fled. All was clear, real, grim, present. Like a child she had been deceived, for no reason she could see. That talk of ransom was false. Likewise Kells's assertion that he had parted company with Halloway and Bill because he would not share the ransom—that, too, was false. The idea of a ransom, in this light, was now ridiculous. From that first moment Kells had wanted her; he had tried to persuade Roberts to leave her, and, failing, had killed him; he had rid himself of the other two men—and now Joan knew she had heard shots back there. Kells's intention loomed out of all his dark brooding, and it stood clear now to her, dastardly, worse than captivity, or torture, or death—the worst fate that could befall a woman.

The reality of it now was so astounding. True—as true as those stories she had deemed impossible! Because she and her people and friends had appeared secure in their mountain camp and happy in their work and trustful of good, they had scarcely credited the rumors of just such things as had happened to her. The stage held up by roadagents, a lonely prospector murdered and robbed, fights in the saloons and on the trails, and useless pursuit of hardriding men out there on the border, elusive as Arabs, swift as Apaches—these facts had been terrible enough, without the dread of worse. The truth of her capture, the meaning of it, were raw, shocking spurs to Joan Randle's intelligence and courage. Since she still lived, which was strange indeed in the illuminating light of her later insight into Kells and his kind, she had to meet him with all that was catlike and subtle and devilish at the command of a woman. She had to win him, foil him, kill him—or go to her death. She was no girl to be dragged into the mountain fastness by a desperado and made a plaything. Her horror and terror had worked its way deep into the depths of her and uncovered powers never suspected, never before required in her scheme of life. She had no longer any fear. She matched herself against this man. She anticipated him. And she felt like a woman who had lately been a thoughtless girl, who, in turn, had dreamed of vague old happenings of a past before she was born, of impossible adventures in her own future. Hate and wrath and outraged womanhood were not wholly the secret of Joan Randle's flaming spirit.

4

◈

Joan Randle rode on and on, through the cañon, out at its head and over a pass into another cañon, and never did she let it be possible for Kells to see her eyes until she knew beyond peradventure of a doubt that they hid the strength and spirit and secret of her soul.

The time came when traveling was so steep and rough that she must think first of her horse and her own safety. Kells led up over a rock-jumbled spur of range, where she had sometimes to follow on foot. It seemed miles across that wilderness of stone. Foxes and wolves trotted over open places, watching stealthily. All around dark mountain peaks stood up. The afternoon was far advanced when Kells started to descend again, and he rode a zigzag course on weathered slopes and over brushy benches, down and down into the cañons again.

A lonely peak was visible, sunset-flushed against the blue, from the point where Kells finally halted. That ended the longest ride Joan had ever made in one day. For miles and miles they had climbed and descended and wound into the mountains. Joan had scarcely any idea of direction. She was completely turned around and lost. This spot was the wildest and most beautiful she had ever seen. A cañon headed here. It was narrow, low-walled, and luxuriant with grass and wild roses and willow and spruce and balsam. There were deer standing with long ears erect, motionless, curious, tame as cattle. There were moving streaks through the long grass, showing the course of smaller animals slipping away.

Then under a giant balsam, that reached aloft to the rim-wall, Joan saw a little log cabin, open in front. It had not been built very long; some of the log ends still showed yellow. It did not resemble the hunters' and prospectors' cabins she had seen on her trips with her uncle.

In a sweeping glance Joan had taken in these features. Kells had dismounted and approached her. She looked frankly, but not directly, at him.

"I'm tired—almost too tired to get off," she said.

"Fifty miles of rock and brush, up and down! Without a kick!" he exclaimed, admiringly. "You've got sand, girl!"

"Where are we?"

"This is Lost Cañon. Only a few men know of it. And they are—attached to me. I intend to keep you here."

"How long?" She felt the intensity of his gaze.

"Why—as long as—" he replied, slowly, "till I get my ransom."

"What amount will you ask?"

"You're worth a hundred thousand in gold right now. . . . Maybe later I might let you go for less."

Joan's keen-wrought perception registered his covert, scarcely veiled implication. He was studying her.

"Oh, poor uncle. He'll never, never get so much."

"Sure he will," replied Kells, bluntly.

Then he helped her out of the saddle. She was stiff and awkward, and she let herself slide. Kells handled her gently and like a gentleman, and for Joan the first agonizing moment of her ordeal was past. Her intuition had guided her correctly. Kells might have been and probably was the most depraved of outcast men; but the presence of a girl like her, however it affected him, must also have brought up associations of a time when by family and breeding and habit he had been infinitely different. His action here, just like the ruffian Bill's, was instinctive, beyond his control. Just this slight thing, this frail link that joined Kells to his past and better life, immeasurably inspirited Joan and outlined the difficult game she had to play.

"You're a very gallant robber," she said.

He appeared not to hear that or to note it; he was eying her up and down; and he moved closer, perhaps to estimate her height compared to his own.

"I didn't know you were so tall. You're above my shoulder."

"Yes, I'm very lanky."

"Lanky! Why you're not that. You've a splendid figure—tall, supple, strong; you're like a Nez Percé girl I knew once. . . . You're a beautiful thing. Didn't you know that?"

"Not particularly. My friends don't dare flatter me. I suppose I'll have to stand it from you. But I didn't expect compliments from Jack Kells of the Border Legion."

"Border Legion? Where'd you hear that name?"

"I didn't hear it. I made it up—thought of it myself."

"Well, you've invented something I'll use. . . . And what's your name—your first name? I heard Roberts use it."

Joan felt a cold contraction of all her internal being, but outwardly she never so much as flicked an eyelash. "My name's Joan."

"Joan!" He placed heavy, compelling hands on her shoulders and turned her squarely toward him.

Again she felt his gaze, strangely, like the reflection of sunlight from ice. She had to look at him. This was her supreme test. For hours she had prepared for it, steeled herself, wrought upon all that was sensitive in her; and now she prayed, and swiftly looked up into his eyes. They were windows of a gray hell. And she gazed into that naked abyss, at that dark, uncovered soul, with only the timid anxiety and fear and the unconsciousness of an innocent, ignorant girl.

"Joan! You know why I brought you here?"

"Yes, of course; you told me," she replied, steadily. "You want to ransom me for gold. . . . And I'm afraid you'll have to take me home without getting any."

"You know what I mean to do to you," he went on, thickly.

"Do to me?" she echoed, and she never quivered a muscle. "You—you didn't say. . . . I haven't thought. . . . But you won't hurt me, will you? It's not my fault if there's no gold to ransom me."

He shook her. His face changed, grew darker. "You *know* what I mean."

"I don't." With some show of spirit she essayed to slip out of his grasp. He held her the tighter.

"How old are you?"

It was only in her height and development that Joan looked anywhere near her age. Often she had been taken for a very young girl.

"I'm seventeen," she replied. This was not the truth. It was a lie that did not falter on lips which had scorned falsehood.

"Seventeen!" he ejaculated in amaze. "Honestly, now?"

She lifted her chin scornfully and remained silent.

"Well, I thought you were a woman. I took you to be twenty-five—at least twenty-two. Seventeen, with that shape! You're only a girl—a kid. You don't know anything."

Then he released her, almost with violence, as if angered at her or himself, and he turned away to the horses. Joan walked toward the little cabin. The strain of that encounter left her weak, but once from under his eyes, certain that she had carried her point, she quickly regained her poise. There might be, probably would be, infinitely more trying ordeals for her to meet than this one had been; she realized, however, that never again would she be so near betrayal of terror and knowledge and self.

The scene of her isolation had a curious fascination for her. Something—and she shuddered—was to happen to her here in this lonely, silent gorge. There were some flat stones made into a rude seat under the balsam-tree, and a swift, yard-wide stream of clear water ran by. Observing something white against the tree, Joan went closer. A card, the ace of hearts, had been pinned to the bark by a small cluster of bullet-holes, every one of which touched the red heart, and one of them had obliterated it. Below the circle of bullet-holes, scrawled in rude letters with a lead-pencil, was the name "Gulden." How little, a few nights back, when Jim Cleve had menaced Joan with the names of Kells and Gulden, had she imagined they were actual men she was to meet and fear! And here she was the prisoner of one of them. She would ask Kells who and what this Gulden was. The log cabin was merely a shed, without fireplace or window, and the floor was a covering of balsam boughs, long dried out and withered. A dim trail led away from it down the cañon. If Joan was any judge of trails, this one had not seen the imprint of a horse track for many months. Kells had indeed brought her to a hiding place, one of those, perhaps, that camp gossip said was inaccessible to any save a border hawk. Joan knew that only an Indian could follow the tortuous and rocky trail by which Kells had brought her in. She would never be tracked there by her own people.

The long ride had left her hot, dusty, scratched, with tangled hair and torn habit. She went over to her saddle, which Kells had removed from her pony, and, opening the saddle-bag, she took inventory of her possessions. They were few enough, but now, in view of an unexpected and enforced sojourn in the wilds, beyond all calculation of value. And they included towel, soap, toothbrush, mirror and comb and brush, a red scarf, and gloves. It occurred to her how seldom she carried that bag on her saddle, and, thinking back, referred the fact to accident, and then with honest amusement owned that the motive might have been also a little vanity. Taking the bag, she went to a flat stone by the brook

34

and, rolling up her sleeves, proceeded to improve her appearance. With deft fingers she rebraided her hair and arranged it as she had worn it when only sixteen. Then, resolutely, she got up and crossed over to where Kells was unpacking.

"I'll help you get supper," she said.

He was on his knees in the midst of a jumble of camp duffle that had been hastily thrown together. He looked up at her—from her shapely, strong, brown arms to the face she had rubbed rosy.

"Say, but you're a pretty girl!"

He said it enthusiastically, in unstinted admiration, without the slightest subtlety or suggestion; and if he had been the devil himself it would have been no less a compliment, given spontaneously to youth and beauty.

"I'm glad if it's so, but please don't tell me," she rejoined, simply.

Then with swift and business-like movements she set to helping him with the mess the inexperienced pack-horse had made of that particular pack. And when that was straightened out she began with the biscuit dough while he lighted a fire. It appeared to be her skill, rather than her willingness, that he yielded to. He said very little, but he looked at her often. And he had little periods of abstraction. The situation was novel, strange to him. Sometimes Joan read his mind and sometimes he was an enigma. But she divined when he was thinking what a picture she looked there, on her knees before the bread-pan, with flour on her arms; of the difference a girl brought into any place; of how strange it seemed that this girl, instead of lying a limp and disheveled rag under a tree, weeping and praying for home, made the best of a bad situation and improved it wonderfully by being a thoroughbred.

Presently they sat down, cross-legged, one on each side of the tarpaulin, and began the meal. That was the strangest supper Joan ever sat down to; it was like a dream where there was danger that tortured her; but she knew she was dreaming and would soon wake up. Kells was almost imperceptibly changing. The amiability of his face seemed to have stiffened. The only time he addressed her was when he

35

offered to help her to more meat or bread or coffee. After the meal was finished he would not let her wash the pans and pots, and attended to that himself.

Joan went to the seat by the tree, near the camp-fire. A purple twilight was shadowing the cañon. Far above, on the bold peak the last warmth of the afterglow was fading. There was no wind, no sound, no movement. Joan wondered where Jim Cleve was then. They had often sat in the twilight. She felt an unreasonable resentment toward him, knowing she was to blame, but blaming him for her plight. Then suddenly she thought of her uncle, of home, of her kindly old aunt who always worried so about her. Indeed, there was cause to worry. She felt sorrier for them than for herself. And that broke her spirit momentarily. Forlorn, and with a wave of sudden sorrow and dread and hopelessness, she dropped her head upon her knees and covered her face. Tears were a relief. She forgot Kells and the part she must play. But she remembered swiftly—at the rude touch of his hand.

"Here! Are you crying?" he asked, roughly.

"Do you think I'm laughing?" Joan retorted. Her wet eyes, as she raised them, were proof enough.

"Stop it."

"I can't help—but cry—a little. I was th—thinking of home—of those who've been father and mother to me— since I was a baby. I wasn't crying—for myself. But they—they'll be so miserable. They loved me so."

"It won't help matters to cry."

Joan stood up then, no longer sincere and forgetful, but the girl with her deep and cunning game. She leaned close to him in the twilight.

"Did *you* ever love any one? Did you ever have a sister—a girl like me?"

Kells stalked away into the gloom.

Joan was left alone. She did not know whether to interpret his abstraction, his temper, and his action as favorable or not. Still she hoped and prayed they meant that he had some good in him. If she could only hide her terror, her abhorrence, her knowledge of him and his motive! She built up a bright camp-fire. There was an abundance of wood.

She dreaded the darkness and the night. Besides, the air was growing chilly. So, arranging her saddle and blankets near the fire, she composed herself in a comfortable seat to await Kells's return and developments. It struck her forcibly that she had lost some of her fear of Kells and she did not know why. She ought to fear him more every hour—every minute. Presently she heard his step brushing the grass and then he emerged out of the gloom. He had a load of fire-wood on his shoulder.

"Did you get over your grief?" he asked, glancing down upon her.

"Yes," she replied.

Kells stooped for a red ember, with which he lighted his pipe, and then he seated himself a little back from the fire. The blaze threw a bright glare over him, and in it he looked neither formidable nor vicious nor ruthless. He asked her where she was born, and upon receiving an answer he followed that up with another question. And he kept this up until Joan divined that he was not so much interested in what he apparently wished to learn as he was in her presence, her voice, her personality. She sensed in him loneliness, hunger for the sound of a voice. She had heard her uncle speak of the loneliness of lonely camp-fires and how all men working or hiding or lost in the wilderness would see sweet faces in the embers and be haunted by soft voices. After all, Kells was human. And she talked as never before in her life, brightly, willingly, eloquently, telling the facts of her eventful youth and girlhood—the sorrow and the joy and some of the dreams—up to the time she had come to Camp Hoadley.

"Did you leave any sweethearts over there at Hoadley?" he asked, after a silence.

"Yes."

"How many?"

"A whole campful," she replied, with a laugh, "but admirers is a better name for them."

"Then there's no one fellow?"

"Hardly—yet."

"How would you like being kept here in this lonesome place for—well, say for ever?"

37

"I wouldn't like that," replied Joan. "I'd like this—camping out like this now—if my folks only knew I am alive and well and safe. I love lonely, dreamy places. I've dreamed of being in just such a one as this. It seems so far away here—so shut in by the walls and the blackness. So silent and sweet! I love the stars. They speak to me. And the wind in the spruces. Hear it. . . . Very low, mournful! That whispers to me—to-morrow I'd like it here if I had no worry. I've never grown up yet. I explore and climb trees and hunt for little birds and rabbits—young things just born, all fuzzy and sweet, frightened, piping or squealing for their mothers. But I won't touch one for worlds. I simply can't hurt anything. I can't spur my horse or beat him. Oh, I *hate* pain!"

"You're a strange girl to live out here on this border," he said.

"I'm no different from other girls. You don't know girls."

"I knew one pretty well. She put a rope round my neck," he replied, grimly.

"A rope!"

"Yes, I mean a halter, a hangman's noose. But I balked her!"

"Oh! . . . A good girl?"

"Bad! Bad to the core of her black heart—bad as I am!" he exclaimed, with fierce, low passion.

Joan trembled. The man, in an instant, seemed transformed, somber as death. She could not look at him, but she must keep on talking.

"Bad? You don't seem bad to me—only violent, perhaps, or wild. . . . Tell me about yourself."

She had stirred him. His neglected pipe fell from his hand. In the gloom of the camp-fire he must have seen faces or ghosts of his past.

"Why not?" he queried, strangely. "Why not do what's been impossible for years—open my lips? It'll not matter—to a girl who can never tell! . . . Have I forgotten? God!—I have not! Listen, so that you'll *know* I'm bad. My name's not Kells. I was born in the East, and went to school there till I ran away. I was young, ambitious, wild. I stole. I

38

ran away—came West in 'fifty-one to the gold-fields in California. There I became a prospector, miner, gambler, robber—and road-agent. I had evil in me, as all men have, and those wild years brought it out. I had no chance. Evil and gold and blood—they are one and the same thing. I committed every crime till no place, bad as it might be, was safe for me. Driven and hunted and shot and starved—almost hanged! . . . And now I'm—Kells! of that outcast crew you named 'the Border Legion!' Every black crime but one—the blackest—and that haunting me, itching my hands to-night"

"Oh, you speak so—so dreadfully!" cried Joan. "What can I say? I'm sorry for you. I don't believe it all. What—what black crime haunts you? Oh! what could be possible tonight—here in this lonely cañon—with only me?"

Dark and terrible the man arose.

"Girl," he said, hoarsely. "To-night—to-night—I'll. . . . What have you done to me? One more day—and I'll be mad to do right by you—instead of *wrong*. . . . Do you understand that?"

Joan leaned forward in the camp-fire light with outstretched hands and quivering lips, as overcome by his halting confession of one last remnant of honor as she was by the dark hint of his passion.

"No—no—I don't understand—nor believe!" she cried. "But you frighten me—so! I am all—all alone with you here. You said I'd be safe. Don't—don't—"

Her voice broke then and she sank back exhausted in her seat. Probably Kells had heard only the first words of her appeal, for he took to striding back and forth in the circle of the camp-fire light. The scabbard with the big gun swung against his leg. It grew to be a dark and monstrous thing in Joan's sight. A marvelous intuition born of that hour warned her of Kells's subjection to the beast in him, even while, with all the manhood left to him, he still battled against it. Her girlish sweetness and innocence had availed nothing, except mock him with the ghost of dead memories. He could not be won or foiled. She must get her hands on that gun—kill him—or—! The alternative was death for

39

herself. And she leaned there, slowly gathering all the unconquerable and unquenchable forces of a woman's nature, waiting, to make one desperate, supreme, and final effort.

5

◆

KELLS strode there, a black, silent shadow, plodding with bent head, as if all about and above him were demons and furies.

Joan's perceptions of him, of the night, of the inanimate and imponderable black walls, and of herself, were exquisitely and abnormally keen. She saw him there, bowed under his burden, gloomy and wroth and sick with himself because the man in him despised the coward. Men of his stamp were seldom or never cowards. Their lives did not breed cowardice or baseness. Joan knew the burning in her breast—that thing which inflamed and swept through her like a wind of fire—was hate. Yet her heart held a grain of pity for him. She measured his forbearance, his struggle, against the monstrous cruelty and passion engendered by a wild life among wild men at a wild time. And, considering his opportunities of the long hours and lonely miles, she was grateful, and did not in the least underestimate what it cost him, how different from Bill or Halloway he had been. But all this was nothing, and her thinking of it useless, unless he conquered himself. She only waited, holding on to that steel-like control of her nerves, motionless and silent.

She leaned back against her saddle, a blanket covering her, with wide-open eyes, and despite the presence of that stalking figure and the fact of her mind being locked round one terrible and inevitable thought, she saw the changing beautiful glow of the fire-logs and the cold, pitiless stars and the mustering shadows under the walls. She heard, too, the low rising sigh of the wind in the balsam and the silvery tinkle of the brook, and sounds only imagined or nameless. Yet a stern and insupportable silence weighed her down. This dark cañon seemed at the ends of the earth. She felt encompassed by illimitable and stupendous upflung mountains, insulated in a vast, dark, silent tomb.

Kells suddenly came to her, treading noiselessly, and he leaned over her. His vasage was a dark blur, but the posture of him was that of a wolf about to spring. Lower he leaned—slowly—and yet lower. Joan saw the heavy gun swing away from his leg; she saw it black and clear against the blaze; a cold, blue light glinted from its handle. And then Kells was near enough for her to see his face and his eyes that were but shadows of flames. She gazed up at him steadily, open-eyed, with no fear or shrinking. His breathing was quick and loud. He looked down at her for an endless moment, then, straightening his bent form, he resumed his walk to and fro.

After that for Joan time might have consisted of moments or hours, each of which was marked by Kells looming over her. He appeared to approach her from all sides; he round her wide-eyed, sleepless; his shadowy glance gloated over her lithe, slender shape; and then he strode away into the gloom. Sometimes she could no longer hear his steps and then she was quiveringly alert, listening, fearful that he might creep upon her like a panther. At times he kept the camp-fire blazing brightly; at others he let it die down. And these dark intervals were frightful for her. The night seemed treacherous, in league with her foe. It was endless. She prayed for dawn—yet with a blank hopelessness for what the day might bring. Could she hold out through more interminable hours? Would she not break from sheer strain? There were moments when she wavered and shook like a leaf in the wind, when the beating of her heart was audible, when a child could have seen her distress. There were other moments when all was ugly, unreal, impossible like things in a nightmare. But when Kells was near or approached to look at her, like a cat returned to watch a captive mouse, she was again strong, waiting, with ever a strange and cold sense of the nearness of that swinging gun. Late in the night she missed him, for how long she had no idea. She had less trust in his absence than his presence. The nearer he came to her the stronger she grew and the clearer of purpose. At last the black void of cañon lost its blackness and turned to gray. Dawn was at hand. The horrible endless night, in which she had aged from girl to woman, had passed. Joan had never closed her eyes a single instant.

When day broke she got up. The long hours in which she had rested motionlessly had left her muscles cramped and dead. She began to walk off the feeling. Kells had just stirred from his blanket under the balsam-tree. His face was dark, haggard, lined. She saw him go down to the brook and plunge his hands into the water and bathe his face with a kind of fury. Then he went up to the smoldering fire. There was a gloom, a somberness, a hardness about him that had not been noticeable the day before.

Joan found the water cold as ice, soothing to the burn beneath her skin. She walked away then, aware that Kells did not appear to care, and went up to where the brook brawled from under the cliff. This was a hundred paces from camp, though in plain sight. Joan looked round for her

43

horse, but he was not to be seen. She decided to slip away the first opportunity that offered, and on foot or horseback, any way, to get out of Kells's clutches if she had to wander, lost in the mountains, till she starved. Possibly the day might be endurable, but another night would drive her crazy. She sat on a ledge, planning and brooding, till she was startled by a call from Kells. Then slowly she retraced her steps.

"Don't you want to eat?" he asked.

"I'm not hungry," she replied.

"Well, eat anyhow—if it chokes you," he ordered.

Joan seated herself while he placed food and drink before her. She did not look at him and did not feel his gaze upon her. Far asunder as they had been yesterday the distance between them to-day was incalculably greater. She ate as much as she could swallow and pushed the rest away. Leaving the camp-fire, she began walking again, here and there, aimlessly, scarcely seeing what she looked at. There was a shadow over her, an impending portent of catastrophe, a moment standing dark and sharp out of the age-long hour. She leaned against the balsam and then she rested in the stone seat, and then she had to walk again. It might have been long, that time; she never knew how long or short. There came a strange flagging, sinking of her spirit, accompanied by vibrating, restless, uncontrollable muscular activity. Her nerves were on the verge of collapse.

It was then that a call from Kells, clear and ringing, thrilled all the weakness from her in a flash, and left her limp and cold. She saw him coming. His face looked amiable again, bright against what seemed a vague and veiled background. Like a mountaineer he strode. And she looked into his strange, gray glance to see unmasked the ruthless power, the leaping devil, the ungovernable passion she had sensed in him.

He grasped her arm and with a single pull swung her to him. *"You've* got to pay that ransom!"

He handled her as if he thought she resisted, but she was unresisting. She hung her head to hide her eyes. Then he placed an arm round her shoulders and half led, half dragged her toward the cabin.

Joan saw with startling distinctness the bits of balsam and pine at her feet and pale pink daisies in the grass, and then the dry withered boughs. She was in the cabin.

"Girl! . . . I'm hungry—for you!" he breathed, hoarsely. And turning her toward him, he embraced her, as if his nature was savage and he had to use a savage force.

If Joan struggled at all, it was only slightly, when she writhed and slipped, like a snake, to get her arm under his as it clasped her neck. Then she let herself go. He crushed her to him. He bent her backward—tilted her face with hard and eager hand. Like a madman, with hot working lips, he kissed her. She felt blinded—scorched. But her purpose was as swift and sure and wonderful as his passion was wild. The first reach of her groping hand found his gun-belt. Swift as light her hand slipped down. Her fingers touched the cold gun—grasped with thrill on thrill—slipped farther down, strong and sure to raise the hammer. Then with a leaping, strung intensity that matched his own she drew the gun. She raised it while her eyes were shut. She lay passive under his kisses—the devouring kisses of one whose manhood had been denied the sweetness, the glory, the fire, the life of woman's lips. It was a moment in which she met his primitive fury of possession with a woman's primitive fury of profanation. She pressed the gun against his side and pulled the trigger.

A thundering, muffled, hollow boom! The odor of burned powder stung her nostrils. Kells's hold on her tightened convulsively, loosened with strange, lessening power. She swayed back free of him, still with tight-shut eyes. A horrible cry escaped him—a cry of mortal agony. It wrenched her. And she looked to see him staggering amazed, stricken, at bay, like a wolf caught in cruel steel jaws. His hands came away from both sides, dripping with blood. They shook till the crimson drops spattered on the wall, on the boughs. Then he seemed to realize and he clutched at her with these bloody hands.

"God Almighty!" he panted. "You shot me! . . . You—you girl! . . . You she-cat . . . You knew—all the time . . . You she-cat! . . . Give me—that gun!"

45

"Kells, get back! I'll kill you!" she cried. The big gun, outstretched between them, began to waver.

Kells did not see the gun. In his madness he tried to move, to reach her, but he could not; he was sinking. His legs sagged under him, let him down to his knees, and but for the wall he would have fallen. Then a change transformed him. The black, turgid, convulsed face grew white and ghastly, with beads of clammy sweat and lines of torture. His strange eyes showed swiftly passing thought— wonder, fear, scorn—even admiration.

"Joan, you've done—for me!" he gasped. "You've broken my back! . . . It'll kill me! Oh the pain—the pain! And I can't stand pain! You—you girl! You innocent seventeen-year-old girl! You that couldn't hurt any creature! You so tender—so gentle! . . . Bah! you fooled me. The cunning of a woman! I ought—to know. A good woman's—more terrible than a—bad woman. . . . But I deserved this. Once I used—to be. . . . Only, the torture! . . . Why didn't you—kill me outright? . . . Joan—Randle—watch me—die! Since I had—to die—by rope or bullet—I'm glad you—you—did for me. . . . Man or beast—I believe—I loved you!"

Joan dropped the gun and sank beside him, helpless, horror-stricken, wringing her hands. She wanted to tell him she was sorry, that he drove her to it, that he must let her pray for him. But she could not speak. Her tongue clove to the roof of her mouth and she seemed strangling.

Another change, slower and more subtle, passed over Kells. He did not see Joan. He forgot her. The white shaded out of his face, leaving a gray like that of his somber eyes. Spirit, sense, life, were fading from him. The quivering of a racked body ceased. And all that seemed left was a lonely soul groping on the verge of the dim borderland between life and death. Presently his shoulders slipped along the wall and he fell, to lie limp and motionless before Joan. Then she fainted.

6

◆

WHEN Joan returned to consciousness she was lying half outside the opening of the cabin and above her was a drift of blue gun-smoke, slowly floating upward. Almost as swiftly as perception of that smoke came a shuddering memory. She lay still, listening. She did not hear a sound except the tinkle and babble and gentle rush of the brook. Kells was dead, then. And overmastering the horror of her act was a relief, a freedom, a lifting of her soul out of the dark dread, a something that whispered justification of the fatal deed.

She got up and, avoiding to look within the cabin, walked away. The sun was almost at the zenith. Where had the morning hours gone?

"I must get away," she said, suddenly. The thought quickened her. Down the cañon the horses were grazing. She hurried along the trail, trying to decide whether to follow this dim old trail or endeavor to get out the way she had been brought in. She decided upon the latter. If she traveled slowly, and watched for familiar landmarks, things she had seen once, and hunted carefully for the tracks, she believed she might be successful. She had the courage to try. Then she caught her pony and led him back to camp.

"What shall I take?" she pondered. She decided upon very little—a blanket, a sack of bread and meat, and a canteen of water. She might need a weapon, also. There was only one, the gun with which she had killed Kells. It seemed utterly impossible to touch that hateful thing. But now that she had liberated herself, and at such cost, she must not yield to sentiment. Resolutely she started for the cabin, but when she reached it her steps were dragging. The long, dull-blue gun lay where she had dropped it. And out of the tail of averted eyes she saw a huddled shape along the wall. It was a sickening moment when she reached a shaking hand for the gun. And at that instant a low moan transfixed her.

She seemed frozen rigid. Was the place already haunted? Her heart swelled in her throat and a dimness came before her eyes. But another moan brought a swift realization—Kells was alive. And the cold, clamping sickness, the strangle in her throat, all the feelings of terror, changed and were lost in a flood of instinctive joy. He was not dead. She had not killed him. She did not have blood on her hands. She was not a murderer.

She whirled to look at him. There he lay, ghastly as a corpse. And all her woman's gladness fled. But there was compassion left to her, and, forgetting all else, she knelt beside him. He was as cold as stone. She felt no stir, no beat of pulse in temple or wrist. Then she placed her ear against his breast. His heart beat weakly.

"He's alive," she whispered. "But—he's dying. . . . What shall I do?"

Many thoughts flashed across her mind. She could not help him now; he would be dead soon; she did not need to wait there beside him; there was a risk of some of his comrades riding into that rendezvous. Suppose his back was not broken after all! Suppose she stopped the flow of blood, tended him, nursed him, saved his life? For if there were one chance of his living, which she doubted, it must be through her. Would he not be the same savage the hour he was well and strong again? What difference could she make in such a nature? The man was evil. He could not conquer evil. She had been witness to that. He had driven Roberts to draw and had killed him. No doubt he had deliberately and coldly murdered the two ruffians, Bill and Halloway, just so he could be free of their glances at her and be alone with her. He deserved to die there like a dog.

What Joan Randle did was surely a woman's choice. Carefully she rolled Kells over. The back of his vest and shirt was wet with blood. She got up to find a knife, towel, and water. As she returned to the cabin he moaned again.

Joan had dressed many a wound. She was not afraid of blood. The difference was that she had shed it. She felt sick, but her hands were firm as she cut open the vest and shirt, rolled them aside, and bathed his back. The big bullet had made a gaping wound, having apparently gone through the small of his back. The blood still flowed. She could not tell whether or not Kell's spine was broken, but she believed that the bullet had gone between bone and muscle, or had glanced. There was a blue welt just over his spine, in line with the course of the wound. She tore her scarf into strips and used it for compresses and bandages. Then she laid him back upon a saddle-blanket. She had done all that was possible for the present, and it gave her a strange sense of comfort. She even prayed for his life, and, if that must go, for his soul. Then she got up. He was unconscious, white, death-like. It seemed that his torture, his near approach to death, had robbed his face of ferocity, of ruthlessness, and of that strange amiable expression. But then, his eyes, those furnace-windows, were closed.

Joan waited for the end to come. The afternoon passed and she did not leave the cabin. It was possible that he might come to and want water. She had once administered to a miner who had been fatally crushed in an avalanche; and never could forget his husky call for water and the gratitude in his eyes.

Sunset, twilight, and night fell upon the cañon. And she began to feel solitude as something tangible. Bringing saddle and blankets into the cabin, she made a bed just inside, and, facing the opening and the stars, she lay down to rest, if not to sleep. The darkness did not keep her from seeing the prostrate figure of Kells. He lay there as silent as if he were already dead. She was exhausted, weary for sleep, and unstrung. In the night her courage fled and she was frightened at shadows. The murmuring of insects seemed augmented into a roar; the mourn of wolf and scream of cougar made her start; the rising wind moaned like a lost spirit. Dark fancies beset her. Troop on troop of specters moved out of the black night, assembling there, waiting for Kells to join them. She thought she was riding homeward over the back trail, sure of her way, remembering every rod of that rough travel, until she got out of the mountains, only to be turned back by dead men. Then fancy and dream, and all the haunted gloom of cañon and cabin, seemed slowly to merge into one immense blackness.

The sun, rimming the east wall, shining into Joan's face, awakened her. She had slept hours. She felt rested, stronger. Like the night, something dark had passed away from her. It did not seem strange to her that she should feel that Kells still lived. She knew it. And examination proved her right. In him there had been no change except that he had ceased to bleed. There was just a flickering of life in him, manifest only in his slow, faint heart-beats.

Joan spent most of that day in sitting beside Kells. The whole day seemed only an hour. Sometimes she would look down the cañon trail, half expecting to see horsemen riding up. If any of Kells's comrades happened to come, what could she tell them? They would be as bad as he, without that one trait which had kept him human for a day. Joan pondered upon this. It would never do to let them suspect she had shot Kells. So, carefully cleaning the gun, she reloaded it. If any men came, she would tell them that Bill had done the shooting.

Kells lingered. Joan began to feel that he would live, though everything indicated the contrary. Her intelligence told her he would die, and her feeling said he would not. At times she lifted his head and got water into his mouth with a spoon. When she did this he would moan. That night, during the hours she lay awake, she gathered courage out of the very solitude and loneliness. She had nothing to fear, unless someone came to the cañon. The next day in no wise differed from the preceding. And then there came the third day, with no change in Kells till near evening, when she thought he was returning to consciousness. But she must have been mistaken. For hours she watched patiently. He might return to consciousness just before the end, and want to speak, to send a message, to ask a prayer, to feel a human hand at the last.

That night the crescent moon hung over the cañon. In the faint light Joan could see the blanched face of Kells, strange and sad, no longer seeming evil. The time came when his lips stirred. He tried to talk. She moistened his lips and gave him a drink. He murmured incoherently, sank again into a stupor, to rouse once more and babble like a madman. Then he lay quietly for long—so long that sleep was claiming Joan. Suddenly he startled her by calling very faintly but distinctly: "Water! Water!"

Joan bent over him, lifting his head, helping him to drink. She could see his eyes, like dark holes in something white.

"Is—that—you—mother?" he whispered.

"Yes," replied Joan.

He sank immediately into another stupor or sleep, from which he did not rouse. That whisper of his—mother—touched Joan. Bad men had mothers just the same as any other kind of men. Even this Kells had a mother. He was still a young man. He had been youth, boy, child, baby. Some mother had loved him, cradled him, kissed his rosy baby hands, watched him grow with pride and glory, built castles in her dreams of his manhood, and perhaps prayed for him still, trusting he was strong and honored among men. And here he lay, a shattered wreck, dying for a wicked act, the last of many crimes. It was a tragedy. It made Joan think of the hard lot of mothers, and then of this unsettled Western wild, where men flocked in packs like wolves, and spilled blood like water, and held life nothing.

Joan sought her rest and soon slept. In the morning she did not at once go to Kells. Somehow she dreaded finding him conscious, almost as much as she dreaded the thought of finding him dead. When she did bend over him he was awake, and at sight of her he showed a faint amaze.

"Joan!" he whispered.

"Yes," she replied.

"Are you—with me still?"

"Of course, I couldn't leave you."

The pale eyes shadowed strangely, darkly. "I'm alive yet. And you stayed! . . . Was it yesterday—you threw my gun—on me?"

"No. Four days ago."

"Four! Is my back broken?"

"I don't know. I don't think so. It's a terrible wound. I—I did all I could."

"You tried to kill me—then tried to save me?"

She was silent to that.

"You're good—and you've been noble," he said. "But I wish—you'd only been bad. Then I'd curse you—and strangle you—presently."

"Perhaps you had best be quiet," replied Joan.

"No. I've been shot before. I'll get over this—if my back's not broken. How can we tell?"

"I've no idea."

"Lift me up."

"But you might open your wound," protested Joan.

"Lift me up!" The force of the man spoke even in his low whisper.

"But why—why?" asked Joan.

"I want to see—if I can sit up. If I can't—give me my gun."

"I won't let you have it," replied Joan. Then she slipped

52

her arms under his and, carefully raising him to a sitting posture, released her hold.

"I'm—a—rank coward—about pain," he gasped, with thick drops standing out on his white face. "I can't—stand it."

But tortured or not, he sat up alone, and even had the will to bend his back. Then with a groan he fainted and fell into Joan's arms. She laid him down and worked over him for some time before she could bring him to. Then he was wan, suffering, speechless. But she believed he would live and told him so. He received that with a strange smile. Later, when she came to him with broth, he drank it gratefully.

"I'll beat this out," he said, weakly. "I'll recover. My back's not broken. I'll get well. Now you bring water and food in here—then go."

"Go?" she echoed.

"Yes. Don't go down the cañon. You'd be worse off. . . . Take the back trail. You've got a chance to get out. . . . Go!"

"Leave you here? So weak you can't lift a cup! I won't."

"I'd rather you did."

"Why?"

"Because in a few days I'll begin to mend. Then I'll grow like—myself. . . . I think—I'm afraid I loved you. . . . It could only be hell for you. Go now, before it's too late! . . . If you stay—till I'm well—I'll never let you go!"

"Kells, I believe it would be cowardly for me to leave you here alone," she replied, earnestly. "You can't help yourself. You'd die."

"All the better. But I won't die. I'm hard to kill. Go, I tell you."

She shook her head. "This is bad for you—arguing. You're exciited. Please be quiet."

"Joan Randle, if you stay—I'll halter you—keep you naked in a cave—curse you—beat you—murder you! Oh, it's in me! . . . Go, I tell you!"

"You're out of your head. Once for all—no!" she replied, firmly.

"*You—you—*" His voice failed in a terrible whisper. . . .

In the succeeding days Kells did not often speak. His

53

recovery was slow—a matter of doubt. Nothing was any plainer than the fact that if Joan had left him he would not have lived long. She knew it. And he knew it. When he was awake, and she came to him, a mournful and beautiful smile lit his eyes. The sight of her apparently hurt him and uplifted him. But he slept twenty hours out of every day, and while he slept he did not need Joan.

She came to know the meaning of solitude. There were days when she did not hear the sound of her own voice. A habit of silence, one of the significant forces of solitude, had grown upon her. Daily she thought less and felt more. For hours she did nothing. When she roused herself, compelled herself to think of these encompassing peaks of the lonely cañon walls, the stately trees, all those eternally silent and changeless features of her solitude, she hated them with a blind and unreasoning passion. She hated them because she was losing her love for them, because they were becoming a part of her, because they were fixed and content and passionless. She liked to sit in the sun, feel its warmth, see its brightness; and sometimes she almost forgot to go back to her patient. She fought at times against an insidious change —a growing older—a going backward; at other times she drifted through hours that seemed quiet and golden, in which nothing happened. And by and by when she realized that the drifting hours were gradually swallowing up the restless and active hours, then strangely, she remembered Jim Cleve. Memory of him came to save her. She dreamed of him during the long, lonely, solemn days, and in the dark, silent climax of unbearable solitude—the night. She remembered his kisses, forgot her anger and shame, accepted the sweetness of their meaning, and so in the interminable hours of her solitude she dreamed herself into love for him.

Joan kept some record of days, until three weeks or thereabout passed, and then she lost track of time. It dragged along, yet looked at as the past, it seemed to have sped swiftly. The change in her, the growing old, the revelation and responsibility of self, as a woman, made this experience appear to have extended over months.

Kells slowly became convalescent and then he had a

relapse. Something happened, the nature of which Joan could not tell, and he almost died. There were days when his life hung in the balance, when he could not talk; and then came a perceptible turn for the better.

The store of provisions grew low, and Joan began to face another serious situation. Deer and rabbit were plentiful in the cañon, but she could not kill one with a revolver. She thought she would be forced to sacrifice one of the horses. The fact that Kells suddenly showed a craving for meat brought this aspect of the situation to a climax. And that very morning while Joan was pondering the matter she saw a number of horsemen riding up the cañon toward the cabin. At the moment she was relieved, and experienced nothing of the dread she had formerly felt while anticipating this very event.

"Kells," she said, quickly, "there are men riding up the trail."

"Good" he exclaimed, weakly, with a light on his drawn face. "They've been long in—getting here. How many?"

Joan counted them—five riders, and several pack-animals.

"Yes. It's Gulden."

"Gulden!" cried Joan, with a start.

Her exclamation and tone made Kells regard her attentively.

"You've heard of him? He's the toughest nut—on this border. . . . I never saw his like. You won't be safe. I'm so helpless. . . . What to say—to tell him! . . . . Joan, if I should happen to croak—you want to get away quick . . . . . . or shoot yourself."

How strange to hear this bandit warn her of peril the like of which she had encountered through him! Joan secured the gun and hid it in a niche between the logs. Then she looked out again.

The riders were close at hand now. The foremost one, a man of Herculean build, jumped his mount across the brook, and leaped off while he hauled the horse to a stop. The second rider came close behind him; the others approached leisurely, with the gait of the pack-animals.

"Ho, Kells!" called the big man. His voice had a loud, bold, sonorous kind of ring.

"Reckon he's here somewheres," said the other man, presently.

"Sure. I seen his hoss. Jack ain't goin' to be far from thet hoss."

Then both of them approached the cabin. Joan had never before seen two such striking, vicious-looking, awesome men. The one was huge—so wide and heavy and deep-set that he looked short—and he resembled a gorilla. The other was tall, slim, with a face as red as flame, and an expression of fierce keenness. He was stoop shouldered, yet he held his head erect in a manner that suggested a wolf scenting blood.

"Someone here, Pearce," boomed the big man.

"Why, Gul, if it ain't a girl!"

Joan moved out of the shadow of the wall of the cabin, and she pointed to the prostrate figure on the blankets.

"Howdy boys!" said Kells, wanly.

Gulden cursed in amaze while Pearce dropped to his knee with an exclamation of concern. Then both began to talk at once. Kells interrupted them by lifting a weak hand.

"No, I'm not going—to cash," he said. "I'm only starved—and in need of stimulants. Had my back half shot off."

"Who plugged you, Jack?"

"Gulden, it was your side-partner, Bill."

"Bill?" Gulden's voice held a queer, coarse constraint. Then he added, gruffly. "Thought you and him pulled together."

"Well, we didn't."

"And—where's Bill now?" This time Joan heard a slow, curious, cold note in the heavy voice, and she interpreted it as either doubt or deceit.

"Bill's dead and Halloway, too," replied Kells.

Gulden turned his massive, shaggy head in the direction of Joan. She had not the courage to meet the gaze upon her. The other man spoke:

"Split over the girl, Jack?"

"No" replied Kells, sharply. "They tried to get familiar with—*my wife*— and I shot them both."

Joan felt a swift leap of hot blood all over her and then a coldness, a sickening, a hateful weakness.

"Wife!" ejaculated Gulden.

"Your real wife, Jack?" queried Pearce.

"Well, I guess. I'll introduce you. . . . Joan, here are two of my friends—Sam Gulden and Red Pearce."

Gulden grunted something.

"Mrs. Kells, I'm glad to meet you," said Pearce.

Just then the other three men entered the cabin and Joan took advantage of the commotion they made to get out into the air. She felt sick, frightened, and yet terribly enraged. She staggered a little as she went out, and she knew she was as pale as death. These visitors thrust reality upon her with a cruel suddenness. There was something terrible in the mere presence of this Gulden. She had not yet dared to take a good look at him. But what she felt was overwhelming. She wanted to run. Yet escape now was infinitely more of a menace than before. If she slipped away it would be these new enemies who would pursue her, track her like hounds. She understood why Kells had introduced her as his wife. She hated the idea with a shameful and burning hate, but a moment's reflection taught her that Kells had answered once more to a good instinct. At the moment he had meant that to protect her. And further reflection persuaded Joan that she would be wise to act naturally and to carry out the deception as far as it was possible for her. It was her only hope. Her position had again grown perilous. She thought of the gun she had secreted, and it gave her strength to control her agitation and to return to the cabin outwardly calm.

The men had Kells half turned over with the flesh of his back exposed.

"Aw, Gul, it's whisky he needs," said one.

"If you let out any more blood he'll croak sure," protested another.

"Look how weak he is," said Red Pearce.

"It's a hell of a lot you know," roared Gulden. "I served my time—but that's none of your business. . . . Look here! See that blue spot!" Gulden pressed a huge finger down upon the blue welt on Kells's back. The bandit moaned. "That's lead—that's the bullet," declared Gulden.

"Wall, if you ain't correct!" exclaimed Pearce.

Kells turned his head. "When you punched that place—it made me numb all over. Gul, if you've located the bullet, cut it out."

Joan did not watch the operation. As she went away to the seat under the balsam she heard a sharp cry and then cheers. Evidently the grim Gulden had been both swift and successful.

Presently the men came out of the cabin and began to attend to their horses and the pack-train.

Pearce looked for Joan, and upon seeing her called out, "Kells wants you."

Joan found the bandit half propped up against a saddle with a damp and pallid face, but an altogether different look.

"Joan, that bullet was pressing on my spine," he said. "Now it's out, all that deadness is gone. I feel alive. I'll get well, soon. . . . Gulden was curious over the bullet. It's a forty-four caliber, and neither Bill Bailey nor Halloway used that caliber of gun. Gulden remembered. He's cunning. Bill was as near being a friend to this Gulden as any man I know of. I can't trust any of these men, particularly Gulden. You stay pretty close by me."

"Kells, you'll let me go soon—help me to get home?" implored Joan in a low voice.

"Girl, it'd never be safe now," he replied.

"Then later—soon—when it is safe?"

"We'll see. . . . But you're my wife now!"

With the latter words the man subtly changed. Something of the power she had felt in him before his illness began again to be manifested. Joan divined that these comrades had caused the difference in him.

"You won't dare—!" Joan was unable to conclude her meaning. A tight band compressed her breast and throat, and she trembled.

"Will you dare go out there and tell them you're *not* my wife?" he queried. His voice had grown stronger and his eyes were blending shadows of thought.

Joan knew that she dared not. She must choose the lesser

58

of two evils. "No man could be such a beast to a woman—after she'd saved his life," she whispered.

"I could be anything. You had your chance. I told you to go. I said if I ever got well I'd be as I was—before."

"But you'd have died."

"That would have been better for you. . . . . Joan, I'll do this. Marry you honestly and leave the country. I've gold. I'm young. I love you. I intend to have you. And I'll begin life over again. What do you say?"

"Say? I'd die before—I'd marry you!" she panted.

"All right, Joan Randle," he replied, bitterly. "For a moment I saw a ghost. My old dead better self! . . . It's gone. . . . And you stay with me."

7

◈

AFTER dark Kells had his men build a fire before the open side of the cabin. He lay propped up on blankets and his saddle, while the others lounged or sat in a half-circle in the light, facing him.

Joan drew her blankets into a corner where the shadows were thick and she could see without being seen. She wondered how she would ever sleep near all these wild men—if she could ever sleep again. Yet she seemed more curious and wakeful than frightened. She had no way to explain it, but she felt the fact that her presence in the camp had a subtle influence, at once restraining and exciting. So she looked out upon the scene with wide-open eyes.

And she received more strongly than ever an impression of wildness. Even the camp-fire seemed to burn wildly; it did not glow and sputter and pale and brighten and sing like an honest camp-fire. It blazed in red, fierce, hurried flames, wild to consume the logs. It cast a baleful and sinister color upon the hard faces there. Then the blackness of the enveloping night was pitchy, without any bold outline of cañon wall or companionship of stars. The coyotes were out in force and from all around came their wild sharp barks. The wind rose and mourned weirdly through the balsams.

But it was in the men that Joan felt mostly that element of wildness. Kells lay with his ghastly face clear in the play of the moving flare of light. It was an intelligent, keen, strong face, but evil. Evil power stood out in the lines, in the strange eyes, stranger then ever, now in shadow; and it seemed once more the face of an alert, listening, implacable man, with wild projects in mind, driving him to the doom he meant for others. Pearce's red face shone redder in that ruddy light. It was hard, lean, almost fleshless, a red mask stretched over a grinning skull. The one they called Frenchy was little, dark, small-featured, with piercing gimlet-like eyes, and a mouth ready to gush forth hate and violence. The next two were not particularly individualized by any striking aspect, merely looking border ruffians after the type of Bill and Halloway. But Gulden, who sat at the end of the half-circle, was an object that Joan could scarcely bring her gaze to study. Somehow her first glance at him put into her mind a strange idea—that she was a woman and therefore of all creatures or things in the world the farthest removed from him. She looked away, and found her gaze returning. fascinated, as if she were a bird and he a snake. The man was of huge frame, a giant whose every move suggested the acme of physical power. He was an animal—a gorilla with a shock of light instead of black hair, of pale instead of black skin. His features might have been hewn and hammered out with coarse, dull, broken chisels. And upon his face, in the

61

lines and cords, in the huge caverns where his eyes hid, and in the huge gash that held strong, white fangs, had been stamped by nature and by life a terrible ferocity. Here was a man or a monster in whose presence Joan felt that she would rather be dead. He did not smoke; he did not indulge in the coarse, good-natured raillery, he sat there like a huge engine of destruction that needed no rest, but was forced to rest because of weaker attachments. On the other hand, he was not sullen or brooding. It was that he did not seem to think.

Kells had been rapidly gaining strength since the extraction of the bullet, and it was evident that his interest was growing proportionately. He asked questions and received most of his replies from Red Pearce. Joan did not listen attentively at first, but presently she regretted that she had not. She gathered that Kells's fame as the master bandit of the whole gold region of Idaho, Nevada, and northeastern California was a fame that he loved as much as the gold he stole. Joan sensed, through the replies of these men and their attitude toward Kells, that his power was supreme. He ruled the robbers and ruffians in his bands, and evidently they were scattered from Bannack to Lewiston and all along the border. He had power, likewise, over the border hawks not directly under his leadership. During the weeks of his enforced stay in the canon there had been a cessation of operations—the nature of which Joan merely guessed—and a gradual accumulation of idle waiting men in the main camp. Also she gathered, but vaguely, that though Kells had supreme power, the organization he desired was yet far from being consummated. He showed thoughtfulness and irritation by turns, and it was the subject of gold that drew his intensest interest.

"Reckon you figgered right, Jack," said Red Pearce, and paused as if before a long talk, while he refilled his pipe. "Sooner or later there'll be the biggest gold strike ever made in the West. Wagon-trains are met every day comin' across from Salt Lake. Prospectors are workin' in hordes down from Bannack. All the gulches an' valleys in the Bear Mountains have their camps. Surface gold everywhere an' easy to get where there's water. But there's diggin's all over.

No big strike yet. It's bound to come sooner or later. An' then when the news hits the main-traveled roads an' reaches back into the mountains there's goin' to be a rush that'll make '49 an' '51 look sick. What do you say, Bate?"

"Shore will," replied a grizzled individual whom Kells had called Bate Wood. He was not so young as his companions, more sober, less wild, and slower of speech. "I saw both '49 and '51. Them was days! But I'm agreein' with Red. There shore will be hell on this Idaho border sooner or later. I've been a prospector, though I never hankered after the hard work of diggin' gold. Gold is hard to dig, easy to lose, an' easy to get from some other feller. I see the signs of a comin' strike somewhere in this region. Mebbe it's on now. There's thousands of prospectors in twos an' threes an' groups, out in the hills all over. They ain't a-goin' to tell when they do make a strike. But the gold must be brought out. An' gold is heavy. It ain't easy hid. Thet's how strikes are discovered. I shore reckon thet this year will beat '49 an' '51. An' fer two reasons. There's a steady stream of broken an' disappointed gold-seekers back-trailin' from California. There's a bigger stream of hopeful an' crazy fortune hunters travelin' in from the East. Then there's the wimmen an' gamblers an' such thet hang on. An' last the men thet the war is drivin' out here. Whenever an' wherever these streams meet, if there's a big gold strike, there'll be the hellishest time the world ever saw!"

"Boys," said Kells, with a ring in his weak voice, "it'll be a harvest for my Border Legion."

"Fer what?" queried Bate Wood, curiously.

All the others except Gulden turned inquiring and interested faces toward the bandit.

"The Border Legion," replied Kells.

"An' what's that?" asked Red Pearce, bluntly.

"Well, if the time's ripe for the great gold fever you say is coming, then it's ripe for the greatest band ever organized. I'll organize. I'll call it the Border Legion."

"Count me in as right-hand, pard," replied Red, with enthusiasm.

"An' shore me, boss," added Bate Wood.

The idea was received vociferously, at which demonstration the giant Gulden raised his massive head and asked, or rather growled, in a heavy voice what the fuss was about. His query, his roused presence, seemed to act upon the others, even Kells, with a strange, disquieting or halting force, as if here was a character or an obstacle to be considered. After a moment of silence Red Pearce explained the project.

"Huh! Nothing new in that," replied Gulden. "I belonged to one once. It was in Algiers. They called it the Royal Legion."

"Algiers. What's thet?" asked Bate Wood.

"Africa," replied Gulden.

"Say, Gul, you've been around some," said Red Pearce, admiringly. "What was the Royal Legion?"

"Nothing but a lot of devils from all over. The border there was the last place. Every criminal was safe from pursuit."

"What'd you do?"

Fought among ourselves. Wasn't many in the Legion when I left."

"Shore thet ain't strange!" exclaimed Wood, significantly. But his inference was lost upon Gulden.

"I won't allow fighting in my Legion," said Kells, coolly. "I'll pick this band myself."

"Thet's the secret," rejoined Wood. "The right fellers. I've been in all kinds of bands. Why, I even was a vigilante in '51"

This elicited a laugh from his fellows, except the wooden-faced Gulden.

"How many do we want?" asked Red Pearce.

"The number doesn't matter. But they must be men I can trust and control. Then as lieutenants I'll need a few young fellows, like you, Red. Nervy, daring, cool, quick of wits."

Red Pearce enjoyed the praise bestowed upon him and gave his shoulders a swagger. "Speakin' of that, boss," he said, "reminds me of a chap who rode into Cabin Gulch a few weeks ago. Braced right into Beard's place, where we was all playin' faro, an' he asks for Jack Kells. Right off we all thought he was a guy who had a grievance, an' some of us was for pluggin' him. But I kinda liked him an' I cooled the gang down. Glad I did that. He wasn't wantin' to throw a gun. His intentions were friendly. Of course I didn't show curious about who or what he was. Reckoned he was a young feller who'd gone bad sudden-like an' was huntin' friends. An' I'm here to say, boss, that he was wild."

"What's his name?" asked Kells.

"Jim Cleve, he said," replied Pearce.

Joan Randle, hidden back in the shadows, forgotten or ignored by this bandit group, heard the name Jim Cleve with pain and fear, but not amaze. From the moment Pearce began his speech she had been prepared for the revelation of her runaway lover's name. She trembled, and grew a little sick. Jim had made no idle threat. What would she have given to live over again the moment that had alienated him?"

"Jim Cleve," mused Kells. "Never heard of him. And I never forget a name or a face. What's he like?"

"Clean, rangy chap, big, but not too big," replied Pearce. "All muscle. Not more'n twenty three. Hard rider, hard fighter, hard gambler an' drinker—reckless as hell. If only you can steady him, boss! Ask Bate what he thinks."

"Well!" exclaimed Kells in surprise. "Strangers are everyday occurrences on this border. But I never knew one to impress you fellows as this Cleve. . . . Bate, what do you say? What's this Cleve done? You're an old head. Talk sense, now."

"Done?" echoed Wood, scratching his grizzled head. "What in the hell ain't he done? . . . He rode in brazener than any feller thet ever stacked up against this outfit. An' straight-off he wins the outfit. I don't know how he done it. Mebbe it was because you seen he didn't care fer anythin' or anybody on earth. He stirred us up. He won all the money we had in camp—broke most of us—an' give it all back. He drank more'n the whole outfit, yet didn't get drunk. He threw his gun on Beady Jones fer cheatin' an' then on Beady's pard, Chick Williams. Didn't shoot to kill—jest winged 'em. But say, he's the quickest and smoothest hand to throw a gun thet ever hit this border. Don't overlook thet. . . . Kells, this Jim Cleve's a great youngster goin' bad quick. An' I'm here to add that he'll take some company along."

65

"Bate, you forgot to tell how he handled Luce," said Red Pearce. "You was there. I wasn't. Tell Kells that."

"Luce. I know the man. Go ahead, Bate," responded Kells.

"Mebbe it ain't any recommendation fer said Jim Cleve," replied Wood. "Though it did sorta warm me to him. . . . Boss, of course, you recollect thet little Brander girl over at Bear Lake village. She's old Brander's girl—worked in his store there. I've seen you talk sweet to her myself. Wal, it seems the old man an' some of his boys took to prospectin' an' fetched the girl along. Thet's how I understood it. Luce came bracin' in over at Cabin Gulch one day. As usual, we was drinkin' an' playin'. But young Cleve wasn't doin' neither. He had a strange, moody spell thet day, as I recollect. Luce sprung a job on us. We never worked with him or his outfit, but mebbe—you can't tell what'd come off if it hadn't been for Cleve. Luce had a job put up to ride down where ole Brander was washin' fer gold, take what he had—*an'* the girl. Fact was the gold was only incidental. When somebody cornered Luce he couldn't swear there was gold worth goin' after. An' about then Jim Cleve woke up. He cussed Luce somethin' fearful. An' when Luce went for his gun, natural-like, why this Jim Cleve took it away from him. An' then he jumped Luce. He knocked an' threw him around an' he near beat him to death before we could interfere. Luce was shore near dead. All battered up—broken bones—an' what-all I can't say. We put him to bed an' he's there yet, an' he'll never be the same man he was."

A significant silence fell upon the group at the conclusion of Wood's narrative. Wood had liked the telling, and it made his listeners thoughtful. All at once the pale face of Kells turned slightly toward Gulden.

"Gulden, did you hear that?" asked Kells.

"Yes," replied the man.

"What do you think about this Jim Cleve—and the job he prevented?"

"Never saw Cleve. I'll look him up when we get back to camp. Then I'll go after the Brander girl."

How strangely his brutal assurance marked a line between him and his companions! There was something wrong, something perverse in this Gulden. Had Kells meant to bring that point out or to get an impression of Cleve?"

Joan could not decide. She divined that there was antagonism between Gulden and all the others. And there was something else, vague and intangible, that might have been fear. Apparently Gulden was a criminal for the sake of crime. Joan regarded him with a growing terror—augmented the more because he alone kept eyes upon the corner where she was hidden—and she felt that compared with him the others, even Kells, of whose cold villainy she was assured, were but insignificant men of evil. She covered her head with a blanket to shut out sight of that shaggy, massive head and the great dark caves of eyes.

Thereupon Joan did not see or hear any more of the bandits. Evidently the conversation died down, or she, in the absorption of new thoughts, no longer heard. She relaxed, and suddenly seemed to quiver all over with the name she whispered to herself. "Jim! Jim! Oh, Jim!" And the last whisper was an inward sob. What he had done was terrible. It tortured her. She had not believed it in him. Yet, now she thought, how like him. All for her—in despair and spite—he had ruined himself. He would be killed out there in some drunken brawl, or, still worse, he would become a member of this bandit crew and drift into crime. That was a great blow to Joan—that the curse she had put upon him. How silly, false, and vain had been her coquetry, her indifference! She loved Jim Cleve. She had not known that when she started out to trail him, to fetch him back, but she knew it now. She ought to have known before.

The situation she had foreseen loomed dark and monstrous and terrible in prospect. Just to think of it made her body creep and shudder with cold terror. Yet there was that strange, inward, thrilling burn round her heart. Somewhere and soon she was coming face to face with this changed Jim Cleve—this boy who had become a reckless devil. What would he do? What could she do? Might he not despise her, scorn her, curse her, taking her at Kells's word, the wife of a bandit? But no! he would divine the truth in the flash of an eye. And then! She could not think what might happen, but it must mean blood-death. If he escaped Kells, how could he ever escape this Gulden—this huge vulture of prey?

Still, with the horror thick upon her, Joan could not wholly give up. The moment Jim Cleve's name and his ruin burst upon her ears, in the gossip of these bandits, she had become another girl—a girl wholly become a woman, and one with a driving passion to save if it cost her life. She lost her fear of Kells, of the others, of all except Gulden. He was not human, and instinctively she knew she could do nothing with him. She might influence the others, but never Gulden.

The torment in her brain eased then, and gradually she quieted down, with only a pang and a weight in her breast. The past seemed far away. The present was nothing. Only the future, that contained Jim Cleve, mattered to her. She would not have left the clutches of Kells, if at that moment she could have walked forth free and safe. She was going on to Cabin Gulch. And that thought was the last one in her weary mind as she dropped to sleep.

8

IN THREE days—during which time Joan attended Kells as faithfully as if she were indeed his wife—he thought that he had gained sufficiently to undertake the journey to the main camp, Cabin Gulch. He was eager to get back there and imperious in his overruling of any opposition. The men could take turns at propping him in a saddle. So on the morning of the fourth day they packed for the ride.

During these few days Joan had verified her suspicion

that Kells had two sides to his character; or it seemed, rather, that her presence developed a latent or a long-dead side. When she was with him, thereby distracting his attention, he was entirely different from what he was when his men surrounded him. Apparently he had no knowledge of this. He showed surprise and gratitude at Joan's kindness though never pity or compassion for her. That he had become infatuated with her Joan could no longer doubt. His strange eyes followed her; there was a dreamy light in them; he was mostly silent with her.

Before those few days had come to an end he had developed two things—a reluctance to let Joan leave his sight and an intolerance of the presence of the other men, particularly Gulden. Always Joan felt the eyes of these men upon her, mostly in unobtrusive glances, except Gulden's. The giant studied her with slow, cavernous stare, without curiosity or speculation or admiration. Evidently a woman was a new and strange creature to him and he was experiencing unfamiliar sensations. Whenever Joan accidentally met his gaze—for she avoided it as much as possible—she shuddered with sick memory of a story she had heard—how a huge and ferocious gorilla had stolen into an African village and run off with a white woman. She could not shake the memory. And it was this that made her kinder to Kells than otherwise would have been possible.

All Joan's faculties sharpened in this period. She felt her own development—the beginning of a bitter and hard education—an instinctive assimilation of all that nature taught its wild people and creatures, the first thing in elemental life—self-preservation. Parallel in her heart and mind ran a hopeless despair and a driving, unquenchable spirit. The former was fear, the latter love. She believed beyond a doubt that she had doomed herself along with Jim Cleve; she felt that she had the courage, the power, the love to save him, if not herself. And the reason that she did not falter and fail in this terrible situation was because her despair, great as it was, did not equal her love.

That morning, before being lifted upon his horse, Kells buckled on his gun-belt. The sheath and full round of shells

70

and the gun made this belt a burden for a weak man. And so Red Pearce insisted. But Kells laughed in his face. The men, always excepting Gulden, were unfailing in kindness and care. Apparently they would have fought for Kells to the death. They were simple and direct in their rough feelings. But in Kells, Joan thought, was a character who was a product of this border wildness, yet one who could stand aloof from himself and see the possibilities, the unexpected, the meaning of that life. Kells knew that a man and yet another might show kindness and faithfulness one moment, but the very next, out of a manhood retrograded to the savage, out of the circumstance or chance, might respond to a primitive force far sundered from thought or reason, and rise to unbridled action. Joan divined that Kells buckled on his gun to be ready to protect her. But his men never dreamed his motive. Kells was a strong, bad man set among men like him, yet he was infinitely different because he had brains.

On the start of the journey Joan was instructed to ride before Kells and Pearce, who supported the leader in his saddle. The pack-drivers and Bate Wood and Frenchy rode ahead; Gulden held to the rear. And this order was preserved till noon, when the cavalcade halted for a rest in a shady, grassy, and well-watered nook. Kells was haggard, and his brow wet with clammy dew, and lined with pain. Yet he was cheerful and patient. Still he hurried the men through their tasks.

In an hour the afternoon travel was begun. The cañon and its surroundings grew more rugged and of larger dimensions. Yet the trail appeared to get broader and better all the time. Joan noticed intersecting trails, running down from side cañons and gulches. The descent was gradual, and scarcely evident in any way except in the running water and warmer air.

Kells, tired before the middle of the afternoon, and he would have fallen from his saddle but for the support of his fellows. One by one they held him up. And it was not easy work to ride alongside, holding him up. Joan observed that Gulden did not offer his services. He seemed a part of this gang, yet not of it. Joan never lost a feeling of his presence behind her, and from time to time, when he rode closer, the feeling grew stronger. Toward the close of that afternoon she became aware of Gulden's strange attention. And when a halt was made for camp she dreaded something nameless.

This halt occurred early, before sunset, and had been necessitated by the fact that Kells was fainting. They laid him out on blankets, with his head in his saddle. Joan tended him, and he recovered somewhat, though he lacked the usual keenness.

It was a busy hour with saddles, packs, horses, with wood to cut and fire to build and meal to cook. Kells drank thirstily, but refused food.

"Joan," he whispered, at an opportune moment, "I'm only tired—dead for sleep. You stay beside me. Wake me quick—if you want to!"

He closed his eyes wearily, without explaining, and soon slumbered. Joan did not choose to allow these men to see that she feared them or distrusted them or disliked them. She ate with them beside the fire. And this was their first opportunity to be close to her. The fact had an immediate and singular influence. Joan had no vanity, though she knew she was handsome. She forced herself to be pleasant, agreeable, even sweet. Their response was instant and growing. At first they were bold, then familiar and coarse. For years she had been used to rough men of the camps. These however, were different, and their jokes and suggestions had no effect because they were beyond her. And when this became manifest to them that aspect of their relation to her changed. She grasped the fact intuitively, and then she verified it by proof. Her heart beat strong and high. If she could hide her hate, her fear, her abhorrence, she could influence these wild men. But it all depended upon her charm, her strangeness, her femininity. Insensibly they had been influenced, and it proved that in the worst of men there yet survived some good. Gulden alone presented a contrast and a problem. He appeared aware of her presence while he sat there eating like a wolf, but it was as if she were only an object. The man watched as might have an animal.

Her experience at the camp-fire meal inclined her to the belief that, if there were such a possibility as her being safe at all, it would be owing to an unconscious and friendly at-

72

litude toward the companions she had been forced to accept. Those men were pleased, stirred at being in her vicinity. Joan came to a melancholy and fearful cognizance of her attraction. While at home she seldom had borne upon her a reality—that she was a woman. Her place, her person were merely natural. Here it was all different. To these wild men, developed by loneliness, fierce-blooded, with pulses like whips, a woman was something that thrilled, charmed, soothed, that incited a strange, insatiable, inexplicable hunger for the very sight of her. They did not realize it, but Joan did.

Presently Joan finished her supper and said: "I'll go hobble my horse. He strays sometimes."

"Shore I'll go, miss," said Bate Wood. He had never called her Mrs. Kells, but Joan believed he had not thought of the significance. Hardened old ruffian that he was. Joan regarded him as the best of a bad lot. He had lived long, and some of his life had not been bad.

"Let me go," added Pearce.

"No, thanks. I'll go myself," she replied.

She took the rope hobble off her saddle and boldly swung down the trail. Suddenly she heard two or more of the men speak at once, and then, low and clear: "Gulden, where'n hell are you goin'?" This was Red Pearce's voice.

Joan glanced back. Gulden had started down the trail after her. Her heart quaked, her knees shook, and she was ready to run back. Gulden halted, then turned away, growling. He acted as if caught in something surprising to himself.

"We're on to you, Gulden," continued Pearce, deliberately. "Be careful or we'll put Kells on."

A booming, angry curse was the response. The men grouped closer and a loud altercation followed. Joan almost ran down the trail and heard no more. If any one of them had started her way now she would have plunged into the thickets like a frightened deer. Evidently, however, they meant to let her alone. Joan found her horse, and before hobbling him she was assailed by a temptation to mount him and ride away. This she did not want to do and would

73

not do under any circumstances; still, she could not prevent the natural instinctive impulse of a woman.

She crossed to the other side of the brook and returned toward camp under the spruce and balsam trees. She did not hurry. It was good to be alone, out of sight of those violent men, away from that constant wearing physical proof of catastrophe. Nevertheless, she did not feel free or safe for a moment; she peered fearfully into the shadows of the rocks and trees; and presently it was a relief to get back to the side of the sleeping Kells. He lay in a deep slumber of exhaustion. She arranged her own saddle and blankets near him, and prepared to meet the night as best she could. Instinctively she took a position where in one swift snatch she could get possession of Kells's gun.

It was about time of sunset, warm and still in the cañon, with rosy lights fading upon the peaks. The men were all busy with one thing and another. Strange it was to see that Gulden, who Joan thought might be a shirker, did twice the work of any man, especially the heavy work. He seemed to enjoy carrying a log that would have overweighted two ordinary men. He was so huge, so active, so powerful that it was fascinating to watch him. They built the camp-fire for the night uncomfortably near Joan's position; however, remembering how cold the air would become later, she made no objection. Twilight set in and the men, through for the day, gathered near the fire.

Then Joan was not long in discovering that the situation had begun to impinge upon the feelings of each of these men. They looked at her differently. Some of them invented pretexts to approach her, to ask something, to offer service—anything to get near her. A personal and individual note had been injected into the attitude of each. Intuitively Joan guessed that Gulden's arising to follow her had turned their eyes inward. Gulden remained silent and inactive at the edge of the camp-fire circle of light, which flickered fitfully around him, making him seem a huge, gloomy ape of a man. So far as Joan could tell, Gulden never cast his eyes in her direction. That was a difference which left cause for reflection. Had that hulk of brawn and bone begun to think? Bate Wood's overtures to Joan were rough, but inexplicable to her because she dared not wholly trust him.

"An' shore, miss," he had concluded, in a hoarse whisper, "we-all know you ain't Kells's wife. Thet bandit wouldn't marry no woman. He's a woman-hater. He was famous fer thet over in California. He's run off with you—kidnapped you, thet's shore. . . . An' Gulden swears he shot his own men an' was in turn shot by you. Thet bullet-hole in his back was full of powder. There's liable to be a muss-up any time. . . . Shore, miss, you'd better sneak off with me to-night when they're all asleep. I'll git grub an' hosses, an' take you off to some prospector's camp. Then you can git home."

Joan only shook her head. Even if she could have felt trust in Wood—and she was of half a mind to believe him—it was too late. Whatever befell her mattered little if in suffering it she could save Jim Cleve from the ruin she had wrought.

Since this wild experience of Joan's had begun she had been sick so many times with raw and naked emotions hitherto unknown to her, that she believed she could not feel another new fear or torture. But these strange sensations grew by what they had been fed upon.

The man called Frenchy, was audacious, persistent, smiling, amorous-eyed, and rudely gallant. He cared no more for his companions than if they had not been there. He vied with Pearce in his attention, and the two of them discomfited the others. The situation might have been amusing had it not been so terrible. Always the portent was a shadow behind their interest and amiability and jealousy. Except for that one abrupt and sinister move of Gulden's— that of a natural man beyond deceit—there was no word, no look, no act at which Joan could have been offended. They were joking, sarcastic, ironical, and sullen in their relation to each other; but to Joan each one presented what was naturally or what he considered his kindest and most friendly front. A young and attractive woman had dropped into the camp of lonely wild men; and in their wild hearts was a rebirth of egotism, vanity, hunger for notice. They seemed as foolish as a lot of cock grouse preening themselves and

75

parading before a single female. Surely in some heart was born real brotherhood for a helpless girl in peril. Inevitably in some of them would burst a flame of passion as it had in Kells.

Between this amiable contest for Joan's glances and replies, with its possibility of latent good to her, and the dark, lurking, unspoken meaning, such as lay in Gulden's brooding, Joan found another new and sickening torture.

"Say, Frenchy, you're no lady's man," declared Red Pearce, "an' you, Bate, you're too old. Move—pass by—sashay!" Pearce, good-naturedly, but deliberately, pushed the two men back.

"Shore she's Kells's lady, ain't she?" drawled Wood. "Ain't you all forgettin' thet?"

"Kells is asleep or dead," replied Pearce, and he succeeded in getting the field to himself.

"Where'd you meet Kells anyway?" he asked Joan, with his red face bending near hers.

Joan had her part to play. It was difficult, because she divined Pearce's curiosity held a trap to catch her in a falsehood. He knew—they all knew she was not Kells's wife. But if she were a prisoner she seemed a willing and contented one. The query that breathed in Pearce's presence was how was he to reconcile the fact of her submission with what he and his comrades had potently felt as her goodness?"

"That doesn't concern anybody," replied Joan.

"Reckon not," said Pearce. Then he leaned nearer with intense face. "What I want to know—is Gulden right? Did you shoot Kells?"

In the dusk Joan reached back and clasped Kells' hand.

For a man as weak and weary as he had been, it was remarkable how quickly a touch awakened him. He lifted his head.

"Hello! Who's that?" he called out, sharply.

Pearce rose guardedly, startled, but not confused. "It's only me, boss," he replied. "I was about to turn in,-an' I wanted to know how you are—if I could do anythin'."

"I'm all right, Red," replied Kells, coolly. "Clear out and let me alone. All of you."

Pearce moved away with an amiable good-night and

joined the others at the camp-fire. Presently they sought their blankets, leaving Gulden hunching there silent in the gloom.

"Joan, why did you wake me?" whispered Kells.

"Pearce asked me if I shot you," replied Joan. "I woke you instead of answering him."

"He did!" exclaimed Kells under his breath. Then he laughed. "Can't fool that gang. I guess it doesn't matter. Maybe it'd be well if they knew you shot me."

He appeared thoughtful, and lay there with the fading flare of the fire on his pale face. But he did not speak again. Presently he fell asleep.

Joan leaned back, within reach of him, with her head in her saddle, and pulling a blanket up over her, relaxed her limbs to rest. Sleep seemed the furthest thing from her. She wondered that she dared to think of it. The night had grown chilly; the wind was sweeping with low roar through the balsams; the fire burned dull and red. Joan watched the black, shapeless hulk that she knew to be Gulden. For a long time he remained motionless. By and by he moved, approached the fire, stood one moment in the dying ruddy glow. his great breadth and bulk magnified, with all about him vague and shadowy, but the more sinister for that. The cavernous eyes were only black spaces in that vast face, yet Joan saw them upon her. He lay down then among the other men and soon his deep and heavy breathing denoted the tranquil slumber of an ox.

For hours through changing shadows and starlight Joan lay awake, while a thousand thoughts besieged her, all centering round that vital and compelling one of Jim Cleve.

Only upon awakening, with the sun in her face, did Joan realize that she had actually slept.

The camp was bustling with activity. The horses were in, fresh and quarrelsome, with ears laid back. Kells was sitting upon a rock near the fire with a cup of coffee in his hand. He was looking better. When he greeted Joan his voice sounded stronger. She walked by Pearce and Frenchy and Gulden on her way to the brook, but they took no notice of her. Bate Wood, however, touched his sombrero and said: "Mornin', miss." Joan wondered if her memory of the preceding night were only a bad dream. There was a different atmosphere by daylight, and it was dominated by Kells. Presently she returned to camp refreshed and hungry. Gulden was throwing a pack, which action he performed with ease and dexterity. Pearce was cinching her saddle. Kells was talking, more like his old self than at any time since his injury.

Soon they were on the trail. For Joan time always passed swiftly on horseback. Movement and changing scene were pleasurable to her. The passing of time now held a strange expectancy, a mingled fear and hope and pain, for at the end of this trail was Jim Cleve. In other days she had flouted him, made fun of him, dominated him, everything except loved and feared him. And now she was assured of her love and almost convinced of her fear. The reputation these wild bandits gave Jim was astounding and inexplicable to Joan. She rode the miles thinking of Jim, dreading to meet him, longing to see him, and praying and planning for him.

About noon the cavalcade rode out of the mouth of a cañon into a wide valley, surrounded by high, rounded foot-hills. Horses and cattle were grazing on the green levels. A wide, shallow, noisy stream split the valley. Joan could tell from the tracks at the crossing that this place, whatever and wherever it was, saw considerable travel; and she concluded the main rendezvous of the bandits was close at hand.

The pack drivers led across the stream and the valley to enter an intersecting ravine. It was narrow, rough-sided, and floored, but the trail was good. Presently it opened out into a beautiful V-shaped gulch, very different from the high-walled, shut-in cañons. It had a level floor, through which a brook flowed, and clumps of spruce and pine, with here and there a giant balsam. Huge patches of wild flowers gave rosy color to the grassy slopes. At the upper end of this gulch Joan saw a number of widely separated cabins. This place, then, was Cabin Gulch.

Upon reaching the first cabin the cavalcade split up. There were men here who hallooed a welcome. Gulden halted with his pack-horse. Some of the others rode on. Wood drove other pack-animals off to the right, up the gentle slope. And Red Pearce, who was beside Kells, instructed Joan to follow them. They rode up to a bench of straggling spruce-trees, in the midst of which stood a large log cabin. It was new, as in fact all the structures in the Gulch appeared to be, and none of them had seen a winter. The chinks between the logs were yet open. This cabin was of the rudest make of notched logs one upon another, and roof of brush and earth. It was low and flat, but very long, and extending before the whole of it was a porch roof supported by posts. At one end was a corral. There were doors and windows with nothing in them. Upon the front wall, outside, hung saddles and bridles.

Joan had a swift, sharp gaze for the men who rose from their lounging to greet the travelers. Jim Cleve was not among them. Her heart left her throat then, and she breathed easier. How could she meet him?

Kells was in better shape than at noon of the preceding day. Still, he had to be lifted off his horse. Joan heard all the men talking at once. They crowded round Pearce, each lending a hand. However, Kells appeared able to walk into the cabin. It was Bate Wood who led Joan inside.

There was a long room, with stone fireplace, rude benches and a table, skins and blankets on the floor, and lanterns and weapons on the wall. At one end Joan saw a litter of cooking utensils and shelves of supplies.

Suddenly Kells's impatient voice silenced the clamor of questions. "I'm not hurt," he said. "I'm all right—only weak and tired. Fellows, this girl is my wife. . . . Joan, you'll find a room there—at the back of the cabin. Make yourself comfortable."

Joan was only too glad to act upon his suggestion. A door had been cut through the back wall. It was covered with a blanket. When she swept this aside she came upon several steep steps that led up to a smaller, lighter cabin of two rooms, separated by a partition of boughs. She dropped the blanket behind her and went up the steps. Then she saw that the new cabin had been built against an old one. It had no door or opening except the one by which she had entered. It was light because the chinks between the logs were open.

The furnishings were a wide bench of boughs covered with blankets, a shelf with a blurred and cracked mirror hanging above it, a table made of boxes, and a lantern. This room was four feet higher than the floor of the other cabin. And at the bottom of the steps leaned a half-dozen slender trimmed poles. She gathered presently that these poles were intended to be slipped under crosspieces above and fastened by a bar below, which means effectually barricaded the opening. Joan could stand at the head of the steps and peep under an edge of the swinging blanket into the large room, but that was the only place she could see through, for the openings between the logs of each wall were not level. These quarters were comfortable, private, and could be shut off from intruders. Joan had not expected so much consideration from Kells and she was grateful.

She lay down to rest and think. It was really very pleasant here. There were birds nesting in the chinks; a ground squirrel ran along one of the logs and chirped at her; through an opening near her face she saw a wild rose-bush and the green slope of the gulch; a soft, warm, fragrant breeze blew in, stirring her hair. How strange that there could be beautiful and pleasant things here in this robber den; that time was the same here as elsewhere; that the sun shone and the sky gleamed blue. Presently she discovered that a lassitude weighted upon her and she could not keep her eyes open. She ceased trying, but intended to remain awake—to think, to listen, to wait. Nevertheless, she did fall asleep and did not awaken till disturbed by some noise. The color of the western sky told her that the afternoon was far spent. She had slept hours. Someone was knocking. She got up and drew aside the blanket. Bate Wood was standing near the door.

"Now, miss, I've supper ready," he said, "an' I was reckonin' you'd like me to fetch yours."

"Yes, thank you, I would," replied Joan.

In a few moments Wood returned carrying the top of a box upon which were steaming pans and cups. He handed this rude tray up to Joan.

"Shore I'm a first-rate cook, miss, when I've somethin' to cook," he said with a smile that changed his hard face.

She returned the smile with her thanks. Evidently Kells had a well-filled larder, and as Joan had fared on coarse and hard food for long, this supper was a luxury and exceedingly appetizing. While she was eating, the blanket curtain moved aside and Kells appeared. He dropped it behind him, but did not step up into the room. He was in his shirt-sleeves, had been clean shaven, and looked a different man.

"How do you like your—home?" he inquired, with a hint of his former mockery.

"I'm grateful for the privacy," she replied.

"You think you could be worse off, then?"

"I know it."

"Suppose Gulden kills me—and rules the gang—and takes you? . . . There's a story about him, the worst I've heard on this border. I'll tell you some day when I want to scare you bad."

"Gulden!" Joan shivered as she pronounced the name. "Are you and he enemies?"

"No man can have a friend on this border. We flock together like buzzards. There's safety in numbers, but we fight together, like buzzards over carrion."

"Kells, you hate this life?"

"I've always hated *my* life, everywhere. The only life I ever loved was adventure. . . . I'm willing to try a new one, if you'll go with me."

Joan shook her head.

"Why not? I'll marry you," he went on, speaking lower. "I've got gold; I'll get more."

"Where did you get the gold?" she asked

"I've relieved a good many overburdened travelers and prospectors," he replied.

"Kells, you're a—a villain!" exclaimed Joan, unable to contain her sudden heat. "You must be utterly mad—to ask me to marry you."

"No, I'm not mad," he rejoined, with a laugh. "Gulden's the mad one. He's crazy. He's got a twist in his brain. I'm no fool. . . . I've only lost my head over you. But compare marrying me, living and traveling among decent people and comfort, to camps like this. If I don't get drunk I'll be half

81

decent to you. But I'll get shot sooner or later. Then you'll be left to Gulden."

"Why do you say *him?*" she queried, in a shudder of curiosity.

"Well, Gulden haunts me."

"He does me, too. He makes me lose my sense of proportion. Beside him you and the others seem good. But you *are* wicked."

"Then you won't marry me and go away somewhere? . . . Your choice is strange. Because I tell you the truth."

"Kells! I'm a woman. Something deep in me says you won't keep me here—you *can't* be so base. Not *now,* after I saved your life! It would be horrible—inhuman. I can't believe any man born of a woman could do it."

"But I want you—I love you!" he said, low and hard.

"Love! That's not love," she replied in scorn. "God only knows what it is."

"Call it what you like," he went on, bitterly. "You're a young, beautiful, sweet woman. It's wonderful to be near you. My life has been hell. I've had nothing. There's only hell to look forward to—and hell at the end. Why shouldn't I keep you here?"

"But, Kells, listen," she whispered, earnestly, "suppose I am young and beautiful and sweet—as you said. I'm utterly in your power. I'm compelled to seek your protection from even worse men. You're different from these others. You're educated. You must have had—a—a good mother. Now you're bitter, desperate, terrible. You hate life. You seem to think this charm you see in me will bring you something. Maybe a glimpse of joy! But how can it? You know better. How can it . . . unless I—I love you?"

Kells stared at her, the evil and hardness of his passion corded in his face. And the shadows of comprehending thought in his strange eyes showed the other side of the man. He was still staring at her while he reached to put aside the curtains; then he dropped his head and went out.

Joan sat motionless, watching the door where he had disappeared, listening to the mounting beats of her heart. She had only been frank and earnest with Kells. But he had taken a meaning from her last few words that she had not intended to convey. All that was woman in her—mounting, fighting, hating—leaped to the power she sensed in herself. If she could be deceitful, cunning, shameless in holding out to Kells a possible return of his love, she could do anything with him. She knew it. She did not need to marry him or sacrifice herself. Joan was amazed that the idea remained an instant before her consciousness. But something had told her this was another kind of life than she had known, and all that was precious to her hung in the balance. Any falsity was justifiable, even righteous, under the circumstances. Could she formulate a plan that this keen bandit would not see through? The remotest possibility of her even caring for Kells—that was as much as she dared hint. But that, together with all the charm and seductiveness she could summon, might be enough. Dared she try it? If she tried and failed Kells would despise her, and then she was utterly lost. She was caught between doubt and hope. All that was natural and true in her shrank from such unwomanly deception; all that had been born of her wild experience inflamed her to play the game, to match Kells's villainy with a woman's unfathomable duplicity.

And while Joan was absorbed in thought the sun set, the light failed, twilight stole into the cabin, and then darkness. All this hour there had been a continual sound of men's voices in the large cabin, sometimes low and at other times loud. It was only when Joan distinctly heard the name Jim Cleve that she was startled out of her absorption, thrilling and flushing. In her eagerness she nearly fell as she stepped and gropped through the darkness to the door, and as she drew aside the blanket her hand shook.

The large room was lighted by a fire and half a dozen lanterns. Through a faint tinge of blue smoke Joan saw men standing and sitting and lounging around Kells, who had a seat where the light fell full upon him. Evidently a lull had intervened in the talk. The dark faces Joan could see were all turned toward the door expectantly.

"Bring him in, Bate, and let's look him over," said Kells.

Then Bate Wood appeared, elbowing his way in, and he had his hand on the arm of a tall, lithe fellow. When they got into the light Joan quivered as if she had been stabbed.

That stranger with Wood was Jim Cleve—Jim Cleve in frame and feature, yet not the same she knew.

"Cleve, glad to meet you," greeted Kells, extending his hand.

"Thanks. Same to you," replied Cleve, and he met the proffered hand. His voice was cold and colorless, unfamiliar to Joan. Was this man really Jim Cleve?

The meeting of Kells and Cleve was significant because of Kells's interest and the silent attention of the men of his clan. It did not seem to mean anything to the white-faced, tragic-eyed Cleve. Joan gazed at him with utter amazement. She remembered a heavily built, florid Jim Cleve, an overgrown boy with a good-natured, lazy smile on his full face and sleepy eyes. She all but failed to recognize him in the man who stood there now, lithe and powerful, with muscles bulging in his coarse, white shirt. Joan's gaze swept over him, up and down, shivering at the two heavy guns he packed, till it was transfixed on his face. The old, or the other, Jim Cleve had been homely, with too much flesh on his face to show force or fire. This man seemed beautiful. But it was a beauty of tragedy. He was as white as Kells, but smoothly, purely white, without shadow or sunburn. His lips seemed to have set with a bitter, indifferent laugh. His eyes looked straight out, piercing, intent, haunted, and as dark as night. Great blue circles lay under them, lending still further depth and mystery. It was a sad, reckless face that wrung Joan's very heartstrings. She had come too late to save his happiness, but she prayed that it was not too late to save his honor and his soul.

While she gazed there had been further exchange of speech between Kells and Cleve, and she had heard, though not distinguished, what was said. Kells was unmistakably friendly. as were the other men within range of Joan's sight. Cleve was surrounded; there were jesting and laughter; and then he was led to the long table where several men were already gambling.

Joan dropped the curtain, and in the darkness of her cabin she saw that white, haunting face, and when she covered her eyes she still saw it. The pain, the reckless violence, the hopeless indifference, the wreck and ruin in that face had been her doing. Why? How had Jim Cleve wronged her? He had loved her at her displeasure and had kissed her against her will. She had furiously upbraided him, and when he had finally turned upon her, threatening to prove he was no coward, she had scorned him with a girl's merciless injustice. All her strength and resolve left her, momentarily, after seeing Jim there. Like a woman, she weakened. She lay on the bed and writhed. Doubt, hopelessness, despair, again seized upon her, and some strange, yearning maddening emotion. What had she sacrificed? His happiness and her own—and both their lives!

The clamor in the other cabin grew so boisterous that suddenly when it stilled Joan was brought shaply to the significance of it. Again she drew aside the curtain and peered out.

Gulden, huge, stolid, gloomy, was entering the cabin. The man fell into the circle and faced Kell with the fire-light dancing in his cavernous eyes.

"Hello, Gulden!" said Kells, coolly. "What ails you?"

"Anybody tell you about Bill Bailey?" asked Gulden, heavily.

Kells did not show the least concern. "Tell me what?"

"That he died in a cabin, down in the valley?"

Kells gave a slight start and his eyes narrowed and shot steely glints. "No. It's news to me."

"Kells, you left Bailey for dead. But he lived. He was shot through, but he got there somehow—nobody knows. He was far gone when Beady Jones happened along. Before he died he sent word to me by Beady. . . . Are you curious to know what it was?"

"Not the least," replied Kells. "Bailey was—well, offensive to my wife. I shot him."

"He swore you drew on him in cold blood," thundered Gulden. "He swore it was for nothing—just so you could be alone with that girl!"

Kells rose in wonderful calmness, with only his pallor and a slight shaking of his hands to betray excitement. An uneasy stir and murmur ran through the room. Red Pearce, nearest at hand, stepped to Kells's side. All in a moment there was a deadly surcharged atmosphere there.

"Well, he swore right! . . . Now what's it to you?"

Apparently the fact and its confession were nothing particular to Gulden, or else he was deep where all considered him only dense and shallow.

"It's done. Bill's dead," continued Gulden. "But why do you double-cross the gang? What's the game? You never did it before. . . . That girl isn't your—"

"Shut up!" hissed Kells. Like a flash his hand flew out with his gun, and all about him was dark menace.

Gulden made no attempt to draw. He did not show surprise nor fear nor any emotion. He appeared plodding in mind.

Red Pearce stepped between Kells and Gulden. There was a realization in the crowd, loud breaths, scraping of feet. Gulden turned away. Then Kells resumed his seat and his pipe as if nothing out of the ordinary had occurred.

9

◈

JOAN turned away from the door in a cold clamp of relief.
The shadow of death hovered over these men. She must fortify herself to live under that shadow, to be prepared for any
sudden violence, to stand a succession of shocks that
inevitably would come. She listened. The men were talking
and laughing now; there came a click of chips, the spat of a
thrown card, the thump of a little sack of gold. Ahead of her
lay the long hours of night in which these men would hold

revel. Only a faint ray of light penetrated her cabin, but it was sufficient for her to distinguish objects. She set about putting the poles in place to barricade the opening. When she had finished she knew she was safe at least from intrusion. Who had constructed that rude door and for what purpose? Then she yielded to the temptation to peep once more under the edge of the curtain.

The room was cloudy and blue with smoke. She saw Jim Cleve at a table gambling with several ruffians. His back was turned, yet Joan felt the contrast of his attitude toward the game, compared with that of the others. They were tense, fierce, and intent upon every throw of a card. Cleve's very poise of head and movement of arm betrayed his indifference. One of the gamblers howled his disgust, slammed down his cards, and got up.

"He's cleaned out," said one, in devilish glee.

"Naw, he ain't," voiced another. "He's got two fruit-cans full of dust. I saw 'em. . . . He's just lay down—like a poisoned coyote."

"Shore I'm glad Cleve's got the luck, fer mebbe he'll give my gold back," spoke up another gamester, with a laugh.

"Wal, he certainlee is the chilvalus card sharp," rejoined the last player. "Jim, was you allus as lucky in love as in cards?"

"Lucky in love? . . . Sure!" answered Jim Cleve, with a mocking, reckless ring in his voice.

"Funny, ain't thet, boys? Now there's the boss. Kells can sure win the gurls, but he's a pore gambler." Kells heard this speech, and he laughed with the others. "Hey, you greaser, you never won any of my money," he said.

"Come an' set in, boss. Come an' see your gold fade away. You can't stop this Jim Cleve. Luck—bull luck straddles his neck. He'll win your gold—your hosses an' saddles an' spurs an' guns—an' your shirt, if you've nerve enough to bet it."

The speaker slapped his cards upon the table while he gazed at Cleve in grieved admiration. Kells walked over to the group and he put his hand on Cleve's shoulder.

"Say youngster," he said, genially, "you said you were

just as lucky in love. . . . Now I had a hunch some *bad* luck with a girl drove you out here to the border."

Kells spoke jestingly, in a way that could give no offense, even to the wildest of boys, yet there was curiosity, keenness, penetration, in his speech. It had not the slightest effect upon Jim Cleve.

"Bad luck and a girl? . . . To hell with both!" he said.

"Shore you're talkin' religion. Thet's where both luck an' gurls come from," replied the unlucky gamester. "Will one of you hawgs pass the whiskey?"

The increased interest with which Kells looked down upon Jim Cleve was not lost upon Joan. But she had seen enough, and, turning away, she stumbled to the bed and lay there with an ache in her heart.

"Oh," she whispered to herself, "he is ruined—ruined—ruined! . . . God forgive me!" She saw bright, cold stars shining between the logs. The night wind swept in cold and pure, with the dew of the mountain in it. She heard the mourn of wolves, the hoot of an owl, the distant cry of a panther, weird and wild. Yet outside there was a thick and lonely silence. In that other cabin, from which she was mercifully shut out, there were different sounds, hideous by contrast. By and by she covered her ears, and at length, weary from thought and sorrow, she drifted into slumber.

Next morning, long after she had awakened, the cabin remained quiet, with no one stirring. Morning had half gone before Wood knocked and gave her a bucket of water, a basin and towels. Later he came with her breakfast. After that she had nothing to do but pace the floor of her two rooms. One appeared to be only an empty shed, long in disuse. Her view from both rooms was resticted to the green slope of the gulch up to yellow crags and the sky. But she would rather have had this to watch than an outlook upon the cabins and the doings of these bandits.

About noon she heard the voice of Kells in low and earnest conversation with someone; she could not, however, understand what was said. That ceased, and then she heard Kells moving around. There came a clatter of hoofs as a horse galloped away from the cabin, after which a knock sounded on the wall.

"Joan," called Kells. Then the curtain was swept aside and Kells, appearing pale and troubled, stepped into her room.

"What's the matter?" asked Joan, hurriedly.

"Gulden shot two men this morning. One's dead. The other's in bad shape, so Red tells me. I haven't seen him."

"Who—who are they?" faltered Joan. She could not think of any man except Jim Cleve.

"Dan Small's the one's dead. The other they call Dick. Never heard his last name."

"Was it a fight?"

"Of course. And Gulden picked it. He's a quarrelsome man. Nobody can go against him. He's all the time like some men when they're drunk. I'm sorry I didn't bore him last night. I would have done it if it hadn't been for Red Pearce."

Kells seemed gloomy and concentrated on his situation and he talked naturally to Joan, as if she were one to sympathize. A bandit, then, in the details of his life, the schemes, troubles, friendships, relations, was no different from any other kind of a man. He was human, and things that might constitute black evil for observers were dear to him, a part of him. Joan feigned the sympathy she could not feel.

"I thought Gulden was your enemy."

Kells sat down on one of the box seats, and his heavy gun-sheath rested upon the floor. He looked at Joan now, forgetting she was a woman and his prisoner.

"I never thought of that till now," he said. "We always got along because I understood him. I managed him. The man hasn't changed in the least. He's always what he *is*. But there's a difference. I noticed that first over in Lost Cañon. And Joan, I believe it's because Gulden saw you."

"Oh, no!" cried Joan, trembling.

"Maybe I'm wrong. Anyway something's wrong. Gulden never had a friend or a partner. I don't misunderstand his position regarding Bailey. What did he care for that soak? Gulden's cross-grained. He opposes anything or anybody. He's got a twist in his mind that makes him dangerous. . . .

I wanted to get rid of him. I decided to—after last night. But now it seems that's no easy job."

"Why?" asked Joan, curiously.

"Pearce and Wood and Beard, all men I rely on, said it won't do. They hint Gulden is strong with my gang here, and all through the border. I was wild. I don't believe it. But as I'm not sure—what can I do? . . . They're all afraid of Gulden. That's it. . . . And I believe I am, too."

"You!" exclaimed Joan.

Kells actually looked ashamed. "I believe I am, Joan," he replied. "That Gulden is not a man. I never was afraid of a real man. He's—he's an animal."

"He made me think of a gorrilla," said Joan.

"There's only one man I know who's not afraid of Gulden. He's a new-comer here on the border. Jim Cleve he calls himself. A youngster I can't figure! But he'd slap the devil himself in the face. Cleve won't last long out here. Yet you can never tell. Men like him, who laugh at death, sometimes avert it for long. I was that way once. . . . Cleve heard me talking to Pearce about Gulden. And he said, 'Kells, I'll pick a fight with this Gulden and drive him out of the camp or kill him.' "

"What did you say?" queried Joan, trying to steady her voice as she averted her eyes.

"I said 'Jim, that wins me. But I don't want you killed.' . . . It certainly was nervy of the youngster. Said it just the same as—as he'd offer to cinch my saddle. Gulden can whip a roomful of men. He's done it. And as for a killer—I've heard of no man with his record."

"And that's why you fear him?"

"It's not," replied Kells, passionately, as if his manhood had been affronted. "It's because he's Gulden. There's something uncanny about him. . . . Gulden's a cannibal!"

Joan looked as if she had not heard aright.

"It's a cold fact. Known all over the border. Gulden's no braggart. But he's been known to talk. He was a sailor—a pirate. Once he was shipwrecked. Starvation forced him to be a cannibal. He told this in California, and in Nevada camps. But no one believed him. A few years ago he got snowed-up in the mountains back of Lewiston. He

91

had two companions with him. They all began to starve. It was absolutely necessary to try to get out. They started out in the snow. Travel was desperately hard. Gulden told that his companions dropped. But he murdered them—and again saved his life by being a cannibal. After this became known his sailor yarns were no longer doubted. . . . There's another story about him. Once he got hold of a girl and took her into the mountains. After a winter he returned alone. He told that he'd kept her tied in a cave, without any clothes, and she froze to death."

"Oh, horrible!" moaned Joan.

"I don't know how true it is. But I believe it. Gulden is not a man. The worst of us have a conscience. We can tell right from wrong. But Gulden can't. He's beneath morals. He has no conception of manhood, such as I've seen in the lowest of outcasts. That cave story with the girl—that betrays him. He belongs back in the Stone Age. He's a thing. . . . And here on the border, if he wants, he can have all the more power because of what he is."

"Kells, don't let him see me!" entreated Joan.

The bandit appeared not to catch the fear in Joan's tone and look. She had been only a listener. Presently with preoccupied and gloomy mien, he left her alone.

Joan did not see him again, except for glimpses under the curtain, for three days. She kept the door barred and saw no one except Bate Wood, who brought her meals. She paced her cabin like a caged creature. During this period few men visited Kells's cabin, and these few did not remain long. Joan was aware that Kells was not always at home. Evidently he was able to go out. Upon the fourth day he called to her and knocked for admittance. Joan let him in, and saw that he was now almost well again, once more cool, easy, cheerful, with his strange, forceful air.

"Good day, Joan. You don't seem to be pining for your—negligent husband."

He laughed as if he mocked himself, but there was gladness in the very sight of her, and some indefinable tone in his voice that suggested respect.

"I didn't miss you," replied Joan. Yet it was a relief to see him.

"No, I imagine not," he said, dryly. "Well, I've been busy with men—with plans. Things are working out to my satisfaction. Red Pearce got around Gulden. There's been no split. Besides, Gulden rode off. Someone said he went after a little girl named Brander. I hope he gets shot. . . . Joan, we'll be leaving Cabin Gulch soon. I'm expecting news that'll change things. I won't leave you here. You'll have to ride the roughest trails. And your clothes are in tatters now. You've got to have something to wear."

"I should think so," replied Joan, fingering the thin, worn, ragged habit that had gone to pieces. "The first brush I ride through will tear this off."

"That's annoying," said Kells, with exasperation at himself. "Where on earth can I get you a dress? We're two hundred miles from everywhere. The wildest kind of country. . . . Say, did you ever wear a man's outfit?"

"Ye-es, when I went prospecting and hunting with my uncle," she replied, reluctantly.

Suddenly he had a daring and brilliant smile that changed his face completely. He rubbed his palms together. He laughed as if at a huge joke. He cast a measuring glance up and down her slender form.

"Just wait till I come back," he said.

He left her and she heard him rummaging around in the pile of trappings she had noted in a corner of the other cabin. Presently he returned carrying a bundle. This he unrolled on the bed and spread out the articles.

"Dandy Dale's outfit," he said, with animation. "Dandy was a would-be knight of the road. He dressed the part. But he tried to hold up a stage over here and an unappreciative passenger shot him. He wasn't killed outright. He crawled away and died. Some of my men found him and they fetched his clothes. That outfit cost a fortune. But not a man among us could get into it."

There was a black sombrero with heavy silver band; a dark-blue blouse and an embroidered buckskin vest; a belt full of cartridges and a pearl-handled gun; trousers of corduroy; high-top leather boots and gold mounted spurs, all of the finest material and workmanship.

"Joan, I'll make you a black mask out of the rim of a felt hat, and then you'll be grand." He spoke with the impulse and enthusiasm of a boy.

"Kells, you don't mean me to wear these?" asked Joan, incredulously.

"Certainly. Why not? Just the thing. A little fancy, but then you're a girl. We can't hide that. I don't want to hide it."

"I won't wear them," declared Joan.

"Excuse me—but you will," he replied, coolly and pleasantly.

"I won't!" cried Joan. She could not keep cool.

"Joan, you've got to take long rides with me. At night sometimes. Wild rides to elude pursuers sometimes. You'll go into camps with me. You'll have to wear strong, easy, free clothes. You'll have to be masked. Here the outfit is—as if made for you. Why, you're dead lucky. For this stuff is good and strong. It'll stand the wear, yet it's fit for a girl. . . . You put the outfit on, right now."

"I said I wouldn't!" Joan snapped.

"But what do you care if it belonged to a fellow who's dead? . . . There! See that hole in the shirt. That's a bullet-hole. Don't be squeamish. It'll only make your part harder."

"Mr. Kells, you seem to have forgotten entirely that I'm a—a girl."

He looked blank astonishment. "Maybe I have. . . . I'll remember. But you said you'd worn a man's things."

"I wore my brother's coat and overalls, and was lost in them," replied Joan.

His face began to work. Then he laughed uproariously. "I—under—stand. This'll fit—you—like a glove. . . . Fine! I'm dying to see you."

"You never will."

At that he grew sober and his eyes glinted. "You can't take a little fun. I'll leave you now for a while. When I come back you'll have that suit on!"

There was that in his voice then which she had heard when he ordered men.

Joan looked her defiance.

"If you don't have it on when I come I'll—I'll tear your rags off! . . . I can do that. You're a strong little devil, and maybe I'm not well enough yet to put this outfit on you. But I can get help. . . . If you anger me I might wait for—Gulden!"

Joan's legs grew weak under her, so that she had to sink on the bed. Kells would do absolutely and literally what he threatened. She understood now the changing secret in his eyes. One moment he was a certain kind of a man and the very next he was incalculably different. She instinctively recognized this latter personality as her enemy. She must use all the strength and wit and cunning and charm to keep his other personality in the ascendancy, else all was futile.

"Since you force me so—then I must," she said.

Kells left her without another word.

Joan removed her stained and torn dress and her worn-out boots; then hurriedly, for fear Kells might return, she put on the dead boy-bandit's outfit. Dandy Dale assuredly must have been her counterpart, for his things fitted her perfectly. Joan felt so strange that she scarcely had courage enough to look into the mirror. When she did look she gave a start that was of both amaze and shame. But for her face she never could have recognized herself. What had become of her height, her slenderness? She looked like an audacious girl in a dashing boy masquerade. Her shame was singular, inasmuch as it consisted of a burning hateful consciousness that she had not been able to repress a thrill of delight at her appearance, and that this costume strangely magnified every curve and swell of her body, betraying her feminity as nothing had ever done.

And just at that moment Kells knocked on the door and called, "Joan, are you dressed?"

"Yes," she replied. But the word seemed involuntary.

Then Kells came in.

It was an instinctive and frantic impulse that made Joan snatch up a blanket and half envelop herself in it. She stood with scarlet face and dilating eyes, trembling in every limb. Kells had entered with an expectant smile and that mocking light in his gaze. Both faded. He stared at the blanket—then

95

at her face. Then he seemed to comprehend this ordeal. And he looked sorry for her.

"Why you—you little—fool!" he exclaimed, with emotion. And that emotion seemed to exasperate him. Turning away from her, he gazed out between the logs. Again, as so many times before, he appeared to be remembering something that was hard to recall, and vague.

Joan, agitated as she was, could not help but see the effect of her unexpected and unconscious girlishness. She comprehended that with the mind of the woman which had matured in her. Like Kells, she too, had different personalities.

"I'm trying to be decent to you," went on Kells, without turning. "I want to give you a chance to make the best of a bad situation. But you're a kid—a girl! . . . And I'm a bandit. A man lost to all good, who means to have you!"

"But you're *not* lost to all good," replied Joan, earnestly. "I can't understand what I do feel. But I know—if it had been Gulden instead of you—that I wouldn't have tried to hide my—myself behind this blanket. I'm no longer—*afraid* of you. That's why I acted—so—just like a girl caught. . . . Oh! can't you see!"

"No, I can't see," he replied. "I wish I hadn't fetched you here. I wish the thing hadn't happened. Now it's too late."

"It's never too late. . . . You—you haven't harmed me yet."

"But I love you," he burst out. "Not like I have. Oh! I see this—that I never really loved any woman before. Something's gripped me. It feels like that rope at my throat—when they were going to hang me."

Then Joan trembled in the realization that a tremendous passion had seized upon this strange, strong man. In the face of it she did not know how to answer him. Yet somehow she gathered courage in the knowledge.

Kells stood silent a long moment, looking out at the green slope. And then, as if speaking to himself, he said: "I stacked the deck and dealt myself a hand—a losing hand— and now I've got to play it!"

With that he turned to Joan. It was the piercing gaze he bent upon her that hastened her decision to resume the part she had to play. And she dropped the blanket. Kells's gloom and that iron hardness vanished. He smiled as she had never seen him smile. In that and his speechless delight she read his estimate of her appearance; and, notwithstanding the unwomanliness of her costume, and the fact of his notorious character, she knew she had never received so great a compliment. Finally he found his voice.

"Joan, if you're not the prettiest thing I ever saw in my life!"

"I can't get used to this outfit," said Joan. "I can't—I won't go away from this room in it."

"Sure you will. See here, this'll make a difference, maybe. You're so shy."

He held out a wide piece of black felt that evidently he had cut from a sombrero. This he measured over her forehead and eyes, and then taking his knife he cut it to a desired shape. Next he cut eyeholes in it and fastened to it a loop made of a short strip of buckskin.

"Try that. . . . Pull it down—even with your eyes. There!—take a look at yourself."

Joan faced the mirror and saw merely a masked stranger. She was no longer Joan Randle. Her identity had been absolutely lost.

"No one—who ever knew me—could recognize me now," she murmured, and the relieving thought centered round Jim Cleve.

"I hadn't figured on that," replied Kells. "But you're right. . . . Joan, if I don't miss my guess, it won't be long till you'll be the talk of mining-towns and camp-fires."

This remark of Kells's brought to Joan proof of his singular pride in the name he bore, and proof of many strange stories about bandits and wild women of the border. She had never believed any of these stories. They had seemed merely a part of the life of this unsettled wild country. A prospector would spend a night at a camp-fire and tell a weird story and pass on, never to be seen there again. Could there have been a stranger story than her life seemed destined to be? Her mind whirled with vague, circling thought—Kells and his gang, the wild trails, the camps, and towns, gold and stage-coaches, robbery, fights, murder, mad rides in the dark, and back to Jim Cleve and his ruin.

Suddenly Kells stepped to her from behind and put his arms around her. Joan grew stiff. She had been taken off her guard. She was in his arms and could not face him.

"Joan, kiss me," he whispered, with a softness, a richer, deeper note in his voice

"No!" cried Joan, violently.

There was a moment of silence in which she felt his grasp slowly tighten—the heave of his breast.

"Then I'll make you," he said. So different was the voice now that another man might have spoken. Then he bent her backward, and, freeing one hand, brought it under her chin and tried to lift her face.

But Joan broke into fierce, violent resistance. She believed she was doomed, but that only made her the fiercer, the stronger. And with her head down, her arms straining, her body hard and rigidly unyielding she fought him all over the room, knocking over the table and seats, wrestling from wall to wall, till at last they fell across the bed and she broke his hold. Then she sprang up, panting, disheveled, and backed away from him. It had been a sharp, desperate struggle on her part and she was stronger than he. He was not a well man. He raised himself and put one hand to his breast. His face was haggard, wet, working with passion, gray with pain. In the struggle she had hurt him, perhaps reopened his wound.

"Did you—knife me—that it hurts so?" he panted, raising a hand that shook.

"I had—nothing. . . . I just—fought," cried Joan, breathlessly.

"You hurt me—again—damn you! I'm never free—from pain. But this's worse. . . . And I'm a coward. . . . And I'm a dog, too! Not half a man!—You slip of a girl—and I couldn't—hold you!"

His pain and shame were dreadful for Joan to see, because she felt sorry for him, and divined that behind them would rise the darker, grimmer force of the man. And she was right, for suddenly he changed. That which had seemed almost to make him abject gave way to a pale and bitter

98

dignity. He took up Dandy Dale's belt, which Joan had left on the bed, and, drawing the gun from its sheath, he opened the cylinder to see if it was loaded, and then threw the gun at Joan's feet.

"There! Take it—and make a better job this time," he said.

The power in his voice seemed to force Joan to pick up the gun.

"What do—you mean?" she queried, haltingly.

"Shoot me again! Put me out of my pain—my misery. . . . I'm sick of it all. I'd be glad to have you kill me!"

"Kells!" exclaimed Joan, weakly.

"Take your chance—now—when I've no strength—to force you. . . . Throw the gun on me . . . . Kill me!"

He spoke with a terrible impelling earnestness, and the strength of his will almost hypnotized Joan into execution of his demand.

"You are mad," she said. "I don't want to kill you. I couldn't. . . . I just want you to—to be—decent to me."

"I have been—for me. I was only in fun this time—when I grabbed you. But the *feel* of you! . . . I can't be decent any more. I see things clear now. . . . Joan Randle, it's my life or your soul!"

He rose now, dark, shaken, stripped of all save the truth. Joan dropped the gun from nerveless grasp.

"Is that your choice?" he asked hoarsely.

"I can't murder you!"

"Are you afraid of the other men—of Gulden? Is that why you can't kill me? You're afraid to be left—to try to get away?"

"I never thought of them."

"Then—my life or your soul!"

He stalked toward her, loomed over her, so that she put out trembling hands. After the struggle a reaction was coming to her. She was weakening. She had forgotten her plan.

"If you're merciless—then it must be—my soul," she whispered. "For I *can't* murder you. . . . Could you take that gun now—and press it here—and murder *me?*"

"No. For I love you."

"You don't love me. It's a blacker crime to murder the soul than the body."

Something in his strange eyes inspired Joan with a flashing, reviving divination. Back upon her flooded all that tide of woman's subtle incalculable power to allure, to charge, to hold. Swiftly she went close to Kells. She stretched out her hands. One was bleeding from rough contract with the log wall during the struggle. Her wrists were red, swollen, bruised from his fierce grasp.

"Look! See what you've done. You were a beast. You made me fight like a beast. My hands were claws—my whole body one hard knot of muscle. You couldn't hold me—you couldn't kiss me. . . . Suppose you *are* able to hold me—later. I'll only be the husk of a woman. I'll just be a cold shell, doubled-up, unrelaxed, a callous thing never to yield. . . . All that's *me,* the girl, the woman you say you love—will be inside, shrinking, loathing, hating, sickened to death. You will only kiss—embrace—a thing you've degraded. The warmth, the sweetness, the quiver, the thrill, the response, the life—all that is the soul of a woman and makes her lovable will be murdered."

Then she drew still closer to Kells, and with all the wondrous subtlety of a woman in a supreme moment where a life and a soul hang in the balance, she made of herself an absolute contrast to the fierce, wild, unyielding creature who had fought him off.

"Let me show—you the difference," she whispered, leaning to him, glowing, soft, eager, terrible, with her woman's charm. "Something tells me—gives me strength. . . . What *might* be! . . . Only barely possible—if in my awful plight —you turned out to be a man, good instead of bad! . . . And—if it were possible—see the differences—in the woman. . . . I show you—to save my soul!"

She gave the fascinated Kells her hands, slipped into his arms, to press against his breast, and leaned against him an instant, all one quivering, surrendered body; and then lifting a white face, true in its radiance to her honest and supreme purpose to give him one fleeting glimpse of the beauty and tenderness and soul of love, she put warm and tremulous lips to his.

Then she fell away from him, shrinking and terrified. But he stood there as if something beyond belief had happened to him, and the evil of his face, the hard lines, the brute softened and vanished in a light of transformation.

"My God!" he breathed softly. Then he awakened as if from a trance, and, leaping down the steps, he violently swept aside the curtain and disappeared.

Joan threw herself upon the bed and spent the last of her strength in the relief of blinding tears. She had won. She believed she need never fear Kells again. In that one moment of abandon she had exalted him. But at what cost!

10

◈

NEXT day, when Kells called Joan out into the other cabin, she verified her hope and belief, not so much in the almost indefinable aging and sadness of the man, as in the strong intuitive sense that her attraction had magnified for him and had uplifted him.

"You mustn't stay shut up in there any longer," he said. "You've lost weight and you're pale. Go out in the air and sun. You might as well get used to the gang. Bate Wood came to me this morning and said he thought you were the ghost of Dandy Dale. That name will stick to you. I don't care how you treat my men. But if you're friendly you'll fare better. Don't go far from the cabin. And if any man says or does a thing you don't like—flash your gun. Don't yell for me. You can bluff this gang to a standstill."

That was a trial for Joan, when she walked out into the light in Dandy Dale's clothes. She did not step very straight, and she could feel the cold prick of her face under the mask. It was not shame, but fear that gripped her. She would rather die than have Jim Cleve recognize her in that bold disguise. A line of dusty saddled horses stood heads and bridles down before the cabin, and a number of lounging men ceased talking when she appeared. It was a crowd that smelled of dust and horses and leather and whisky and tobacco. Joan did not recognize any one there, which fact aided her in a quick recovery of her composure. Then she found amusement in the absolute sensation she made upon these loungers. They stared, open-mouthed and motionless. One old fellow dropped his pipe from bearded lips and did not seem to note the loss. A dark young man, dissipated and wild-looking, with years of lawlessness stamped upon his face, was the first to move; and he, with awkward gallantry, but with amiable disposition. Joan wanted to run, yet she forced herself to stand there, apparently unconcerned before this battery of bold and curious eyes. That, once done, made the rest easier. She was grateful for the mask. And with her first low, almost incoherent, words in reply Joan entered upon the second phase of her experience with these bandits. Naturalness did not come soon, but it did come, and with it her wit and courage.

Used as she had become to the villainous countenances of the border ruffians, she yet upon closer study discovered wilder and more abandoned ones. Yet despite that, and a brazen, unconcealed admiration, there was not lacking kindliness and sympathy and good nature. Presently Joan sauntered away, and she went among the tired, shaggy horses and made friends with them. An occasional rider swung up the trail to dismount before Kells's cabin, and once two riders rode in, both staring—all eyes—at her. The meaning of her intent alertness dawned upon her then. Always, whatever she was doing or thinking or saying, behind it all hid the driving watchfulness for Jim Cleve. And the consciousness of this fixed her mind upon him. Where was he? What was he doing? Was he drunk or gambling or fighting or sleeping? Was he still honest? When she did meet him what would happen? How could she make herself and circumstances known to him before he killed somebody? A new fear had birth and grew—Cleve would recognize her in that disguise, mask and all.

She walked up and down for a while, absorbed with this new idea. Then an unusual commotion among the loungers drew her attention to a group of men on foot surrounding and evidently escorting several horsemen. Joan recognized Red Pearce and Frenchy, and then, with a start, Jim Cleve. They were riding up the trail. Joan's heart began to pound. She could not meet Jim; she dared not trust this disguise; all her plans were as if they had never been. She forgot Kells. She even forgot her fear of what Cleve might do. The meeting—the inevitable recognition—the pain Jim Cleve must suffer when the fact and apparent significance of her presence there burst upon him, these drove all else from Joan's mind. Mask or no mask, she could not face his piercing eyes, and like a little coward she turned to enter the cabin.

Before she got in, however, it was forced upon her that something unusual had roused the loungers. They had arisen and were interested in the approaching group. Loud talk dinned in Joan's ears. Then she went in the door as Kells stalked by, eyes agleam, without even noticing her. Once inside her cabin, with the curtain drawn, Joan's fear gave place to anxiety and curiosity.

There was no one in the large cabin. Through the outer door she caught sight of a part of the crowd, close together, heads up, all noisy. Then she heard Kells's authoritative voice, but she could understand nothing. The babel of hoarse voices grew louder. Kells appeared, entering the door with Pearce. Jim Cleve came next, and, once the three were inside, the crowd spilled itself after them like angry bees. Kells was talking, Pearce was talking, but their voices were lost. Suddenly Kells vented his temper.

"Shut up—the lot of you!" he yelled, and his power and position might have been measured by the menace he showed.

The gang became suddenly quiet.

"Now—what's up?" demanded Kells.

"Keep your shirt on, boss," replied Pearce, with good humor. "There ain't much wrong. . . . Cleve, here, throwed a gun on Gulden, that's all."

Kells gave a slight start, barely perceptible, but the intensity of it, and a fleeting tigerish gleam across his face, impressed Joan with the idea that he felt a fiendish joy. Her own heart clamped in a cold amaze.

"Gulden!" Kells's exclamation was likewise a passionate query.

"No, he ain't cashed," replied Pearce. "You can't kill that bull so easy. But he's shot up some. He's layin' over at Beard's. Reckon you'd better go over an' dress them shots."

"He can rot before I doctor him," replied Kells. "Where's Bate Wood? . . . Bate, you can take my kit and go fix Gulden up. And now, Red, what was all the roar about?"

"Reckon that was Gulden's particular pards tryin' to mix it with Cleve an' Cleve tryin' to mix it with them—an' *me* in between! . . . I'm here to say, boss, that I had a time stavin' off a scrap."

During this rapid exchange between Kells and his lieutenant, Jim Cleve sat on the edge of the table, one dusty boot swinging so that his spur jangled, a wisp of a cigarette in his lips. His face was white except where there seemed to be bruises under his eyes. Joan had never seen him look like this. She guessed that he had been drunk—perhaps was still drunk. That utterly abandoned face Joan was so keen to read made her bite her tongue to keep from crying out. Yes, Jim was lost.

"What'd they fight about?" queried Kells.

"Ask Cleve," replied Pearce. "Reckon I'd just as lief not talk any more about him."

Then Kells turned to Cleve and stepped before him. Somehow these two men face to face thrilled Joan to her depths. They presented such contrasts. Kells was keen, imperious, vital, strong, and complex, with an unmistakable

105

friendly regard for this young outcast. Cleve seemed aloof, detached, indifferent to everything, with a white, weary, reckless scorn. Both men were far above the gaping ruffians around them.

"Cleve, why'd you draw on Gulden?" asked Kells, sharply.

"That's my business," replied Cleve, slowly, and with his piercing eyes on Kells he blew a long, thin, blue stream of smoke upward.

"Sure. . . . But I remember what you asked me the other day—about Gulden. Was that why?"

"Nope," replied Cleve. "This was my affair."

"All right. But I'd like to know. Pearce says you're in bad with Gulden's friends. If I can't make peace between you I'll have to take sides."

"Kells, I don't need any one on my side," said Cleve, and he flung the cigarette away.

"Yes, you do," replied Kells, persuasively. "Every man on this border needs that. And he's lucky when he gets it."

"Well, I don't ask for it; I don't want it."

"That's your own business, too. I'm not insisting or advising."

Kells's force and ability to control men manifested itself in his speech and attitude. Nothing could have been easier than to rouse the antagonism of Jim Cleve, abnormally responding as he was to the wild conditions of this border environment.

"Then you're not calling my hand?" queried Cleve, with his dark, piercing glance on Kells.

"I pass, Jim," replied the bandit, easily.

Cleve began to roll another cigarette. Joan saw his strong, brown hands tremble, and she realized that this came from his nervous condition, not from agitation. Her heart ached for him. What a white, somber face, so terribly expressive of the overthrow of his soul! He had fled to the border in reckless fury at her—at himself. There in its wildness he had, perhaps, lost thought of himself and memory of her. He had plunged into the unrestrained border life. Its changing, raw, and fateful excitement might have made him forget, but behind all was the terrible seek-

106

ing to destroy and be destroyed. Joan shuddered when she remembered how she had mocked this boy's wounded vanity—how scathingly she had said he did not possess manhood and nerve enough even to be bad.

"See here, Red," said Kells to Pearce, "tell me what happened—what you saw. Jim can't object to that."

"Sure," replied Pearce, thus admonished. "We was all over at Beard's an' several games was on. Gulden rode into camp last night. He's always sore, but last night it seemed more'n usual. But he didn't say much an' nothin' happened. We all reckoned his trip fell through. To-day he was restless. He walked an' walked just like a cougar in a pen. You know how Gulden has to be on the move. Well, we let him alone, you can bet. But suddenlike he comes up to our table—me an' Cleve an' Beard an' Texas was playin' cards—an' he nearly kicks the table over. I grabbed the gold an' Cleve he saved the whisky. We'd been drinkin' an' Cleve most of all. Beard was white at the gills with rage an' Texas was soffocatin'. But we all was afraid of Gulden, except Cleve, as it turned out. But he didn't move or look mean. An' Gulden pounded on the table an' addressed himself to Cleve.

"'I've a job you'll like. Come on.'

"'Job? Say, man, you couldn't have a job I'd like,' replied Cleve, slow an' cool.

"You know how Gulden gets when them spells come over him. It's just plain cussedness. I've seen gun-fighters lookin' for trouble—for someone to kill. But Gulden was worse than that. You all take my hunch—he's got a screw loose in his nut.

"'Cleve,' he said, 'I located the Brander gold-diggin's—an' the girl was there.'

"Some kind of a white flash went over Cleve. An' we all, rememberin' Luce, began to bend low, ready to duck. Gulden didn't look no different from usual. You can't see any change in him. But I for one felt all hell burnin' in him.

"'Oho! You have,' said Cleve, quick, like he was pleased. 'An' did you get her?'

"'Not yet. Just looked over the ground. I'm pickin' you to go with me. We'll split on the gold, an' I'll take the girl.'

"Cleve swung the whisky-bottle an' it smashed on Gulden's mug, knockin' him flat. Cleve was up, like a cat, gun burnin' red. The other fellers were dodgin' low. An' as I ducked I seen Gulden, flat on his back, draggin' at his gun. He stopped short an' his hand flopped. The side of his face went all bloody. I made sure he'd cashed, so I leaped up an' grabbed Cleve.

"It'd been all right if Gulden had only cashed. But he hadn't. He came to an' bellered fer his gun an' fer his pards. Why, you could have heard him for a mile. . . . Then, as I told you, I had trouble in holdin' back a general mix-up. An' while he was hollerin' about it I led them all over to you. Gulden is layin' back there with his ear shot off. An' that's all."

Kells, with thoughtful mien, turned from Pearce to the group of dark-faced men. "This fight settles one thing," he said to them. "We've got to have organization. If you're not all a lot of fools you'll see that. You need a head. Most of you swear by me, but some of you are for Gulden. Just because he's a bloody devil. These times are the wildest the West ever knew, and they're growing wilder. Gulden is a great machine for execution. He has no sense of fear. He's a giant. He loves to fight—to kill. But Gulden's all but crazy. This last deal proves that. I leave it to your common sense. He rides around hunting for some lone camp to rob. Or some girl to make off with. He does not plan with me or the men whose judgment I have confidence in. He's always without gold. And so are most of his followers. I don't know who they are. And I don't care. But here we split—unless they and Gulden take advice and orders from me. I'm not so much siding with Cleve. Any of you ought to admit that Gulden's kind of work will disorganize a gang. He's been with us for long. And he approaches Cleve with a job. Cleve is a stranger. He may belong here, but he's not yet one of us. Gulden oughtn't have approached him. It was no straight deal. We can't figure what Gulden meant exactly, but it isn't likely he wanted Cleve to go. It was a bluff. He got called. . . . You men think this over—whether you'll stick to Gulden or to me. Clear out now."

His strong, direct talk evidently impressed them, and in

108

silence they crowded out of the cabin, leaving Pearce and Cleve behind.

"Jim, are you just hell-bent on fighting or do you mean to make yourself the champion of every poor girl in these wilds?"

Cleve puffed a cloud of smoke that enveloped his head "I don't pick quarrels," he replied.

"Then you get red-headed at the very mention of a girl."

A savage gesture of Cleve's suggested that Kells was right.

"Here, don't get red-headed at me," called Kells, with piercing sharpness. "I'll be your friend if you let me. . . . But declare yourself like a man—if you want me for a friend!"

"Kells, I'm much obliged," replied Cleve, with a semblance of earnestness. "I'm no good or I wouldn't be out here. . . . But I can't stand for these—these deals with girls."

"You'll change," rejoined Kells, bitterly. "Wait till you live a few lonely years out here! You don't understand the border. You're young. I've seen the gold-fields of California and Nevada. Men go crazy with the gold fever. It's gold that makes men wild. If you don't get killed you'll change. If you live you'll see life on this border. War debases the moral force of a man, but nothing like what you'll experience here the next few years. Men with their wives and daughters are pouring into this range. They're all over. They're finding gold. They've tasted blood. Wait till the great gold strike comes! Then you'll see men and women go back ten thousand years. . . . And then what'll one girl more or less matter?"

"Well, you see, Kells, I was loved so devotedly by one and made such a hero of—that I just can't bear to see any girl mistreated."

He almost drawled the words, and he was suave and cool, and his face was inscrutable, but a bitterness in his tone gave the lie to all he said and looked.

Pearce caught the broader inference and laughed as if at a great joke. Kells shook his head doubtfully, as if Cleve's transparent speech only added to the complexity. And

Cleve turned away, as if in an instant he had forgotten his comrades.

Afterward, in the silence and darkness of night, Joan Randle lay upon her bed sleepless, haunted by Jim's white face, amazed at the magnificent madness of him, thrilled to her soul by the meaning of his attack on Gulden, and tortured by a love that had grown immeasurably full of the strength of these hours of suspense and the passion of this wild border.

Even in her dreams Joan seemed to be bending all her will toward that inevitable and fateful moment when she must stand before Jim Cleve. It had to be. Therefore she would absolutely compel herself to meet it, regardless of the tumult that must rise within her. When all had been said, her experience so far among the bandits, in spite of the shocks and suspense that had made her a different girl, had been infinitely more fortunate than might have been expected. She prayed for this luck to continue and forced herself into a belief that it would.

That night she had slept in Dandy Dale's clothes, except for the boots; and sometimes while turning in restless slumber she had been awakened by rolling on the heavy gun, which she had not removed from the belt. And at such moments she had to ponder in the darkness, to realize that she, Joan Randle, lay a captive in a bandit's camp, dressed in a dead bandit's garb, and packing his gun—even while she slept. It was such an improbable, impossible thing. Yet the cold feel of the polished gun sent a thrill of certainty through her.

In the morning she at least did not have to suffer the shame of getting into Dandy Dale's clothes, for she was already in them. She found a grain of comfort even in that. When she had put on the mask and sombrero she studied the effect in her little mirror. And she again decided that no one, not even Jim Cleve, could recognize her in that disguise. Likewise she gathered courage from the fact that even her best girl friend would have found her figure unfamiliar and striking where once it had been merely tall and slender and strong, ordinarily dressed. Then how would Jim Cleve ever recognize her? She remembered her voice that had been called a contralto, low and deep; and how she used to sing the simple songs she knew. She could not disguise that voice. But she need not let Jim hear it. Then there was a return of the idea that he would instinctively recognize her—that no disguise could be proof to a lover who had ruined himself for her. Suddenly she realized how futile all her worry and shame. Sooner or later she must reveal her identity to Jim Cleve. Out of all this complexity of emotion Joan divined that what she yearned most for was to spare Cleve the shame consequent upon recognition of her and then the agony he must suffer at a false conception of her presence there. It was a weakness in her. When death menaced her lover and the most inconceivably horrible situation yawned for her, still she could only think of her passionate yearning to have him know, all in a flash, that she loved him, that she had followed him in remorse, that she was true to him and would die before being anything else.

And when she left her cabin she was in a mood to force an issue.

Kells was sitting at the table and being served by Bate Wood.

"Hello, Dandy!" he greeted her, in surprise and pleasure. "This's early for you."

Joan returned his greeting and said that she could not sleep all the time.

"You're coming round. I'll bet you hold up a stage before a month is out."

"Hold up a stage?" echoed Joan.

"Sure. It'll be great fun," replied Kells, with a laugh. "Here—sit down and eat with me. . . . Bate, come along lively with breakfast. . . . It's fine to see you there. That mask changes you, though. No one can see how pretty you are. . . . Joan, your admirer, Gulden, has been incapacitated for the present."

Then in evident satisfaction Kells repeated the story that Joan had heard Red Pearce tell the night before; and in the telling Kells enlarged somewhat upon Jim Cleve.

"I've taken a liking to Cleve," said Kells. "He's a strange

youngster. But he's more man than boy. I think he's broken-hearted over some rotten girl who's been faithless or something. Most women are no good, Joan. A while ago I'd have said *all* women were that, but since I've known you I think —I know different. Still, one girl out of a million doesn't change a world."

"What will this J-jim C-cleve do—when he sees—me?" asked Joan, and she choked over the name.

"Don't eat so fast, girl," said Kells. "You're only seventeen years old and you've plenty of time. . . . Well, I've thought some about Cleve. He's not crazy like Gulden, but he's just as dangerous. He's dangerous because he doesn't know what he's doing—has absolutely no fear of death—and then he's swift with a gun. That's a bad combination. Cleve will kill a man presently. He's shot three already, and in Gulden's case he meant to kill. If once he kills a man—that'll make him a gun-fighter. I've worried a little about his seeing you. But I can manage him, I guess. He can't be scared or driven. But he may be led. I've had Red Pearce tell him you are my wife. I hope he believes it, for none of the other fellows believe it. Anyway, you'll meet this Cleve soon, maybe to-day, and I want you to be friendly. If I can steady him—stop his drinking—he'll be the best man for me on this border."

"I'm to help persuade him to join your band?" asked Joan, and she could not yet control her voice.

"Is that so black a thing?" queried Kells, evidently nettled, and he glared at her.

"I—I don't know," faltered Joan. "Is this—this boy a criminal yet?"

"No. He's only a fine, decent young chap gone wild—gone bad for some girl. I told you that. You don't seem to grasp the point. If I can control him he'll be of value to me—he'll be a bold and clever and dangerous man—he'll last out here. If I can't win him, why, he won't last a week longer. He'll be shot or knifed in a brawl. Without my control Cleve'll go straight to the hell he's headed for."

Joan pushed back her plate and, looking up, steadily eyed the bandit.

"Kells, I'd rather he ended his—his career quick—and

112

went to—to—than live to be a bandit and murderer at your command."

Kells laughed mockingly, yet the savage action with which he threw his cup against the wall attested to the fact that Joan had strange power to hurt him.

"That's your sympathy, because I told you some girl drove him out here," said the bandit. "He's done for. You'll know that the moment you see him. I really think he or any man out here would be the better for my interest. Now, I want to know if you'll stand by me—put in a word to help influence this wild boy."

"I'll—I'll have to see him first," replied Joan.

"Well, you take it sort of hard," growled Kells. Then presently he brightened. "I seem always to forget that you're only a kid. Listen! Now you do as you like. But I want to warn you that you've got to get back the same kind of nerve"—here he lowered his voice and glanced at Bate Wood—"that you showed when you shot me. You're going to see some sights. . . . A great gold strike! Men grown gold-mad! Woman of no more account than a puff of cottonseed! . . . Hunger, toil, pain, disease, starvation, robbery, blood, murder, hanging, death—all nothing, nothing! There will be only gold. Sleepless nights—days of hell—rush and rush—all strangers with greedy eyes! The things that made life will be forgotten and life itself will be cheap. There will be only that yellow stuff—gold—over which men go mad and women sell their souls!"

After breakfast Kells had Joan's horse brought out of the corral and saddled.

"You must ride some every day. You must keep in condition," he said. "Pretty soon we may have a chase, and I don't want it to tear you to pieces."

"Where shall I ride?" asked Joan.

"Anywhere you like up and down the gulch."

"Are you going to have me watched?"

"Not if you say you won't run off."

"You trust me?"

"Yes."

113

"All right. I promise. And if I change my mind I'll tell you."

"Lord! don't do it, Joan. I—I— Well, you've come to mean a good deal to me. I don't know what I'd do if I lost you." As she mounted the horse Kells added, "Don't stand any raw talk from any of the gang."

Joan rode away, pondering in mind the strange fact that though she hated this bandit, yet she had softened toward him. His eyes lit when he saw her; his voice mellowed; his manner changed. He had meant to tell her again that he loved her, yet he controlled it. Was he ashamed? Had he seen into the depths of himself and despised what he had imagined love? There were antagonistic forces at war within him.

It was early morning and a rosy light tinged the fresh green. She let the eager horse break into a canter and then a gallop; and she rode up the gulch till the trail started into rough ground. Then turning, she went back, down under the pines and by the cabins, to where the gulch narrowed its outlet into the wide valley. Here she met several dusty horsemen driving a pack-train. One, a jovial ruffian, threw up his hands in mock surrender.

"Hands up, pards!" he exclaimed. "Reckon we've run agin' Dandy Dale come to life."

His companions made haste to comply and then the three regarded her with bold and roguish eyes. Joan had run square into them round a corner of slope and, as there was no room to pass, she had halted.

"Shore it's the Dandy Dale we heerd of," vouchsafed another.

"Thet's Dandy's outfit with a girl inside," added the third.

Joan wheeled her horse and rode back up the trail. The glances of these ruffians seemed to scorch her with the reality of her appearance. She wore a disguise, but her womanhood was more manifest in it than in her feminine garb. It attracted the bold glances of these men. If there were any possible decency among them, this outrageous bandit costume rendered it null. How could she ever continue to wear it? Would not something good and sacred within her be

114

sullied by a constant exposure to the effect she had upon these vile border men? She did not think it could while she loved Jim Cleve; and with thought of him came a mighty throb of her heart to assure her that nothing mattered if only she could save him.

Upon the return trip up the gulch Joan found men in sight leading horses, chopping wood, stretching arms in cabin doors. Joan avoided riding near them, yet even at a distance she was aware of their gaze. One rowdy, half hidden by a window, curved hands round his mouth and called, softly, "Hullo, sweetheart!"

Joan was ashamed that she could feel insulted. She was amazed at the temper which seemed roused in her. This border had caused her feelings she had never dreamed possible to her. Avoiding the trail, she headed for the other side of the gulch. There were clumps of willows along the brook through which she threaded a way, looking for a good place to cross. The horse snorted for water. Apparently she was not going to find any better crossing, so she turned the horse into a narrow lane through the willows and, dismounting on a mossy bank, she slipped the bridle so the horse could drink.

Suddenly she became aware that she was not alone. But she saw no one in front of her or on the other side of her horse. Then she turned. Jim Cleve was in the act of rising from his knees. He had a towel in his hand. His face was wet. He stood no more than ten steps from her.

Joan could not have repressed a little cry to save her life. The surprise was tremendous. She could not move a finger. She expected to hear him call her name.

Cleve stared at her. His face, in the morning light, was as drawn and white as that of a corpse. Only his eyes seemed alive and they were flames. A lightning flash of scorn leaped to them. He only recognized in her a woman, and his scorn was for the creature that bandit garb proclaimed her to be. A sad and bitter smile crossed his face; and then it was followed by an expression that was a lash upon Joan's bleeding spirit. He looked at her shapely person with something of the brazen and evil glance that had been so revolting to her in the eyes of those ruffians. That was the unexpected—the impossible—in connection with Jim Cleve. How could she stand there under it—and live?

She jerked at the bridle, and, wading blindly across the brook, she mounted somehow, and rode with blurred sight back to the cabin. Kells appeared busy with men outside and did not accost her. She fled to her cabin and barricaded the door.

Then she hid her face on her bed, covered herself to shut out the light, and lay there, broken-hearted. What had been that other thing she had imagined was shame—that shrinking and burning she had suffered through Kells and his men? What was that compared to this awful thing? A brand of red-hot pitch, blacker and bitterer than death, had been struck brutally across her soul. By the man she loved—whom she would have died to save! Jim Cleve had seen in her only an abandoned creature of the camps. His sad and bitter smile had been for the thought that he could have loved anything of her sex. His scorn had been for the betrayed youth and womanhood suggested by her appearance. And then the thing that struck into Joan's heart was the fact that her grace and charm of person, revealed by this costume forced upon her, had aroused Jim Cleve's first response to the evil surrounding him, the first call to that baseness he must be assimilating from these border ruffians. That he could look at her so! The girl he had loved! Joan's agony lay not in the circumstance of his being as mistaken in her character as he had been in her identity, but that she, of all women, had to be the one who made him answer, like Kells and Gulden and all those ruffians, to the instincts of a beast.

"Oh, he'd been drunk—he was drunk!" whispered Joan. "He isn't to be blamed. He's not my old Jim. He's suffering—he's changed—he doesn't care. What could I expect—standing there like a hussy before him—in this—this indecent rig? . . . I must see him. I must tell him. If he recognized me now—and I had no chance to tell him why I'm here—why I look like this—that I love him—am still good—and true to him—if I couldn't tell him I'd—I'd shoot myself!"

Joan sobbed out the final words and then broke down.

And when the spell had exercised its sway, leaving her limp and shaken and weak, she was the better for it. Slowly calmness returned so that she could look at her wild and furious rush from the spot where she had faced Jim Cleve, at the storm of shame ending in her collapse. She realized that if she had met Jim Cleve here in the dress in which she had left home there would have been the same shock of surprise and fear and love. She owed part of that breakdown to the suspense she had been under and then the suddenness of the meeting. Looking back at her agitation, she felt that it had been natural—that if she could only tell the truth to Jim Cleve the situation was not impossible. But the meeting, and all following it, bore tremendous revelation of how through all this wild experience she had learned to love Jim Cleve. But for his reckless flight and her blind pursuit, and then the anxiety, fear, pain, toil, and despair, she would never have known her woman's heart and its capacity for love.

11

◆

FOLLOWING that meeting, with all its power to change and strengthen Joan, there were uneventful days in which she rode the gulch trails and grew able to stand the jests and glances of the bandit's gang. She thought she saw and heard everything, yet insulated her true self in a callous and unreceptive aloofness from all that affronted her.

The days were uneventful because, while always looking for Jim Cleve, she never once saw him. Several times she heard his name mentioned. He was here and there—at Beard's off in the mountains. But he did not come to Kells's cabin, which fact, Joan gathered, had made Kells anxious. He did not want to lose Cleve. Joan peered from her covert in the evenings, and watched for Jim, and grew weary of the loud talk and laughter, the gambling and smoking and drinking. When there seemed no more chance of Cleve's coming, then Joan went to bed.

On these occasions Joan learned that Kells was passionately keen to gamble, that he was a weak hand at cards, an honest gambler, and, strangely enough, a poor loser. Moreover, when he lost he drank heavily, and under the influence of drink he was dangerous. There were quarrels when curses rang throughout the cabin, when guns were drawn, but whatever Kells's weaknesses might be, he was strong and implacable in the governing of these men.

That night when Gulden strode into the cabin was certainly not uneventful for Joan. Sight of him sent a chill to her marrow while a strange thrill of fire inflamed her. Was that great hulk of a gorilla prowling about to meet Jim Cleve? Joan thought that it might be the worse for him if he were. Then she shuddered a little to think that she had already been influenced by the wildness around her.

Gulden appeared well and strong, and but for the bandage on his head would have been as she remembered him. He manifested interest in the gambling of the players by surly grunts. Presently he said something to Kells.

"What?" queried the bandit, sharply, wheeling, the better to see Gulden.

The noise subsided. One gamester laughed knowingly.

"Lend me a sack of dust?" asked Gulden.

Kells's face showed amaze and then a sudden brightness. "What! You want gold from me?"

"Yes. I'll pay it back."

"Gulden, I wasn't doubting that. But does your asking mean you've taken kindly to my proposition?"

"You can take it that way," growled Gulden. "I want gold."

"I'm mighty glad, Gulden," replied Kells, and he looked

as if he meant it. "I need you. We ought to get along. . . . Here."

He handed a small buckskin sack to Gulden. Someone made room for him on the other side of the table, and the game was resumed. It was interesting to watch them gamble. Red Pearce had a scale at his end of the table, and he was always measuring and weighing out gold-dust. The value of the gold appeared to be fifteen dollars to the ounce, but the real value of money did not actuate the gamblers. They spilled the dust on the table and ground as if it were as common as sand. Still there did not seem to be any great quantity of gold in sight. Evidently these were not profitable times for the bandits. More than once Joan heard them speak of a gold strike as honest people spoke of good fortune. And these robbers could only have meant that in case of a rich strike there would be gold to steal. Gulden gambled as he did everything else. At first he won and then he lost, and then he borrowed more from Kells, to win again. He paid back as he had borrowed and lost and won—without feeling. He had no excitement. Joan's intuition convinced her that if Gulden had any motive at all in gambling it was only an antagonism to men of his breed. Gambling was a contest, a kind of fight.

Most of the men except Gulden drank heavily that night. There had been fresh liquor come with the last pack-train. Many of them were drunk when the game broke up. Red Pearce and Wood remained behind with Kells after the others had gone, and Pearce was clever enough to cheat Kells before he left.

"Boss—thet there Red double-crossed you," said Bate Wood.

Kells had lost heavily, and he was under the influence of drink. He drove Wood out of the cabin, cursing him sullenly. Then he put in place the several bars that served as a door of his cabin. After that he walked unsteadily around, and all about his action and manner that was not aimless seemed to be dark and intermittent staring toward Joan's cabin. She felt sickened again with this new aspect of her situation, but she was not in the least afraid of Kells. She watched him till he approached her door and then she drew

120

back a little. He paused before the blanket as if he had been impelled to halt from fear. He seemed to be groping in thought. Then he cautiously and gradually, by degrees, drew aside the blanket. He could not see Joan in the darkness, but she saw him plainly. He fumbled at the poles, and, finding that he could not budge them, he ceased trying. There was nothing forceful or strong about him, such as was manifest when he was sober. He stood there a moment, breathing heavily, in a kind of forlorn, undecided way, and then he turned back. Joan heard him snap the lanterns. The lights went out and all grew dark and silent.

Next morning at breakfast he was himself again, and if he had any knowledge whatever of his actions while he was drunk, he effectually concealed it from Joan.

Later, when Joan went outside to take her usual morning exercise, she was interested to see a rider tearing up the slope on a foam-flecked horse. Men shouted at him from the cabins and then followed without hats or coats. Bate Wood dropped Joan's saddle and called to Kells. The bandit came hurriedly out.

"Blicky!" he exclaimed, and then he swore under his breath in elation.

"Shore is Blicky!" said Wood, and his unusually mild eyes snapped with a glint unpleasant for Joan to see.

The arrival of this Blicky appeared to be occasion for excitement and Joan recalled the name as belonging to one of Kells's trusted men. He swung his leg and leaped from his saddle as the horse plunged to a halt. Blicky was a lean, bronzed young man, scarcely out of his teens, but there were years of hard life in his face. He slapped the dust in little puffs from his gloves. At sight of Kells he threw the gloves aloft and took no note of them when they fell. "*Strike!*" he called, piercingly.

"No!" ejaculated Kells, intensely.

Bate Wood let out a whoop which was answered by the men hurrying up the slope.

"Been on—for weeks!" panted Blicky. "It's big. Can't tell how big. Me an' Jesse Smith an' Handy Oliver hit a new road—over here fifty miles as a crow flies—a hundred by

121

trail. We was plumb surprised. An' when we met pack-trains an' riders an' prairie-schooners an' a stage-coach we knew there was doin's over in the Bear Mountain range. When we came to the edge of the diggin's an' seen a whalin' big camp—like a beehive—Jesse an' Handy went on to get the lay of the land an' I hit the trail back to you. I've been a-comin' on an' off since before sundown yesterday. . . . Jesse gave one look an' then hollered. He said, 'Tell Jack it's big an' he wants to plan big. We'll be back there in a day or so with all details.'"

Joan watched Kells intently while he listened to this breathless narrative of a gold strike, and she was repelled by the singular flash of brightness—a radiance—that seemed to be in his eyes and on his face. He did not say a word, but his men shouted hoarsely around Blicky. He walked a few paces to and fro with hands strongly clenched, his lips slightly parted, showing teeth close-shut like those of a mastiff. He looked eager, passionate, cunning, hard as steel, and that strange brightness of elation slowly shaded to a dark, brooding menace. Suddenly he wheeled to silence the noisy men.

"Where're Pearce and Gulden? Do they know?" he demanded.

"Reckon no one knows but who's right here," replied Blicky.

"Red an' Gul are sleepin' off last night's luck," said Bate Wood.

"Have any of you seen young Cleve?" Kells went on. His voice rang quick and sharp.

No one spoke, and presently Kells cracked his fist into his open hand.

"Come on. Get the gang together at Beard's. . . . Boys, the time we've been gambling on has come. Jesse Smith saw '49 and '51. He wouldn't send me word like this—unless there was hell to pay. . . . Come on!"

He strode off down the slope with the men close around him, and they met other men on the way, all of whom crowded into the group, jostling, eager, gesticulating.

Joan was left alone. She felt considerably perturbed, especially at Kells's sharp inquiry for Jim Cleve. Kells

122

might persuade him to join that bandit legion. These men made Joan think of wolves, with Kells the keen and savage leader. No one had given a thought to Blicky's horse and that neglect in border men was a sign of unusual preoccupation. The horse was in bad shape. Joan took off his saddle and bridle, and rubbed the dust-caked lather from his flanks, and led him into the corral. Then she fetched a bucket of water and let him drink sparingly, a little at a time.

Joan did not take her ride that morning. Anxious and curious, she waited for the return of Kells. But he did not come. All afternoon Joan waited and watched, and saw no sign of him or any of the other men. She knew Kells was forging with red-hot iron and blood that organization which she undesignedly had given a name—the Border Legion. It would be a terrible legion, of that she was assured. Kells was the evil genius to create an unparalleled scheme of crime; this wild and remote border, with its inaccessible fastness for hiding-places, was the place; all that was wanting was the time, which evidently had arrived. She remembered how her uncle had always claimed that the Bear Mountain range would see a gold strike which would disrupt the whole West and amaze the world. And Blicky had said a big strike had been on for weeks. Kells's prophecy of the wild life Joan would see had not been without warrant. She had already seen enough to whiten her hair, she thought, yet she divined her experience would shrink in comparison with what was to come. Always she lived in the future. She spent sleeping and waking hours in dreams, thoughts, actions, broodings, over all of which hung an ever-present shadow of suspense. When would she meet Jim Cleve again? When would he recognize her? What would he do? What could she do? Would Kells be a devil or a man at the end? Was there any justification of her haunting fear of Gulden—of her suspicion that she alone was the cause of his attitude toward Kells—of her horror at the unshakable presentiment and fancy that he was a gorilla and meant to make off with her? These, and a thousand other fears, some groundless, but many real and present, besieged Joan and left her little peace. What would happen next?

Toward sunset she grew tired of waiting, and hungry,

besides, so she went into the cabin and prepared her own meal. About dark Kells strode in, and it took but a glance for Joan to see that matters had not gone to his liking. The man seemed to be burning inwardly. Sight of Joan absolutely surprised him. Evidently in the fever of this momentous hour he had forgotten his prisoner. Then, whatever his obsession, he looked like a man whose eyes were gladdened at sight of her and who was sorry to behold her there. He apologized that her supper had not been provided for her and explained that he had forgotten. The men had been crazy—hard to manage—the issue was not yet settled. He spoke gently. Suddenly he had that thoughtful mien which Joan had become used to associating with weakness in him.

"I wish I hadn't dragged you here," he said, taking her hands. "It's too late. I *can't* lose you. . . . But the—*other way*—isn't too late!"

"What way? What do you mean?" asked Joan.

"Girl, will you ride off with me to-night?" he whispered, hoarsely. "I swear I'll marry you—and become an honest man. To-morrow will be too late! . . . Will you?"

Joan shook her head. She was sorry for him. When he talked like this he was not Kells, the bandit. She could not resist a strange agitation at the intensity of his emotion. One moment he had entered—a bandit leader, planning blood, murder; the next, as his gaze found her, he seemed weakened, broken in the shaking grip of a hopeless love for her.

"Speak, Joan!" he said, with his hands tightening and his brow clouding.

"No, Kells," she replied.

"Why? Because I'm a red-handed bandit?"

"No. Because I—I don't love you."

"But wouldn't you rather be my wife—and have me honest—than become a slave here, eventually abandoned to—to Gulden and his cave and his rope?" Kells's voice rose as that other side of him gained dominance.

"Yes, I would. . . . But I *know* you'll never harm me—or abandon me to—to that Gulden."

"*How* do you know?" he cried, with the blood thick at his temples.

124

"Because you're no beast any more. . . . And you—you do love me."

Kells thrust her from him so fiercely that she nearly fell.

"I'll get over it. . . . Then look out!" he said, with dark bitterness.

With that he waved her back, apparently ordering her to her cabin, and turned to the door, through which the deep voices of men sounded nearer and nearer.

Joan stumbled in the darkness up the rude steps to her room, and, softly placing the poles in readiness to close her door, she composed herself to watch and wait. The keen edge of her nerves, almost amounting to pain, told her that this night of such moment for Kells would be one of singular strain and significance for her. But why she could not fathom. She felt herself caught by the changing tide of events—a tide that must sweep her on to flood. Kells had gone outside. The strong, deep voices grew less distinct. Evidently the men were walking away. In her suspense Joan was disappointed. Presently, however, they returned; they had been walking to and fro. After a few moments Kells entered alone. The cabin was now so dark that Joan could barely distinguish the bandit. Then he lighted the lanterns. He hung up several on the wall and placed two upon the table. From somewhere among his effects he produced a small book and a pencil; these, with a heavy, gold-mounted gun, he laid on the table before the seat he manifestly meant to occupy. That done, he began a slow pacing up and down the room, his hands behind his back, his head bent in deep and absorbing thought. What a dark, sinister, plotting figure! Joan had seen many men in different attitudes of thought, but here was a man whose mind seemed to give forth intangible yet terrible manifestations of evil. The inside of that gloomy cabin took on another aspect; there was a meaning in the saddles and bridles and weapons on the wall; that book and pencil and gun seemed to contain the dark deeds of wild men; and all about the bandit hovered a power sinister in its menace to the unknown and distant toilers for gold.

Kells lifted his head, as if listening, and then the whole manner of the man changed. The burden that weighed upon him was thrown aside. Like a general about to inspect a line of soldiers Kells faced the door, keen, stern, commanding. The heavy tread of booted men, the clink of spurs, the low, muffled sound of voices, warned Joan that the gang had arrived. Would Jim Cleve be among them?

Joan wanted a better position in which to watch and listen. She thought a moment, and then carefully felt her way around to the other side of the steps, and here, sitting down with her feet hanging over the drop, she leaned against the wall and through a chink between the logs had a perfect view of the large cabin. The men were filing in silent and intense. Joan counted twenty-seven in all. They appeared to fall into two groups, and it was significant that the larger group lined up on the side nearest Kells, and the smaller back of Gulden. He had removed the bandage, and with a raw, red blotch where his right ear had been shot away, he was hideous. There was some kind of power emanating from him, but it was not that which was so keenly vital and impelling in Kells. It was brute ferocity, dominating by sheer physical force. In any but muscular clash between Kells and Gulden the latter must lose. The men back of Gulden were a bearded, check-shirted, heavily armed group, the worst of that bad lot. All the younger, cleaner-cut men like Red Pearce and Frenchy and Beady Jones and Williams and the scout Blicky, were on the other side. There were two factions here, yet scarcely an antagonism, except possibly in the case of Kells. Joan felt that the atmosphere was supercharged with suspense and fatality and possibility—and anything might happen. To her great joy, Jim Cleve was not present.

"Where're Beard and Wood?" queried Kells.

"Workin' over Beard's sick hoss," replied Pearce. "They'll show up by an' by. Anythin' you say goes with them, you know."

"Did you find young Cleve?"

"No. He camps up in the timber somewheres. Reckon he'll be along, too."

Kells sat down at the head of the table, and, taking up the little book, he began to finger it while his pale eyes studied the men before him.

"We shuffled the deck pretty well over at Beard's," he

126

said. "Now for the deal. . . . Who wants cards? . . . I've organized my Border Legion. I'll have absolute control, whether there're ten men or a hundred. Now, whose names go down in my book?"

Red Pearce stepped up and labored over the writing of his name. Blicky, Jones, Williams, and others followed suit. They did not speak, but each shook hands with the leader. Evidently Kells exacted no oath, but accepted each man's free action and his word of honor. There was that about the bandit which made such action as binding as ties of blood. He did not want men in his Legion who had not loyalty to him. He seemed the kind of leader to whom men would be true.

"Kells, say them conditions over again," requested one of the men, less eager to hurry with the matter.

At this juncture Joan was at once thrilled and frightened to see Jim Cleve enter the cabin. He appeared whiter of face, almost ghastly, and his piercing eyes swept the room, from Kells to Gulden, from men to men. Then he leaned against the wall, indistinct in the shadow. Kells gave no sign that he had noted the advent of Cleve.

"I'm the leader," replied Kells, deliberately. "I'll make the plans. I'll issue orders. No jobs without my knowledge. Equal shares in gold—man to man. . . . Your word to stand by me!"

A muttering of approval ran through the listening group.

"Reckon I'll join," said the man who had wished the conditions repeated. With that he advanced to the table and, apparently not being able to write, he made his mark in the book. Kells wrote the name below. The other men of this contingent one by one complied with Kells's requirements. This action left Gulden and his group to be dealt with.

"Gulden, are you still on the fence?" demanded Kells, coolly.

The giant strode stolidly forward to the table. As always before to Joan, he seemed to be a ponderous hulk, slow, heavy, plodding, with a mind to match.

"Kells, if we can agree I'll join," he said in his sonorous voice.

"You can bet you won't join unless we do agree," snapped Kells. "But—see here, Gulden. Let's be friendly. The border is big enough for both of us. I want you. I need you. Still, if we can't agree, let's not split and be enemies. How about it?"

Another muttering among the men attested to the good sense and good will of Kells's suggestion.

"Tell me what you're going to do—how you'll operate," replied Gulden.

Kells had difficulty in restraining his impatience and annoyance.

"What's that to you or any of you?" he queried. "You all know I'm the man to think of things. That's been proved. First it takes brains. I'll furnish them. Then it takes execution. You and Pearce and the gang will furnish that. What more do you need to know?"

"How're you going to operate?" persisted Gulden.

Kells threw up both hands as if it was useless to argue or reason with this desperado.

"All right, I'll tell you," he replied. "Listen. . . . I can't say what definite plans I'll make till Jesse Smith reports, and then when I get on the diggings. But here's a working basis. Now don't miss a word of this, Gulden—nor any of you men. We'll pack our outfits down to this gold strike. We'll build cabins on the outskirts of the town, and we won't hang together. The gang will be spread out. Most of you must make a bluff at digging gold. Be like other miners. Get in with cliques and clans. Dig, drink, gamble like the rest of them. Beard will start a gambling-place. Red Pearce will find some other kind of work. I'll buy up claims—employ miners to work them. I'll disguise myself and get in with the influential men and have a voice in matters. You'll all be scouts. You'll come to my cabin at night to report. We'll not tackle any little jobs. Miners going out with fifty or a hundred pounds of gold—the wagons—the stage-coach—these we'll have timed to rights, and whoever I detail on the job will hold them up. You must all keep sober, if that's possible. You must all absolutely trust to my judgment. You must all go masked while on a job. You must never speak a word that might direct suspicion to you. In this way we may work all summer without detection. The Border Legion will become mysterious and famous. It will appear to be a large number of men, operating all over. The more secretive we are the more powerful the effect on the diggings. In gold-camps, when there's a strike, all men are mad. They suspect each other. They can't organize. We shall have them helpless. . . . And in short, if it's as rich a strike as looks due here in these hills, before winter we can pack out all the gold our horses can carry."

Kells had begun under restraint, but the sound of his voice, the liberation of his great idea, roused him to a passion. The man radiated with passion. This, then, was his dream—the empire he aspired to.

He had a powerful effect upon his listeners, except Gulden; and it was evident to Joan that the keen bandit was conscious of his influence. Gulden, however, showed nothing that he had not already showed. He was always a strange, dominating figure. He contested the relations of things. Kells watched him—the men watched him—and Jim Cleve's piercing eyes glittered in the shadow, fixed upon that massive face. Manifestly Gulden meant to speak, but in his slowness there was no laboring, no pause from emotion. He had an idea and it moved like he moved.

"Dead men tell no tales!" The words boomed deep from his cavernous chest, a mutter that was a rumble, with something almost solemn in its note and certainly menacing, breathing murder. As Kells had propounded his ideas, revealing his power to devise a remarkable scheme and his passion for gold, so Gulden struck out with the driving inhuman blood-lust that must have been the twist, the knot, the clot in his brain. Kells craved notoriety and gold; Gulden craved to kill. In the silence that followed his speech these wild border ruffians judged him, measured him, understood him, and though some of them grew farther aloof from him, more of them sensed the safety that hid in his terrible implication.

But Kells rose against him.

"Gulden, you mean when we steal gold—to leave only dead men behind?" he queried, with a hiss in his voice.

The giant nodded grimly.

129

"But only fools kill—unless in self-defense," declared Kells, passionately.

"We'd last longer," replied Gulden, imperturbably.

"No—no. We'd never last so long. Killings rouse a mining-camp after a while—gold fever or no. That means a vigilante band."

"We can belong to the vigilantes, just as well as to your Legion," said Gulden.

The effect of this was to make Gulden appear less of a fool than Kells supposed him. The ruffians nodded to one another. They stirred restlessly. They were animated by a strange and provocative influence. Even Red Pearce and the others caught its subtlety. It was evil predominating in evil hearts. Blood and death loomed like a shadow here. The keen Kells saw the change working toward a transformation and he seemed craftily fighting something within him that opposed this cold ruthlessness of his men.

"Gulden, suppose I don't see it your way?" he asked.

"Then I won't join your Legion."

"What *will* you do?"

"I'll take the men who stand by me and go clean up that gold-camp."

From the fleeting expression on Kells's face Joan read that he knew Gulden's project would defeat his own and render both enterprises fatal.

"Gulden, I don't want to lose you," he said.

"You won't lose me if you see this thing right," replied Gulden. "You've got the brains to direct us. But, Kells, you're losing your nerve. . . . It's this girl you've got here!"

Gulden spoke without rancor or fear or feeling of any kind. He merely spoke the truth. And it shook Kells with an almost ungovernable fury.

Joan saw the green glare of his eyes—his gray working face—the flutter of his hand. She had an almost superhuman insight into the workings of his mind. She knew that then he was fighting whether or not to kill Gulden on the spot. And she recognized that this was the time when Kells must kill Gulden or from that moment see a gradual diminishing of his power on the border. But Kells did not recognize that crucial height of his career. His struggle with his fury and hate showed that the thing uppermost in his mind was the need of conciliating Gulden and thus regaining a hold over the men.

"Gulden, suppose we waive the question till we're on the grounds?" he suggested.

"Waive nothing. It's one or the other with me," declared Gulden.

"Do you want to be leader of this Border Legion?" went on Kells, deliberately.

"No."

"Then what do you want?"

Gulden appeared at a loss for an instant reply. "I want plenty to do," he replied, presently. "I want to be in on everything. I want to be free to kill a man when I like."

"When you like!" retorted Kells, and added a curse. Then as if by magic his dark face cleared and there was infinite depth and craftiness in him. His opposition, and that hint of hate and loathing which detached him from Gulden, faded from his bearing. "Gulden, I'll split the difference between us. I'll leave you free to do as you like. But all the others— every man—must take orders from me."

Gulden reached out a huge hand. His instant acceptance evidently amazed Kells and the others.

"Let her rip!" Gulden exclaimed. He shook Kells's hand and then laboriously wrote his name in the little book.

In that moment Gulden stood out alone in the midst of wild abandoned men. What were Kells and this Legion to him? What was the stealing of more or less gold?

"Free to do as you like except fight my men," said Kells. "That's understood."

"If they don't pick a fight with me," added the giant, and he grinned.

One by one his followers went through with the simple observances that Kells's personality made a serious and binding compact.

"Anybody else?" called Kells, glancing round. The somberness was leaving his face.

"Here's Jim Cleve," said Pearce, pointing toward the wall.

131

"Hello, youngster! Come here. I'm wanting you bad," said Kells.

Cleve sauntered out of the shadow, and his glittering eyes were fixed on Gulden. There was an instant of waiting. Gulden looked at Cleve. Then Kells quickly strode between them.

"Say, I forgot you fellows had trouble," he said. He attended solely to Gulden. "You can't renew your quarrel now. Gulden, we've all fought together more or less, and then been good friends. I want Cleve to join us, but not against your ill will. How about it?"

"I've no ill will," replied the giant, and the strangeness of his remark lay in its evident truth. "But I won't stand to lose my other ear!"

Then the ruffians guffawed in hoarse mirth. Gulden, however, did not seem to see any humor in his remark. Kells laughed with the rest. Even Cleve's white face relaxed into a semblance of a smile.

"That's good. We're getting together," declared Kells. Then he faced Cleve, all about him expressive of elation, of assurance, of power. "Jim, will you draw cards in this deal?"

"What's the deal?" asked Cleve.

Then in swift, eloquent speech Kells launched the idea of his Border Legion, its advantages to any loose-footed, young outcast, and he ended his brief talk with much the same argument he had given Joan. Back there in her covert Joan listened and watched, mindful of the great need of controlling her emotions. The instant Jim Cleve had stalked into the light she had been seized by a spasm of trembling.

"Kells, I don't care two straws one way or another," replied Cleve.

The bandit appeared nonplussed. "You don't care whether you join my Legion or whether you don't?"

"Not a damn," was the indifferent answer.

"Then do me a favor," went on Kells. "Join to please me. We'll be good friends. You're in bad out here on the border. You might as well fall in with us."

"I'd rather go alone."

"But you won't last."

"It's a lot I care."

The bandit studied the reckless, white face. "See here, Cleve—haven't you got the nerve to be bad—thoroughly bad?"

Cleve gave a start as if he had been stung. Joan shut her eyes to blot out what she saw in his face. Kells had used part of the very speech with which she had driven Jim Cleve to his ruin. And those words galvanized him. The fatality of all this! Joan hated herself. Those very words of hers would drive this maddened and heartbroken boy to join Kells's band. She knew what to expect from Jim even before she opened her eyes; yet when she did open them it was to see him transformed and blazing.

Then Kells either gave way to leaping passion or simulated it in the interest of his cunning.

"Cleve, you're going down for a woman?" he queried, with that sharp, mocking ring in his voice.

"If you don't shut up you'll get there first," replied Cleve, menacingly.

"Bah! . . . Why do you want to throw a gun on me? I'm your friend. You're sick. You're like a poisoned pup. I say if you've got nerve you won't quit. You'll take a run for your money. You'll see life. You'll fight. You'll win some gold. There are other women. Once I thought I would quit for a woman. But I didn't. I never found the right one till I *had* gone to hell—out here on this border. . . . If you've got nerve, show me. Be a man instead of a crazy youngster. Spit out the poison. . . . Tell it before us all! . . . Some girl drove you to us?"

"Yes—a girl!" replied Cleve, hoarsely, as if goaded.

"It's too late to go back?"

"Too late!"

"There's nothing left but wild life that makes you forget?"

"Nothing. . . . Only I—can't forget!" he panted.

Cleve was in a torture of memory, of despair, of weakness. Joan saw how Kells worked upon Jim's feelings. He was only a hopeless, passionate boy in the hands of a strong, implacable man. He would be like wax to a sculptor's touch. Jim would bend to this bandit's will, and through his very tenacity of love and memory be driven farther on the road to drink, to gaming, and to crime.

Joan got to her feet, and with all her woman's soul uplifting and inflaming her she stood ready to meet the moment that portended.

Kells made a gesture of savage violence. "Show your nerve! . . . Join with me! . . . You'll make a name on this border that the West will never forget!"

That last hint of desperate fame was the crafty bandit's best trump. And it won. Cleve swept up a weak and nervous hand to brush the hair from his damp brow. The keenness, the fire, the aloofness had departed from him. He looked shaken as if by something that had been pointed out as his own cowardice.

"Sure, Kells," he said, recklessly. "Let me in the game. . . . And—by God—I'll play—the hand out!" He reached for the pencil and bent over the book.

"Wait! . . . Oh, *wait!*" cried Joan. The passion of that moment, the consciousness of its fateful portent and her situation, as desperate as Cleve's, gave her voice a singularly high and piercingly sweet intensity. She glided from behind the blanket—out of the shadow—into the glare of the lanterns—to face Kells and Cleve.

Kells gave one astounded glance at her, and then, divining her purpose, he laughed thrillingly and mockingly, as if the sight of her was a spur, as if her courage was a thing to admire, to permit, and to regret.

"Cleve, my wife, Dandy Dale," he said, suave and cool. "Let her persuade you—one way or another!"

The presence of a woman, however disguised, following her singular appeal, transformed Cleve. He stiffened erect and the flush died out of his face, leaving it whiter than ever, and the eyes that had grown dull quickened and began to burn. Joan felt her cheeks blanch. She all but fainted under that gaze. But he did not recognize her, though he was strangely affected.

"Wait!" she cried again, and she held to that high voice, so different from her natural tone. "I've been listening. I've heard all that's been said. Don't join this Border Legion. . . . You're young—and still honest. For God's sake—don't go

134

the way of these men! Kells will make you a bandit. . . . Go home—boy—go home!"

"Who are you—to speak to me of honesty—of home?" Cleve demanded.

"I'm only a—a woman. . . . But I can feel how wrong you are. . . . Go back to that girl—who—who drove you to the border. . . . She must repent. In a day you'll be too late. . . . Oh, boy, go home! Girls never know their minds—their hearts. Maybe your girl—loved you! . . . Oh, maybe her heart is breaking now!"

A strong, muscular ripple went over Cleve, ending in a gesture of fierce protest. Was it pain her words caused, or disgust that such as she dared mention the girl he had loved? Joan could not tell. She only knew that Cleve was drawn by her presence, fascinated and repelled, subtly responding to the spirit of her, doubting what he heard and believing with his eyes.

"You beg me not to become a bandit?" he asked, slowly, as if revolving a strange idea.

"Oh, I implore you!"

"Why?"

"I told you. Because you're still good at heart. You've only been wild. . . . Because—"

"Are you the wife of Kells?" he flashed at her.

A reply seemed slowly wrenched from Joan's reluctant lips. "No!"

The denial left a silence behind it. The truth that all knew when spoken by her was a kind of shock. The ruffians gaped in breathless attention. Kells looked on with a sardonic grin, but he had grown pale. And upon the face of Cleve shone an immeasurable scorn.

"Not his wife!" exclaimed Cleve, softly.

His tone was unendurable to Joan. She began to shrink. A flame curled within her. How he must hate any creature of her sex!

"And you appeal to me!" he went on. Suddenly a weariness came over him. The complexity of women was beyond him. Almost he turned his back upon her. "I reckon such as you can't keep me from Kells—or blood—or hell!"

"Then you're a narrow-souled weakling—born to crime!"

she burst out in magnificent wrath. "For however appearances are against me—I am a good woman!"

That stunned him, just as it drew Kells upright, white and watchful. Cleve seemed long in grasping its significance. His face was half averted. Then he turned slowly, all strung, and his hands clutched quiveringly at the air. No man of coolness and judgment would have addressed him or moved a step in that strained moment. All expected some such action as had marked his encounter with Luce and Gulden.

Then Cleve's gaze in unmistakable meaning swept over Joan's person. How could her appearance and her appeal be reconciled? One was a lie! And his burning eyes robbed Joan of spirit.

"He forced me to—to wear these," she faltered. "I'm his prisoner. I'm helpless."

With catlike agility Cleve leaped backward, so that he faced all the men, and when his hands swept to a level they held gleaming guns. His utter abandon of daring transfixed these bandits in surprise as much as fear. Kells appeared to take most to himself the menace.

"*I crawl!*" he said, huskily. "She speaks the God's truth. . . . But you can't help matters by killing me. Maybe she'd be worse off!"

He expected this wild boy to break loose, yet his wit directed him to speak the one thing calculated to check Cleve.

"Oh, don't shoot!" moaned Joan.

"You go outside," ordered Cleve. "Get on a horse and lead another near the door. . . . Go! I'll take you away from this."

Both temptation and terror assailed Joan. Surely that venture would mean only death to Jim and worse for her. She thrilled at the thought—at the possibility of escape—at the strange front of this erstwhile nerveless boy. But she had not the courage for what seemed only desperate folly.

"I'll stay," she whispered. "You go!"

"Hurry, woman!"

"No! No!"

"Do you want to stay with this bandit?"

"Oh, I must!"

"Then you love him?"

All the fire of Joan's heart flared up to deny the insult and all her woman's cunning fought to keep back words that inevitably must lead to revelation. She drooped, unable to hold up under her shame, yet strong to let him think vilely of her, for his sake. That way she had a barest chance.

"Get out of my sight!" he ejaculated, thickly. "I'd have fought for you."

Again that white, weary scorn radiated from him. Joan bit her tongue to keep from screaming. How could she live under this torment? It was she, Joan Randle, that had earned that scorn, whether he knew her or not. She shrank back, step by step, almost dazed, sick with a terrible inward coldness, blinded by scalding tears. She found her door and stumbled in.

"Kells, I'm what you called me." She heard Cleve's voice, strangely far off. "There's no excuse . . . unless I'm not just right in my head about women. . . . Overlook my break or don't—as you like. But if you want me I'm ready for your Border Legion!"

12

◆

THOSE bitter words of Cleve's, as if he mocked himself, were the last Joan heard, and they rang in her ears and seemed to reverberate through her dazed mind like a knell of doom. She lay there, all blackness about her, weighed upon by an insupportable burden; and she prayed that day might never dawn for her; a nightmare of oblivion ended at last with her eyes opening to the morning light.

She was cold and stiff. She had lain uncovered all the

long hours of night. She had not moved a finger since she had fallen upon the bed, crushed by those bitter words with which Cleve had consented to join Kells's Legion. Since then Joan felt that she had lived years. She could not remember a single thought she might have had during those black hours; nevertheless, a decision had been formed in her mind, and it was that to-day she would reveal herself to Jim Cleve if it cost both their lives. Death was infinitely better than the suspense and fear and agony she had endured; and as for Jim, it would at least save him from crime.

Joan got up, a little dizzy and unsteady upon her feet. Her hands appeared clumsy and shaky. All the blood in her seemed to surge from heart to brain and it hurt her to breathe. Removing her mask, she bathed her face and combed her hair. At first she conceived an idea to go out without her face covered, but she thought better of it. Cleve's reckless defiance had communicated itself to her. She could not now be stopped.

Kells was gay and excited that morning. He paid her compliments. He said they would soon be out of this lonely gulch and she would see the sight of her life—a gold strike. She would see men wager a fortune on the turn of a card, lose, laugh, and go back to the digging. He said he would take her to Sacramento and 'Frisco and buy her everything any girl could desire. He was wild, voluble, unreasoning—obsessed by the anticipated fulfilment of his dream.

It was rather late in the morning and there were a dozen or more men in and around the cabin, all as excited as Kells. Preparations wre already under way for the expected journey to the gold-field. Packs were being laid out, overhauled, and repacked; saddles and bridles and weapons were being worked over; clothes were being awkwardly mended. Horses were being shod, and the job was as hard and disagreeable for men as for horses. Whenever a rider swung up the slope, and one came every now and then, all the robbers would leave off their tasks and start eagerly for the newcomer. The name Jesse Smith was on everybody's lips. Any hour he might be expected to arrive and corroborate Blicky's alluring tale.

Joan saw or imagined she saw that the glances in the eyes

of these men were yellow, like gold fire. She had seen miners and prospectors whose eyes shone with a strange glory of light that gold inspired, but never as those of Kells's bandit Legion. Presently Joan discovered that, despite the excitement, her effect upon them was more marked then ever, and by a difference that she was quick to feel. But she could not tell what this difference was—how their attitude had changed. Then she set herself the task of being useful. First she helped Bate Wood. He was roughly kind. She had not realized that there was sadness about her until he whispered: "Don't be downcast, miss. Mebbe it'll come out right yet!" That amazed Joan. Then his mysterious winks and glances, the sympathy she felt in him, all attested to some kind of a change. She grew keen to learn, but she did not know how. She felt the change in all the men. Then she went to Pearce and with all a woman's craft she exaggerated the silent sadness that had brought quick response from Wood. Red Pearce was even quicker. He did not seem to regard her proximity as that of a feminine thing which roused the devil in him. Pearce could not be other than coarse and vulgar, but there was pity in him. Joan sensed pity and some other quality still beyond her. This lieutenant of the bandit Kells was just as mysterious as Wood. Joan mended a great jagged rent in his buckskin shirt. Pearce appeared proud of her work; he tried to joke; he said amiable things. Then as she finished he glanced furtively round; he pressed her hand: "I had a sister once!" he whispered. And then with a dark and baleful hate: "Kells!—he'll get his over in the gold-camp!"

Joan turned away from Pearce still more amazed. Some strange, deep undercurrent was working here. There had been unmistakable hate for Kells in his dark look and a fierce implication in his portent of fatality. What had caused this sudden impersonal interest in her situation? What was the meaning of the subtle animosity toward the bandit leader? Was there no honor among evil men banded together for evil deeds? Were jealousy, ferocity, hate and faithlessness fostered by this wild and evil border life, ready at an instant's notice to break out? Joan divined the vain and futile and tragical nature of Kell's great enter-

140

prise. It could not succeed. It might bring a few days or weeks of fame, of blood-stained gold, of riotous gambling, but by its very nature it was doomed. It embraced failure and death.

Joan went from man to man, keener now on the track of this inexplicable change, sweetly and sadly friendly to each; and it was not till she encountered the little Frenchman that the secret was revealed. Frenchy was of a different race. Deep in the fiber of his being inculcated a sentiment, a feeling, long submerged in the darkness of a wicked life, and now that something came fleeting out of the depths—and it was respect for a woman. To Joan it was a flash of light. Yesterday these ruffians despised her; to-day they respected her. So they had believed what she had so desperately flung at Jim Cleve. They believed her good, they pitied her, they respected her, they responded to her effort to turn a boy back from a bad career. They were bandits, desperados, murderers, lost, but each remembered in her a mother or a sister. What each might have felt or done had he possessed her, as Kells possessed her, did not alter the case as it stood. A strange inconsistency of character made them hate Kells for what they might not have hated in themselves. Her appeal to Cleve, her outburst of truth, her youth and misfortune, had discovered to each a human quality. As in Kells something of nobility still lingered, a ghost among his ruined ideals, so in the others some goodness remained. Joan sustained an uplifting divination—no man was utterly bad. Then came the hideous image of the giant Gulden, the utter absence of soul in him, and she shuddered. Then came the thought of Jim Cleve, who had not believed her, who had bitterly made the fatal step, who might in the strange reversion of his character be beyond influence.

And it was at the precise moment when this thought rose to counteract the hope revived by the changed attitude of the men that Joan looked out to see Jim Cleve sauntering up, careless, untidy, a cigarette between his lips, blue blotches on his white face, upon him the stamp of abandonment. Joan suffered a contraction of heart that benumbed her breast. She stood a moment battling with herself. She was brave enough, desperate enough, to walk

141

straight up to Cleve, remove her mask and say, "I am Joan!" But that must be a last resource. She had no plan, yet she might force an opportunity to see Cleve alone.

A shout rose above the hubbub of voices. A tall man was pointing across the gulch where dust-clouds showed above the willows. Men crowded round him, all gazing in the direction of his hand, all talking at once.

"Jesse Smith's hoss, I swear!" shouted the tall man. "Kells, come out here!"

Kells appeared, dark and eager, at the door, and nimbly he leaped to the excited group. Pearce and Wood and others followed.

"What's up?" called the bandit. "Hello! Who's that riding bareback?"

"He's shore cuttin' the wind," said Wood.

"Blicky!" exclaimed the tall man. "Kells, there's news. I seen Jesse's hoss."

Kells let out a strange, exultant cry. The excited talk among the men gave place to a subdued murmur, then subsided. Blicky was running a horse up the road, hanging low over him, like an Indian. He clattered to the bench, scattered the men in all directions. The fiery horse plunged and pounded. Blicky was gray of face and wild of aspect.

"Jesse's come!" he yelled, hoarsely, at Kells. "He jest fell off his hoss—all in! He wants you—an' all the gang! *He's seen a million dollars in gold-dust!*"

Absolute silence ensued after that last swift and startling speech. It broke to a commingling of yells and shouts. Blicky wheeled his horse and Kells started on a run. And there was a stampede and rush after him.

Joan grasped her opportunity. She had seen all this excitement, but she had not lost sight of Cleve. He got up from a log and started after the others. Joan flew to him, grasped him, startled him with the suddenness of her onslaught. But her tongue seemed cloven to the roof of her mouth, her lips weak and mute. Twice she strove to speak.

"Meet me—there!—among the pines—right away!" she whispered, with breathless earnestness. "*It's life—or death—for me!*"

As she released his arm he snatched at her mask. But she eluded him.

"Who *are* you?" he flashed.

Kells and his men were piling into the willows, leaping the brook, hurrying on. They had no thought but to get to Jesse Smith to hear of the gold strike. That news to them was as finding gold in the earth was to honest miners.

"Come!" cried Joan. She hurried away toward the corner of the cabin, then halted to see if he was following. He was, indeed. She ran round behind the cabin, out on the slope, halting at the first trees. Cleve came striding after her. She ran on, beginning to pant and stumble. The way he strode, the white grimness of him, frightened her. What would he do? Again she went on, but not running now. There were straggling pines and spruces that soon hid the cabins. Beyond, a few rods, was a dense clump of pines, and she made for that. As she reached it she turned fearfully. Only Cleve was in sight. She uttered a sob of mingled relief, joy, and thankfulness. She and Cleve had not been observed. They would be out of sight in this little pine grove. At last! She could reveal herself, tell him why she was there, that she loved him, that she was as good as ever she had been. Why was she shaking like a leaf in the wind? She saw Cleve through a blur. He was almost running now. Involuntarily she fled into the grove. It was dark and cool; it smelled sweetly of pine; there were narrow aisles and little sunlit glades. She hurried on till a fallen tree blocked her passage. Here she turned—she would wait—the tree was good to lean against. There came Cleve, a dark, stalking shadow. She did not remember him like that. He entered the glade.

"Speak again!" he said, thickly. "Either I'm drunk or crazy!"

But Joan could not speak. She held out hands that shook—swept them to her face—tore at the mask. Then with a gasp she stood revealed.

If she had stabbed him straight through the heart he could not have been more ghastly. Joan saw him, in all the terrible transfiguration that came over him, but she had no conceptions, no thought of what constituted that change. After that check to her mind came a surge of joy.

143

"Jim! . . . Jim! It's Joan!" she breathed, with lips almost mute.

"Joan!" he gasped, and the sound of his voice seemed to be the passing from horrible doubt to certainty.

Like a panther he leaped at her, fastened a powerful hand at the neck of her blouse, jerked her to her knees, and began to drag her. Joan fought his iron grasp. The twisting and tightening of her blouse choked her utterance. He did not look down upon her, but she could see him, the rigidity of his body set in violence, the awful shade upon his face, the upstanding hair on his head. He dragged her as if she had been an empty sack. Like a beast he was seeking a dark place—a hole to hide her. She was strangling; a distorted sight made objects dim; and now she struggled instinctively. Suddenly the clutch at her neck loosened; gaspingly came the intake of air to her lungs; the dark-red veil left her eyes. She was still upon her knees. Cleve stood before her, like a gray-faced demon, holding his gun level, ready to fire.

"Pray for your soul—and mine!"

"Jim! Oh Jim! . . . Will you kill yourself, too?"

"Yes! But pray, girl—quick!"

"Then I pray to God—not for my soul—but just for one more moment of life . . . *to tell you, Jim!*"

Cleve's face worked and the gun began to waver. Her reply had been a stroke of lightning into the dark abyss of his jealous agony.

Joan saw it, and she raised her quivering face, and she held up her arms to him. "To tell—you—Jim!" she entreated.

"What?" he rasped out.

"That I'm innocent—that I'm as good—a girl—as ever. . ever. . . . Let me tell you. . . . Oh, you're mistaken—terribly mistaken."

"Now, I know I'm drunk. . . . You, Joan Randle! You in that rig! You the companion of Jack Kells! Not even his wife! The jest of these foul-mouthed bandits! And you say you're innocent—good? . . . When you refused to leave him!"

"I was afraid to go—afraid you'd be killed," she moaned, beating her breast.

It must have seemed madness to him, a monstrous nightmare, a delirium of drink, that Joan Randle was there on her knees in a brazen male attire, lifting her arms to him, beseeching him, not to spare her life, but to believe in her innocence.

Joan burst into swift, broken utterance: "Only listen! I trailed you out—twenty miles from Hoadley. I met Roberts. He came with me. He lamed his horse—we had to camp. Kells rode down on us. He had two men. They camped there. Next morning he—killed Roberts—made off with me. . . . Then he killed his men—just to have me—alone to himself. . . . We crossed a range—camped in the cañon. There he attacked me—and I—I shot him! . . . But I couldn't leave him—to die!" Joan hurried on with her narrative, gaining strength and eloquence as she saw the weakening of Cleve. "First he said I was his wife to fool that Gulden—and the others," she went on. "He meant to save me from them. But they guessed or found out. . . . Kells forced me into these bandit clothes. He's depraved, somehow. And I had to wear something. Kells hasn't harmed me—no one has. I've influence over him. He can't resist it. He's tried to force me to marry him. And he's tried to give up to his evil intentions. But he can't. There's good in him. I can make him feel it. . . . Oh, he loves me, and I'm not afraid of him any more. . . . It has been a terrible time for me, Jim, but I'm still—the same girl you knew—you used to—"

Cleve dropped the gun and he waved his hand before his eyes as if to dispel a blindness.

"But why—*why?*" he asked, incredulously. "Why did you leave Hoadley? That's forbidden. You knew the risk."

Joan gazed steadily up at him, to see the whiteness slowly fade out of his face. She had imagined it would be an overcoming of pride to betray her love, but she had been wrong. The moment was so full, so overpowering, that she seemed dumb. He had ruined himself for her, and out of that ruin had come the glory of her love. Perhaps it was all too late, but at least he would know that for love of him she had in turn sacrificed herself.

"Jim," she whispered, and with the first word of that

betrayal a thrill, a tremble, a rush went over her, and all her blood seemed hot at her neck and face, "that night when you kissed me I was furious. But the moment you had gone I repented. I must have—cared for you then, but I didn't know. . . . Remorse seized me. And I set out on your trail to save you from yourself. And with the pain and fear and terror there was sometimes—the—the sweetness of your kisses. Then I knew I cared. . . . And with the added days of suspense and agony—all that told me of your throwing your life away—there came love. . . . Such love as otherwise I'd never have been big enough for! I meant to find you—to save you—to send you home! . . . I have found you, maybe too late to save your life, but not your soul, thank God! . . . That's why I've been strong enough to hold back Kells. I love you, Jim! . . . I love you! I couldn't tell you enough. My heart is bursting. . . . Say you believe me! Say you know I'm good—true to you—your Joan! . . . And kiss me—like you did that night when we were such blind fools. A boy and a girl who didn't know—and couldn't tell!—Oh, the sadness of it! . . . . Kiss me, Jim, before I—drop—at your feet! . . . If only you—believe—"

Joan was blinded by tears and whispering she knew not what when Cleve broke from his trance and caught her to his breast. She was fainting—hovering at the border of unconsciousness when his violence held her back from oblivion. She seemed wrapped to him and held so tightly there was no breath in her body, no motion, no stir of pulse. That vague, dreamy moment passed. She heard his husky, broken accents—she felt the pound of his heart against her breast. And he began to kiss her as she had begged him to. She quickened to thrilling, revivifying life. And she lifted her face, and clung round his neck, and kissed him, blindly, sweetly, passionately, with all her heart and soul in her lips, wanting only one thing in the world—to give that which she had denied him.

"Joan! . . . Joan! . . . Joan!" he murmured when their lips parted. "Am I dreaming—drunk—or crazy?"

"Oh, Jim, I'm real—you have me in your arms," she whispered. "Dear Jim—kiss me again—and say you believe me."

"Believe you? . . . I'm out of my mind with joy. . . . You loved me! You followed me! . . . And—that idea of mine—only an absurd, vile suspicion! I might have known—had I been sane!"

"There. . . . Oh, Jim! . . . Enough of madness. We've got to plan. Remember where we are. There's Kells, and this terrible situation to meet!"

He stared at her, slowly realizing, and then it was his turn to shake. "My God! I'd forgotten. I'll *have* to kill you now!"

A reaction set in. If he had any self-control left he lost it, and like a boy whose fling into manhood had exhausted his courage he sank beside her and buried his face against her. And he cried in a low, tense, heartbroken way. For Joan it was terrible to hear him. She held his hand to her breast and implored him not to weaken now. But he was stricken with remorse—he had run off like a coward, he had brought her to this calamity—and he could not rise under it. Joan realized that he had long labored under stress of morbid emotion. Only a supreme effort could lift him out of it to strong and reasoning equilibrium, and that must come from her.

She pushed him away from her, and held him back where he must see her, and white-hot with passionate purpose, she kissed him. "Jim Cleve, if you've *nerve* enough to be *bad* you've nerve enough to save the girl who *loves* you—who *belongs* to you!"

He raised his face and it flashed from red to white. He caught the subtlety of her antithesis With the very two words which had driven him away under the sting of cowardice she uplifted him; and with all that was tender and faithful and passionate in her meaning of surrender she settled at once and forever the doubt of his manhood. He arose trembling in every limb. Like a dog he shook himself. His breast heaved. The shades of scorn and bitterness and abandon might never have haunted his face. In that moment he had passed from the reckless and wild, sick rage of a weakling to the stern, realizing courage of a man. His suffering on this wild border had developed a different fiber of character; and at the great moment, the climax, when his moral force hung balanced between elevation and destruction, the woman had called to him, and her unquenchable spirit passed into him.

"There's only one thing—to get away," he said.

"Yes, but that's a terrible risk," she replied.

"We've a good chance now. I'll get horses. We can slip away while they're all excited."

"No—no. I daren't risk so much. Kells would find out at once. He'd be like a hound on our trail. But that's not all. I've a horror of Gulden. I can't explain. I *feel* it. He would know—he would take the trail. I'd never try to escape with Gulden in camp. . . . Jim, do you know what he's done?"

"He's a cannibal. I hate the sight of him. I tried to kill him. I wish I had killed him."

"I'm never safe while he's near."

"Then I will kill him."

"Hush! you'll not be desperate unless you have to be. . . . Listen. I'm safe with Kells for the present. And he's friendly to you. Let us wait. I'll keep trying to influence him. I have won the friendship of some of his men. We'll stay with him—travel with him. Surely we'd have a better chance to excape after we reach that gold-camp. You must play your part. But do it without drinking and fighting. I couldn't bear that. We'll see each other somehow. We'll plan. Then we'll take the first chance to get away."

"We might never have a better chance than we've got right now," he remonstrated.

"It may seem so to you. But I *know*. I haven't watched these ruffians for nothing. I tell you Gulden has split with Kells because of me. I don't know how I know. And I think I'd die of terror out on the trail with two hundred miles to go—and that gorilla after me."

"But, Joan, if we once got away Gulden would never take you alive," said Jim, earnestly. "So you needn't fear that."

"I've uncanny horror of him. It's as if he were a gorilla—and would take me off even if I were dead! . . . No, Jim, let us wait. Let me select the time. I can do it. Trust me. Oh, Jim, now that I've saved you from being a bandit, I can do anything. I can fool Kells or Pearce or Wood—any of them, except Gulden."

"If Kells had to choose now between trailing you and rushing for the gold-camp, which would he do?"

"He'd trail me," she said.

"But Kells is crazy over gold. He has two passions. To steal gold, and to gamble with it."

"That may be. But he'd go after me first. So would Gulden. We can't ride these hills as they do. We don't know the trails—the water. We'd get lost. We'd be caught. And somehow I know that Gulden and his gang would find us first."

"You're probably right, Joan," replied Cleve. "But you condemn me to a living death. . . . To let you out of my sight with Kells or any of them! It'll be worse almost than my life was before."

"But, Jim, I'll be safe," she entreated. "It's the better choice of two evils. Our lives depend on reason, waiting, planning. And, Jim, I want to live for you."

"My brave darling, to hear you say that!" he exclaimed, with deep emotion. "When I never expected to see you again! . . . But the past is past. I begin over from this hour. I'll be what you want—do what you want."

Joan seemed irresistibly drawn to him again, and the supplication, as she lifted her blushing face, and the yielding, were perilously sweet.

"Jim, kiss me and hold me—the way—you did that night!"

And it was not Joan who first broke that embrace.

"Find my mask," she said.

Cleve picked up his gun and presently the piece of black felt. He held it as if it were a deadly thing.

"Put it on me."

He slipped the cord over her head and adjusted the mask so the holes came right for her eyes.

"Joan, it hides the—the *goodness* of you," he cried. "No one can see your eyes now. No one will look at your face. That rig shows your—shows you off so! It's not decent. . . . But, O Lord! I'm bound to confess how pretty, how devilish, how seductive you are! And I hate it."

"Jim, I hate it, too. But we must stand it. Try not to

149

shame me any more. . . . And now good-by. Keep watch for me—as I will for you—all the time."

Joan broke from him and glided out of the grove, away under the straggling pines, along the slope. She came upon her horse and she led him back to the corral. Many of the horses had strayed. There was no one at the cabin, but she saw men striding up the slope, Kells in the lead. She had been fortunate. Her absence could hardly have been noted. She had just strength left to get to her room, where she fell upon the bed, weak and trembling and dizzy and unutterably grateful at her deliverance from the hateful, unbearable falsity of her situation.

13

$\diamond$

IT WAS afternoon before Joan could trust herself sufficiently to go out again, and when she did she saw that she attracted very little attention from the bandits.

Kells had a springy step, a bright eye, a lifted head, and he seemed to be listening. Perhaps he was—to the music of his sordid dreams. Joan watched him sometimes with woner. Even a bandit—plotting gold robberies, with violence and blood merely means to an end—built castles in the air and lived with joy!

All that afternoon the bandits left camp in twos and threes, each party with pack burros and horses, packed as Joan had not seen them before on the border. Shovels and picks and old sieves and pans, these swinging or tied in prominent places, were evidence that the bandits meant to assume the characters of miners and prospectors. They whistled and sang. It was a lark. The excitement had subsided and the action begun. Only in Kells, under his radiance, could be felt the dark and sinister plot. He was the heart of the machine.

By sundown Kells, Pearce, Wood, Jim Cleve, and a robust, grizzled bandit, Jesse Smith, were left in camp. Smith was lame from his ride, and Joan gathered that Kells would have left camp but for the fact that Smith needed rest. He and Kells were together all the time, talking endlessly. Joan heard them argue a disputed point—would the men abide by Kells's plan and go by twos and threes into the gold-camp, and hide their relations as a larger band? Kells contended they would and Smith had his doubts.

"Jack, wait till you see Alder Creek!" ejaculated Smith, wagging his grizzled head. "Three thousand men, old an' young, of all kinds—gone gold-crazy! Alder Creek has got California's '49 and' '51 cinched to the last hole!" And the bandit leader rubbed his palms in great glee.

That evening they all had supper together in Kell's cabin. Bate Wood grumbled because he had packed most of his outfit. It so chanced that Joan sat directly opposite Jim Cleve, and while he ate he pressed her foot with his under the table. The touch thrilled Joan. Jim did not glance at her, but there was such a change in him that she feared it might rouse Kells's curiosity. This night, however, the bandit could not have seen anything except a gleam of yellow. He talked, he sat at table, but did not eat. After supper he sent Joan to her cabin, saying they would be on the trail at daylight. Joan watched them awhile from her covert. They had evidently talked themselves out, and Kells grew thoughtful. Smith and Pearce went outside, apparently to roll their beds on the ground under the porch roof. Wood, who said he was never a good sleeper, smoked his pipe. And

Jim Cleve spread blankets along the wall in the shadow and and lay down. Joan could see his eyes shining toward the door. Of course he was thinking of her. But could he see her eyes? Watching her chance, she slipped a hand from behind the curtain, and she knew Cleve saw it. What a comfort that was! Joan's heart swelled. All might yet be well. Jim Cleve would be near her while she slept. She could sleep now without those dark dreams—without dreading to awaken to the light. Again she saw Kells pacing the room, silent, bent, absorbed, hands behind his back, weighted with his burden. It was impossible not to feel sorry for him. With all his intelligence and cunning power, his cause was hopeless. Joan knew that as she knew so many other things without understanding why. She had not yet sounded Jesse Smith, but not a man of all the others was true to Kells. They would be of his Border Legion, do his bidding, revel in their ill-gotten gains, and then, when he needed them most, be false to him.

When Joan was awakened her room was shrouded in gray gloom. A bustle sound from the big cabin, and outside horses stamped and men talked.

She sat alone at breakfast and ate by lantern-light. It was necessary to take a lantern back to her cabin, and she was so long in her preparations there that Kells called again. Somehow she did not want to leave this cabin. It seemed protective and private, and she feared she might not find such quarters again. Besides, upon the moment of leaving she discovered that she had grown attached to the place where she had suffered and thought and grown so much.

Kells had put out the lights. Joan hurried through the cabin and outside. The gray obscurity had given way to dawn. The air was cold, sweet, bracing with the touch of mountain purity in it. The men, except Kells, were all mounted, and the pack-train was in motion. Kells dragged the rude door into position, and then, mounting, he called to Joan to follow. She trotted her horse after him, down the slope, across the brook and through the wet willows, and out upon the wide trail. She glanced ahead, discerning that the third man from her was Jim Cleve; and that fact, in the start for Alder Creek, made all the difference in the world.

When they rode out of the narrow defile into the valley the sun was rising red and bright in a notch of the mountains. Clouds hung over distant peaks, and the patches of snow in the high cañons shone blue and pink. Smith in the lead turned westward up the valley. Horses trooped after the cavalcade and had to be driven back. There were also cattle in the valley, and all these Kells left behind like an honest rancher who had no fear for his stock. Deer stood off with long ears pointed forward, watching the horses go by. There were flocks of quail, and whirring grouse, and bounding jack-rabbits, and occasionally a brace of sneaking coyotes. These and the wild flowers, and the waving meadow-grass, the yellow-stemmed willows, and the patches of alder, all were pleasurable to Joan's eyes and restful to her mind.

Smith soon led away from this valley up out of the head of a ravine, across a rough rock-strewn ridge, down again into a hollow that grew to be a cañon. The trail was bad. Part of the time it was the bottom of a boulder-strewn brook where the horses slipped on the wet, round stones. Progress was slow and time passed. For Joan, however, it was a relief; and the slower they might travel the better she would like it. At the end of that journey there were Gulden and the others, and the gold-camp with its illimitable possibilities for such men.

At noon the party halted for a rest. The camp site was pleasant and the men were all agreeable. During the meal Kells found occasion to remark to Cleve:

"Say youngster, you've brightened up. Must be because of our prospects over here."

"Not that so much," replied Cleve. "I quit the whisky. To be honest, Kells, I was almost seeing snakes."

"I'm glad you quit. When you're drinking you're wild. I never yet saw the man who could drink hard and keep his head. I can't. But I don't drink much."

His last remark brought a response in laughter. Evidently his companions thought he was joking. He laughed himself and actually winked at Joan.

It happened to be Cleve whom Kells told to saddle Joan's horse, and as Joan tried the cinches, to see if they were too tight to suit her, Jim's hand came in contact with hers. That touch was like a message. Joan was thrilling all over as she looked at Jim, but he kept his face averted. Perhaps he did not trust his eyes.

Travel was resumed up the cañon and continued steadily, though leisurely. But the trail was so rough, and so winding, that Joan believed the progress did not exceed three miles an hour. It was the kind of travel in which a horse could be helped and that entailed attention to the lay of the ground. Before Joan realized the hours were flying, the afternoon had waned. Smith kept on, however, until nearly dark before halting for camp.

The evening camp was a scene of activity, and all except Joan had work to do. She tried to lend a hand, but Wood told her to rest. This she was glad to do. When called to supper she had almost fallen asleep. After a long day's ride the business of eating precluded conversation. Later, however, the men began to talk between puffs on their pipes, and from the talk no one could have guessed that here was a band of robbers on their way to a gold camp. Jesse Smith had a sore foot and he was compared to a tenderfoot on his first ride. Smith retaliated in kind. Every consideration was shown Joan, and Wood particularly appeared assiduous in his desire for her comfort. All the men except Cleve paid her some kind attention; and he, of course, neglected her because he was afraid to go near her. Again she felt in Red Pearce a condemnation of the bandit leader who was dragging a girl over hard trails, making her sleep in the open, exposing her to danger and to men like himself and Gulden. In his own estimate Pearce, like every one of his kind, was not so slow as the others.

Joan watched and listened from her blankets, under a leafy tree, some few yards from the camp-fire. Once Kells turned to see how far distant she was, and then, lowering his voice, he told a story. The others laughed. Pearce followed with another, and he, too, took care that Joan could not hear. They grew closer for the mirth, and Smith, who evidently was a jolly fellow, set them to roaring. Jim Cleve laughed with them.

"Say, Jim, you're getting over it," remarked Kells.

"Over what?"

Kells paused, rather embarrassed for a reply, as evidently in the humor of the hour he had spoken a thought better left unsaid. But there was no more forbidding atmosphere about Cleve. He appeared to have rounded to good-fellowship after a moody and quarrelsome drinking spell.

"Why, over what drove you out here—and gave me a lucky chance at you," replied Kells, with a constrained laugh.

"Oh, you mean the girl? . . . Sure, I'm getting over that, except when I drink."

"Tell us, Jim," said Kells, curiously.

"Aw, you'll give me the laugh!" retorted Cleve.

"No, we won't unless your story's funny."

"You can gamble it wasn't funny," put in Red Pearce.

They all coaxed him, yet none of them, except Kells, was particularly curious; it was just that hour when men of their ilk were lazy and comfortable and full fed and good-humored round the warm, blazing camp-fire.

"All right," replied Cleve, and apparently, for all his complaisance, a call upon memory had its pain. "I'm from Montana. Range-rider in winter and in summer I prospected. Saved quite a little money, in spite of a fling now and then at faro and whisky. . . . Yes, there was a girl, I guess yes. She was pretty. I had a bad case over her. Not long ago I left all I had—money and gold and things—in her keeping, and I went prospecting again. We were to get married on my return. I stayed out six months, did well, and got robbed of all my dust."

Cleve was telling this fabrication in a matter-of-fact way, growing a little less frank as he proceeded, and he paused while he lifted sand and let it drift through his fingers, watching it curiously. All the men were interested and Kells hung on every word.

"When I got back," went on Cleve, "my girl had married another fellow. She'd given him all I left with her. Then I got drunk. While I was drunk they put up a job on me. It was her word that disgraced me and run me out of town. . . . So I struck west and drifted to the border."

"That's not all," said Kells, bluntly.

"Jim, I reckon you ain't tellin' what you did to thet lyin' girl an' the feller. How'd you leave them?" added Pearce.

But Cleve appeared to become gloomy and reticent.

"Wimmen can hand the double-cross to a man, hey, Kells?" queried Smith, with a broad grin.

"By gosh! I thought you'd been treated powerful mean!" exclaimed Bate Wood, and he was full of wrath.

"A treacherous woman!" exclaimed Kells, passionately. He had taken Cleve's story hard. The man must have been betrayed by women, and Cleve's story had irritated old wounds.

Directly Kells left the fire and repaired to his blankets, near where Joan lay. Probably he believed her asleep, for he neither looked nor spoke. Cleve sought his bed, and likewise Wood and Smith. Pearce was the last to leave, and as he stood up the light fell upon his red face, lean and bold like an Indian's. Then he passed Joan, looking down upon her and then upon the recumbent figure of Kells; and if his glance was not baleful and malignant, as it swept over the bandit, Joan believed her imagination must be vividly weird, and running away with her judgment.

The next morning began a day of toil. They had to climb over the mountain divide, a long, flat-topped range of broken rocks. Joan spared her horse to the limit of her own endurance. If there were a trail Smith alone knew it, for none was in evidence to the others. They climbed out of the notched head of the cañon, and up a long slope of weathered shale that let the horses slide back a foot for every yard gained, and through a labyrinth of broken cliffs, and over bench and ridge to the height of the divide. From there Joan had a magnificent view. Foot-hills rolled round heads below, and miles away, in a curve of the range, glistened Bear Lake. The rest here at this height was counteracted by the fact that the altitude affected Joan. She was glad to be on the move again, and now the travel was downhill, so that she could ride. Still it was difficult, for horses were more easily lamed in a descent. It took two hours to descend the distance that had consumed all the morning to ascend. Smith led through valley after valley between

157

foot-hills, and late in the afternoon halted by a spring in a timbered spot.

Joan ached in every muscle and she was too tired to care what happened round the camp-fire. Jim had been close to her all day and that had kept up her spirit. It was not yet dark when she lay down for the night.

"Sleep well, Dandy Dale," said Kells, cheerfully, yet not without pathos. "Alder Creek to-morrow! . . . Then you'll never sleep again!"

At times she seemed to feel that he regretted her presence, and always this fancy came to her with mocking or bantering suggestion that the costume and mask she wore made her a bandit's consort, and she could not escape the wildness of this gold-seeking life. The truth was that Kells saw the insuperable barrier between them, and in the bitterness of his love he lied to himself, and hated himself for the lie.

About the middle of the afternoon of the next day the tired cavalcade rode down out of the brush and rock into a new, broad, dusty road. It was so new that the stems of the cut brush along the borders were still white. But that road had been traveled by a multitude.

Out across the valley in the rear Joan saw a canvas-topped wagon, and she had not ridden far on the road when she saw a bobbing pack-burros to the fore. Kells had called Wood and Smith and Pearce and Cleve together, and now they went on in a bunch, all driving the pack-train. Excitement again claimed Kells; Pearce was alert and hawk-eyed; Smith looked like a hound on a scent; Cleve showed genuine feeling. Only Bate Wood remained proof to the meaning of that broad road.

All along, on either side, Joan saw wrecks of wagons, wheels, harness, boxes, old rags of tents blown into the brush, dead mules and burros. It seemed almost as if an army had passed that way. Presently the road crossed a wide, shallow brook of water, half clear and half muddy; and on the other side the road followed the course of the brook. Joan heard Smith call the stream Alder Creek, and he asked Kells if he knew what muddied water meant. The bandit's eyes flashed fire. Joan thrilled, for she, too, knew that up-stream there were miners washing earth for gold.

A couple of miles farther on creek and road entered the mouth of a wide spruce-timbered gulch. These trees hid any view of the slopes or floor of the gulch, and it was not till several more miles had been passed that the bandit rode out into what Joan first thought was a hideous slash in the forest made by fire. But it was only the devastation wrought by men. As far as she could see the timber was down, and everywhere began to be manifested signs that led her to expect habitations. No cabins showed, however, in the next mile. They passed out of the timbered part of the gulch into one of rugged, bare, and stony slopes, with bunches of sparse alder here and there. The gulch turned at right angles and a great gray slope shut out sight of what lay beyond. But, once round that obstruction, Kells halted his men with short, tense exclamation.

Joan saw that she stood high up on the slope, looking down upon the gold-camp. It was an interesting scene, but not beautiful. To Kells it must have been so, but to Joan it was even more hideous than the slash in the forest. Here and there, everywhere, were rude dugouts, little huts of brush, an occasional tent, and an occasional log cabin; and as she looked farther and farther these crude habitations of miners magnified in number and in dimensions till the white and black broken mass of the town choked the narrow gulch.

"Wal, boss, what do you say to thet diggin's?" demanded Jesse Smith.

Kells drew a deep breath. "Old forty-niner, this beats all I ever saw!"

"Shore I've seen Sacramento look like thet!" added Bate Wood.

Pearce and Cleve gazed with fixed eyes, and, however different their emotions, they rivaled each other in attention.

"Jesse, what's the word?" queried Kells, with a sharp return to the business of the matter.

"I've picked a site on the other side of camp. Best fer us," he replied.

"Shall we keep to the road?"

"Certain-lee," he returned, with his grin.

Kells hesitated, and felt of his beard, probably conjecturing the possibilities of recognition.

"Whiskers make another man of you. Reckon you needn't expect to be known over here."

That decided Kells. He pulled his sombrero well down, shadowing his face. Then he remembered Joan and made a slight significant gesture at her mask.

"Kells, the people in this here camp wouldn't look at an army ridin' through," responded Smith. "It's every man fer hisself. An' wimmen, say! there's all kinds. I seen a dozen with veils, an' them's the same as masks."

Nevertheless, Kells had Joan remove the mask and pull her sombrero down, and instructed her to ride in the midst of the group. Then they trotted on, soon catching up with the jogging pack-train.

What a strange ride that was for Joan! The slope resembled a magnified ant-hill with a horde of frantic ants in action. As she drew closer she saw these ants were men, digging for gold. Those near at hand could be plainly seen—rough, ragged, bearded men and smooth-faced boys. Farther on and up the slope, along the waterways and ravines, were miners so close they seemed almost to interfere with one another. The creek bottom was alive with busy, silent, violent men, bending over the water, washing and shaking and paddling, all desperately intent upon something. They had not time to look up. They were ragged, unkempt, barearmed and bare-legged, every last one of them with back bent. For a mile or more Kells's party trotted through this part of the diggings, and everywhere, on rocky bench and gravel bar and gray slope, were holes with men picking and shoveling in them. Some were deep and some were shallow; some long trenches and others mere pits. If all of these prospectors were finding gold, then gold was everywhere. And presently Joan did not need to have Kells tell her that all of these diggers were finding dust. How silent they were—how tense! They were not mechanical. It was a soul that drove them. Joan had seen many men dig for gold, and find a little now and then, but

160

she had never seen men dig when they knew they were going to strike gold. That made the strange difference.

Joan calculated she must have seen a thousand miners in less than two miles of the gulch, and then she could not see up the draws and washes that intersected the slope, and she could not see beyond the camp.

But it was not a camp which she was entering; it was a tent-walled town, a city of squat log cabins, a long, motley, checkered jumble of structures thrown up and together in mad haste. The wide road split it in the middle and seemed a stream of color and life. Joan rode between two lines of horses, burros, oxen, mules, packs and loads and canvas-domed wagons and gaudy vehicles resembling gipsy cara-vans. The street was as busy as a beehive and as noisy as a bedlam. The sidewalks were rough-hewn planks and they rattled under the tread of booted men. There were tents on the ground and tents on floors and tents on log walls. And farther on began the lines of cabins—stores and shops and saloons—and then a great, square, flat structure with a flaring sign in crude gold letters, "Last Nugget," from which came the creak of fiddles and scrape of boots, and hoarse mirth. Joan saw strange, wild-looking creatures—women that made her shrink; and several others of her sex, hurry-ing along, carrying sacks or buckets, worn and bewildered-looking women, the sight of whom gave her a pang. She saw lounging Indians and groups of lazy, bearded men, just like Kells's band, and gamblers in long, black coats, and fron-tiersmen in fringed buckskin, and Mexicans with swarthy faces under wide, peaked sombreros; and then in great ma-jority, dominating that stream of life, the lean and stalwart miners, of all ages, in their check shirts and high boots, all packing guns, jostling along, dark-browed, somber, and in-tent. These last were the workers of this vast beehive; the others were the drones, the parasites.

Kell's party rode on through the town, and Smith halted them beyond the outskirts, near a grove of spruce-trees, where camp was to be made.

Joan pondered over her impression of Alder Creek. It was confused; she had seen too much. But out of what she had seen and heard loomed two contrasting features: a

161

throng of toiling miners, slaves to their lust for gold and actuated by ambitions, hopes, and aims, honest, rugged, tireless workers, but frenzied in that strange pursuit; and a lesser crowd, like leeches, living for and off the gold they did not dig with blood of hand and sweat of brow.

Manifestly Jesse Smith had selected the spot for Kells's permanent location at Alder Creek with an eye for the bandit's peculiar needs. It was out of sight of town, yet within a hundred rods of the nearest huts, and closer than that to a sawmill. It could be approached by a shallow ravine that wound away toward the creek. It was backed up against a rugged bluff in which there was a narrow gorge, choked with pieces of weathered cliff; and no doubt the bandits could go and come in that direction. There was a spring near at hand and a grove of spruce-trees. The ground was rocky, and apparently unfit for the digging of gold.

While Bate Wood began preparations for supper, and Cleve built the fire, and Smith looked after the horses, Kells and Pearce stepped off the ground where the cabin was to be erected. They selected a level bench down upon which a huge cracked rock, as large as a house, had rolled. The cabin was to be backed up against this stone, and in the rear, under cover of it, a secret exit could be made and hidden. The bandit wanted two holes to his burrow.

When the group sat down to the meal the gulch was full of sunset colors. And, strangely, they were all some shade of gold. Beautiful golden veils, misty, ethereal, shone in rays across the gulch from the broken ramparts; and they seemed so brilliant, so rich, prophetic of the treasures of the hills. But that golden sunset changed. The sun went down red, leaving a sinister shadow over the gulch, growing darker and darker. Joan saw Cleve thoughtfully watching this transformation, and she wondered if he had caught the subtle mood of nature. For whatever had been the hope and brightness, the golden glory of this new Eldorado, this sudden uprising Alder Creek with its horde of brave and toiling miners, the truth was that Jack Kells and Gulden had ridden into the camp and the sun had gone down red. Joan knew that great mining-camps were always happy, rich, free, lucky, honest places till the fame of gold brought evil men. And she had not the slightest doubt that the sun of Alder Creek's brief and glad day had set forever.

Twilight was stealing down from the hills when Kells announced to his party: "Bate, you and Jesse keep camp. Pearce, you look out for any of the gang. But meet in the dark! . . . Cleve, you can go with me." Then he turned to Joan. "Do you want to go with us to see the sights or would you rather stay here?"

"I'd like to go, if only I didn't look so—so dreadful in this suit," she replied.

Kells laughed, and the camp-fire glare lighted the smiling faces of Pearce and Smith.

"Why, you'll not be seen. And you look far from dreadful."

"Can't you give me a—a longer coat?" faltered Joan.

Cleve heard, and without speaking he went to his saddle and unrolled his pack. Inside a slicker he had a gray coat. Joan had seen it many a time, and it brought a pang with memories of Hoadley. Had that been years ago? Cleve handed this coat to Joan.

"Thank you," she said.

Kells held the coat for her and she slipped into it. She seemed lost. It was long, coming way below her hips, and for the first time in days she felt she was Joan Randle again.

"Modesty is all very well in a woman, but it's not always becoming," remarked Kells. "Turn up your collar. . . . Pull down your hat—farther— There! If you won't go as a youngster now I'll eat Dandy Dale's outfit and get you silk dresses. Ha-ha!"

Joan was not deceived by his humor. He might like to look at her in that outrageous bandit costume; it might have pleased certain vain and notoriety-seeking proclivities of his, habits of his California road-agent days; but she felt that notwithstanding this, once she had donned the long coat he was relieved and glad in spite of himself. Joan had a little rush of feeling. Sometimes she almost liked this bandit. Once he must have been something very different.

163

They set out, Joan between Kells and Cleve. How strange for her! She had daring enough to feel for Jim's hand in the dark and to give it a squeeze. Then he nearly broke her fingers. She felt the fire in him. It was indeed a hard situation for him. The walking was rough, owing to the uneven road and the stones. Several times Joan stumbled and her spurs jangled. They passed ruddy camp-fires, where steam and smoke arose with savory odors, where red-faced men were eating; and they passed other camp-fires, burned out and smoldering. Some tents had dim lights, throwing shadows on the canvas, and others were dark. There were men on the road, all headed for town, gay, noisy and profane.

Then Joan saw uneven rows of lights, some dim and some bright, and crossing before them were moving dark figures. Again Kells bethought himself of his own disguise, and buried his chin in his scarf and pulled his wide-brimmed hat down so that hardly a glimpse of his face could be seen. Joan could not have recognized him at the distance of a yard.

They walked down the middle of the road, past the noisy saloons, past the big, flat structure with its sign "Last Nugget" and its open windows, where shafts of light shone forth, and all the way down to the end of town. Then Kells turned back. He scrutinized each group of men he met. He was looking for members of his Border Legion. Several times he left Cleve and Joan standing in the road while he peered into saloons. At these brief intervals Joan looked at Cleve with all her heart in her eyes. He never spoke. He seemed under a strain. Upon the return, when they reached the Last Nugget, Kells said:

"Jim, hang on to her like grim death! She's worth more than all the gold in Alder Creek!"

Then they started for the door.

Joan clung to Cleve on one side, and on the other, instinctively with a frightened girl's action, she let go Kells's arm and slipped her hand in his. He seemed startled. He bent to her ear, for the din made ordinary talk indistinguishable. That involuntary hand in his evidently had pleased and touched him, even hurt him, for his whisper was husky.

"It's all right—you're perfectly safe."

First Joan made out a glare of smoky lamps, a huge place full of smoke and men and sounds. Kells led the way slowly. He had his own reason for observance. There was a stench that sickened Joan—a blended odor of tobacco and rum and wet sawdust and smoking oil. There was a noise that appeared almost deafening—the loud talk and vacant laughter of drinking men, and a din of creaky fiddles and scraping boots and boisterous mirth. This last and dominating sound came from an adjoining room, which Joan could see through a wide opening. There was dancing, but Joan could not see the dancers because of the intervening crowd. Then her gaze came back to the features nearer at hand. Men and youths were lined up to a long bar nearly as high as her head. Then there were excited shouting groups round gambling games. There were men in clusters, sitting on up-turned kegs, round a box for a table, and dirty bags of gold-dust were in evidence. The gamblers at the cards were silent, in strange contrast with the others; and in each group was at least one dark-garbed, hard-eyed gambler who was not a miner. Joan saw boys not yet of age, flushed and haggard, wild with the frenzy of winning and cast down in defeat. There were jovial, grizzled, old prospectors to whom this scene and company were pleasant reminders of bygone days. There were desperados whose glittering eyes showed they had no gold with which to gamble.

Joan suddenly felt Kells start and she believed she heard a low, hissing exclamation. And she looked for the cause. Then she saw familiar dark faces; they belonged to men of Kells's Legion. And with his broad back to her there sat the giant Gulden. Already he and his allies had gotten together in defiance of or indifference to Kells's orders. Some of them were already under the influence of drink, but, though they saw Kells, they gave no sign of recognition. Gulden did not see Joan, and for that she was thankful. And whether or not his presence caused it, the fact was that she suddenly felt as much of a captive as she had in Cabin Gulch, and feared that here escape would be harder because in a community like this Kells would watch her closely.

Kells led Joan and Cleve from one part of the smoky hall

to another, and they looked on at the games and the strange raw life manifested there. The place was getting packed with men. Kells's party encountered Blicky and Beady Jones together. They passed by as strangers. Then Joan saw Beard and Chick Williams arm in arm, strolling about, like royster-ing miners. Williams telegraphed a keen, fleeting glance at Kells, then went on, to be lost in the crowd. Handy Oliver brushed by Kells, jostled him, apparently by accident, and he said, "Excuse me, mister!" There were other familiar faces. Kells's gang were all in Alder Creek and the dark machinations of the bandit leader had been put into opera-tion. What struck Joan forcibly was that, though there were hilarity and comradeship, they were not manifested in any general way. These miners were strangers to one another; the groups were strangers; the gamblers were strangers; the newcomers were strangers; and over all hung an atmosphere of distrust. Good fellowship abided only in the many small companies of men who stuck together. The mining-camps that Joan had visited had been composed of an assort-ment of prospectors and hunters who made one big, jolly family. This was a gold strike, and the difference was obvious. The hunting for gold was one thing, in its relation to the searchers; after it had been found, in a rich field, the conditions of life and character changed. Gold had always seemed wonderful and beautiful to Joan; she absorbed here something that was the nucleus of hate. Why could not these miners, young and old, stay in their camps and keep their gold? That was the fatality. The pursuit was a dream—a glittering allurement; the possession incited a lust for more, and that was madness. Joan felt that in these reckless, honest miners there was a liberation of the same wild ele-ment which was the driving passion of Kells's Border Legion. Gold, then, was a terrible thing.

"Take me in there," said Joan, conscious of her own ex-citement, and she indicated the dance-hall.

Kells laughed as if at her audacity. But he appeared reluctant.

"Please take me—unless—" Joan did not know what to add, but she meant unless it was not right for her to see any more. A strange curiosity had stirred in her. After all, this place where she now stood was not greatly different from the picture imagination had conjured up. That dance-hall, however, was beyond any creation of Joan's mind.

"Let me have a look first," said Kells, and he left Joan with Cleve.

When he had gone Joan spoke without looking at Cleve, though she held fast to his arm.

"Jim, it could be dreadful here—all in a minute!" she whispered.

"You've struck it exactly," he replied. "All Alder Creek needed to make it hell was Kells and his gang."

"Thank Heaven I turned you back in time! . . . Jim, you'd have—have gone the pace here."

He nodded grimly. Then Kells returned and led them back through the room to another door where spectators were fewer. Joan saw perhaps a dozen couples of rough, whirling, jigging dancers in a half-circle of watching men. The hall was a wide platform of boards with posts holding a canvas roof. The sides were open; the lights were situated at each end—huge, round, circus tent lamps. There were rude benches and tables where reeling men surrounded a woman. Joan saw a young miner in dusty boots and corduroys lying drunk or dead in the sawdust. Her eyes were drawn back to the dancers, and to the dance that bore some semblance to a waltz. In the din the music could scarcely be heard. As far as the men were concerned this dance was a bold and violent expression of excitement on the part of some, and for the rest a drunken, mad fling. Sight of the women gave Joan's curiosity a blunt check. She felt queer. She had not seen women like these, and their dancing, their actions, their looks, were beyond her understanding. Nevertheless, they shocked her, disgusted her, sickened her. And suddenly when it dawned upon her in unbelievable vivid suggestion that they were the wildest and most terrible element of this dark stream of humanity lured by gold, then she was appalled.

"Take me out of here!" she besought Kells, and he led her out instantly. They went through the gambling-hall and into the crowded street, back toward camp.

"You saw enough," said Kells, "but nothing to what will

167

break out by and by. This camp is new. It's rich. Gold is the cheapest thing. It passes from hand to hand. Ten dollars an ounce. Buyers don't look at the scales. Only the gamblers are crooked. But all this will change."

Kells did not say what that change might be, but the click of his teeth was expressive. Joan did not, however, gather from it, and the dark meaning of his tone, that the Border Legion would cause this change. That was in the nature of events. A great strike of gold might enrich the world, but it was a catastrophe.

Long into the night Joan lay awake, and at times, stirring the silence, there was wafted to her on a breeze the low, strange murmur of the gold-camp's strife.

Joan slept late next morning, and was awakened by the unloading of lumber. Teams were drawing planks from the sawmill. Already a skeleton framework for Kells's cabin had been erected. Jim Cleve was working with the others, and they were sacrificing thoroughness to haste. Joan had to cook her own breakfast, which task was welcome, and after it had been finished she wished for something more to occupy her mind. But nothing offered. Finding a comfortable seat among some rocks where she would be inconspicuous, she looked on at the building of Kells's cabin. It seemed strange, and somehow comforting, to watch Jim Cleve work. He had never been a great worker. Would this experience on the border make a man of him? She felt assured of that.

If ever a cabin sprang up like a mushroom, that bandit rendezvous was the one. Kells worked himself, and appeared no mean hand. By noon the roof of clapboards was on, and the siding of the same material had been started. Evidently there was not to a be a fireplace inside.

Then a teamster drove up with a wagon-load of purchases Kells had ordered. Kells helped unload this and evidently was in search of articles. Presently he found them, and then approached Joan, to deposit before her an assortment of bundles little and big.

"There Miss Modestly," he said. "Make yourself some clothes. You can shake Dandy Dale's outfit, except when we're on the trail. . . . And, say, if you knew what I had to

168

pay for this stuff you'd think there was a bigger robber in Alder Creek than Jack Kells. . . . And, come to think of it, my name's now Blight. You're my daughter, if any one asks."

Joan was so grateful to him for the goods and the permission to get out of Dandy Dale's suit as soon as possible, that she could only smile her thanks. Kells stared at her, then turned abruptly away. Those little unconscious acts of hers seemed to affect him strangely. Joan remembered that he had intended to parade her in Dandy Dale's costume to gratify some vain abnormal side of his bandit's proclivities. He had weakened. Here was another subtle indication of the deterioration of the evil of him. How far would it go? Joan thought dreamily, and with a swelling heart, of her influence upon this hardened bandit, upon that wild boy, Jim Cleve.

All that afternoon, and part of the evening in the camp-fire light, and all of the next day Joan sewed, so busy that she scarcely lifted her eyes from her work. The following day she finished her dress, and with no little pride, for she had both taste and skill. Of the men, Bate Wood had been most interested in her task; and he would let things burn on the fire to watch her.

That day the rude cabin was completed. It contained one long room; and at the back a small compartment partitioned off from the rest, and built against and around a shallow cavern in the huge rock. This compartment was for Joan. There were a rude board door with padlock and key, a bench upon which blankets had been flung, a small square hole cut in the wall to serve as a window. What with her own few belongings and the articles of furniture that Kells bought for her, Joan soon had a comfortable room, even a luxury compared to what she had been used to for weeks. Certain it was that Kells meant to keep her a prisoner, or virtually so. Joan had no sooner spied the little window than she thought that it would be possible for Jim Cleve to talk to her there from the outside.

Kells verified Joan's suspicion by telling her that she was not to leave the cabin of her own accord, as she had been permitted to do back in Cabin Gulch; and Joan retorted that there she had made him a promise not to run away, which promise she now took back. That promise had worried her.

She was glad to be honest with Kells. He gazed at her somberly.

"You'll be worse off if you do—and I'll be better off," he said. And then as an afterthought he added: "Gulden might not think you—a white elephant on his hands! . . . Remember his way, the cave and the rope!"

So, instinctively or cruelly he chose the right name to bring shuddering terror into Joan's soul.

14

◈

JOAN'S opportunity for watching Kells and his men and overhearing their colloquies was as good as it had been back in Cabin Gulch. But it developed that where Kells had been open and frank he now became secret and cautious. She was aware that men, singly and in couples, visited him during the early hours of the night, and they had conferences in low, earnest tones. She could peer out of her little window and see dark, silent forms come up from the ravine at the back of the cabin, and leave the same way. None of them went round to the front door, where Bate Wood smoked and kept guard. Joan was able to hear only scraps of these earnest talks; and from part of one she gathered that for some reason or other Kells desired to bring himself into notice. Alder Creek must be made to know that a man of importance had arrived. It seemed to Joan that this was the very last thing which Kells ought to do. What magnificent daring the bandit had! Famous years before in California—with a price set upon his life in Nevada—and now the noted, if unknown, leader of border robbers in Idaho, he sought to make himself prominent, respected, and powerful. Joan found that in spite of her horror at the sinister and deadly nature of the bandit's enterprise she could not avoid an absorbing interest in his fortunes.

Next day Joan watched for an opportunity to tell Jim Cleve that he might come to her little window any time after dark to talk and plan with her. No chance presented itself. Joan wore the dress she had made, to the evident pleasure of Bate Wood and Pearce. They had conceived as strong an interest in her fortunes as she had in Kells's. Wood nodded his approval and Pearce said she was a lady once more. Strange it was to Joan that this villain Pearce, whom she could not have dared trust, grew open in his insinuating hints of Kells's blackguardism. Strange because Pearce was absolutely sincere!

When Jim Cleve did see Joan in her dress the first time he appeared so glad and relieved and grateful that she feared he might betray himself, so she got out of his sight.

Not long after that Kells called her from her room. He wore his somber and thoughtful cast of countenance. Red Pearce and Jesse Smith were standing at attention. Cleve was sitting on the threshold of the door and Wood leaned against the wall.

"Is there anything in the pack of stuff I bought you that you could use for a veil?" asked Kells of Joan.

"Yes," she replied.

"Get it," he ordered. "And your hat, too."

Joan went to her room and returned with the designated

articles, the hat being that which she had worn when she left Hoadley.

"That'll do. Put it on—over your face—and let's see how you look."

Joan complied with this request, all the time wondering what Kells meant.

"I want it to disguise you, but not to hide your youth—your good looks," he said, and he arranged it differently about her face. "There! . . . You'd sure make any man curious to see you now. . . . Put on the hat."

Joan did so. Then Kells appeared to become more forcible.

"You're to go down into the town. Walk slow as far as the Last Nugget. Cross the road and come back. Look at every man you meet or see standing by. Don't be in the least frightened. Pearce and Smith will be right behind you. They'd get to you before anything could happen. . . . Do you understand?"

"Yes," replied Joan.

Red Pearce stirred uneasily. "Jack, I'm thinkin' some rough talk'll come her way," he said, darkly.

"Will you shut up!" replied Kells in quick passion. He resented some implication. "I've thought of that. She won't hear what's said to her. . . . Here," and he turned again to Joan, "take some cotton—or anything—and stuff up your ears. Make a good job of it."

Joan went back to her room and, looking about for something with which to execute Kells's last order, she stripped some soft, woolly bits from a fleece-lined piece of cloth. With these she essayed to deaden her hearing. Then she returned. Kells spoke to her, but, though she seemed dully to hear his voice, she could not distinguish what he said. She shook her head. With that Kells waved her out upon her strange errand.

Joan brushed against Cleve as she crossed the threshold. What would he think of this? She would not see his face. When she reached the first tents she could not resist the desire to look back. Pearce was within twenty yards of her and Smith about the same distance farther back. Joan was more curious than anything else. She divined that Kells wanted her to attract attention, but for what reason she was at a loss to say. It was significant that he did not intend to let her suffer any indignity while fulfilling this mysterious mission.

Not until Joan got well down the road toward the Last Nugget did any one pay any attention to her. A Mexican jabbered at her, showing his white teeth, flashing his sloe-black eyes. Young miners eyed her curiously, and some of them spoke. She met all kinds of men along the plank walk, most of whom passed by, apparently unobserving. She obeyed Kells to the letter. But for some reason she was unable to explain, when she got to the row of saloons, where lounging, evil-eyed rowdies accosted her, she found she had to disobey him, at least in one particular. She walked faster. Still that did not make her task much easier. It began to be an ordeal. The farther she got the bolder men grew. Could it have been that Kells wanted this sort of thing to happen to her? Joan had no idea what these men meant, but she believed that was because for the time being she was deaf. Assuredly their looks were not a compliment to any girl. Joan wanted to hurry now, and she had to force herself to walk at a reasonable gait. One persistent fellow walked beside her for several steps. Joan was not fool enough not to realize now that these wayfarers wanted to make her acquaintance. And she decided she would have something to say to Kells when she got back.

Below the Last Nugget she crossed the road and started upon the return trip. In front of this gambling-hell there were scattered groups of men, standing, and going in. A tall man in black detached himself and started out, as if to intercept her. He wore a long black coat, a black bow tie, and a black sombrero. He had little, hard, piercing eyes, as black as his dress. He wore gloves and looked immaculate, compared with the other men. He, too, spoke to Joan, turned to walk with her. She looked straight ahead now, frightened, and she wanted to run. He kept beside her, apparently talking. Joan heard only the low sound of his voice. Then he took her arm, gently, but with familiarity. Joan broke from him and quickened her pace.

"Say, there! Leave thet girl alone!"

174

This must have been yelled, for Joan certainly heard it. She recognized Red Pearce's voice. And she wheeled to look. Pearce had overhauled the gambler, and already men were approaching. Involuntarily Joan halted. What would happen? The gambler spoke to Pearce, made what appeared deprecating gestures, as if to explain. But Pearce looked angry.

"I'll tell her daddy!" he shouted.

Joan waited for no more. She almost ran. There would surely be a fight. Could that have been Kells's intention? Whatever it was, she had been subjected to a mortifying and embarrassing affront. She was angry, and she thought it might be just as well to pretend to be furious. Kells must not use her for his nefarious schemes. She hurried on, and, to her surprise, when she got within sight of the cabin both Pearce and Smith had almost caught up with her. Jim Cleve sat where she had last seen him. Also Kells was outside. The way he strode to and fro showed Joan his anxiety. There was more to this incident than she could fathom. She took the padding from her ears, to her intense relief, and, soon reaching the cabin, she tore off the veil and confronted Kells.

"Wasn't that a—a fine thing for you to do?" she demanded, furiously. And with the outburst she felt her face blazing. "If I'd any idea what you meant—you couldn't—have driven me! . . . I trusted you. And you sent me down there on some—shameful errand of yours. You're no gentleman!"

Joan realized that her speech, especially the latter part, was absurd. But it had a remarkable effect upon Kells. His face actually turned red. He stammered something and halted, seemingly at a loss for words. How singularly the slightest hint of any act or word of hers that approached a possible respect or tolerance worked upon this bandit! He started toward Joan appealingly, but she passed him in contempt and went to her room. She heard him cursing Pearce in a rage, evidently blaming his lieutenant for whatever had angered her.

"But you wanted her insulted!" protested Pearce, hotly.

"You mullet-head!" roared Kells. "I wanted some

175

man—any man—to get just near enough to her so I could *swear* she'd been insulted. You let her go through that camp to meet real insult! . . . Why—! Pearce, I've a mind to shoot you!"

"Shoot!" retorted Pearce. "I obeyed orders as I saw them. . . . An' I want to say right here thet when it comes to anythin' concernin' this girl you're plumb off your nut. That's what. An' you can like it or lump it! I said before you'd split over this girl. An' I say it now!"

Through the door Joan had a glimpse of Cleve stepping between the angry men. This seemed unnecessary, however, for Pearce's stinging assertion had brought Kells to himself. There were a few more words, too low for Joan's ears, and then, accompanied by Smith, the three started off, evidently for the camp. Joan left her room and watched them from the cabin door. Bate Wood sat outside smoking.

"I'm declarin' my hand," he said to Joan, feelingly. "I'd never hev stood for thet scurvy trick. Now, miss, this's the toughest camp I ever seen. I mean tough as to wimmen! For it ain't begun to fan guns an' steal gold yet."

"Why did Kells want me insulted?" asked Joan.

"Wal, he's got to hev a reason for raisin' an orful fuss," replied Wood.

"Fuss?"

"Shore," replied Wood, dryly.

"What for?"

"Jest so he can walk out on the stage," rejoined Wood, evasively.

"It's mighty strange," said Joan.

"I reckon all about Mr. Kells is some strange these days. Red Pearce had it correct. Kells is a-goin' to split on you!"

"What do you mean by that?"

"Wal, he'll go one way an' the gang another."

"Why?" asked Joan, earnestly.

"Miss, there's some lot of reasons," said Wood, deliberately. "Fust, he did for Halloway an' Bailey, not because they wanted to treat you as he meant to, but just because he wanted to be alone. We're all wise thet you shot him—an' thet you wasn't his wife. An' since then we've seen him gradually lose his nerve. He organized his Legion an'

176

makes his plan to run this Alder Creek red. He still hangs on to you. He'd kill any man thet batted an eye at you. . . . An' through all this, because he's not Jack Kells of old, he's lost his pull with the gang. Sooner or later he'll split."

"Have I any real friends among you?" asked Joan.

"Wal, I reckon."

"Are you my friend, Bate Wood?" she went on in sweet wistfulness.

The grizzled old bandit removed his pipe and looked at her with a glint in his bloodshot eyes.

"I shore am. I'll sneak you off now if you'll go. I'll stick a knife in Kells if you say so."

"Oh, no, I'm afraid to run off—and you needn't harm Kells. After all, he's good to me."

"Good to you! . . . When he keeps you captive like an Indian would? When he's given me orders to watch you—keep you locked up?"

Wood's snort of disgust and wrath was thoroughly genuine. Still Joan knew that she dared not trust him, any more than Pearce or the others. Their raw emotions would undergo a change if Kells's possession of her were transferred to them. It occurred to Joan, however, that she might use Wood's friendliness to some advantage.

"So I'm to be locked up?" she asked.

"You're supposed to be."

"Without any one to talk to?"

"Wal, you'll hev me, when you want. I reckon thet ain't much to look forward to. But I can tell you a heap of stories. An' when Kells ain't around, if you're careful not to get me ketched, you can do as you want."

"Thank you, Bate. I'm going to like you," replied Joan, sincerely, and then she went back to her room. There was sewing to do, and while she worked she thought, so that the hours sped. When the light got so poor that she could sew no longer she put the work aside and stood at her little window, watching the sunset. From the front of the cabin came the sound of subdued voices. Probably Kells and his men had returned, and she was sure of this when she heard the ring of Bate Wood's ax.

All at once an object darker than the stones arrested

Joan's gaze. There was a man sitting on the far side of the little ravine. Instantly she recognized Jim Cleve. He was looking at the little window—at her. Joan believed he was there for just that purpose. Making sure that no one else was near to see, she put out her hand and waved it. Jim gave a guarded perceptible sign that he had observed her action, and almost directly got up and left. Joan needed no more than that to tell her how Jim's idea of communicating with her corresponded with her own. That night she would talk with him and she was thrilled through. The secrecy, the peril, somehow lent this prospect a sweetness, a zest, a delicious fear. Indeed, she was not only responding to love, but to daring, to defiance, to a wilder nameless element born of her environment and the needs of the hour.

Presently, Bate Wood called her in to supper. Pearce, Smith, and Cleve were finding seats at the table, but Kells looked rather sick. Joan observed him then more closely. His face was pale and damp, strangely shaded as if there were something dark under the pale skin. Joan had never seen him appear like this, and she shrank as from another and forbidding side of the man. Pearce and Smith acted naturally, ate with relish, and talked about the gold-diggings. Cleve, however, was not as usual; and Joan could not quite make out what constituted the dissimilarity. She hurried through her own supper and back to her room.

Already it was dark outside. Joan lay down to listen and wait. It seemed long, but probably was not long before she heard the men go outside, and the low thump of their footsteps as they went away. Then came the rattle and bang of Bate Wood's attack on the pans and pots. Bate liked to cook, but he hated to clean up afterward. By and by he settled down outside for his evening smoke and there was absolute quiet. Then Joan rose to stand at the window. She could see the dark mass of rock overhanging the cabin, the bluff beyond, and the stars. For the rest all was gloom.

She did not have to wait long. A soft step, almost indistinguishable, made her pulse beat quicker. She put her face out of the window, and on the instant a dark form seemed to loom up to meet her out of the shadow. She could not recognize that shape, yet she knew it belonged to Cleve.

"Joan," he whispered.

"Jim," she replied, just as low and gladly.

He moved closer, so that the hand she had gropingly put out touched him, then seemed naturally to slip along his shoulder, round his neck. And his face grew clearer in the shadow. His lips met hers, and Joan closed her eyes to that kiss. What hope, what strength for him and for her now in that meeting of lips!

"Oh, Jim! I'm so glad—to have you near—to touch you," she whispered.

"Do you love me still?" he whispered back, tensely.

"Still? More—more!"

"Say it, then."

"Jim, I love you!"

And their lips met again and clung, and it was he who drew back first.

"Dearest, why didn't you let me make a break to get away with you—before we came to this camp?"

"Oh, Jim, I told you. I was afraid. We'd have been caught. And Gulden—"

"We'll never have half the chance here. Kells means to keep you closely guarded. I heard the order. He's different now. He's grown crafty and hard. And the miners of this Alder Creek! Why, I'm more afraid to trust them than men like Wood or Pearce. They've gone clean crazy. Gold-mad! If you shouted for your life they wouldn't hear you. And if you could make them hear they wouldn't believe. This camp has sprung up in a night. It's not like any place I ever heard of. It's not human. It's so strange—so— Oh, I don't know what to say. I think I mean that men in a great gold strike become like coyotes at a carcass. You've seen that. No relation at all!"

"I'm frightened, too, Jim. I wish I'd had the courage to run when we were back in Cabin Gulch. But don't ever give up, not for a second! We can get away. We must plan and wait. Find out where we are—how far from Hoadley— what we must expect—whether it's safe to approach any one in this camp."

"Safe! I guess not, after to-day," he whispered, grimly.

"Why? What's happened?" she asked quickly.

"Joan, have you guessed yet why Kells sent you down into camp alone?"

"No."

"Listen. . . . I went with Kells and Smith and Pearce. They hurried straight to the Last Nugget. There was a crowd of men in front of the place. Pearce walked straight up to one—a gambler by his clothes. And he said in a loud voice. 'Here's the man!' . . . The gambler looked startled, turned pale, and went for his gun. But Kells shot him! . . . He fell dead, without a word. There was a big shout, then silence. Kells stood there with his smoking gun. I never saw the man so cool—so masterful. Then he addressed the crowd: 'This gambler insulted my daughter! My men here saw him. My name's Blight. I came here to buy up gold claims. And I want to say this: Your Alder Creek has got the gold. But it needs some of your best citizens to run it right, so a girl can be safe on the street.'

"Joan, I tell you it was a magnificent bluff," went on Jim, excitedly. "And it worked. Kells walked away amid cheers. He meant to give an impression of character and importance. He succeeded. So far as I could tell, there wasn't a man present who did not show admiration for him. I saw that dead gambler kicked."

"Jim!" breathed Joan. "He killed him—just for that?"

"Just for that—the bloody devil!"

"But still—what for? Oh, it was cold-blooded murder."

"No, an even break. Kells made the gambler go for his gun. I'll have to say that for Kells."

"It doesn't change the thing. I'd forgotten what a monster he is."

"Joan, his motive is plain. This new gold-camp has not reached the blood-spilling stage yet. It hadn't, I should say. The news of this killing will fly. It'll focus minds on this claim-buyer, Blight. His deed rings true—like that of an honest man with a daughter to protect. He'll win sympathy. Then he talks as if he were prosperous. Soon he'll be represented in this changing, growing population as a man of importance. He'll play the card for all he's worth. Meanwhile, secretly he'll begin to rob the miners. It'll be hard to suspect him. His plot is just like the man—great!"

"Jim, oughtn't we tell?" whispered Joan, trembling.

"I've thought of that. Somehow I seem to feel guilty. But whom on earth could we tell? We wouldn't dare speak here. . . . Remember—you're a prisoner. I'm supposed to be a bandit—one of the Border Legion. How to get away from here and save our lives—that's what tortures me."

"Something tells me we'll escape, if only we can plan the right way. Jim, I'll have to be penned here, with nothing to do but wait. You must come every night! . . . Won't you?"

For an answer he kissed her again.

"Jim, what'll you do meanwhile?" she asked, anxiously.

"I'm going to work a claim. Dig for gold. I told Kells so to-day, and he was delighted. He said he was afraid his men wouldn't like the working part of his plan. It's hard to dig gold. Easy to steal it. But I'll dig a hole as big as a hill! . . . Wouldn't it be funny if I struck it rich?"

"Jim, you're getting the fever."

"Joan, if I did happen to run into a gold-pocket—there're lots of them found—would—you—marry me?"

The tenderness, the timidity, and the yearning in Cleve's voice told Joan as never before how he had hoped and feared and despaired. She patted his cheek with her hand, and in the darkness, with her heart swelling to make up for what she had done to him, she felt a boldness and a recklessness, sweet, tumultuous, irresistible.

"Jim, I'll marry you—whether you strike gold or not," she whispered.

And there was another blind, sweet moment. Then Cleve tore himself away, and Joan leaned at the window, watching the shadow, with tears in her eyes and an ache in her breast.

From that day Joan lived a life of seclusion in the small room. Kells wanted it so, and Joan thought best for the time being not to take advantage of Bate Wood's duplicity. Her meals were brought to her by Wood, who was supposed to unlock and lock her door. But Wood never turned the key in that padlock.

Prisoner though Joan was, the days and nights sped swiftly.

Kells was always up till late in the night and slept half of the next morning. It was his wont to see Joan every day about noon. He had a care for his appearance. When he came in he was dark, forbidding, weary, and cold. Manifestly he came to her to get rid of the imponderable burden of the present. He left it behind him. He never spoke a word of Alder Creek, of gold, of the Border Legion. Always he began by inquiring for her welfare, by asking what he could do for her, what he could bring her. Joan had an abhorrence of Kells in his absence that she never felt when he was with her; and the reason must have been that she thought of him, remembered him as the bandit, and saw him as another and growing character. Always mindful of her influence, she was as companionable, as sympathetic, as cheerful, and sweet as it was possible for her to be. Slowly he would warm and change under her charm, and the grim gloom, the dark strain, would pass from him. When that left he was indeed another person. Frankly he told Joan that the glimpse of real love she had simulated back there in Cabin Gulch was seldom out of his mind. No woman had ever kissed him like she had. That kiss had transfigured him. It haunted him. If he could not win kisses like that from Joan's lips, of her own free will, then he wanted none. No other woman's lips would ever touch his. And he begged Joan in the terrible earnestness of a stern and hungering outcast for her love. And Joan could only sadly shake her head and tell him she was sorry for him, that the more she really believed he loved her the surer she was that he would give her up. Then always he passionately refused. He must have her to keep, to look at as his treasure, to dream over, and hope against hope that she would love him some day. Women sometimes learned to love their captors, he said; and if she only learned, then he would take her away to Australia, to distant lands. But most of all he begged her to show him again what it meant to be loved by a good woman. And Joan, who knew that her power now lay in her unattainableness, feigned a wavering reluctance, when in truth any surrender was impossible. He left her with a spirit that her presence gave him, in a kind of trance, radiant, yet with mocking smile, as if he foresaw the overthrow of his soul through her,

182

and in the light of that his waning power over his Legion was as nothing.

In the afternoon he went down into camp to strengthen the associations he had made, to buy claims, and to gamble. Upon his return Joan, peeping through a crack between the boards, could always tell whether he had been gambling, whether he had won or lost.

Most of the evenings he remained in his cabin, which after dark became a place of mysterious and stealthy action. The members of his Legion visited him, sometimes alone, never more than two together. Joan could hear them slipping in at the hidden aperture in the back of the cabin; she could hear the low voices, but seldom what was said; she could hear these night prowlers as they departed. Afterward Kells would have the lights lit, and then Joan could see into the cabin. Was that dark, haggard man Kells? She saw him take little buckskin sacks full of gold-dust and hide them under the floor. Then he would pace the room in his old familiar manner, like a caged tiger. Later his mood usually changed with the advent of Wood and Pearce and Smith and Cleve, who took turns at guard and going down into camp. Then Kells would join them in a friendly game for small stakes. Gambler though he was, he refused to allow any game there that might lead to heavy wagering. From the talk sometimes Joan learned that he played for exceedingly large stakes with gamblers and prosperous miners, usually with the same result—a loss. Sometimes he won, however, and then he would crow over Pearce and Smith, and delight in telling them how cunningly he had played.

Jim Cleve had his bed up under the bulge of bluff, in a sheltered nook. Kells had appeared to like this idea, for some reason relative to his scout system, which he did not explain. And Cleve was happy about it because this arrangement left him absolutely free to have his nightly rendezvous with Joan at her window, sometime between dark and midnight. Her bed was right under the window: if awake she could rest on her knees and look out; and if she was asleep he could thrust a slender stick between the boards to awaken her. But the fact was that Joan lived for these stolen meetings, and unless he could not come until very late she waited wide-eyed and listening for him. Then, besides, as long as Kells was stirring in the cabin she spent her time spying upon him.

Jim Cleve had gone to an unfrequented part of the gulch, for no particular reason, and here he had located his claim. The very first day he struck gold. And Kells, more for advertisement than for any other motive, had his men stake out a number of claims near Cleve's, and bought them. Then they had a little field of their own. All found the rich pay-dirt, but it was Cleve to whom the goddess of fortune turned her bright face. As he had been lucky at cards, so he was lucky at digging. His claim paid big returns. Kells spread the news, and that part of the gulch saw a rush of miners.

Every night Joan had her whispered hour with Cleve, and each succeeding one was the sweeter. Jim had become a victim of the gold fever. But, having Joan to steady him, he did not lose his head. If he gambled it was to help out with his part. He was generous to his comrades. He pretended to drink, but did not drink at all. Jim seemed to regard his good fortune as Joan's also. He believed if he struck it rich he could buy his sweetheart's freedom. He claimed that Kells was drunk for gold to gamble away. Joan let Jim talk, but she coaxed him and persuaded him to follow a certain line of behavior, she planned for him, she thought for him, she influenced him to hide the greater part of his gold-dust, and let it be known that he wore no gold-belt. She had a growing fear that Jim's success was likely to develop a temper in him inimical to the cool, waiting, tolerant policy needed to outwit Kells in the end. It seemed the more gold Jim acquired the more passionate he became, the more he importuned Joan, the more he hated Kells. Gold had gotten into his blood, and it was Joan's task to keep him sane. Naturally she gained more by yielding herself to Jim's caresses than by any direct advice or admonishment. It was her love that held Jim in check.

One night, the instant their hands met Joan knew that Jim was greatly excited or perturbed.

"Joan," he whispered, thrillingly, with his lips at her ear, "I've made myself solid with Kells! Oh, the luck of it!"

"Tell me!" whispered Joan, and she leaned against those lips.

"It was early to-night at the Nugget. I dropped in as usual. Kells was playing faro again with that gambler they call Flash. He's won a lot of Kells's gold—a crooked gambler. I looked on. And some of the gang were there—Pearce, Blicky, Handy Oliver, and of course Gulden, but all separated. Kells was losing and sore. But he was game. All at once he caught Flash in a crooked trick, and he yelled in a rage. He sure had the gang and everybody else looking. I expected—and so did all the gang—to see Kells pull his gun. But strange how gambling affects him! He only cursed Flash—called him right. You know that's about as bad as death to a professional gambler in a place like Alder Creek. Flash threw a derringer on Kells. He had it up his sleeve. He meant to kill Kells, and Kells had no chance. But Flash, having the drop, took time to talk, to make his bluff go strong with the crowd. And that's where he made a mistake. I jumped and knocked the gun out of his hand. It went off—burned my wrist. Then I slugged Mr. Flash good—he didn't get up. . . . Kells called the crowd around and, showing the cards as they lay, coolly proved that Flash was what everybody suspected. Then Kells said to me—I'll never forget how he looked: 'Youngster, he meant to do for me. I never thought of my gun. You see! . . . I'll kill him the next time we meet. . . . I've owed my life to men more than once. I never forget. You stood pat with me before. And now you're ace high!'"

"Was it fair of you?" asked Joan.

"Yes. Flash is a crooked gambler. I'd rather be a bandit. . . . Besides, all's fair in love! And I was thinking of you when I saved Kells!"

"Flash will be looking for you," said Joan, fearfully.

"Likely. And if he finds me he wants to be quick. But Kells will drive him out of camp or kill him. I tell you, Kells is the biggest man in Alder Creek. There's talk of office—a mayor and all that—and if the miners can forget gold long enough they'll elect Kells. But the riffraff, these blood-suckers who live off the miners, they'd rather not have any office in Alder Creek."

And upon another night Cleve in serious and somber mood talked about the Border Legion and its mysterious workings. The name had found prominence, no one knew how, and Alder Creek knew no more peaceful sleep. This Legion was supposed to consist of a strange, secret band of unknown bandits and road-agents, drawing its members from all that wild and trackless region called the border. Rumor gave it a leader of cunning and ruthless nature. It operated all over the country at the same time, and must have been composed of numerous smaller bands, impossible to detect. Because its victims never lived to tell how or by whom they had been robbed! This Legion worked slowly and in the dark. It did not bother to rob for little gain. It had strange and unerring information of large quantities of gold-dust. Two prospectors going out on the Bannack road, packing fifty pounds of gold, were found shot to pieces. A miner named Black, who would not trust his gold to the stage-express, and who left Adler Creek against advice, was never seen or heard of again. Four other miners of the camp, known to carry considerable gold, were robbed and killed at night on their way to their cabins. And another was found dead in his bed. Robbers had crept to his tent, slashed the canvas, murdered him while he slept, and made off with his belt of gold.

An evil day of blood had fallen upon Alder Creek. There were terrible and implacable men in the midst of the miners, by day at honest toil, learning who had gold, and murdering by night. The camp had never been united, but this dread fact disrupted any possible unity. Every man, or every little group of men, distrusted the other, watched and spied and lay awake at night. But the robberies continued, one every few days, and each one left no trace. For dead men could not talk.

Thus was ushered in at Alder Creek a régime of wildness that had no parallel in the earlier days of '49 and '51. Men frenzied by the possession of gold or greed for it responded to the wildness of that time and took their cue from this deadly and mysterious Border Legion. The gold-lust created its own blood-lust. Daily the population of Alder Creek grew in the new gold-seekers and its dark records kept pace. With distrust came suspicion and with suspicion came fear, and with fear came hate—and these, in already distorted minds, inflamed a hell. So that the most primitive passions of mankind found outlet and held sway. The operations of the Border Legion were lost in deeds done in the gambling dens, in the saloons, and on the street, in broad day. Men fought for no other reason than that the incentive was in the charged air. Men were shot at gaming-tables—and the game went on. Men were killed in the dance-halls, dragged out, marking a line of blood on the rude floor—and the dance went on. Still the pursuit of gold went on, more frenzied than ever, and still the greater and richer claims were struck. The price of gold soared and the commodities of life were almost beyond the dreams of avarice. It was a time in which the worst of men's natures stalked forth, hydra-headed and deaf, roaring for gold, spitting fire, and shedding blood. It was a time when gold and fire and blood were one. It was a time when a horde of men from every class and nation, of all ages and characters, met on a field were motives and ambitions and faiths and traits merged into one mad instinct of gain. It was worse than the time of the medieval crimes of religion; it made war seem a brave and honorable thing; it robbed manhood of that splendid and noble trait, always seen in shipwrecked men or those hopelessly lost in the barren north, the divine will not to retrograde to the savage. It was a time, for all it enriched the world with yellow treasure, when might was right, when men were hopeless, when death stalked rampant. The sun rose gold and it set red. It was the hour of Gold!

One afternoon late, while Joan was half dreaming, half dozing the hours away, she was thoroughly aroused by the tramp of boots and loud voices of excited men. Joan slipped to the peephole in the partition. Bate Wood had raised a warning hand to Kells, who stood up, facing the door. Red Pearce came bursting in, wild-eyed and violent. Joan imagined he was about to cry out that Kells had been betrayed.

"Kells, have you—heard?" he panted.

"Not so loud, you—!" replied Kells, coolly. "My name's Blight. . . . Who's with you?"

"Only Jesse an' some of the gang. I couldn't steer them away. But there's nothin' to fear."

"What's happened? What haven't I heard?"

"The camp's gone plumb ravin' crazy. . . . Jim Cleve found the biggest nugget ever dug in Idaho! . . . *Thirty pounds!*"

Kells seemed suddenly to inflame, to blaze with white passion. "Good for Jim!" he yelled, ringingly. He could scarcely have been more elated if he had made the strike himself.

Jesse Smith came stamping in, with a crowd elbowing their way behind him. Joan had a start of the old panic at sight of Gulden. For once the giant was not slow nor indifferent. His big eyes glared. He brought back to Joan the sickening sense of the brute strength of his massive presence. Some of his cronies were with him. For the rest, there were Blicky and Handy Oliver and Chick Williams. The whole group bore resemblance to a pack of wolves about to leap upon its prey. Yet, in each man, excepting Gulden, there was that striking aspect of exultation.

"Where's Jim?" demanded Kells.

"He's comin' along," replied Pearce. "He's sure been runnin' a gantlet. His strike stopped work in the diggin's. What do you think of that, Kells? The news spread like smoke before wind. Every last miner in camp has jest got to see thet lump of gold."

"Maybe I don't want to see it!" exclaimed Kells. "A thirty-pounder! I heard of one once, sixty pounds, but I never saw it. You can't believe till you see."

"Jim's comin' up the road now," said one of the men near the door. "Thet crowd hangs on. . . . But I reckon he's shakin' them."

"What'll Cleve do with this nugget?"

Gulden's big voice, so powerful, yet feelingless, caused a momentary silence. The expression of many faces changed. Kells looked startled, then annoyed.

"Why, Gulden, that's not my affair—nor yours," replied Kells. "Cleve dug it and it belongs to him."

"Dug or stole—it's all the same," responded Gulden.

Kell's threw up his hands as if it were useless and impossible to reason with this man.

Then the crowd surged round the door with shuffling boots and hoarse, mingled greetings to Cleve, who presently came plunging in out of the mêlée.

His face wore a flush of radiance; his eyes were like diamonds. Joan thrilled and thrilled at sight of him. He was beautiful. Yet there was about him a more striking wildness. He carried a gun in one hand and in the other an object wrapped in his scarf. He flung this upon the table in front of Kells. It made a heavy, solid thump. The ends of the scarf flew aside, and there lay a magnificent nugget of gold, black and rusty in parts, but with a dull, yellow glitter in others.

"Boss, what'll you bet against that?" cried Cleve, with exulting laugh. He was like a boy.

Kells reached for the nugget as if it were not an actual object, and when his hands closed on it he fondled it and weighed it and dug his nails into it and tasted it.

"My God!" he ejaculated, in wondering ecstasy. Then this, and the excitement, and the obsession all changed into sincere gladness. "Jim, you're born lucky. You, the youngster born unlucky in love! Why, you could buy any woman with this!"

"Could I? Find me one," responded Cleve, with swift boldness.

Kells laughed. "I don't know any worth so much."

"What'll I do with it?" queried Cleve.

"Why, you fool youngster! Has it turned your head, too? What'd you do with the rest of your dust? You've certainly been striking it rich."

"I spent it—lost it—lent it—gave some away and—saved a little."

"Probably you'll do the same with this. You're a good fellow, Jim."

"But this nugget means a lot of money. Between six and seven thousand dollars."

"You won't need advice how to spend it, even if it was a million. . . . Tell me, Jim, how'd you strike it?"

"Funny about that," replied Cleve. "Things were poor

for several days. Dug off branches into my claim. One grew to be a deep hole in gravel, hard to dig. My claim was once the bed of a stream, full of rocks that the water had rolled down once. This hole sort of haunted me. I'd leave it when my back got so sore I couldn't bend, but always I'd return. I'd say there wasn't a darned grain of gold in that gravel; then like a fool I'd go back and dig for all I was worth. No chance of finding blue dirt down there! But I kept on. And to-day when my pick hit what felt like a soft rock—I looked and saw the gleam of gold! . . . You ought to have seen me claw out that nugget! I whooped and brought everybody around. The rest was a parade. . . . Now I'm embarrassed by riches. What to do with it?"

"Wal, go back to Montana an' make thet fool girl sick," suggested one of the men who had heard Jim's fictitious story of himself.

"Dug or stole is all the same!" boomed the imperturbable Gulden.

Kells turned white with rage, and Cleve swept a swift and shrewd glance at the giant.

"Sure, that's my idea," declared Cleve. "I'll divide as—as we planned."

"You'll do nothing of the kind," retorted Kells. "You dug for that gold and it's yours."

"Well, boss, then say a quarter share to you and the same to me—and divide the rest among the gang."

"No!" exclaimed Kells, violently.

Joan imagined he was actuated as much by justice to Cleve as opposition to Gulden.

"Jim Cleve, you're a square pard if I ever seen one," declared Pearce, admiringly. "An' I'm here to say thet I wouldn't hev a share of your nugget."

"Nor me," spoke up Jesse Smith.

"I pass, too," said Chick Williams.

"Jim, if I was dyin' fer a drink I wouldn't stand fer thet deal," added Blicky, with a fine scorn.

These men, and others who spoke or signified their refusal, attested to the living truth that there was honor even among robbers. But there was not the slightest suggestion of change in Gulden's attitude or of those back of him.

"Share and share alike for me!" he muttered, grimly, with those great eyes upon the nugget.

Kells, with an agile bound, reached the table and pounded it with his fist, confronting the giant.

"So you say!" he hissed in dark passion. "You've gone too far, Gulden. Here's where I call you! ... You don't get a grain of that gold nugget. Jim's worked like a dog. If he digs up a million I'll see he gets it all. Maybe you loafers haven't a hunch what Jim's done for you. He's helped our big deal more than you or I. His honest work has made it easy for me to look honest. He's supposed to be engaged to marry my daughter. That more than anything was a blind. It made my stand, and I tell you that stand is high in this camp. Go down there and swear Blight is Jack Kells! See what you get! ... That's all. ... I'm dealing the cards in this game!"

Kells did not cow Gulden—for it was likely the giant lacked the feeling of fear—but he overruled him by sheer strength of spirit.

Gulden backed away stolidly, apparently dazed by his own movements; then he plunged out the door, and the ruffians who had given silent but sure expression of their loyalty tramped after him.

"Reckon thet starts the split!" declared Red Pearce.

"Suppose you'd been in Jim's place!" flashed Kells.

"Jack, I ain't sayin' a word. You was square. I'd want you to do the same by me. ... But fetchin' the girl into the deal—"

Kells's passionate and menacing gesture shut Pearce's lips. He lifted a hand, resignedly, and went out.

"Jim," said Kells, earnestly, "take my hunch. Hide your nugget. Don't send it out with the stage to Bannack. It'd never get there. ... And change the place where you sleep!"

"Thanks," replied Cleve, brightly. "I'll hide my nugget all right. And I'll take care of myself."

Later that night Joan waited at her window for Jim. It was so quiet that she could hear the faint murmur of the shallow creek. The sky was dusky blue; the stars were white, the night breeze sweet and cool. Her first flush of elation for Jim having passed, she experienced a sinking of courage.

Were they not in peril enough without Jim's finding a fortune? How dark and significant had been Kells's hint! There was something splendid in the bandit. Never had Joan felt so grateful to him. He was a villain, yet he was a man. What hatred he showed for Gulden! These rivals would surely meet in a terrible conflict—for power—for gold. And for her!—she added, involuntarily, with a deep, inward shudder. Once the thought had flashed through her mind, it seemed like a word of revelation.

Then she started as a dark form rose out of the shadow under her and a hand clasped hers. Jim! and she lifted her face.

"Joan! Joan! I'm rich! rich!" he babbled, wildly.

"Sssssh!" whispered Joan, softly, in his ear. "Be careful. You're wild to-night. . . . I saw you come in with the nugget. I heard you. . . . Oh, you lucky Jim! *I'll* tell you what to do with it!"

"Darling! It's all yours. You'll marry me now?"

"Sir! Do you take me for a fortune-hunter? I marry you for your gold? Never!"

"Joan!"

"I've promised," she said.

"I won't go away now. I'll work my claim," he began, excitedly. And he went on so rapidly that Joan could not keep track of his words. He was not so cautious as formerly. She remonstrated with him, all to no purpose. Not only was he carried away by possession of gold and assurance of more, but he had become masterful, obstinate, and illogical. He was indeed hopeless to-night—the gold had gotten into his blood. Joan grew afraid he would betray their secret and realized there had come still greater need for a woman's wit. So she resorted to a never-failing means of silencing him, of controlling him—her lips on his.

15

◈

FOR SEVERAL nights these stolen interviews were apparently the safer because of Joan's tender blinding of her lover. But it seemed that in Jim's condition of mind this yielding of her lips and her whispers of love had really been a mistake. Not only had she made the situation perilously sweet for herself, but in Jim's case she had added the spark to the powder. She realized her blunder when it was too late. And the fact that she did not regret it very much, and seemed to have lost herself in a defiant, reckless spell, warned her again that she, too, was answering to the wildness of the time and place. Joan's intelligence had broadened wonderfully in this period of her life, just as all her feelings had quickened. If gold had developed and intensified and liberated the worst passions of men, so the spirit of that atmosphere had its baneful effect upon her. Joan deplored this, yet she had the keenness to understand that it was nature fitting her to survive.

Back upon her fell that weight of suspense—what would happen next? Here in Alder Creek there did not at present appear to be the same peril which had menaced her before, but she would suffer through fatality to Cleve or Kells. And these two slept at night under a shadow that held death, and by day they walked on a thin crust over a volcano. Joan grew more and more fearful of the disclosures made when Kells met his men nightly in the cabin. She feared to hear, but she must hear, and even if she had not felt it necessary to keep informed of events, the fascination of the game would have impelled her to listen. And gradually the suspense she suffered augmented into a magnified, though vague, assurance of catastrophe, of impending doom. She could not shake off the gloomy presentiment. Something terrible was going to happen. An experience begun as tragically as hers could only end in a final and annihilating stroke. Yet hope was unquenchable, and with her fear kept pace a driving and relentless spirit.

One night at the end of a week of these interviews, when Joan attempted to resist Jim, to plead with him, lest in his growing boldness he betray them, she found him a madman.

"I'll pull you right out of this window," he said, roughly, and then with his hot face pressed against hers tried to accomplish the thing he threatened.

"Go on—pull me to pieces!" replied Joan, in despair and pain. "I'd be better off dead! And—you—hurt me—so!"

"Hurt you!" he whispered, hoarsely, as if he had never dreamed of such possibility. And then suddenly he was remorseful. He begged her to forgive him. His voice was broken, husky, pleading. His remorse, like every feeling of his these days, was exaggerated, wild, with that raw tinge of gold-blood in it. He made so much noise that Joan, more fearful than ever of discovery, quieted him with difficulty.

"Does Kells see you often—these days?" asked Jim, suddenly.

Joan had dreaded this question, which she had known would inevitably come. She wanted to lie; she knew she ought to lie; but it was impossible.

"Every day," she whispered. "Please—Jim—never mind that. Kells is good—he's all right to me. . . . And you and I have so little time together."

"Good!" exclaimed Cleve. Joan felt the leap of his body under her touch. "Why, if I'd tell you what he sends that gang to do—you'd—you'd kill him in his sleep."

"Tell me," replied Joan. She had a morbid, irresistible desire to learn.

"No. . . . And *what* does Kells do—when he sees you every day?"

"He talks."

"What about?"

"Oh, everything except about what holds him here. He talks to me to forget himself."

"Does he make love to you?"

Joan maintained silence. What would she do with this changed and hopeless Jim Cleve?

"Tell me!" Jim's hands gripped her with a force that made her wince. And now she grew as afraid of him as she had been for him. But she had spirit enough to grow angry, also.

"Certainly he does."

Jim Cleve echoed her first word, and then through grinding teeth he cursed. "I'm going to—stop it!" he panted, and his eyes looked big and dark and wild in the starlight.

"You can't. I belong to Kells. You at least ought to have sense enough to see that."

"Belong to him! . . . For God's sake! By what right?"

"By the right of possession. Might is right here on the border. Haven't you told me that a hundred times? Don't you hold your claim—your gold—by the right of your strength? It's the law of this border. To be sure Kells stole me. But just now I belong to him. And lately I see his consideration—his kindness in the light of what he could do if he held to that border law. . . . And of all the men I've met out here Kells is the least wild with this gold fever. He sends his men out to do murder for gold; he'd sell his soul to gamble for gold; but just the same, he's more of a man than—"

"Joan!" he interrupted, piercingly. "You love this bandit!"

"You're a fool!" burst out Joan.

"I guess—I—am," he replied in terrible, slow earnestness. He raised himself and appeared to loom over her and released his hold.

But Joan fearfully retained her clasp on his arm, and when he surged to get away she was hard put to it to hold him.

"Jim! Where are you going?"

He stood there a moment, a dark form against the night shadow, like an outline of a man cut from black stone.

"I'll just step around—there."

"Oh, what for?" whispered Joan.

"I'm going to kill Kells."

Joan got both arms round his neck and with her head against him she held him tightly, trying, praying to think how to meet this long-dreaded moment. After all, what was the use to try? This was the hour of Gold! Sacrifice, hope, courage, nobility, fidelity—these had no place here now. Men were the embodiment of passion—ferocity. They breathed only possession, and the thing in the balance was death. Women were creatures to hunger and fight for, but womanhood was nothing. Joan knew all this with a desperate hardening certainty, and almost she gave in. Strangely, thought of Gulden flashed up to make her again strong! Then she raised her face and began the old pleading with Jim, but different this time, when it seemed that absolutely all was at stake. She begged him, she importuned him, to listen to reason, to be guided by her, to fight the wildness that had obsessed him, to make sure that she would not be left alone. All in vain! He swore he would kill Kells and any other bandit who stood in the way of his leading her free out of that cabin. He was wild to fight. He might never have felt fear of these robbers. He would not listen to

196

any possibility of defeat for himself, or the possibility that in the event of Kells's death she would be worse off. He laughed at her strange, morbid fears of Gulden. He was immovable.

"Jim! . . . Jim! You'll break my heart!" she whispered, wailingly. "Oh! *what* can I do?"

Then Joan released her clasp and gave up to utter defeat. Cleve was silent. He did not seem to hear the shuddering little sobs that shook her. Suddenly he bent close to her.

"There's one thing you can do. If you'll do it I won't kill Kells. I'll obey your every word."

"What is it? Tell me!"

"Marry me!" he whispered, and his voice trembled.

"*Marry you!*" exclaimed Joan. She was confounded. She began to fear Jim was out of his head.

"I mean it. Marry me. Oh, Joan, will you—will you? It'll make the difference. That'll steady me. Don't you want to?"

"Jim, I'd be the happiest girl in the world if—if I only *could* marry you!" she breathed, passionately.

"But will you—will you? Say yes! Say yes!"

"*Yes!*" replied Joan in her desperation. "I hope that pleases you. But what on earth is the use to talk about it now?"

Cleve seemed to expand, to grow taller, to thrill under her nervous hands. And then he kissed her differently. She sensed a shyness, a happiness, a something hitherto foreign to his attitude. It was spiritual, and somehow she received an uplift of hope.

"Listen," he whispered. "There's a preacher down in camp. I've seen him—talked with him. He's trying to do good in that hell down there. I know I can trust him. I'll confide in him—enough. I'll fetch him up here tomorrow night—about this time. Oh, I'll be careful—very careful. And he can marry us right here by the window. Joan, will you do it? . . . Somehow, whatever threatens you or me—that'll be my salvation! . . . I've suffered so. It's been burned in my heart that *you* would never marry me. Yet you say you love me! . . . Prove it! . . . *My wife!* . . . Now, girl, a word will make a man of me!"

"Yes!" And with the word she put her lips to his with all

her heart in them. She felt him tremble. Yet almost instantly he put her from him.

"Look for me to-morrow about this time," he whispered. "Keep your nerve. . . . Good night."

That night Joan dreamed strange, weird, unremembered dreams. The next day passed like a slow, unreal age. She ate little of what was brought to her. For the first time she denied Kells admittance and she only vaguely sensed his solicitations. She had no ear for the murmur of voices in Kells's room. Even the loud and angry notes of a quarrel between Kells and his men did not distract her.

At sunset she leaned out of the little window, and only then, with the gold fading on the peaks and the shadow gathering under the bluff, did she awaken to reality. A broken mass of white cloud caught the glory of the sinking sun. She had never seen a golden radiance like that. It faded and dulled. But a warm glow remained. At twilight and then at dusk this glow lingered.

Then night fell. Joan was exceedingly sensitive to the sensations of light and shadow, of sound and silence, of dread and hope, of sadness and joy.

That pale, ruddy glow lingered over the bold heave of the range in the west. It was like a fire that would not go out, that would live to-morrow, and burn golden. The sky shone with deep, rich blue color fired with a thousand stars, radiant, speaking, hopeful. And there was a white track across the heavens. The mountains flung down their shadows, impenetrable, like the gloomy minds of men; and everywhere under the bluffs and slopes, in the hollows and ravines, lay an enveloping blackness, hiding its depth and secret and mystery.

Joan listened. Was there sound or silence? A faint and indescribably low roar, so low that it might have been real or false, came on the soft night breeze. It was the roar of the camp down there—the strife, the agony, the wild life in ceaseless action—the strange voice of gold, roaring greed and battle and death over the souls of men. But above that, presently, rose the murmur of the creek, a hushed and dreamy flow of water over stones. It was hurrying to get by this horde of wild men, for it must bear the taint of gold and blood. Would it purge itself and clarify in the valleys below, on its way to the sea? There was in its murmur an imperishable and deathless note of nature, of time; and this was only a fleeting day of men and gold.

Only by straining her ears could Joan hear these sounds, and when she ceased that, then she seemed to be weighed upon and claimed by silence. It was not a silence like that of Lost Cañon, but a silence of solitude where her soul stood alone. She was there on earth, yet no one could hear her mortal cry. The thunder of avalanches or the boom of the sea might have lessened her sense of utter loneliness.

And that silence fitted the darkness, and both were apostles of dread. They spoke to her. She breathed dread on that silent air and it filled her breast. There was nothing stable in the night shadows. The ravine seemed to send forth stealthy, noiseless shapes, specter and human, man and phantom, each on the other's trail.

If Jim would only come and let her see that he was safe for the hour! A hundred times she imagined she saw him looming darker than the shadows. She had only to see him now, to feel his hand, and dread might be lost. Love was something beyond the grasp of mind. Love had confounded Jim Cleve; it had brought up kindness and honor from the black depths of a bandit's heart; it had transformed her from a girl into a woman. Surely with all its greatness it could not be lost; surely in the end it must triumph over evil.

Joan found that hope was fluctuating, but eternal. It took no stock of intelligence. It was a matter of feeling. And when she gave rein to it for a moment, suddenly it plunged her into sadness. To hope was to think! Poor Jim! It was his fool's paradise. Just to let her be his wife! That was the apex of his dream. Joan divined that he might yield to her wisdom, he might become a man, but his agony would be greater. Still, he had been so intense, so strange, so different that she could not but feel joy in his joy.

Then at a soft footfall, a rustle, and a moving shadow Joan's mingled emotions merged into a poignant sense of the pain and suspense and tenderness of the actual moment.

"Joan—Joan," came the soft whisper.

She answered, and there was a catch in her breath.

The moving shadow split into two shadows that stole closer, loomed before her. She could not tell which belonged to Jim till he touched her. His touch was potent. It seemed to electrify her.

"Dearest, we're here—this is the parson," said Jim, like a happy boy. "I—"

"Ssssh!" whispered Joan. "Not so loud. . . . Listen!"

Kells was holding a rendezvous with members of his Legion. Joan even recognized his hard and somber tone, and the sharp voice of Red Pearce, and the drawl of Handy Oliver.

"All right. I'll be quiet," responded Cleve, cautiously. "Joan, you're to answer a few questions."

Then a soft hand touched Joan, and a voice differently keyed from any she had heard on the border addressed her.

"What is your name?" asked the preacher.

Joan told him.

"Can you tell anything about yourself? This young man is—is almost violent. I'm not sure. Still I want to—"

"I can't tell much," replied Joan, hurriedly. "I'm an honest girl. I'm free to—to marry him. I—I love him! . . . Oh, I want to help him. We—we are in trouble here. I daren't say how."

"Are you over eighteen?"

"Yes, sir."

"Do your parents object to this young man?"

"I have no parents. And my uncle, with whom I lived before I was brought to this awful place, he loves Jim. He always wanted me to marry him."

"Take his hand, then."

Joan felt the strong clasp of Jim's fingers, and that was all which seemed real at the moment. It seemed so dark and shadowy round these two black forms in front of her window. She heard a mournful wail of a lone wolf and it intensified the weird dream that bound her. She heard her shaking, whispered voice repeating the preacher's words. She caught a phrase of a low-murmured prayer. Then one dark form moved silently away. She was alone with Jim.

"Dearest Joan!" he whispered. "It's over! It's done! . . . Kiss me!"

She lifted her lips and Jim seemed to kiss her more sweetly, with less violence.

"Oh, Joan, that you'd really have me! I can't believe it. . . . Your *husband.*"

That word dispelled the dream and the pain which had held Joan, leaving only the tenderness, magnified now a hundredfold.

And that instant when she was locked in Cleve's arms, when the silence was so beautiful and full, she heard the heavy pound of a gun-butt upon the table in Kells's room.

"Where is Cleve?" That was the voice of Kells, stern, demanding.

Joan felt a start, a tremor run over Jim. Then he stiffened.

"I can't locate him," replied Red Pearce. "It was the same last night an' the one before. Cleve jest disappears these nights—about this time. . . . Some woman's got him!"

"He goes to bed. Can't you find where he sleeps?"

"No."

"This job's got to go through and he's got to do it."

"Bah!" taunted Pearce. "Gulden swears you can't make Cleve do a job. And so do I!"

"Go out and yell for Cleve! . . . Damn you all! I'll show you!"

Then Joan heard the tramp of heavy boots, then a softer tramp on the ground outside the cabin. Joan waited, holding her breath. She felt Jim's heart beating. He stood like a post. He, like Joan, was listening, as if for a trumpet of doom.

"HALLO, JIM!" rang out Pearce's stentorian call. It murdered the silence. It boomed under the bluff, and clapped in echo, and wound away, mockingly. It seemed to have shrieked to the whole wild borderland the breaking-point of the bandit's power.

So momentous was the call that Jim Cleve seemed to forget Joan, and she let him go without a word. Indeed, he was gone before she realized it, and his dark form dissolved in the shadows. Joan waited, listening with abated breathing. On this side of the cabin there was absolute silence. She

201

believed that Jim would slip around under cover of night and return by the road from camp. Then what would he do? The question seemed to puzzle her.

Joan leaned there at her window for moments greatly differing from those vaguely happy ones just passed. She had sustained a shock that had left her benumbed with a dull pain. What a rude, raw break the voice of Kells had made in her brief forgetfulness! She was returning now to reality. Presently she would peer through the crevice between the boards into the other room, and she shrank from the ordeal. Kells, and whoever was with him, maintained silence. Occasionally she heard the shuffle of a boot and a creak of the loose floor boards. She waited till anxiety and fear compelled her to look.

The lamps were burning; the door was wide open. Apparently Kells's rule of secrecy had been abandoned. One glance at Kells was enough to show Joan that he was sick and desperate. Handy Oliver did not wear his usual lazy good humor. Red Pearce sat silent and sullen, a smoking, unheeded pipe in his hand. Jesse Smith was gloomy. The only other present was Bate Wood, and whatever had happened had in no wise affected him. These bandits were all waiting.

Presently quick footsteps on the path outside caused them all to look toward the door. That tread was familiar to Joan, and suddenly her mouth was dry, her tongue stiff. What was Jim Cleve coming to meet? How sharp and decided his walk! Then his dark form crossed the bar of light outside the door, and he entered, bold and cool, and with a weariness that must have been simulated.

"Howdy boys!" he said.

Only Kells greeted him in response. The bandit eyed him curiously. The others added suspicion to their glances.

"Did you hear Red's yell?" queried Kells, presently.

"I'd have heard that roar if I'd been dead," replied Cleve, bluntly. "And I didn't like it! . . . I was coming up the road and I heard Pearce yell. I'll bet every man in camp heard it."

"How'd you know Pearce yelled for you?"

"I recognized his voice."

Cleve's manner recalled to Joan her first sight of him over

202

in Cabin Gulch. He was not so white or haggard, but his eyes were piercing, and what had once been recklessness now seemed to be boldness. He deliberately studied Pearce. Joan trembled, for she divined what none of these robbers knew, and it was that Pearce was perilously near death. It was there for Joan to read in Jim's dark glance.

"Where've you been all these nights?" queried the bandit leader.

"Is that any of your business—when you haven't had need of me?" returned Cleve.

"Yes, it's my business. And I've sent for you. You couldn't be found."

"I've been here for supper every night."

"I don't talk to any men in daylight. You know my hours for meeting. And you've not come."

"You should have told me. How was I to know?"

"I guess you're right. But where've you been?"

"Down in camp. Faro, most of the time. Bad luck, too."

Red Pearce's coarse face twisted into a scornful sneer. It must have been a lash to Kells.

"Pearce says you're chasing a woman," retorted the bandit leader.

"Pearce lies!" flashed Cleve. His action was as swift. And there he stood with a gun thrust hard against Pearce's side.

"*Jim!* Don't kill him!" yelled Kells, rising.

Pearce's red face turned white. He stood still as a stone, with his gaze fixed in fascinated fear upon Cleve's gun.

A paralyzing surprise appeared to hold the group.

"Can you prove what you said?" asked Cleve, low and hard.

Joan knew that if Pearce did have the proof which would implicate her he would never live to tell it.

"Cleve—I don't—know nothin'," choked out Pearce. "I jest figgered—it was a woman!"

Cleve slowly lowered the gun and stepped back. Evidently that satisfied him. But Joan had an intuitive feeling that Pearce lied.

"You want to be careful how you talk about me," said Cleve.

Kells puffed out a suspended breath and he flung the

sweat from his brow. There was about him, perhaps more than the others, a dark realization of how close the call had been for Pearce.

"Jim, you're not drunk?"

"No."

"But you're sore?"

"Sure I'm sore. Pearce put me in bad with you, didn't he?"

"No. You misunderstood me. Red hasn't a thing against you. And neither he nor anybody else could put you in bad with me."

"All right. Maybe I was hasty. But I'm not wasting time these days," replied Cleve. "I've no hard feelings. . . . Pearce, do you want to shake hands—or hold that against me?"

"He'll shake, of course," said Kells.

Pearce extended his hand, but with a bad grace. He was dominated. This affront of Cleve's would rankle in him.

"Kells, what do you want with me?" demanded Cleve.

A change passed over Kells, and Joan could not tell just what it was, but somehow it seemed to suggest a weaker man.

"Jim, you've been a great card for me," began Kells, impressively. "You've helped my game—and twice you saved my life. I think a lot of you. . . . If you stand by me now I swear I'll return the trick some day. . . . Will you stand by me?"

"Yes," replied Cleve, steadily, but he grew pale. "What's the trouble?"

"By——, it's bad enough!" exclaimed Kells, and as he spoke the shade deepened in his haggard face. "Gulden has split my Legion. He has drawn away more than half my men. They have been drunk and crazy ever since. They've taken things into their own hands. You see the result as well as I. That camp down there is fire and brimstone. Some one of that drunken gang has talked. We're none of us safe any more. I see suspicion everywhere. I've urged getting a big stake and then hitting the trail for the border. But not a man sticks to me in that. They all want the free, easy, wild life of this gold-camp. So we're anchored till—till . . . But maybe it's not too late. Pearce, Oliver, Smith—all the best of my Legion—profess loyalty to me. If we all pull together maybe we can win yet. But they've threatened to split, too. And it's all on your account!"

"Mine?" ejaculated Cleve.

"Yes. Now it's nothing to make you flash your gun. Remember you said you'd stand by me. . . . Jim, the fact is—all the gang to a man believe you're double-crossing me!"

"In what way?" queried Cleve, blanching.

"They think you're the one who has talked. They blame you for the suspicion that's growing."

"Well, they're absolutely wrong," declared Cleve, in a ringing voice.

"I know they are. Mind you I'm not hinting I distrust you. I don't. I swear by you. But Pearce—"

"So it's Pearce," interrupted Cleve, darkly. "I thought you said he hadn't tried to put me in bad with you."

"He hasn't. He simply spoke his convictions. He has a right to them. So have all the men. And, to come to the point, they all think you're crooked because you're honest!"

"I don't understand," replied Cleve, slowly.

"Jim, you rode into Cabin Gulch, and you raised some trouble. But you were no bandit. You joined my Legion, but you've never become a bandit. Here you've been an honest miner. That suited my plan and it helped. But it's got so it doesn't suit my men. You work every day hard. You've struck it rich. You're well thought of in Alder Creek. You've never done a dishonest thing. Why, you wouldn't turn a crooked trick in a card game for a sack full of gold. This has hurt you with my men. They can't see as I see, that you're as square as you are game. They see you're an honest miner. They believe you've got into a clique—that you've given us away. I don't blame Pearce or any of my men. This is a time when men's intelligence, if they have any, doesn't operate. Their brains are on fire. They see gold and whisky and blood, and they feel gold and whisky and blood. That's all. I'm glad that the gang gives you the benefit of a doubt and a chance to stand by me."

"A chance!"

"Yes. They've worked out a job for you alone. Will you undertake it?"

"I'll have to," replied Cleve.

"You certainly will if you want the gang to justify my faith in you. Once you pull off a crooked deal, they'll switch and swear by you. Then we'll get together, all of us, and plan what to do about Gulden and his outfit. They'll run our heads, along with their own, right into the noose."

"What is this—this job?" labored Cleve. He was sweating now and his hair hung damp over his brow. He lost that look which had made him a bold man and seemed a boy again, weak, driven, bewildered.

Kells averted his gaze before speaking again. He hated to force this task upon Cleve. Joan felt, in the throbbing pain of the moment, that if she never had another reason to like this bandit, she would like him for the pity he showed.

"Do you know a miner named Creede?" asked Kells, rapidly.

"A husky chap, short, broad, something like Gulden for shape, only not so big—fellow with a fierce red beard?" asked Cleve.

"I never saw him," replied Kells. "But Pearce has. How does Cleve's description fit Creede?"

"He's got his man spotted," answered Pearce.

"All right, that's settled," went on Kells, warming to his subject. "This fellow Creede wears a heavy belt of gold. Blicky never makes a mistake. Creede's partner left on yesterday's stage for Bannack. He'll be gone a few days. Creede is a hard worker—one of the hardest. Sometimes he goes to sleep at his supper. He's not the drinking kind. He's slow, thick-headed. The best time for this job will be early in the evening—just as soon as his lights are out. Locate the tent. It stands at the head of a little wash and there's a bleached pine-tree right by the tent. To-morrow night as soon as it gets dark crawl up this wash—be careful—wait till the right time—then finish the job quick!"

"How—finish—it?" asked Cleve, hoarsely.

Kells was scintillating now, steely, cold, radiant. He had forgotten the man before him in the prospect of the gold.

"Creede's cot is on the side of the tent opposite the tree.

You won't have to go inside. Slit the canvas. It's a rotten old tent. Kill Creede with your knife. . . . Get his belt. . . . Be bold, cautious, swift! That's your job. Now what do you say?"

"All right," responded Cleve, somberly, and with a heavy tread he left the room.

After Jim had gone Joan still watched and listened. She was in distress over his unfortunate situation, but she had no fear that he meant to carry out Kells's plan. This was a critical time for Jim, and therefore for her. She had no idea what Jim could do; all she thought was what he would not do.

Kells gazed triumphantly at Pearce. "I told you the youngster would stand by me. I never put him on a job before."

"Reckon I figgered wrong, boss," replied Pearce.

"He looked sick to me, but game," said Handy Oliver. "Kells is right, Red, an' you've been sore-headed over nothin'!"

"Mebbe. But ain't it good figgerin' to make Cleve do some kind of a job, even if he is on the square?"

They all acquiesced to this, even Kells slowly nodding his head.

"Jack, I've thought of another an' better job for young Cleve," spoke up Jesse Smith, with his characteristic grin.

"You'll all be setting him jobs now," replied Kells. "What's yours?"

"You spoke of plannin' to get together once more—what's left of us. An' there's thet bull-head Gulden."

"You're sure right," returned the leader, grimly, and he looked at Smith as if he would welcome any suggestion.

"I never was afraid to speak my mind," went on Smith. Here he lost his grin and his coarse mouth grew hard. "Gulden will have to be killed if we're goin' to last!"

"Wood, what do you say?" queried Kells, with narrowing eyes.

Bate Wood nodded as approvingly as if he had been asked about his bread.

"Oliver, what do you say?"

"Wal, I'd love to wait an' see Gul hang, but if you press me, I'll agree to stand pat with the cards Jesse's dealt," replied Handy Oliver.

Then Kells turned with a bright gleam upon his face. "And you—Pearce?"

"I'd say yes in a minute if I'd not have to take a hand in thet job," replied Pearce, with a hard laugh. "Gulden won't be so easy to kill. He'll pack a gunful of lead. I'll gamble if the gang of us cornered him in this cabin he'd do for most of us before we killed him."

"Gul sleep alone, no one knows where," said Handy Oliver. "An' he can't be surprised. Red's correct. How're we goin' to kill him?"

"If you gents will listen you'll find out," rejoined Jesse Smith. "Thet's the job for young Cleve. He can do it. Sure Gulden never was afraid of any man. But somethin' about Cleve bluffed him. I don't know what. Send Cleve out after Gulden. He'll call him face to face, anywhere, an' beat him to a gun! . . . Take my word for it."

"Jesse, that's the grandest idea you ever had," said Kells, softly. His eyes shone. The old power came back to his face. "I split on Gulden. With him once out of the way—!"

"Boss, are you goin' to make thet Jim Cleve's second job?" inquired Pearce, curiously.

"I am," replied Kells, with his jaw corded and stiff.

"If he pulls thet off you'll never hear a yap from me so long as I live. An' I'll eat out of Cleve's hand."

Joan could bear to hear no more. She staggered to her bed and fell there, all cramped as if in a cold vise. However Jim might meet the situation planned for murdering Creede, she knew he would not shirk facing Gulden with deadly intent. He hated Gulden because she had a horror of him. Would these hours of suspense never end? Must she pass from one torture to another until—?

Sleep did not come for a long time. And when it did she suffered with nightmares from which it seemed she could never awaken.

The day, when at last it arrived, was no better than the night. It wore on endlessly, and she who listened so intently found it one of the silent days. Only Bate Wood remained at the cabin. He appeared kinder than usual, but Joan did not want to talk. She ate her meals, and passed the hours watching from the window and lying on the bed. Dusk brought Kells and Pearce and Smith, but not Jim Cleve. Handy Oliver and Blicky arrived at supper-time.

"Reckon Jim's appetite is pore," remarked Bate Wood, reflectively. "He ain't been in to-day."

Some of the bandits laughed, but Kells had a twinge, if Joan ever saw a man have one. The dark, formidable, stern look was on his face. He alone of the men ate sparingly, and after the meal he took to his bent posture and thoughtful pacing. Joan saw the added burden of another crime upon his shoulders. Conversation, which had been desultory, and such as any miners or campers might have indulged in, gradually diminished to a word here and there, and finally ceased. Kells always at this hour had a dampening effect upon his followers. More and more he drew aloof from them, yet he never realized that. He might have been alone. But often he glanced out of the door, and appeared to listen. Of course he expected Jim Cleve to return, but what did he expect of him? Joan had a blind faith that Jim would be cunning enough to fool Kells and Pearce. So much depended upon it!

Some of the bandits uttered an exclamation. Then silently, like a shadow, Jim Cleve entered.

Joan's heart leaped and seemed to stand still. Jim could not have looked more terrible if he were really a murderer. He opened his coat. Then he flung a black object upon the table and it fell with a soft, heavy, sodden thud. It was a leather belt packed with gold.

When Kells saw that he looked no more at the pale Cleve. His clawlike hand swept out for the belt, lifted and weighed it. Likewise the other bandits, with gold in sight, surged round Kells, forgetting Cleve.

"Twenty pounds!" exclaimed Kells, with a strange rapture in his voice.

"Let me heft it?" asked Pearce, thrillingly.

Joan saw and heard so much, then through a kind of dimness, that she could not wipe away, her eyes beheld Jim.

What was the awful thing that she interpreted from his face, his mien? Was this a part he was playing to deceive Kells? The slow-gathering might of her horror came with the meaning of that gold-belt. Jim had brought back the gold-belt of the miner Creede. He had, in his passion to remain near her, to save her in the end, kept his word to Kells and done the ghastly deed.

Joan reeled and sank back upon the bed, blindly, with darkening sight and mind.

16

◇

JOAN returned to consciousness with a sense of vague and
unlocalized pain which she thought was that old, familiar
pang of grief. But once fully awakened, as if by a sharp
twinge, she became aware that the pain was some kind of
muscular throb in her shoulder. The instant she was fully
sure of this the strange feeling ceased. Then she lay wide-
eyed in the darkness, waiting and wondering.

Suddenly the slight sharp twing was repeated. It seemed

to come from outside her flesh. She shivered a little, thinking it might be a centipede. When she reached for her shoulder her hand came in contact with a slender stick that had been thrust through a crack between the boards. Jim was trying to rouse her. This had been his method on several occasions when she had fallen asleep after waiting long for him.

Joan got up to the window, dizzy and sick with the resurging memory of Jim's return to Kells with that gold-belt.

Jim rose out of the shadow and felt for her, clasped her close. Joan had none of the old thrill; her hands slid loosely round his; and every second the weight inwardly grew heavier.

"Joan! I had a time waking you," whispered Jim, and then he kissed her. "Why, you're as cold as ice."

"Jim—I—I must have fainted," she replied.

"What for?"

"I was peeping into Kells's cabin, when you—you—"

"Poor kid!" he interrupted, tenderly. "You've had so much to bear! . . . Joan, I fooled Kells. Oh, I was slick! . . . He ordered me out on a job—to kill a miner! Fancy that! And what do you think? I know Creede well. He's a good fellow. I traded my big nugget for his gold-belt!"

"You *traded*—you—didn't—kill him!" faltered Joan.

"Hear the child talk!" exclaimed Cleve, with a low laugh.

Joan suddenly clung to him with all her might, quivering in a silent joy. It had not occurred to Jim what she might have thought.

"Listen," he went on. "I traded my nugget. It was worth a great deal more than Creede's gold-belt. He knew this. He didn't want to trade. But I coaxed him. I persuaded him to leave camp—to walk out on the road to Bannack. To meet the stage somewhere and go on to Bannack, and stay a few days. He sure was curious. But I kept my secret. . . . Then I came back here, gave the belt to Kells, told him I had followed Creede in the dark, had killed him and slid him into a deep hole in the creek. . . . Kells and Pearce—none of them paid any attention to my story. I had the gold-belt. That was enough. Gold talks—fills the ears of these bandits. . . . I have my share of Creede's gold-dust in my pocket. Isn't that funny? Alas for my—*your* big nugget! But we've got to play the game. Besides, I've sacks and cans of gold hidden away. Joan, what'll we do with it all? You're my wife now. And, oh! If we can only get away with it you'll be rich!"

Joan could not share his happiness any more than she could understand his spirit. She remembered.

"Jim—dear—did Kells tell you what your—next job was to be?" she whispered, haltingly.

Cleve swore under his breath, but loud enough to make Joan swiftly put her hand over his lips and caution him.

"Joan, did you hear that about Gulden?" he asked.

"Oh yes."

"I'm sorry. I didn't mean to tell you. Yes, I've got my second job. And this one I can't shirk or twist around."

Joan held to him convulsively. She could scarcely speak.

"Girl, don't lose your nerve!" he said, sternly. "When you married me you made me a man. I'll play my end of the game. Don't fear for me. You plan when we can risk escape. I'll obey you to the word."

"But Jim—oh, Jim!" she moaned. "You're as wild as these bandits. You can't see your danger. . . . That terrible Gulden! . . . You don't mean to meet him—fight him? . . . *Say* you won't!"

"Joan, I'll meet him—and I'll *kill* him," whispered Jim, with a piercing intensity. "You never knew I was swift with a gun. Well, I didn't, either, till I struck the border. I know now. Kells is the only man I've seen who can throw a gun quicker than I. Gulden is a big bull. He's slow. I'll get into a card-game with him—I'll quarrel over gold—I'll smash him as I did once before—and this time I won't shoot off his ear. I've my nerve now. Kells swore he'd do anything for me if I stand by him now. I will. You never can tell. Kells is losing his grip. And my standing by him may save you."

Joan drew a deep breath. Jim Cleve had indeed come into manhood. She crushed down her womanish fears and rose dauntless to the occasion. She would never weaken him by a lack of confidence.

"Jim, Kells's plot draws on to a fatal close," she said, earnestly. "I feel it. He's doomed. He doesn't realize that yet. He hopes and plots on. When he falls, then he'll be

213

great—terrible. We must get away before that comes. What you said about Creede has given me an idea. Suppose we plan to slip out some night soon, and stop the stage next day on its way to Bannack?"

"I've thought of that. But we must have horses."

"Let's go afoot. We'd be safer. There'd not be so much to plan."

"But if we go on foot we must pack guns and grub—and there's my gold-dust. Fifty pounds or more! It's yours, Joan. . . . .You'll need it all. You love pretty clothes and things. And now I'll get them for you or—or die."

"Hush! That's foolish talk, with our very lives at stake. Let me plan some more. Oh, I think so hard! . . . And, Jim, there's another thing. Red Pearce was more than suspicious about your absence from the cabin at certain hours. What he hinted to Kells about a woman in the case! I'm afraid he suspects or knows."

"He had me cold, too," replied Cleve, thoughtfully. "But he swore he *knew* nothing."

"Jim, trust a woman's instinct. Pearce lied. That gun at his side made him a liar. He knew you'd kill him if he betrayed himself by a word. Oh, look out for him!"

Cleve did not reply. It struck Joan that he was not listening, at least to her. His head was turned, rigid and alert. He had his ear to the soft wind. Suddenly Joan heard a faint rustle—then another. They appeared to come from the corner of the cabin. Silently Cleve sank down into the shadow and vanished. Low, stealthy footsteps followed, but Joan was not sure whether or not Cleve made them. They did not seem to come from the direction he usually took. Besides, when he was careful he never made the slightest noise. Joan strained her ears, only to catch the faint sounds of the night. She lay back upon her bed, worried and anxious again, and soon the dread returned. There were to be no waking or sleeping hours free from this portent of calamity.

Next morning Joan awaited Kells, as was her custom, but he did not appear. This was the third time in a week that he had forgotten or avoided her or had been prevented from

214

seeing her. Joan was glad, yet the fact was not reassuring. The issue for Kells was growing from trouble to disaster.

Early in the afternoon she heard Kells returning from camp. He had men with him. They conversed in low, earnest tones. Joan was about to spy up on them when Kells's step approached her door. He rapped and spoke:

"Put on Dandy Dale's suit and mask, and come out here," he said.

The tone of his voice as much as the content of his words startled Joan so that she did not at once reply.

"Do you hear?" he called, sharply.

"Yes," replied Joan.

Then he went back to his men, and the low, earnest conversation was renewed.

Reluctantly Joan took down Dandy Dale's things from the pegs, and with a recurring shame she divested herself of part of her clothes and donned the suit and boots and mask and gun. Her spirit rose, however, at the thought that this would be a disguise calculated to aid her in the escape with Cleve. But why had Kells ordered the change? Was he in danger and did he mean to flee from Alder Creek? Joan found the speculation a relief from that haunting, persistent thought of Jim Cleve and Gulden. She was eager to learn, still she hesitated at the door. It was just as hard as ever to face those men.

But it must be, so with a wrench she stepped out boldly.

Kells looked worn and gray. He had not slept. But his face did not wear the shade she had come to associate with his gambling and drinking. Six other men were present, and Joan noted coats and gloves and weapons and spurs. Kells turned to address her. His face lighted fleetingly.

"I want you to be ready to ride any minute," he said.

"Why?" asked Joan.

"We may *have* to, that's all," he replied.

His men, usually so keen when they had a chance to ogle Joan, now scarcely gave her a glance. They were a dark, grim group, with hard eyes and tight lips. Handy Oliver was speaking.

"I tell you, Gulden swore he seen Creede—on the road—in the lamplight—last night *after* Jim Cleve got here."

"Gulden must have been mistaken," declared Kells, impatiently.

"He ain't the kind to make mistakes," replied Oliver.

"Gul's seen Creede's ghost, thet's what," suggested Blicky, uneasily. "I've seen a few in my time."

Some of the bandits nodded gloomily.

"Aw!" burst out Red Pearce. "Gulden never seen a ghost in his life. If he seen Creede he's seen him *alive!*"

"Shore you're right, Red," agreed Jesse Smith.

"But, men—Cleve brought in Creede's belt—and we've divided the gold," said Kells. "You all know Creede would have to be dead before that belt could be unbuckled from him. There's a mistake."

"Boss, it's my idee thet Gul is only makin' more trouble," put in Bate Wood. "I seen him less than an hour ago. I was the first one Gul talked to. An' he knew Jim Cleve did for Creede. How'd he know? Thet was supposed to be a secret. What's more, Gul told me Cleve was on the job to kill him. How'd he ever find thet out? . . . Sure as God made little apples Cleve never told him!"

Kells's face grew livid and his whole body vibrated. "Maybe one of Gulden's gang was outside, listening when we planned Cleve's job," he suggested. But his look belied his hope.

"Naw! There's a nigger in the wood-pile, you can gamble on thet," blurted out the sixth bandit, a lean faced, bold-eye, blond-mustached fellow whose name Joan had never heard.

"I won't believe it," replied Kells, doggedly. "And you, Budd, you're accusing somebody present of treachery—or else Cleve. He's the only one not here who knew."

"Wal, I always said thet youngster was slick," replied Budd.

"Will you accuse him to his face?"

"I shore will. Glad of the chance."

"Then you're drunk or just a fool."

"Thet so?"

"Yes, that's so," flashed Kells. "You don't know Cleve. He'll kill you. He's lightning with a gun. Do you suppose I'd set him on Gulden's trail if I wasn't sure? Why I wouldn't care to—"

"Here comes Cleve," interrupted Pearce, sharply.

Rapid footsteps sounded without. Then Joan saw Jim Cleve darken the doorway. He looked keen and bold. Upon sight of Joan in her changed attire he gave a slight start.

"Budd, here's Cleve," called out Red Pearce, mockingly. "Now, say it to his face!"

In the silence that ensued Pearce's spirit dominated the moment with its cunning, hate, and violence. But Kells savagely leaped in front of the men, still master of the situation.

"Red, what's got into you?" he hissed. "You're cross-grained lately. You're sore. Any more of this and I'll swear you're a disorganizer. . . . Now, Budd, you keep your mouth shut. And you, Cleve, you pay no heed to Budd if he does gab. . . . We're in bad and all the men have chips on their shoulders. We've got to stop fighting among ourselves."

"Wal, boss, there's a power of sense in a good example," dryly remarked Bate Wood. His remark calmed Kells and eased the situation.

"Jim, did you meet Gulden?" queried Kells, eagerly.

"Can't find him anywhere," replied Cleve. "I've loafed in the saloons and gambling-hells where he hangs out. But he didn't show up. He's in camp. I know that for a fact. He's laying low for some reason."

"Gulden's been tipped off, Jim," said Kells, earnestly. "He told Bate Wood you were out to kill him."

"I'm glad. It wasn't a fair hand you were going to deal him," responded Cleve. "But who gave my job away? Someone in this gang wants me done for—more than Gulden."

Cleve's flashing gaze swept over the motionless men and fixed hardest upon Red Pearce. Pearce gave back hard look for hard look.

"Gulden told Oliver more," continued Kells, and he pulled Cleve around to face him. "Gulden swore he saw Creede alive last night. . . . *Late last night!*"

"That's funny," replied Cleve, without the flicker of an eyelash.

"It's not funny. But it's queer. Gulden hasn't the moral sense to lie. Bate says he wants to make trouble between

217

you and me. I doubt that. I don't believe Gulden could see a ghost, either. He's simply mistaken some miner for Creede."

"He sure has, unless Creede came back to life. I'm not sitting on his chest now, holding him down."

Kells drew back, manifestly convinced and relieved. This action seemed to be a magnet for Pearce. He detached himself from the group, and, approaching Kells, tapped him significantly on the shoulder; and whether by design or accident the fact was that he took a position where Kells was between him and Cleve.

"Jack, you're being double-crossed here—an' by more 'n one," he said, deliberately. "But if you want me to talk you've got to guarantee no gun-play."

"Speak up, Red," replied Kells, with a glinting eye. "I swear there won't be a gun pulled."

The other men shifted from one foot to another and there were deep-drawn breaths. Jim Cleve alone seemed quiet and cool. But his eyes were ablaze.

"Fust off an' for instance here's one who's double-crossin' you," said Pearce, in slow, tantalizing speech, as if he wore out this suspense to torture Kells. And without ever glancing at Joan he jerked a thumb, in significant gesture, at her.

Joan leaned back against the wall, trembling and cold all over. She read Pearce's mind. He knew her secret and meant to betray her and Jim. He hated Kells and wanted to torture him. If only she could think quickly and speak! But she seemed dumb and powerless.

"Pearce, what do you mean?" demanded Kells.

"The girl's double-crossin' you," replied Pearce. With the uttered words he grew pale and agitated.

Suddenly Kells appeared to become aware of Joan's presence and that the implication was directed toward her. Then, many and remarkable as had been the changes Joan had seen come over him, now occurred one wholly greater. It had all his old amiability, his cool, easy manner, veiling a deep and hidden ruthlessness, terrible in contrast.

"Red, I thought our talk concerned men and gold and—things," he said, with a cool, slow softness that had a sting, "but since you've nerve enough or are crazy enough to speak of—her—why, explain your meaning."

Pearce's jaw worked so that he could scarcely talk. He had gone too far—realized it too late.

"She meets a man—back there—at her window," he panted. "They whisper in the dark for hours. I've watched an' heard them. An' I'd told you before, but I wanted to make sure who he was. . . . I know him now! . . . An' remember I seen him climb in an' out—"

Kells's whole frame leaped. His gun was a flash of blue and red and white all together. Pearce swayed upright, like a tree chopped at the roots, and then fell, face up, eyes set—dead. The bandit leader stood over him with the smoking gun.

"My Gawd, Jack!" gasped Handy Oliver. "You swore no one would pull a gun—an' here you've killed him yourself! . . . *You've double-crossed yourself!* An' if I die for it I've got to tell you Red wasn't lyin' then!"

Kells's radiance fled, leaving him ghastly. He stared at Oliver.

"You've double-crossed yourself an' your pards," went on Oliver, pathetically. "What's your word amount to? Do you expect the gang to stand for this? . . . There lays Red Pearce dead. An' for what? Jest once—relyin' on your oath—he speaks out what might have showed you. An' you kill him! . . . If I knowed what he knowed I'd tell you now with thet gun in your hand! But I don't know. Only I know he wasn't lyin' . . . . Ask the girl! . . . An' as for me, I reckon I'm through with you an' your Legion. You're done, Kells—your head's gone—you've broke over thet slip of a woman!"

Oliver spoke with a rude and impressive dignity. When he ended he strode out into the sunlight.

Kells was shaken by this forceful speech, yet he was not in any sense a broken man. "Joan—you heard Pearce," said he, passionately. "He lied about you. I had to kill him. He hinted— Oh, the low-lived dog! He could not know a good woman. He lied—and there he is—dead! I wouldn't fetch him back for a hundred Legions!"

"But it—it wasn't—all—a lie," said Joan, and her words

219

came haltingly because a force stronger than her cunning made her speak. She had reached a point where she could not deceive Kells to save her life.

"WHAT!" he thundered.

"Pearce told the truth—except that no one ever climbed in my window. That's false. No one could climb in. It's too small. . . . But I did whisper—to someone."

Kells had to moisten his lips to speak. "Who?"

"I'll never tell you."

"*Who?*" . . . I'll kill him!"

"No—no. I won't tell. I won't let you kill another man on my account."

"I'll choke it out of you."

"You can't. There's no use to threaten me, or hurt me, either."

Kells seemed dazed. "Whisper! For hours! In the dark! . . . But, Joan, what for? Why such a risk?"

Joan shook her head.

"Were you just unhappy—lonesome? Did some young miner happen to see you there in daylight—then come at night? Wasn't it only accident? Tell me."

"I won't—and I won't because I don't want you to spill more blood."

"For my sake," he queried, with the old, mocking tone. Then he grew dark with blood in his face, fierce with action of hands and body as he bent nearer her. "Maybe you like him too well to see him shot? . . . Did you—whisper often to this stranger?"

Joan felt herself weakening. Kells was so powerful in spirit and passion that she seemed unable to fight him. She strove to withhold her reply, but it burst forth, involuntarily.

"Yes—often."

That roused more than anger and passion. Jealousy flamed from him and it transformed him into a devil.

"You held hands out of that window—and kissed—in the dark?" he cried, with working lips.

Joan had thought of this so fearfully and intensely—she had battled so to fortify herself to keep it secret—that he had divined it, had read her mind. She could not control herself. The murder of Pearce had almost overwhelmed her.

She had not the strength to bite her tongue. Suggestion alone would have drawn her then—and Kells's passionate force was hypnotic.

"Yes," she whispered.

He appeared to control a developing paroxysm of rage.

"That settles you," he declared darkly. "But I'll do one more decent thing by you. I'll marry you." Then he wheeled to his men. "Blicky, there's a parson down in camp. Go on the run. Fetch him back if you have to push him with a gun."

Blicky darted through the door and his footsteps thudded out of hearing.

"You can't force me to marry you," said Joan. "I—I won't open my lips."

"That's your affair. I've no mind to coax you," he replied, bitterly. "But if you don't I'll try Gulden's way with a woman. . . . You remember. Gulden's way! A cave and a rope!"

Joan's legs gave out under her and she sank upon a pile of blankets. Then beyond Kells she saw Jim Cleve. With all that was left of her spirit she flashed him a warning—a meaning—a prayer not to do the deed she divined was his deadly intent. He caught it and obeyed. And he flashed back a glance which meant that, desperate as her case was, it could never be what Kells threatened.

"Men, see me through this," said Kells to the silent group. "Then any deal you want—I'm on. Stay here or—sack the camp! Hold up the stage express with gold for Bannack! Anything for a big stake! Then the trail and the border."

He began pacing the floor. Budd and Smith strolled outside. Bate Wood fumbled in his pockets for pipe and tobacco. Cleve sat down at the table and leaned on his hands. No one took notice of the dead Pearce. Here was somber and terrible sign of the wildness of the border clan—that Kells could send out for a parson to marry him to a woman he hopelessly loved, there in the presence of murder and death, with Pearce's distorted face upturned in stark and ghastly significance.

It might have been a quarter of an hour, though to Joan it seemed an endless time, until footsteps and voices outside announced the return of Blicky.

He held by the arm a slight man whom he was urging along with no gentle force. This stranger's face presented as great a contrast to Blicky's as could have been imagined. His apparel proclaimed his calling. There were consternation and bewilderment in his expression, but very little fear.

"He was preachin' down there in a tent," said Blicky, "an I jest waltzed him up without explainin'."

"Sir, I want to be married at once," declared Kells, peremptorily.

"Certainly. I'm at your service," replied the preacher. "But I deplore the—the manner in which I've been approached."

"You'll excuse haste," rejoined the bandit. "I'll pay you well." Kells threw a small buckskin sack of gold-dust upon the table, and then he turned to Joan. "Come, Joan," he said, in the tone that brooked neither resistance nor delay.

It was at that moment that the preacher first noticed Joan. Was her costume accountable for his start? Joan had remembered his voice and she wondered if he would remember hers. Certainly Jim had called her Joan more than once on the night of the marriage. The preacher's eyes grew keener. He glanced from Joan to Kells, and then at the other men, who had come in. Jim Cleve stood behind Jesse Smith's broad person, and evidently the preacher did not see him. That curious gaze, however, next discovered the dead man on the floor. Then to the curiosity and anxiety upon the preacher's face was added horror.

"A minister of God is needed here, but not in the capacity you name," he said. "I'll perform no marriage ceremony in the presence of—murder."

"Mr. Preacher, you'll marry me quick or you'll go along with him," replied Kells, deliberately.

"I cannot be forced." The preacher still maintained some dignity, but he had grown pale.

"*I* can force you. Get ready now! . . . Joan, come here!" Kells spoke sternly, yet something of the old, self-

222

mocking spirit was in his tone. His intelligence was deriding the flesh and blood of him, the beast, the fool. It spoke that he would have his way and that the choice was fatal for him.

Joan shook her head. In one stride Kells reached her and swung her spinning before him. The physical violence acted strangely upon Joan—roused her rage.

"I wouldn't marry you to save my life—even if I *could!*" she burst out.

At her declaration the preacher gave a start that must have been suspicion or confirmation, or both. He bent low to peer into the face of the dead Pearce. When he arose he was shaking his head. Evidently he had decided that Pearce was not the man to whom he had married Joan.

"Please remove your mask," he said to Joan.

She did so, swiftly, without a tremor. The preacher peered into her face again, as he had upon the night he had married her to Jim. He faced Kells again.

"I am beyond your threats," he said, now with calmness. "I can't marry you to a woman who already has a husband. . . . But I don't see that husband here."

"You don't see that husband here!" echoed the bewildered Kells. He stared with open mouth. "Say, have you got a screw loose?"

The preacher, in his swift glance, had apparently not observed the half-hidden Cleve. Certainly it appeared now that he would have no attention for any other than Kells. The bandit was a study. His astonishment was terrific and held him like a chain. Suddenly he lurched.

"What did you say?" he roared, his face flaming.

"I can't marry you to a woman who already has a husband."

Swift as light the red flashed out of Kells's face. "Did you ever see her before?" he asked.

"Yes," replied the preacher.

"Where and when?"

"Here—at the back of this cabin—a few nights ago."

It hurt Joan to look at Kells now, yet he seemed wonderful to behold. She felt as guilty as if she had really been false to him. Her heart labored high in her breast. This was the climax—the moment of catastrophe. Another word and

223

Jim Cleve would be facing Kells. The blood pressure in Joan's throat almost strangled her.

"At the back of this cabin! . . . At her window?"

"Yes."

"What were you there for?"

"In my capacity as minister. I was summoned to marry her."

"To marry her?" gasped Kells.

"Yes. She is Joan Randle, from Hoadley, Idaho. She is over eighteen. I understood she was detained here against her will. She loved an honest young miner of the camp. He brought me up here one night. And I married them."

"You—married—them!"

"Yes."

Kells was slow in assimilating the truth and his action corresponded with his mind. Slowly his hand moved toward his gun. He drew it, threw it aloft. And then all the terrible evil in the man flamed forth. But as he deliberately drew down on the preacher Blicky leaped forward and knocked up the gun. Flash and report followed; the discharge went into the roof. Blicky grasped Kells's arm and threw his weight upon it to keep it down.

"I fetched thet parson here," he yelled, "an you ain't a-goin' to kill him! . . . Help, Jesse! . . . He's crazy! He'll do it!"

Jesse Smith ran to Blicky's aid and tore the gun out of Kells's hand. Jim Cleve grasped the preacher by the shoulders and, whirling him around, sent him flying out of the door.

"Run for your life!" he shouted.

Blicky and Jesse Smith were trying to hold the lunging Kells.

"Jim, you block the door," called Jesse. "Bate, you grab any loose guns an' knives. . . . Now, boss, rant an' be damned!"

They released Kells and backed away, leaving him the room. Joan's limbs seemed unable to execute her will.

"Joan! It's true," he exclaimed, with whistling breath.

"Yes."

"Who?" he bellowed.

"I'll never tell."

He reached for her with hands like claws, as if he meant to tear her, rend her. Joan was helpless, weak, terrified. Those shaking, clutching hands reached for her throat and yet never closed round it. Kells wanted to kill her, but he could not. He loomed over her, dark, speechless, locked in his paroxysm of rage. Perhaps then came a realization of ruin through her. He hated her because he loved her. He wanted to kill her because of that hate, yet he could not harm her, even hurt her. And his soul seemed in conflict with two giants—the evil in him that was hate, and the love that was good. Suddenly he flung her aside. She stumbled over Pearce's body, almost falling, and staggered back to the wall. Kells had the center of the room to himself. Like a mad steer in a corral he gazed about, stupidly seeking some way to escape. But the escape Kells longed for was from himself. Then either he let himself go or was unable longer to control his rage. He began to plunge around. His actions were violent, random, half insane. He seemed to want to destroy himself and everything. But the weapons were guarded by his men and the room contained little he could smash. There was something magnificent in his fury, yet childish and absurd. Even under its influence and his abandonment he showed a consciousness of its futility. In a few moments the inside of the cabin was in disorder and Kells seemed a disheveled, sweating, panting wretch. The rapidity and violence of his action, coupled with his fury, soon exhausted him. He fell from plunging here and there to pacing the floor. And even the dignity of passion passed from him. He looked a hopeless, beaten, stricken man, conscious of defeat.

Jesse Smith approached the bandit leader. "Jack, here's your gun," he said. "I only took it because you was out of your head. . . . An' listen, boss. There's a few of us left."

That was Smith's expression of fidelity, and Kells received it with a pallid, grateful smile.

"Bate, you an' Jim clean up this mess," went on Smith. "An', Blicky, come here an' help me with Pearce. We'll have to plant him."

The stir begun by the men was broken by a sharp exclamation from Cleve.

"Kells, here comes Gulden—Beady Jones, Williams, Beard!"

The bandit raised his head and paced back to where he could look out.

Bate Wood made a violent and significant gesture. "Somethin' wrong," he said, hurriedly. "An' it's more'n to do with Gul! . . . Look down the road. See thet gang. All excited an' wavin' hands an' runnin'. But they're goin' down into camp.'

Jesse Smith turned a gray face toward Kells. "Boss, there's hell to pay! I've seen *thet* kind of excitement before."

Kells thrust the men aside and looked out. He seemed to draw upon a reserve strength, for he grew composed even while he gazed. "Jim, get in the other room," he ordered, sharply. "Joan—you go, too. Keep still."

Joan hurried to comply. Jim entered after her and closed the door. Instinctively they clasped hands, drew close together.

"Jim, what does it mean?" she whispered, fearfully. "Gulden!"

"He must be looking for me," replied Jim. But there's more doing. Did you see that crowd down the road?"

"No. I couldn't see out."

"Listen."

Heavy tramp boots sounded without. Silently Joan led Jim to the crack between the boards through which she had spied upon the bandits. Jim peeped through, and Joan saw his hand go to his gun. Then she looked.

Gulden was being crowded into the cabin by fierce, bulging-jawed men who meant some kind of dark business. The strangest thing about that entrance was its silence. In a moment they were inside, confronting Kells with his little group. Beard, Jones, Williams, former faithful allies of Kells, showed a malignant opposition. And the huge Gulden resembled an enraged gorilla. For an instant his great, pale, cavernous eyes glared. He had one hand under his coat and his position had a sinister suggestion. But Kells stood cool and sure. When Gulden moved Kells's gun was leaping forth. But he withheld his fire, for Gulden had only a heavy round object wrapped in a handkerchief.

226

"Look there!" he boomed, and he threw the object on the table.

The dull, heavy, sodden thump had a familiar ring. Joan heard Jim gasp and his hand tightened spasmodically upon hers.

Slowly the ends of the red scarf slid down to reveal an irregularly round, glinting lump. When Joan recognized it her heart seemed to burst.

"Jim Cleve's nugget!" ejaculated Kells. "Where'd you get that?"

Gulden leaned across the table, his massive jaw working. "I found it on the miner Creede," replied the giant, stridently.

Then came a nervous shuffling of boots on the creaky boards. In the silence a low, dull murmur of distant voices could be heard, strangely menacing. Kells stood transfixed, white as a sheet.

"On Creede!"

"Yes."

"Where was his—his body?"

"I left it out on the Bannack trail."

The bandit leader appeared mute.

"Kells, I followed Creede out of camp last night," fiercely declared Gulden. . . . "I killed him! . . . I found this nugget on him!"

17

❖

APPARENTLY to Kells that nugget did not accuse Jim Cleve of treachery. Not only did this possibility seem lost upon the bandit leader, but also the sinister intent of Gulden and his associates.

"Then Jim didn't kill Creede!" cried Kells.

A strange light flashed across his face. It fitted the note of gladness in his exclamation. How strange that in his amaze there should be relief instead of suspicion! Joan thought she understood Kells. He was glad that he had not yet made a murderer out of Cleve.

Gulden appeared slow in rejoining. "I told you I got Creede," he said. "And we want to know if this says to you what it says to us."

His huge, hairy hand tapped the nugget. Then Kells caught the implication.

"What does it say to you?" he queried, coolly, and he eyed Gulden and then the grim men behind him.

"Somebody in the gang is crooked. Somebody's giving you the double-cross. We've known that for long. Jim Cleve goes out to kill Creede. He comes in with Creede's gold-belt—and a lie! . . . We think Cleve is the crooked one."

"No! You're way off, Gulden," replied Kells, earnestly. "That boy is absolutely square. He's lied to me about Creede. But I can excuse that. He lost his nerve. He's only a youngster. To knife a man in his sleep—that was too much for Jim! . . . And I'm glad! I see it all now. Jim's swapped his big nugget for Creede's belt. And in the bargain he exacted that Creede hit the trail out of camp. You happened to see Creede and went after him yourself. . . . Well, I don't see where you've any kick coming. For you've ten times the money in Cleve's nugget that there was in a share of Creede's gold."

"That's not my kick," declared Gulden. "What you say about Cleve may be true. But I don't believe it. And the gang is sore. Things have leaked out. We're watched. We're not welcome in the gambling-places any more. Last night I was not allowed to sit in the game at Belcher's."

"You think Cleve has squealed?" queried Kells.

"Yes."

"I'll bet you every ounce of dust I've got that you're wrong," declared Kells. "A straight, square bet against anything you want to put up!"

Kells's ringing voice was nothing if not convincing.

"Appearances are against Cleve," growled Gulden, dubiously. Always he had been swayed by the stronger mind of the leader.

"Sure they are," agreed Kells.

"Then what do you base your confidence on?"

"Just my knowledge of men. Jim Cleve wouldn't squeal. . . . Gulden, did anybody tell you that?"

"Yes," replied Gulden, slowly. "Red Pearce."

"Pearce was a liar," said Kells, bitterly. "I shot him for lying to me."

Gulden stared. His men muttered and gazed at one another and around the cabin.

"Pearce told me you set Cleve to kill me," suddenly spoke up the giant.

If he expected to surprise Kells he utterly failed.

"That's another and bigger lie," replied the bandit leader, disgustedly. "Gulden, do you think my mind's gone?"

"Not quite," replied Gulden, and he seemed as near a laugh as was possible for him.

"Well, I've enough mind left not to set a boy to kill such a man as you."

Gulden might have been susceptible to flattery. He turned to his men. They, too, had felt Kells's subtle influence. They were ready to veer round like weather-vanes.

"Red Pearce has cashed, an' he can't talk for himself," said Beady Jones, as if answering to the unspoken thought of all.

"Men, between you and me, I had more queer notions about Pearce than Cleve," announced Gulden, gruffly. "But I never said so because I had no proof."

"Red shore was sore an' strange lately," added Chick Williams. "Me an' him were pretty thick onct—but not lately."

The giant Gulden scratched his head and swore. Probably he had no sense of justice and was merely puzzled.

"We're wastin' a lot of time," put in Beard, anxiously. "Don't fergit there's somethin' comin' off down in camp, an' we ain't sure what."

"Bah! Haven't we heard whispers of vigilantes for a week?" queried Gulden.

Then some one of the men looked out of the door and suddenly whistled.

"Who's thet on a hoss?"

Gulden's gang crowded to the door.

"Thet's Handy Oliver."

"No!"

"Shore is. I know him. But it ain't his hoss. . . . Say, he's hurryin'."

Low exclamations of surprise and curiosity followed. Kells and his men looked attentively, but no one spoke. The clatter of hoofs on the stony road told of a horse swiftly approaching—pounding to a halt before the cabin.

"Handy! . . . Air you chased? . . . What's wrong? . . . You shore look pale round the gills." These and other remarks were flung out the door.

"Where's Kells? Let me in," replied Oliver, hoarsely.

The crowd jostled and split to admit the long, lean Oliver. He stalked straight toward Kells, till the table alone stood between them. He was gray of face, breathing hard, resolute and stern.

"Kells, I throwed—you—down!" he said, with outstretched hand. It was a gesture of self-condemnation and remorse.

"What of that?" demanded Kells, with his head leaping like the strike of an eagle.

"I'm takin' it back!"

Kells met the outstretched hand with his own and wrung it. "Handy, I never knew you to right-about-face. But I'm glad. . . . What's changed you so quickly?"

"*Vigilantes!*"

Kells's animation and eagerness suddenly froze. "*Vigilantes!*" he ground out.

"No rumor, Kells, this time. I've sure some news. . . . Come close, all you fellows. You, Gulden, come an' listen. Here's where we git together closer 'n ever."

Gulden surged forward with his group. Handy Oliver was surrounded by pale, tight faces, dark-browed and hardeyed.

He gazed at them, preparing them for a startling revelation. "Men, of all the white-livered traitors as ever was Red Pearce was the worst!" he declared, hoarsely.

No one moved or spoke.

"*An' he was a vigilante!*"

A low, strange sound, almost a roar, breathed through the group.

"Listen now an' don't interrupt. We ain't got a lot of

231

time. . . . So never mind how I happened to find out about Pearce. It was all accident, an' jest because I put two an' two together. . . . Pearce was approached by one of this secret vigilante band, an' he planned to sell the Border Legion outright. There was to be a big stake in it for him. He held off day after day, only tippin' off some of the gang. There's Dartt an' Singleton an' Frenchy an' Texas all caught red-handed at jobs. Pearce put the vigilantes to watchin' them jest to prove his claim. . . . Aw! I've got the proofs! Jest wait. Listen to me! . . . You all never in your lives seen a snake like Red Pearce. An' the job he had put up on us was grand. To-day he was to squeal on the whole gang. You know how he began on Kells—an' how with his oily tongue he asked a guarantee of no gun-play. But he figgered Kells wrong for once. He accused Kells's girl an' got killed for his pains. Mebbe it was part of his plan to git the girl himself. Anyway, he had agreed to betray the Border Legion to-day. An' if he hadn't been killed by this time we'd all be tied up, ready for the noose! . . . Mebbe thet wasn't a lucky shot of the boss's. Men, I was the first to declare myself against Kells, an' I'm here now to say thet I was a fool. So you've all been fools who've bucked against him. If this ain't provin' it, what can!

"But I must hustle with my story. . . . They was havin' a trial down at the big hall, an' thet place was sure packed. No diggin' gold to-day! . . . Think of what thet means for Alder Creek. I got inside where I could stand on a barrel an' see. Dartt an' Singleton an' Frenchy an' Texas was bein' tried by a masked court. A man near me said two of them had been proved guilty. It didn't take long to make out a case against Texas an' Frenchy. Miners there recognized them an' identified them. They was convicted an' sentenced to be hung! . . . Then the offer was made to let them go free out of the border if they'd turn state's evidence an' give away the leader an' men of the Border Legion. Thet was put up to each prisoner. Dartt he never answered at all. An' Singleton told them to go to hell. An' Texas he swore he was only a common an' honest road-agent, an' never heard of the Legion. But the Frenchman showed a yellow streak. He might have taken the offer. But Texas cussed him turrible, an' made him ashamed to talk. But if they git Frenchy away from

Texas they'll make him blab. He's like a greaser. Then there was a delay. The big crowd of miners yelled for ropes. But the vigilantes are waitin', an' it's my hunch they're waitin' for Pearce."

"So! And where do we stand?" cried Kells, clear and cold.

"We're not spotted yet, thet's certain," replied Oliver, "else them masked vigilantes would have been on the job before now. But it's not sense to figger we can risk another day. . . . I reckon it's hit the trail back to Cabin Gulch."

"Gulden, what do you say?" queried Kells, sharply.

"I'll go or stay—whatever you want," replied the giant. In this crisis he seemed to be glad to have Kells decide the issue. And his followers resembled sheep ready to plunge after the leader.

But though Kells, by a strange stroke, had been made wholly master of the Legion, he did not show the old elation or radiance. Perhaps he saw more clearly than ever before. Still he was quick, decisive, strong, equal to the occasion.

"Listen—all of you," he said. "Our horses and outfits are hidden in a gulch several miles below camp. We've got to go that way. We can't pack any grub or stuff from here. We'll risk going through camp. Now leave here two or three at a time, and wait down there on the edge of the crowd for me. When I come we'll stick together. Then all do as I do."

Gulden put the nugget under his coat and strode out, accompanied by Budd and Jones. They hurried away. The others went in couples. Soon only Bate Wood and Handy Oliver were left with Kells.

"Now you fellows go," said Kells. "Be sure to round up the gang down there and wait for me."

When they had gone he called for Jim and Joan to come out.

All this time Joan's hand had been gripped in Jim's, and Joan had been so absorbed that she had forgotten the fact. He released her and faced her, silent, pale. Then he went out. Joan swiftly followed.

Kells was buckling on his spurs. "You heard?" he said, the moment he saw Jim's face.

"Yes," replied Jim.

"So much the better. We've got to rustle. . . . Joan, put on that long coat of Cleve's. Take off your mask. . . . Jim, get what gold you have, and hurry. If we're gone when you come back hurry down the road. I want you with me."

Cleve stalked out, and Joan ran into her room and put on the long coat. She had little time to choose what possessions she could take; and that choice fell upon the little saddle-bag, into which she hurriedly stuffed comb and brush and soap—all it would hold. Then she returned to the larger room.

Kells had lifted a plank of the floor, and was now in the act of putting small buckskin sacks of gold into his pockets. They made his coat bulge at the sides.

"Joan, stick some meat and biscuits in your pockets," he said. "I'd never get hungry with my pockets full of gold. But you might."

Joan rummaged around in Bate Wood's rude cupboard.

"These biscuits are as heavy as gold—and harder," she said.

Kells flashed a glance at her that held pride, admiration, and sadness. "You are the gamest girl I ever knew! I wish I'd— But that's too late! . . . Joan, if anything happens to me stick close to Cleve. I believe you can trust him. Come on now."

Then he strode out of the cabin. Joan had almost to run to keep up with him. There were no other men now in sight. She knew that Jim would follow soon, because his gold-dust was hidden in the cavern back of her room, and he would not need much time to get it. Nevertheless, she anxiously looked back. She and Kells had gone perhaps a couple of hundred yards before Jim appeared, and then he came on the run. At a point about opposite the first tents he joined Kells.

"Jim, how about guns?" asked the bandit.

"I've got two," replied Cleve.

"Good! There's no telling— Jim, I'm afraid of the gang. They're crazy. What do you think?"

"I don't know. It's a hard proposition."

"We'll get away, all right. Don't worry about that. But

the gang will never come together again." This singular man spoke with melancholy. "Slow up a little now," he added. "We don't want to attract attention. . . . But where is there any one to see us? . . . Jim, did I have you figured right about the Creede job?"

"You sure did. I just lost my nerve."

"Well, no matter."

Then Kells appeared to forget that. He stalked on with keen glances searching everywhere, until suddenly, when he saw round a bend of the road, he halted with grating teeth. That road was empty all the way to the other end of camp, but there surged a dark mob of men. Kells stalked forward again. The Last Nugget appeared like an empty barn. How vacant and significant the whole center of camp! Kells did not speak another word.

Joan hurried on between Kells and Cleve. She was trying to fortify herself to meet what lay at the end of the road. A strange, hoarse roar of men and an upflinging of arms made her shudder. She kept her eyes lowered and clung to the arms of her companions.

Finally they halted. She felt the crowd before she saw it. A motley assemblage with what seemed craned necks and intent backs! They were all looking forward and upward. But she forced her glance down.

Kells stood still. Jim's grip was hard upon her arm. Presently men grouped round Kells. She heard whispers. They began to walk slowly, and she was pushed and led along. More men joined the group. Soon she and Kells and Jim were hemmed in a circle. Then she saw the huge form of Gulden, the towering Oliver, and Smith and Blicky, Beard, Jones, Williams, Budd, and others. The circle they formed appeared to be only one of many groups, all moving, whispering, facing from her. Suddenly a sound like the roar of a wave agitated that mass of men. It was harsh, piercing, unnatural, yet it had a note of wild exultation. Then came the stamp and surge, and then the upflinging of arms, and then the abrupt strange silence, broken only by a hiss or an escaping breath, like a sob. Beyond all Joan's power to resist was a deep, primitive desire to look.

There over the heads of the mob—from the bench of the

slope—rose grotesque structures of new-hewn lumber. On a platform stood black, motionless men in awful contrast with a dangling object that doubled up and curled upon itself in terrible convulsions. It lengthened while it swayed; it slowed its action while it stretched. It took on the form of a man. He swung by a rope round his neck. His head hung back. His hands beat. A long tremor shook the body; then it was still, and swayed to and fro, a dark, limp thing.

Joan's gaze was riveted in horror. A dim, red haze made her vision imperfect. There was a sickening riot within her.

There were masked men all around the platform—a solid phalanx of them on the slope above. They were heavily armed. Other masked men stood on the platform. They seemed rigid figures—stiff, jerky when they moved. How different from the two forms swaying below!

The structure was a rude scaffold and the vigilantes had already hanged two bandits.

Two others with hands bound behind their backs stood farther along the platform under guard. Before each dangled a noose.

Joan recognized Texas and Frenchy. And on the instant the great crowd let out a hard breath that ended in silence.

The masked leader of the vigilantes was addressing Texas: "We'll spare your life if you confess. Who's the head of this Border Legion?"

"Shore it's Red Pearce! . . . Haw! Haw! Haw!"

"We'll give you one more chance," came the curt reply.

Texas appeared to become serious and somber. "I swear to God it's Pearce!" he declared.

"A lie won't save you. Come, the truth! We think we know, but we want proof! Hurry!"

"You can go where it's hot!" responded Texas.

The leader moved his hand and two other masked men stepped forward.

"Have you any message to send any one—anything to say?" he asked.

"Nope."

"Have you any request to make?"

"Hang that Frenchman before me! I want to see him kick."

Nothing more was said. The two men adjusted the noose round the doomed man's neck. Texas refused the black cap. And he did not wait for the drop to be sprung. He walked off the platform into space as Joan closed her eyes.

Again that strange, full, angry, and unnatural roar waved through the throng of watchers. It was terrible to hear. Joan felt the violent action of that crowd, although the men close round her were immovable as stones. She imagined she could never open her eyes to see Texas hanging there. Yet she did—and something about his form told her that he had died instantly. He had been brave and loyal even in dishonor. He had more than once spoken a kind word to her. Who could tell what had made him an outcast? She breathed a prayer for his soul.

The vigilantes were bolstering up the craven Frenchy. He could not stand alone. They put the rope round his neck and lifted him off the platform—then let him down. He screamed in his terror. They cut short his cries by lifting him again. This time they held him up several seconds. His face turned black. His eyes bulged. His breast heaved. His legs worked with the regularity of a jumping-jack. They let him down and loosened the noose. They were merely torturing him to wring a confession from him. He had been choked severely and needed a moment to recover. When he did it was to shrink back in abject terror from that loop of rope dangling before his eyes.

The vigilante leader shook the noose in his face and pointed to the swaying forms of the dead bandits.

Frenchy frothed at the mouth as he shrieked out words in his native tongue, but any miner there could have translated their meaning.

The crowd heaved forward, as if with one step, then stood in a strained silence.

"Talk English!" ordered the vigilante.

"I'll tell! I'll tell!"

Joan became aware of a singular tremor in Kells's arm, which she still clasped. Suddenly it jerked. She caught a gleam of blue. Then the bellow of a gun almost split her ears. Powder burned her cheek. She saw Frenchy double up and collapse on the platform.

For an instant there was a silence in which every man seemed petrified. Then burst forth a hoarse uproar and the stamp of many boots. All in another instant pandemonium broke out. The huge crowd split in every direction. Joan felt Cleve's strong arm around her—felt herself borne on a resistless tide of yelling, stamping, wrestling men. She had a glimpse of Kells's dark face drawing away from her; another of Gulden's giant form in Herculean action, tossing men aside like ninepins; another of weapons aloft. Savage, wild-eyed men fought to get into the circle whence that shot had come. They broke into it, but did not know then whom to attack or what to do. And the rushing of the frenzied miners all around soon disintegrated Kells's band and bore its several groups in every direction. There was not another shot fired.

Joan was dragged and crushed in the mêlée. Not for rods did her feet touch the ground. But in the clouds of dust and confusion of struggling forms she knew Jim still held her, and she clasped him with all her strength. Presently her feet touched the earth; she was not jostled and pressed; then she felt free to walk; and with Jim urging her they climbed a rock-strewn slope till a cabin impeded further progress. But they had escaped the stream.

Below was a strange sight. A scaffold shrouded in dust-clouds; a band of bewildered vigilantes with weapons drawn, waiting for they knew not what; three swinging, ghastly forms and a dead man on the platform; and all below, a horde of men trying to escape from one another. That shot of Kells's had precipitated a rush. No miner knew who the vigilantes were nor the members of the Border Legion. Every man there expected a bloody battle —distrusted the man next to him—and had given way to panic. The vigilantes had tried to crowd together for defense and all the others had tried to escape. It was a wild scene, born of wild justice and blood at fever-heat, the climax of a disordered time where gold and violence reigned supreme. It could only happen once, but it was terrible while it lasted. It showed the craven in men; it proved the baneful influence of gold; it brought, in its fruition, the destiny of Alder Creek Camp. For it must have been that the really brave and honest men in vast majority retraced their steps while the vicious kept running. So it seemed to Joan.

She huddled against Jim there in the shadow of the cabin wall, and not for long did either speak. They watched and listened. The streams of miners turned back toward the space around the scaffold where the vigilantes stood grouped, and there rose a subdued roar of excited voices. Many small groups of men conversed together, until the vigilante leader brought all to attention by addressing the populace in general. Joan could not hear what he said and had no wish to hear.

"Joan, it all happened so quickly, didn't it?" whispered Jim, shaking his head as if he was not convinced of reality.

"Wasn't he—terrible!" whispered Joan in reply.

"He! Who?"

"Kells." In her mind the bandit leader dominated all that wild scene.

"Terrible, if you like. But I'd say great! . . . The nerve of him! In the face of a hundred vigilantes and thousands of miners! But he knew what that shot would do!"

"Never! He never thought of that," declared Joan, earnestly. "I felt him tremble. I had a glimpse of his face. . . . Oh! . . . First in his mind was his downfall, and, second, the treachery of Frenchy. I think that shot showed Kells as utterly desperate, but weak. He couldn't have helped it—if that had been the last bullet in his gun."

Jim Cleve looked strangely at Joan, as if her eloquence was both persuasive and incomprehensible.

"Well, that was a lucky shot for us—and him, too."

"Do you think he got away?" she asked, eagerly.

"Sure. They all got away. Wasn't that about the maddest crowd you ever saw?"

"No wonder. In a second every man there feared the man next to him would shoot. That showed the power of Kells's Border Legion. If his men had been faithful and obedient he never would have fallen."

"Joan! You speak as if you regret it!"

"Oh, I am ashamed," replied Joan. "I don't mean that. I

don't know what I do mean. But still I'm sorry for Kells. I suffered so much. . ... Those long, long hours of suspense. . . . And his fortunes seemed my fortunes—my very life—and yours, too, Jim."

"I think I understand, dear," said Jim, soberly.

"Jim, what'll we do now? Isn't it strange to feel free?"

"I feel as queer as you. Let me think," replied Jim.

They huddled there in comparative seclusion for a long time after that. Joan tried to think of plans, but her mind seemed unproductive. She felt half dazed. Jim, too, appeared to be laboring under the same kind of burden. Moreover, responsibility had been added to his.

The afternoon waned till the sun tipped the high range in the west. The excitement of the mining populace gradually wore away, and toward sunset strings of men filed up the road and across the open. The masked vigilantes disappeared, and presently only a quiet and curious crowd was left round the grim scaffold and its dark swinging forms. Joan's one glance showed that the vigilantes had swung Frenchy's dead body in the noose he would have escaped by treachery. They had hanged him dead. What a horrible proof of the temper of these newborn vigilantes! They had left the bandits swinging. What sight was so appalling as these limp, dark, swaying forms? Dead men on the ground had a dignity—at least the dignity of death. And death sometimes had a majesty. But here both life and death had been robbed and there was only horror. Joan felt that all her life she would be haunted.

"Joan, we've got to leave Alder Creek," declared Cleve, finally. He rose to his feet. The words seemed to have given him decision. "At first I thought every bandit in the gang would run as far as he could from here. But—you can't tell what these wild men will do. Gulden, for instance! Common sense ought to make them hide for a spell. Still, no matter what's what, we must leave. . . . Now, how to go?"

"Let's walk. If we buy horses or wait for the stage we'll have to see men here—and I'm afraid—"

"But, Joan, there'll be bandits along the road sure. And the trails, wherever they are, would be less safe."

"Let's travel by night and rest by day."

"That won't do, with so far to go and no pack."

"Then part of the way."

"No. We'd better take the stage for Bannack. If it starts at all it'll be under armed guard. The only thing is—will it leave soon? . . . Come, Joan, we'll go down into camp."

Dusk had fallen and lights had begun to accentuate the shadows. Joan kept close beside Jim, down the slope, and into the road. She felt like a guilty thing and every passing man or low-conversing group frightened her. Still she could not help but see that no one noticed her or Jim, and she began to gather courage. Jim also acquired confidence. The growing darkness seemed a protection. The farther up the street they passed, the more men they met. Again the saloons were in full blast. Alder Creek had returned to the free, careless tenor of its way. A few doors this side of the Last Nugget was the office of the stage and express company. It was a wide tent with the front canvas cut out and a shelf-counter across the opening. There was a dim, yellow lamplight. Half a dozen men lounged in front, and inside were several more, two of whom appeared to be armed guards. Jim addressed no one in particular.

"When does the next stage leave for Bannack?"

A man looked up sharply from the papers that littered a table before him. "It leaves when we start it," he replied, curtly.

"Well, when will that be?"

"What's that to you?" he replied, with a question still more curt.

"I want to buy seats for two."

"That's different. Come in and let's look you over. . . . Hello! it's young Cleve. I didn't recognize you. *Ex*cuse me. We're a little particular these days."

The man's face lighted. Evidently he knew Jim and thought well of him. This reassured Joan and stilled the furious beating of her heart. She saw Jim hand over a sack of gold, from which the agent took the amount due for the passage. Then he returned the sack and whispered something in Jim's ear. Jim rejoined her and led her away, pressing her arm close to his side.

"It's all right," he whispered, excitedly. "Stage leaves just before daylight. It used to leave in the middle of the fore-noon. But they want a good start to-morrow."

"They think it might be held up?"

"He didn't say so. But there's every reason to suspect that. . . . Joan, I sure hope it won't. Me with all this gold. Why, I feel as if I weighed a thousand pounds."

"What'll we do now?" she inquired.

Jim halted in the middle of the road. It was quite dark now. The lights of the camp were flaring; men were passing to and fro; the loose boards on the walks rattled to their tread; the saloons had begun to hum; and there was a discordant blast from the Last Nugget.

"That's it—what'll we do?" he asked in perplexity.

Joan had no idea to advance, but with the lessening of her fear and the gradual clearing of her mind she felt that she would not much longer be witless.

"We've got to eat and get some rest," said Jim, sensibly.

"I'll try to eat—but I don't think I'll be able to sleep tonight," replied Joan.

Jim took her to a place kept by a Mexican. It appeared to consist of two tents, with opening in front and door be-tween. The table was a plank resting upon two barrels, and another plank, resting upon kegs, served as a seat. There was a smoking lamp that flickered. The Mexican's tableware was of a crudeness befitting his house, but it was clean and he could cook—two facts that Joan appreciated after her long experience of Bate Wood. She and Jim were the only customers of the Mexican, who spoke English rather well and was friendly. Evidently it pleased him to see the meal enjoyed. Both the food and the friendliness had good effect upon Jim Cleve. He ceased to listen all the time and to glance furtively out at every footstep.

"Joan, I guess it'll turn out all right," he said, clasping her hand as it rested upon the table. Suddenly he looked bright-eyed and shy. He leaned toward her. "Do you remem-ber—we are married?" he whispered.

Joan was startled. "Of course," she replied hastily. But had she forgotten?

"You're my wife."

Joan looked at him and felt her nerves begin to tingle. A soft, warm wave stole over her.

Like a boy he laughed. "This was our first meal together—on our honeymoon!"

"Jim!" The blood burned in Joan's face.

"There you sit—you beautiful . . . But you're not a girl now. You're Dandy Dale."

"Don't call me that!" exclaimed Joan.

"But I shall—always. We'll keep that bandit suit always. You can dress up sometimes to show off—to make me remember—to scare the—the kids—"

"Jim Cleve!"

"Oh, Joan, I'm afraid to be happy. But I can't help it. We're going to get away. You belong to me. And I've sacks and sacks of gold-dust. Lord! I've no idea how much! But you can never spend all the money. Isn't it just like a dream?"

Joan smiled through tears, and failed trying to look severe.

"Get me and the gold away—safe—before you crow," she said.

That sobered him. He led her out again into the dark street with its dark forms crossing to and fro before the lights.

"It's a long time before morning. Where can I take you—so you can sleep a little?" he muttered.

"Find a place where we can sit down and wait," she suggested.

"No." He pondered a moment. "I guess there's no risk."

Then he led her up the street and through that end of camp out upon the rough, open slope. They began to climb. The stars were bright, but even so Joan stumbled often over the stones. She wondered how Jim could get along so well in the dark and she clung to his arm. They did not speak often, and then only in whispers. Jim halted occasionally to listen or to look up at the bold, black bluff for his bearings. Presently he led her among broken fragments of cliff, and half carried her over rougher ground, into a kind of shadowy pocket or niche.

"Here's where I slept," he whispered.

He wrapped a blanket round her, and then they sat down against the rock, and she leaned upon his shoulder.

"I have your coat and the blanket, too," she said. "Won't you be cold?"

He laughed. "Now don't talk any more. You're white and fagged-out. You need to rest—to sleep."

"Sleep? How impossible!" she murmured.

"Why, your eyes are half shut now. . . . Anyway, I'll not talk to you. I want to think."

"Jim! . . . kiss me—good night," she whispered.

He bent over rather violently, she imagined. His head blotted out the light of the stars. He held her tightly for a moment. She felt him shake. Then he kissed her on the cheek and abruptly drew away. How strange he seemed!

For that matter, everything was strange. She had never seen the stars so bright, so full of power, so close. All about her the shadows gathered protectingly, to hide her and Jim. The silence spoke. She saw Jim's face in the starlight and it seemed so keen, so listening, so thoughtful, so beautiful. He would sit there all night, wide-eyed and alert, guarding her, waiting for the gray of dawn. How he had changed! And she was his wife! But that seemed only a dream. It needed daylight and sight of her ring to make that real.

A warmth and languor stole over her; she relaxed comfortably; after all, she would sleep. But why did that intangible dread hang on to her soul? The night was so still and clear and perfect—a radiant white night of stars—and Jim was there, holding her—and to-morrow they would ride away. That might be, but dark, dangling shapes haunted her, back in her mind, and there, too, loomed Kells. Where was he now? Gone—gone on his bloody trail with his broken fortunes and his desperate bitterness! He had lost her. The lunge of that wild mob had parted them. A throb of pain and shame went through her, for she was sorry. She could not understand why, unless it was because she had possessed some strange power to instil or bring up good in him. No woman could have been proof against that. It was monstrous to know that she had power to turn him from an evil life, yet she could not do it. It was more than monstrous to realize that he had gone on spilling blood and would continue to go on when she could have prevented it—could have saved many poor miners who perhaps had wives or sweethearts somewhere. Yet there was no help for it. She loved Jim Cleve. She might have sacrificed herself, but she would not sacrifice him for all the bandits and miners on the border.

Joan felt that she would always be haunted and would always suffer that pang for Kells. She would never lie down in the peace and quiet of her home, wherever that might be, without picturing Kells, dark and forbidding and burdened, pacing some lonely cabin or riding a lonely trail or lying with his brooding face upturned to the lonely stars. Sooner or later he would meet his doom. It was inevitable. She pictured over that sinister scene of the dangling forms; but no—Kells would never end that way. Terrible as he was, he had not been born to be hanged. He might be murdered in his sleep, by one of that band of traitors who were traitors because in the nature of evil they had to be. But more likely some gambling-hell, with gold and life at stake, would see his last fight. These bandits stole gold and gambled among themselves and fought. And that fight which finished Kells must necessarily be a terrible one. She seemed to see into a lonely cabin where a log fire burned low and lamps flickered and blue smoke floated in veils and men lay prone on the floor—Kells, stark and bloody, and the giant Gulden, dead at last and more terrible in death, and on the rude table bags of gold and dull, shining heaps of gold, and scattered on the floor, like streams of sand and useless as sand, dust of gold—the Destroyer.

18

◆

ALL JOAN'S fancies and dreams faded into obscurity, and when she was aroused it seemed she had scarcely closed her eyes. But there was the gray gloom of dawn. Jim was shaking her gently.

"No, you weren't sleepy—it's just a mistake," he said, helping her to arise. "Now we'll get out of here."

They threaded a careful way out of the rocks, then hurried down the slope. In the grayness Joan saw the dark shape of a cabin and it resembled the one Kells had built. It disappeared. Presently when Jim led her into a road she felt sure that this cabin had been the one where she had been a prisoner for so long. They hurried down the road and entered the camp. There were no lights. The tents and cabins looked strange and gloomy. The road was empty. Not a sound broke the stillness. At the bend Joan saw a stage-coach and horses looming up in what seemed gray distance. Jim hurried her on.

They reached the stage. The horses were restive. The driver was on the seat, whip and reins in hand. Two men sat beside him with rifles across their knees. The door of the coach hung open. There were men inside, one of whom had his head out of the window. The barrel of a rifle protruded near him. He was talking in a low voice to a man apparently busy at the traces.

"Hello, Cleve! You're late," said another man, evidently the agent. "Climb aboard. When'll you be back?"

"I hardly know," replied Cleve, with hesitation.

"All right. Good luck to you." He closed the coach door after Joan and Jim. "Let 'em go, Bill."

The stage started with a jerk. To Joan what an unearthly creak and rumble it made, disturbing the silent dawn! Jim squeezed her hand with joy. They were on the way!

Joan and Jim had a seat to themselves. Opposite sat three men—the guard with his head half out of the window, a bearded miner who appeared stolid or drowsy, and a young man who did not look rough and robust enough for a prospector. None of the three paid any particular attention to Joan and Jim.

The road had a decided slope down-hill, and Bill, the driver, had the four horses on a trot. The rickety old stage appeared to be rattling to pieces. It lurched and swayed, and sometimes jolted over rocks and roots. Joan was hard put to it to keep from being bumped off the seat. She held to a brace on one side and to Jim on the other. And when the stage rolled down into the creek and thumped over boulders Joan made sure that every bone in her body would be broken. This crossing marked the mouth of the gulch, and on the other side the road was smooth.

"We're going the way we came," whispered Jim in her ear.

This was surprising, for Joan had been sure that Bannack lay in the opposite direction. Certainly this fact was not reassuring to her. Perhaps the road turned soon.

Meanwhile the light brightened, the day broke, and the sun reddened the valley. Then it was as light inside the coach as outside. Joan might have spared herself concern as to her fellow-passengers. The only one who noticed her was the young man, and he, after a stare and a half-smile, lapsed into abstraction. He looked troubled, and there was about him no evidence of prosperity. Jim held her hand under a fold of the long coat, and occasionally he spoke of something or other outside that caught his eye. And the stage rolled on rapidly, seemingly in pursuit of the steady roar of hoofs.

Joan imagined she recognized the brushy ravine out of which Jesse Smith had led that day when Kells's party came upon the new road. She believed Jim thought so, too, for he gripped her hand unusually hard. Beyond that point Joan began to breathe more easily. There seemed no valid reason now why every mile should not separate them farther from the bandits, and she experienced relief.

Then the time did not drag so. She wanted to talk to Jim, yet did not, because of the other passengers. Jim himself appeared influenced by their absorption in themselves. Besides, the keen, ceaseless vigilance of the guard was not without its quieting effect. Danger lurked ahead in the bends of that road. Joan remembered hearing Kells say that the Bannack stage had never been properly held up by road-agents, but that when he got ready for the job it would be done right. Riding grew to be monotonous and tiresome. With the warmth of the sun came the dust and flies, and all these bothered Joan. She did not have her usual calmness, and as the miles steadily passed her nervousness increased.

The road left the valley and climbed between foot-hills and wound into rockier country. Every dark gulch brought to Joan a trembling, breathless spell. What places for ambush! But the stage bowled on.

At last her apprehensions wore out and she permitted

herself the luxury of relaxing, of leaning back and closing her eyes. She was tired, drowsy, hot. There did not seem to be a breath of air.

Suddenly Joan's ears burst to an infernal crash of guns. She felt the whip and sting of splinters sent flying by bullets. Harsh yells followed, then the scream of a horse in agony, the stage lurching and slipping to a halt, and thunder of heavy guns overhead.

Jim yelled at her—threw her down on the seat. She felt the body of the guard sink against her knees. Then she seemed to feel, to hear through an icy, sickening terror.

A scattering volley silenced the guns above. Then came the pound of hoofs, the snort of frightened horses.

"Jesse Smith! Stop!" called Jim, piercingly.

"Hold on thar, Beady!" replied a hoarse voice. "Damn if it ain't Jim Cleve!"

"Ho, Gul!" yelled another voice, and Joan recognized it as Blicky's.

Then Jim lifted her head, drew her up. He was white with fear.

"Dear—are—you—hurt?"

"No. I'm only—scared," she replied.

Joan looked out to see bandits on foot, guns in hand, and others mounted, all gathering near the coach. Jim opened the door, and, stepping out, bade her follow. Joan had to climb over the dead guard. The miner and the young man huddled down on their seat.

"If it ain't Jim an' Kells's girl—Dandy Dale!" ejaculated Smith. "Fellers, this means somethin'. . . . Say, youngster, hope you ain't hurt—or the girl?"

"No. But that's not your fault," replied Cleve. "Why did you want to plug the coach full of lead?"

"This beats me," said Smith. "Kells sent you out in the stage! But when he gave us the job of holdin' it up he didn't tell us you'd be in there. . . . When an' where'd you leave him?"

"Sometime last night—in camp—near our cabin," replied Jim, quick as a flash. Manifestly he saw his opportunity "He left Dandy Dale with me. Told us to take the stage this morning. I expected him to be in it or to meet us."

"Didn't you have no orders?"

"None, except to take care of the girl till he came. But he did tell me he'd have more to say."

Smith gazed blankly from Cleve to Blicky, and then at Gulden, who came slowly forward, his hair ruffed, his gun held low. Joan followed the glance of his great gray eyes, and she saw the stage-driver hanging dead over his seat, and the guards lying back of him. The off-side horse of the leaders lay dead in his traces, with his mate nosing at him.

"Who's in there?" boomed Gulden, and he thrust hand and gun in at the stage door. "Come out!"

The young man stumbled out, hands above his head, pallid and shaking, so weak he could scarcely stand.

Gulden prodded the bearded miner. "Come out here, you!"

The man appeared to be hunched forward in a heap.

"Guess he's plugged," said Smith. "But he ain't cashed. Hear him breathe? . . . . Heaves like a sick hoss."

Gulden reached with brawny arm and with one pull he dragged the miner off the seat and out into the road, where he flopped with a groan. There was blood on his neck and hands. Gulden bent over him, tore at his clothes, tore harder at something, and then, with a swing, he held aloft a broad, black belt, sagging heavy with gold.

"Hah!" he boomed. It was just an exclamation, horrible to hear, but it did not express satisfaction or exultation. He handed the gold-belt to the grinning Budd, and turned to the young man.

"Got any gold?"

"No. I—I wasn't a miner," replied the youth huskily.

Gulden felt for a gold-belt, then slapped at his pockets. "Turn round!" ordered the giant.

"Aw, Gul let him go!" remonstrated Jesse Smith.

Blicky laid a restraining hand upon Gulden's broad shoulder.

"Turn round!" repeated Gulden, without the slightest sign of noticing his colleagues.

But the youth understood and he turned a ghastly livid hue.

"For God's sake—don't murder me!" he gasped. "I had —nothing—no gold—no gun!"

Gulden spun him round like a top and pushed him forward. They went half a dozen paces, then the youth staggered, and turning, he fell on his knees.

"Don't—kill—me!" he entreated.

Joan, seeing Jim Cleve stiffen and crouch, thought of him even in that horrible moment; and she gripped his arm with all her might. They must endure.

The other bandits muttered, but none moved a hand.

Gulden thrust out the big gun. His hair bristled on his head, and his huge frame seemed instinct with strange vibration, like some object of tremendous weight about to plunge into resistless momentum.

Even the stricken youth saw his doom. "Let—me—pray!" he begged.

Joan did not faint, but a merciful unclamping of muscle-bound rigidity closed her eyes.

"Gul!" yelled Blicky, with passion. "I ain't a-goin' to let you kill this kid! There's no sense in it. We're spotted back in Alder Creek. . . . Run, kid! Run!"

Then Joan opened her eyes to see the surly Gulden's arm held by Blicky, and the youth running blindly down the road. Joan's relief and joy were tremendous. But still she answered to the realizing shock of what Gulden had meant to do. She leaned against Cleve, all within and without a whirling darkness of fire. The border wildness claimed her then. She had the spirit, though not the strength, to fight. She needed the sight and sound of other things to restore her equilibrium. She would have welcomed another shock, an injury. And then she was looking down upon the gasping miner. He was dying. Hurriedly Joan knelt beside him to lift his head. At her call Cleve brought a canteen. But the miner could not drink and he died with some word unspoken.

Dizzily Joan arose, and with Cleve half supporting her she backed off the road to a seat on the bank. She saw the bandits now at business-like action. Blicky and Smith were cutting the horses out of their harness; Beady Jones, like a ghoul, searched the dead men; the three bandits whom Joan knew only by sight were making up a pack; Budd was standing beside the stage with his expectant grin; and Gulden, with the agility of the gorilla he resembled, was clambering over the top of the stage. Suddenly from under the driver's seat he hauled a buckskin sack. It was small, but heavy. He threw it down to Budd, almost knocking over that bandit. Budd hugged the sack and yelled like an Indian. The other men whooped and ran toward him. Gulden hauled out another sack. Hands to the number of a dozen stretched clutchingly. When he threw the sack there was a mad scramble. They fought, but it was only play. They were gleeful. Blicky secured the prize and he held it aloft in triumph. Assuredly he would have waved it had it not been so heavy. Gulden drew out several small sacks, which he provokingly placed on the seat in front of him. The bandits below howled in protest. Then the giant, with his arm under the seat, his huge frame bowed, heaved powerfully upon something, and his face turned red. He halted in his tugging to glare at his bandit comrades below. If his great cavernous eyes expressed any feeling it was analogous to the reluctance manifest in his posture—he regretted the presence of his gang. He would rather have been alone. Then with deep-muttered curse and mighty heave he lifted out a huge buckskin sack, tied and placarded and marked.

"*One hundred pounds!*" he boomed.

It seemed to Joan then that a band of devils surrounded the stage, all roaring at the huge, bristling demon above, who glared and bellowed down at them.

Finally Gulden stilled the tumult, which, after all, was one of frenzied joy.

"Share and share alike!" he thundered, now black in the face. "Do you fools want to waste time here on the road, dividing up this gold?"

"What you say goes," shouted Budd.

There was no dissenting voice.

"What a stake!" ejaculated Blicky. "Gul, the boss had it figgered. Strange, though, he hasn't showed up!"

"Where'll we go?" queried Gulden. "Speak up, you men."

The unanimous selection was Cabin Gulch. Plainly Gulden did not like this, but he was just.

"All right. Cabin Gulch it is. But nobody outside of Kells and us gets a share in this stake."

Many willing hands made short work of preparation. Gulden insisted on packing all the gold upon his saddle, and had his will. He seemed obsessed; he never glanced at Joan. It was Jesse Smith who gave the directions and orders. One of the stage-horses was packed. Another, with a blanket for a saddle, was given Cleve to ride. Blicky gallantly gave his horse to Joan, shortened his stirrups to fit her, and then whistled at the ridgy back of the stage-horse he elected to ride. Gulden was in a hurry, and twice he edged off, to be halted by impatient calls. Finally the cavalcade was ready. Jesse Smith gazed around upon the scene with the air of a general overlooking a vanquished enemy.

"Whoever fust runs acrost this job will have blind staggers, don't you forgit thet!"

"What's Kells goin' to figger?" asked Blicky, sharply.

"Nothin' fer Kells! He wasn't in at the finish!" declared Budd.

Blicky gazed darkly at him, but made no comment.

"I tell you Blick, I can't git this all right in my head," said Smith.

"Say, ask Jim again. Mebbe, now the job's done, he can talk," suggested Blicky.

Jim Cleve heard and appeared ready for that question.

"I don't *know* much more than I told you. But I can guess. Kells had this big shipment of gold spotted. He must have sent us in the stage for some reason. He said he'd tell me what to expect and do. But he didn't come back. Sure he knew you'd do the job. And just as sure he expected to be on hand. He'll turn up soon."

This ruse of Jim's did not sound in the least logical or plausible to Joan, but it was readily accepted by the bandits. Apparently what they knew of Kells's movements and plans since the break-up at Alder Creek fitted well with Cleve's suggestions.

"Come on!" boomed Gulden, from the fore. "Do you want to rot here?"

Then without so much as a backward glance at the ruin they left behind the bandits fell into line. Jesse Smith led

253

straight off the road into a shallow brook and evidently meant to keep in it. Gulden followed; next came Beady Jones; then the three bandits with the pack-horse and the other horses; Cleve and Joan, close together, filed in here; and last came Budd and Blicky. It was rough, slippery traveling and the riders spread out. Cleve, however, rode beside Joan. Once, at an opportune moment, he leaned toward her.

"We'd better run for it at the first chance," he said, somberly.

"No! . . . *Gulden!*" Joan had to moisten her lips to speak the monster's name.

"He'll never think of you while he has all that gold."

Joan's intelligence grasped this, but her morbid dread, terribly augmented now, amounted almost to a spell. Still, despite the darkness of her mind, she had a flash of inspiration and of spirit.

"Kells is my only hope! . . . If he doesn't join us soon— then we'll run! . . . And if we can't escape that"—Joan made a sickening gesture toward the fore—"you must kill me before—before—"

Her voice trailed off, failing.

"I will!" he promised through locked teeth.

And then they rode on, with dark faces bent over the muddy water and treacherous stones.

When Jesse Smith led out of that brook it was to ride upon bare rock. He was not leaving any trail. Horses and riders were of no consideration. And he was a genius for picking hard ground and covering it. He never slackened his gait, and it seemed next to impossible to keep him in sight.

For Joan the ride became toil and the toil became pain. But there was no rest. Smith kept mercilessly onward. Sunset and twilight and night found the cavalcade still moving. Then it halted just as Joan was about to succumb. Jim lifted her off her horse and laid her upon the grass. She begged for water, and she drank and drank. But she wanted no food. There was a heavy, dull beating in her ears, a band tight round her forehead. She was aware of the gloom, of the crackling of fires, of leaping shadows, of the passing of men to and fro near her, and, most of all, rendering her capable of a saving shred of self-control, she was aware of Jim's constant companionship and watchfulness. Then sounds grew far off and night became a blur.

Morning when it came seemed an age removed from that hideous night. Her head had cleared, and but for the soreness of body and limb she would have begun the day strong. There appeared little to eat and no time to prepare it. Gulden was rampant for action. Like a miser he guarded the saddle packed with gold. This time his comrades were as eager as he to be on the move. All were obsessed by the presence of gold. Only one hour loomed in their consciousness—that of the hour of division. How fatal and pitiful and terrible! Of what possible use or good was gold to them?

The ride began before sunrise. It started and kept on at a steady trot. Smith led down out of the rocky slopes and fastnesses into green valleys. Jim Cleve, riding bareback on a lame horse, had his difficulties. Still he kept close beside or behind Joan all the way They seldom spoke, and then only a word relative to this stern business of traveling in the trail of a hard-riding bandit. Joan bore up better this day, as far as her mind was concerned. Physically she had all she could do to stay in the saddle. She learned of what steel she was actually made—what her slender frame could endure. That day's ride seemed a thousand miles long, and never to end. Yet the implacable Smith did finally halt, and that before dark.

Camp was made near water. The bandits were a jovial lot, despite a lack of food. They talked of the morrow. All—the world—lay beyond the next sunrise. Some renounced their pipes and sought their rest just to hurry on the day. But Gulden, tireless, sleepless, eternally vigilant, guarded the saddle of gold and brooded over it, and seemed a somber giant carved out of the night. And Blicky, nursing some deep and late-developed scheme, perhaps in Kells's interest or his own, kept watch over Gulden and all.

Jim cautioned Joan to rest, and importuned her and promised to watch while she slept.

Joan saw the stars through her shut eyelids. All the night

seemed to press down and softly darken.

The sun was shining red when the cavalcade rode up Cabin Gulch. The grazing cattle stopped to watch and the horses pranced and whistled. There were flowers and flitting birds, and glistening dew on leaves, and a shining swift flow of water—the brightness of morning and nature smiled in Cabin Gulch.

Well indeed Joan remembered the trail she had ridden so often. How that clump of willow where first she had confronted Jim thrilled her now! The pines seemed welcoming her. The gulch had a sense of home in it for her, yet it was fearful. How much had happened there! What might yet happen!

Then a clear, ringing call stirred her pulse. She glanced up the slope. Tall and straight and dark, there on the bench, with hand aloft, stood the bandit Kells.

19

◆

THE weary, dusty cavalcade halted on the level bench
before the bandit's cabin. Gulden boomed a salute to Kells.
The other men shouted greeting. In the wild exultation of
triumph they still held him as chief. But Kells was not
deceived. He even passed by that heavily laden, gold-
weighted saddle. He had eyes only for Joan.

"Girl, I never was so glad to see any one!" he exclaimed
in husky amaze. "How did it happen? I never—"

Jim Cleve leaned over to interrupt Kells. "It was great, Kells—that idea of yours putting us in the stagecoach you meant to hold up," said Cleve, with a swift, meaning glance. "But it nearly was the end of us. You didn't catch up. The gang didn't know we were inside, and they shot the old stage full of holes."

"Aha! So that's it," replied Kells, slowly. "But the main point is—you brought her through. Jim, I can't ever square that."

"Oh, maybe you can," laughed Cleve, as he dismounted.

Suddenly Kells became aware of Joan's exhaustion and distress. "Joan, you're not hurt?" he asked in swift anxiety.

"No, only played out."

"You look it. Come." He lifted her out of the saddle and, half carrying, half leading her, took her into the cabin, and through the big room to her old apartment. How familiar it seemed to Joan! A ground-squirrel frisked along a chink between the logs, chattering welcome. The place was exactly as Joan had left it.

Kells held Joan a second, as if he meant to embrace her, but he did not. "Lord, it's good to see you! I never expected to again. . . . But you can tell me all about yourself after you rest. . . . I was just having breakfast. I'll fetch you some."

"Were you alone here?" asked Joan.

"Yes. I was with Bate and Handy—"

"Hey, Kells!" roared the gang, from the outer room.

Kells held aside the blanket curtain so that Joan was able to see through the door. The men were drawn up in a half-circle round the table, upon which were the bags of gold.

Kells whistled low. "Joan, there'll be trouble now," he said, "but don't you fear. I'll not forget you."

Despite his undoubted sincerity Joan felt a subtle change in him, and that, coupled with the significance of his words, brought a return of the strange dread. Kells went out and dropped the curtain behind him. Joan listened.

"Share and share alike!" boomed the giant Gulden.

"Say!" called Kells, gaily, "aren't you fellows going to eat first?"

Shouts of derision greeted his sally.

"I'll eat gold-dust," added Budd.

"Have it your own way, men," responded Kells. "Blicky, get the scales down off of that shelf. . . . Say, I'll bet anybody I'll have the most dust by sundown."

More shouts of derision were flung at him.

"Who wants to gamble now?"

"Boss, I'll take thet bet."

"Haw! Haw! You won't look so bright by sundown."

Then followed a moment's silence, presently broken by a clink of metal on the table.

"Boss, how'd you ever git wind of this big shipment of gold?" asked Jesse Smith.

"I've had it spotted. But Handy Oliver was the scout."

"We'll shore drink to Handy!" exclaimed one of the bandits.

"An' who was sendin' out this shipment?" queried the curious Smith. "Them bags are marked all the same."

"It was a one-man shipment," replied Kells. "Sent out by the boss miner of Alder Creek. They call him Overland something."

That name brought Joan to her feet with a thrilling fire. Her uncle, old Bill Hoadley, was called "Overland." Was it possible that the bandits meant him? It could hardly be; that name was a common one in the mountains.

"Shore, I seen Overland lots of times," said Budd. "An' he got wise to my watchin' him."

"Somebody tipped it off that the Legion was after his gold," went on Kells. "I suppose we have Pearce to thank for that. But it worked out well for us. The hell we raised there at the lynching must have thrown a scare into Overland. He had nerve enough to try to send his dust to Bannack on the very next stage. He nearly got away with it, too. For it was only lucky accident that Handy heard the news."

The name Overland drew Joan like a magnet and she arose to take her old position, where she could peep in upon the bandits. One glance at Jim Cleve told her that he, too, had been excited by the name. Then it occurred to Joan that her uncle could hardly have been at Alder Creek without Jim knowing it. Still, among thousands of men, all wild and toiling and self-sufficient, hiding their identities, anything might be possible. After a few moments, however, Joan leaned to the improbability of the man being her uncle.

Kells sat down before the table and Blicky stood beside him with the gold-scales. The other bandits lined up opposite. Jim Cleve stood to one side, watching, brooding.

"You can't weigh it all on these scales," said Blicky.

"That's sure," replied Kells. "We'll divide the small bags first. . . . Ten shares—ten equal parts! . . . Spill out the bags. Blick. And hurry. Look how hungry Gulden looks! . . . Somebody cook your breakfast while we divide the gold."

"Haw! Haw!"

"Ho! Ho!"

"Who wants to eat?"

The bandits were gay, derisive, scornful, eager, like a group of boys, half surly, half playful, at a game.

"Wal, I shore want to see my share weighted," drawled Budd.

Kells moved—his gun flashed—he slammed it hard upon the table.

"Budd, do you question my honesty?" he asked, quick and hard.

"No offense, boss. I was just talkin'."

That quick change of Kells's marked a subtle difference in the spirit of the bandits and the occasion. Gaiety and good humor and badinage ended. There were no more broad grins or friendly leers or coarse laughs. Gulden and his groups clustered closer to the table, quiet, intense, watchful, suspicious.

It did not take Kells and his assistant long to divide the smaller quantity of the gold.

"Here, Gulden," he said, and handed the giant a bag. Jesse. . . . Bossert. . . . Pike. . . . Beady. . . . Braverman. . . "Blicky."

"Here, Jim Cleve, get in the game," he added, throwing a bag at Jim. It was heavy. It hit Jim with t thud and dropped to the ground. He stooped to reach it.

"That leaves one for Handy and one for me," went on Kells. "Blicky, spill out the big bag."

Presently Joan saw a huge mound of dull, gleaming yellow. The color of it leaped to the glinting eyes of the bandits. And it seemed to her that a shadow hovered over them. The movements of Kells grew tense and hurried. Beads of sweat stood out upon his brow. His hands were not steady.

Soon larger bags were distributed to the bandits. That broke the waiting, the watchfulness, but not the tense eagerness. The bandits were now like leashed hounds. Blicky leaned before Kells and hit the table with his fist.

"Boss, I've a kick comin'," he said.

"Come on with it," replied the leader.

"Ain't Gulden a-goin' to divide up thet big nugget?"

"He is if he's square."

A chorus of affirmatives from the bandits strengthened Kells's statement. Gulden moved heavily and ponderously, and he pushed some of his comrades aside to get nearer to Kells.

"Wasn't it my right to do a job by myself—when I wanted?" he demanded.

"No. I agreed to let you fight when you wanted. To kill a man when you liked! . . . That was the agreement."

"What'd I kill a man for?"

No one answered that in words, but the answer was there, in dark faces.

"I know what I meant," continued Gulden. "And I'm going to keep this nugget."

There was a moment's silence. It boded ill to the giant.

"So—he declares himself," said Blicky, hotly. "Boss, what you say goes."

"Let him keep it," declared Kells, scornfully. "I'll win it from him and divide it with the gang."

That was received with hoarse acclaims by all except Gulden. He glared sullenly. Kells stood up and shook a long finger in the giant's face.

"I'll win your nugget," he shouted. "I'll beat you at any game. . . . I call your hand. . . . Now if you've got any nerve!"

"Come on!" boomed the giant, and he threw his gold down upon the table with a crash.

The bandits closed in around the table with sudden, hard violence, all crowding for seats.

"I'm a-goin' to set in the game!" yelled Blicky.

"We'll all set in," declared Jesse Smith.

"Come on!" was Gulden's acquiescence.

"But we all can't play at once," protested Kells. "Let's make up two games."

"Naw!"

"Some of you eat, then, while the others get cleaned out."

"Thet's it—cleaned out!" ejaculated Budd, meanly. "You seem to be sure, Kells. An' I guess I'll keep shady of thet game."

"That's twice for you, Budd," flashed the bandit leader. "Beware of the third time!"

"Hyar, fellers, cut the cards fer who sets in an' who sets out," called Blicky, and he slapped a deck of cards upon the table.

With grim eagerness, as if drawing lots against fate, the bandits bent over and drew cards. Budd, Braverman, and Beady Jones were the ones excluded from the game.

"Beady, you fellows unpack those horses and turn them loose. And bring the stuff inside," said Kells.

Budd showed a surly disregard, but the other two bandits got up willingly and went out.

Then the game began, with only Cleve standing, looking on. The bandits were mostly silent; they moved their hands, and occasionally bent forward. It was every man against his neighbor. Gulden seemed implacably indifferent and played like a machine. Blicky sat eager and excited, under a spell. Jesse Smith was a slow, cool, shrewed gambler. Bossert and Pike, two ruffians almost unknown to Joan, appeared carried away by their opportunity. And Kells began to wear that strange, rapt, weak expression that gambling gave him.

Presently Beady Jones and Braverman bustled in, carrying the packs. Then Budd jumped up and ran to them. He returned to the table, carrying a demijohn, which he banged upon the table.

"Whisky!" exclaimed Kells. "Take that away. We can't drink and gamble."

"Watch me!" replied Blicky.

"Let them drink, Kells," declared Gulden. "We'll get their dust quicker. Then we can have our game."

Kells made no more comment. The game went on and the

aspect of it changed. When Kells himself began to drink, seemingly unconscious of the fact, Joan's dread increased greatly, and, leaving the peep-hole, she lay back upon the bed. Always a sword had hung over her head. Time after time by some fortunate circumstance or by courage or wit or by an act of Providence she had escaped what strangely menaced. Would she escape it again? For she felt the catastrophe coming. Did Jim recognize that fact? Remembering the look on his face, she was assured that he did. Then he would be quick to seize upon any possible chance to get her away; and always he would be between her and those bandits. At most, then, she had only death to fear—death that he would mercifully deal to her if the worst came. And as she lay there listening to the slow-rising murmur of the gamblers, with her thought growing clearer, she realized it was love of Jim and fear for him—fear that he would lose her—that caused her cold dread and the laboring breath and the weighted heart. She had cost Jim this terrible experience and she wanted to make up to him for it, to give him herself and all her life.

Joan lay there a long time, thinking and suffering, while the strange, morbid desire to watch Kells and Gulden grew stronger and stronger, until it was irresistible. Her fate, her life, lay in the balance between these two men. She divined that.

She returned to her vantage-point, and as she glanced through she vibrated to a shock. The change that had begun subtly, intangibly, was now a terrible and glaring difference. That great quantity of gold, the equal chance of every gambler, the marvelous possibilities presented to evil minds, and the hell that hid in that black bottle—these had made playthings of every bandit except Gulden. He was exactly the same as ever. But to see the others sent a chill of ice along Joan's veins. Kells was white and rapt. Plain to see—he had won! Blicky was wild with rage. Jesse Smith sat darker, grimmer, but no longer cool. There was hate in the glance he fastened upon Kells as he bet. Beady Jones and Braverman showed an inflamed and impotent eagerness to take their turn. Budd sat in the game now, and his face wore a terrible look. Joan could not tell what passion drove him, but she knew he was a loser. Pike and Bossert likewise were losers, and stood apart, sullen, watching with sick, jealous rage. Jim Cleve had reacted to the strain, and he was white, with nervous, clutching hands and piercing glances. And the game went on with violent slap of card or pound of fist upon the table, with the slide of a bag of gold or the little, sodden thump of its weight, with savage curses at loss and strange, raw exultation at gain, with hurry and violence—more than all, with the wildness of the hour and the wildness of these men, drawing closer and closer to the dread climax that from the beginning had been foreshadowed.

Suddenly Budd rose and bent over the table, his cards clutched in a shaking hand, his face distorted and malignant, his eyes burning at Kells. Passionately he threw the cards down.

"There!" he yelled, hoarsely, and he stilled the noise.

"No good!" replied Kells, tauntingly. "Is there any other game you play?"

Budd bent low to see the cards in Kells's hand, and then, straightening his form, he gazed with haggard fury at the winner. "You've done me! . . . I'm cleaned—I'm busted!" he raved.

"You were easy. Get out of the game," replied Kells, with an exultant contempt. It was not the passion of play that now obsessed him, but the passion of success.

"I said you done me," burst out Budd, insanely. "You're slick with the cards!"

The accusation acted like magic to silence the bandits, to check movement, to clamp the situation. Kells was white and radiant; he seemed careless and nonchalant.

"All right, Budd," he replied, but his tone did not suit his strange look. "That's three times for you!"

Swift as a flash he shot. Budd fell over Gulden, and the giant with one sweep of his arm threw the stricken bandit off. Budd fell heavily, and neither moved nor spoke.

"Pass me the bottle," went on Kells, a little hoarse shakiness in his voice. "And go on with the game!"

"Can I set in now?" asked Beady Jones, eagerly.

"You and Jack wait. This's getting to be all between Kells an' me," said Gulden.

"We've sure got Blicky done!" exclaimed Kells. There was something taunting about the leader's words. He did not care for the gold. It was the fight to win. It was his egotism.

"Make this game faster an' bigger, will you?" retorted Blicky, who seemed inflamed.

"Boss, a little luck makes you lofty," interposed Jesse Smith in dark disdain. "Pretty soon you'll show yellow clear to your gizzard!"

The gold lay there on the table. It was only a means to an end. It signified nothing. The evil, the terrible greed, the brutal lust, were in the hearts of the men. And hate, liberated, rampant, stalked out unconcealed, ready for blood.

"Gulden, change the game to suit these gents," taunted Kells.

"Double stakes. Cut the cards!" boomed the giant, instantly.

Blicky lasted only a few more deals of the cards, then he rose, loser of all his share, a passionate and venomous bandit, ready for murder. But he kept his mouth shut and looked wary.

"Boss, can't we set in now?" demanded Beady Jones.

"Say, Beady, you're in a hurry to lose your gold," replied Kells. "Wait till I beat Gulden and Smith."

Luck turned against Jesse Smith. He lost first to Gulden, then to Kells, and presently he rose, a beaten, but game man. He reached for the whisky.

"Fellers, I reckon I can enjoy Kells's yellow streak more when I ain't playin'," he said.

The bandit leader eyed Smith with awakening rancor, as if a persistent hint of inevitable weakness had its effect. He frowned, and the radiance left his face for the forbidding cast.

"Stand around, you men, and see some real gambling," he said.

At this moment in the contest Kells had twice as much gold as Gulden, there being a huge mound of little buckskin sacks in front of him.

They began staking a bag at a time and cutting the cards,

the higher card winning. Kells won the first four cuts. How strangely that radiance returned to his face! Then he lost and won, and won and lost. The other bandits grouped around, only Jones and Braverman now manifesting any eagerness. All were silent. There were suspense, strain, mystery in the air. Gulden began to win consistently and Kells began to change. It was a sad and strange sight to see this strong man's nerve and force gradually deteriorate under a fickle fortune. The time came when half the amount he had collected was in front of Gulden. The giant was imperturbable. He might have been a huge animal, or destiny, or something inhuman that knew the run of luck would be his. As he had taken losses so he greeted gains—with absolute indifference. While Kells's hands shook the giant's were steady and slow and sure. It must have been hateful to Kells—this faculty of Gulden's to meet victory identically as he met defeat. The test of a great gambler's nerve was not in sustaining loss, but in remaining cool with victory. The fact grew manifest that Gulden was a great gambler and Kells was not. The giant had no emotion, no imagination. And Kells seemed all fire and whirling hope and despair and rage. His vanity began to bleed to death. This game was the deciding contest. The scornful and exultant looks of his men proved how that game was going. Again and again Kells's unsteady hand reached for one of the whisky bottles. Once with a low curse he threw an empty bottle through the door.

"Hey, boss, ain't it about time—" began Jesse Smith. But whatever he had intended to say, he thought better of, withholding it. Kells's sudden look and movement were unmistakable.

The goddess of chance, as false as the bandit's vanity, played with him. He brightened under a streak of winning. But just as his face began to lose its haggard shade, to glow, the tide again turned against him. He lost and lost, and with each bag of gold-dust went something of his spirit. And when he was reduced to his original share he indeed showed that yellow streak which Jesse Smith had attributed to him. The bandit's effort to pull himself together, to be a man before that scornful gang, was pitiful and futile. He might have been magnificent, confronted by other issues, of peril or circumstance, but there he was craven. He was a man who should never have gambled.

One after the other, in quick succession, he lost the two bags of gold, his original share. He had lost utterly. Gulden had the great heap of dirty little buckskin sacks, so significant of the hidden power within.

Joan was amazed and sick at sight of Kells then, and if it had been possible she would have withdrawn her gaze. But she was chained there. The catastrophe was imminent.

Kells stared down at the gold. His jaw worked convulsively. He had the eyes of a trapped wolf. Yet he seemed not wholly to comprehend what had happened to him.

Gulden rose, slow, heavy, ponderous, to tower over his heap of gold. Then this giant, who had never shown an emotion, suddenly, terribly blazed.

"One more bet—a cut of the cards—my whole stake of gold!" he boomed.

The bandits took a stride forward as one man, then stood breathless.

"One bet!" echoed Kells, aghast. "Against what?"

"Against the girl!"

Joan sank against the wall, a piercing torture in her breast. She clutched the logs to keep from falling. So that was the impending horror. She could not unrivet her eyes from the paralyzed Kells, yet she seemed to see Jim Cleve leap straight up, and then stand, equally motionless, with Kells.

"One cut of the cards—my gold against the girl!" boomed the giant.

Kells made a movement as if to go for his gun. But it failed. His hand was a shaking leaf.

"You always bragged on your nerve!" went on Gulden, mercilessly. "You're the gambler of the border! . . . Come on."

Kells stood there, his doom upon him. Plain to all was his torture, his weakness, his defeat. It seemed that with all his soul he combated something, only to fail.

"One cut—my gold against your girl!"

The gang burst into one concerted taunt. Like snarling, bristling wolves they craned their necks at Kells.

"No, damn—you! No!" cried Kells, in hoarse, broken fury. With both hands before him he seemed to push back the sight of that gold, of Gulden, of the malignant men, of a horrible temptation.

"Reckon, boss, thet yellow streak is operatin'!" sang out Jesse Smith.

But neither gold, nor Gulden, nor men, nor taunts ruined Kells at this perhaps most critical crisis of his life. It was the mad, clutching, terrible opportunity presented. It was the strange and terrible nature of the wager. What vision might have flitted through the gambler's mind! But neither vision of loss nor gain moved him. There, licking like a flame at his soul, consuming the good in him at a blast, overpowering his love, was the strange and magnificent gamble. He could not resist it.

Speechless, with a motion of his hand, he signified his willingness.

"Blicky, shuffle the cards," boomed Gulden.

Blicky did so and dropped the deck with a slap in the middle of the table.

"Cut!" called Gulden.

Kells's shaking hand crept toward the deck.

Jim Cleve suddenly appeared to regain power of speech and motion. "Don't, Kells, don't!" he cried, piercingly, as he leaped forward.

But neither Kells nor the others heard him, or even saw his movement.

Kells cut the deck. He held up his card. It was the king of hearts. What a transformation! His face might have been that of a corpse suddenly revivified with glorious, leaping life.

"Only an ace can beat thet!" muttered Jesse Smith into the silence.

Gulden reached for the deck as if he knew every card left was an ace. His cavernous eyes gloated over Kells. He cut, and before he looked himself he let Kells see the card.

"You can't beat my streak!" he boomed.

Then he threw the card upon the table. It was the ace of spades.

Kells seemed to shrivel, to totter, to sink. Jim Cleve went quickly to him, held to him.

"Kells, go say good-by to your girl!" boomed Gulden. "I'll want her pretty soon. . . . Come on, you Beady and Braverman. Here's your chance to get even."

Gulden resumed his seat, and the two bandits invited to play were eager to comply, while the others pressed close once more.

Jim Cleve led the dazed Kells toward the door into Joan's cabin. For Joan just then all seemed to be dark.

When she recovered she was lying on the bed and Jim was bending over her. He looked frantic with grief and desperation and fear.

"Jim! Jim!" she moaned, grasping his hands. He helped her to sit up. Then she saw Kells standing there. He looked abject, stupid, drunk. Yet evidently he had begun to comprehend the meaning of his deed.

"Kells," began Cleve, in low, hoarse tones, as he stepped forward with a gun. "I'm going to kill you—and Joan—and myself!"

Kells stared at Cleve. "Go ahead. Kill me. And kill the girl, too. That'll be better for her now. But why kill yourself?"

"I love her. She's my wife!"

The deadness about Kells suddenly changed. Joan flung herself before him.

"Kells—listen," she whispered in swift, broken passion. "Jim Cleve was—my sweetheart—back in Hoadley. We quarreled. I taunted him. I said he hadn't nerve enough— even to be bad. He left me—bitterly enraged. Next day I trailed him. I wanted to fetch him back. . . . You remember—how you met me with Roberts—how you killed Roberts? And all the rest? . . . When Jim and I met out here—I was afraid to tell you. I tried to influence him. I succeeded—till we got to Alder Creek. There he went wild. I married him—hoping to steady him. . . . Then the day of the lynching—we were separated from you in the crowd. That night we hid—and next morning took the stage. Gulden and his gang held up the stage. They thought you had put us there. We fooled them, but we had to come on—here to

Cabin Gulch—hoping to tell—that you'd let us go. . . . And now—now—"

Joan had not strength to go on. The thought of Gulden made her faint.

"It's true, Kells," added Cleve, passionately, as he faced the incredulous bandit. "I swear it. Why, you ought to see now!"

"My God, boy, I *do* see!" gasped Kells. That dark, sodden thickness of comprehension and feeling, indicative of the hold of drink, passed away swiftly. The shock had sobered him.

Instantly Joan saw it—saw in him the return of the other and better Kells, now stricken with remorse. She slipped to her knees and clasped her arms around him. He tried to break her hold, but she held on.

"Get up!" he ordered, violently. "Jim, pull her away! . . . Girl, don't do that in front of me . . . I've just gambled away—"

"Her life, Kells, only that, I swear," cried Cleve.

"Kells, listen," began Joan, pleadingly. "You will not let that—that *cannibal* have me?"

"No, by God!" replied Kells, thickly. "I was drunk—crazy. . . . Forgive me, girl! You see—how did I know—what was coming? . . . Oh, the whole thing is hellish!"

"You loved me once," whispered Joan, softly. "Do you love me still? . . . Kells, can't you see? It's not too late to save my life—and *your* soul! . . . Can't you see? You have been bad. But if you save me now—from Gulden—save me for this boy I've almost ruined—you—you. . . . God will forgive you! . . . Take us away—go with us—and never come back to the border."

"Maybe I can save you," he muttered, as if to himself. He appeared to want to think, but to be bothered by the clinging arms around him. Joan felt a ripple go over his body and he seemed to heighten, and the touch of his hands thrilled.

Then, white and appealing, Cleve added his importunity.

"Kells, I saved your life once. You said you'd remember it some day. Now—now! . . . For God's sake don't make me shoot her!"

Joan rose from her knees, but she still clasped Kells. She seemed to feel the mounting of his spirit, to understand how in this moment he was rising out of the depths. How strangely glad she was for him!

"Joan, once you showed me what the love of a good woman really was. I've never seen the same since then. I've grown better in one way—worse in all others. . . . I let down. I was no man for the border. Always that haunted me. Believe me, won't you—despite all?"

Joan felt the yearning in him for what he dared not ask. She read his mind. She knew he meant, somehow, to atone for his wrong.

"I'll show you again," she whispered. "I'll tell you more. If I'd never loved Jim Cleve—if I'd met you, I'd have loved *you*. . . . And, bandit or not, I'd have gone with you to the end of the world!"

"Joan!" The name was almost a sob of joy and pain. Sight of his face then blinded Joan with her tears. But when he caught her to him, in a violence that was a terrible renunciation, she gave her embrace, her arms, her lips without the vestige of a lie, with all of womanliness and sweetness and love and passion. He let her go and turned away, and in that instant Joan had a final divination that this strange man could rise once to heights as supreme as the depths of his soul were dark. She dashed away her tears and wiped the dimness from her eyes. Hope resurged. Something strong and sweet gave her strength.

When Kells wheeled he was the Kells of her earlier experience—cool, easy, deadly, with the smile almost amiable, and the strange, pale eyes. Only the white radiance of him was different. He did not look at her.

"Jim, will you do exactly what I tell you?"

"Yes, I promise," replied Jim.

"How many guns have you?"

"Two."

"Give me one of them."

Cleve held out the gun that all the while he had kept in his hand. Kells took it and put it in his pocket.

"Pull your other gun—be ready," said he, swiftly. "But

271

don't you shoot once till I go down! . . . Then do your best. . . . Save the last bullet for Joan—in case—"

"I promise," replied Cleve, steadily.

Then Kells drew a knife from a sheath at his belt. It had a long, bright blade. Joan had seen him use it many a time round the camp-fire. He slipped the blade up his sleeve, retaining the haft of the knife in his hand. He did not speak another word. Nor did he glance at Joan again. She had felt his gaze while she had embraced him, as she raised her lips. That look had been his last. Then he went out. Jim knelt beside the door, peering between post and curtain.

Joan staggered to the chink between the logs. She would see that fight if it froze her blood—the very marrow of her bones.

The gamblers were intent upon their game. Not a dark face looked up as Kells sauntered toward the table. Gulden sat with his back to the door. There was a shaft of sunlight streaming in, and Kells blocked it, sending a shadow over the bent heads of the gamesters. How significant that shadow—a blackness barring gold! Still no one paid any attention to Kells.

He stepped closer. Suddenly he leaped into swift and terrible violence. Then with a lunge he drove the knife into Gulden's burly neck.

Up heaved the giant, his mighty force overturning table and benches and men. An awful boom, strangely distorted and split, burst from him.

Then Kells blocked the door with a gun in each hand, but only the one in his right hand spurted white and red. Instantly there followed a mad scramble—hoarse yells, over which that awful roar of Gulden's predominated—and the bang of guns. Clouds of white smoke veiled the scene, and with every shot the veil grew denser. Red flashes burst from the ground where men were down, and from each side of Kells. His form seemed less instinct with force; it had shortened; he was sagging. But at intervals the red spurt and report of his gun showed he was fighting. Then a volley from one side made him stagger against the door. The clear spang of a Winchester spoke above the heavy boom of the guns.

Joan's eyesight recovered from its blur or else the haze of

smoke drifted, for she saw better. Gulden's actions fascinated her, horrified her. He had evidently gone crazy. He groped about the room, through the smoke, to and fro before the fighting, yelling bandits, grasping with huge hands for something. His sense of direction, his equilibrium, had become affected. His awful roar still sounded above the din, but it was weakening. His giant's strength was weakening. His legs bent and buckled under him. All at once he whipped out his two big guns and began to fire as he staggered—at random. He killed the wounded Blicky. In the mêlée he ran against Jesse Smith and thrust both guns at him. Jesse saw the peril and with a shriek he fired pointblank at Gulden. Then as Gulden pulled triggers both men fell. But Gulden rose, bloody-browed, bawling, still a terrible engine of destruction. He seemed to glare in one direction and shoot in another. He pointed the guns and apparently pulled the triggers long after the shots had all been fired.

Kells was on his knees now with only one gun. This wavered and fell, wavered and fell. His left arm hung broken. But his face flashed white through the thin, drifting clouds of smoke.

Besides Gulden the bandit Pike was the only one not down, and he was hard hit. When he shot his last he threw the gun away, and, drawing a knife, he made at Kells. Kells shot once more, and hit Pike, but did not stop him. Silence, after the shots and yells, seemed weird, and the groping giant, trying to follow Pike, resembled a huge phantom. With one wrench he tore off a leg of the overturned table and brandished that. He swayed now, and there was a whistle where before there had been a roar.

Pike fell over the body of Blicky and got up again. The bandit leader staggered to his feet, flung the useless gun in Pike's face, and closed with him in weak but final combat. They lurched and careened to and fro, with the giant Gulden swaying after them. Thus they struggled until Pike moved under Gulden's swinging club. The impetus of the blow carried Gulden off his balance. Kells seized the haft of the knife still protruding from the giant's neck, and he pulled upon it with all his might. Gulden heaved up again, and the move-

273

ment enabled Kells to pull out the knife. A bursting gush of blood, thick and heavy, went flooding before the giant as he fell.

Kells dropped the knife, and, tottering, surveyed the scene before him—the gasping Gulden, and all the quiet forms. Then he made a few halting steps, and dropped near the door.

Joan tried to rush out, but what with the unsteadiness of her limbs and Jim holding her as he went out, too, she seemed long in getting to Kells.

She knelt beside him, lifted his head. His face was white—his eyes were open. But they were only the windows of a retreating soul. He did not know her. Consciousness was gone. Then swiftly life fled.

20

◈

CLEVE steadied Joan in her saddle, and stood a moment beside her, holding her hands. The darkness seemed clearing before her eyes and the sick pain within her seemed numbing out.

"Brace up! Hang to your saddle!" Jim was saying, earnestly. "Any moment some of the other bandits might come. . . . You lead the way. I'll follow and drive the pack-horse."

"But, Jim, I'll never be able to find the back-trail," said Joan.

"I think you will. You'll remember every yard of the trail on which you were brought in here. You won't realize that till you see."

Joan started and did not look back. Cabin Gulch was like a place in a dream. It was a relief when she rode out into the broad valley. The grazing horses lifted their heads to whistle. Joan saw the clumps of bushes and the flowers, the waving grass, but never as she had seen them before. How strange that she knew exactly which way to turn, to head, to cross! She trotted her horse so fast that Jim called to say he could not drive a pack-animal and keep to her gait. Every rod of the trail lessened a burden. Behind was something hideous and incomprehensible and terrible; before beckoned something beginning to seem bright. And it was not the ruddy, calm sunset, flooding the hills with color. That something called from beyond the hills.

She led straight to a camp-site she remembered long before she came to it; and the charred logs of the fire, the rocks, the tree under which she had lain—all brought back the emotions she had felt there. She grew afraid of the twilight, and when night settled down there were phantoms stalking in the shadows. When Cleve, in his hurried camp duties, went out of her sight, she wanted to cry out to him, but had not the voice; and when he was close still she trembled and was cold. He wrapped blankets round her and held her in his arms, yet the numb chill and the dark clamp of mind remained with her. Long she lay awake. The stars were pitiless. When she shut her eyes the blackness seemed unendurable. She slept, to wake out of nightmare, and she dared sleep no more. At last the day came.

For Joan that faint trail seemed a broad road, blazoned through the wild cañons and up the rocky fastness and through the thick brakes. She led on and on and up and down, never at fault, with familiar landmarks near and far. Cleve hung close to her, and now his call to her or to the pack-horse took on a keener note. Every rough and wild mile behind them meant so much. They did not halt at the noon hour. They did not halt at the next camp-site, still more darkly memorable to Joan. And sunset found them miles farther on, down on the divide, at the head of Lost Cañon.

Here Joan ate and drank, and slept the deep sleep of exhaustion. Sunrise found them moving, and through the winding, wild cañon they made fast travel. Both time and miles passed swiftly. At noon they reached the little open cabin, and they dismounted for a rest and a drink at the spring. Joan did not speak a word here. That she could look into the cabin where she had almost killed a bandit, and then, through silent, lonely weeks, had nursed him back to life, was a proof that the long ride and distance were helping her, sloughing away the dark deadlock to hope and brightness. They left the place exactly as they had found it, except that Cleve plucked the card from the bark of the balsam-tree—Gulden's ace-of-hearts target with its bullet-holes.

Then they rode on, out of that cañon, over the rocky ridge, down into another cañon, on and on, past an old camp-site, along a babbling brook for miles, and so at last out into the foot-hills.

Toward noon of the next day, when approaching a clump of low trees in a flat valley, Joan pointed ahead.

"Jim—it was in there—where Roberts and I camped—and—"

"You ride around. I'll catch up with you," replied Cleve.

She made a wide détour, to come back again to her own trail, so different here. Presently Cleve joined her. His face was pale and sweaty, and he looked sick. They rode on silently, and that night they camped without water on her own trail, made months before. The single tracks were there, sharp and clear in the earth, as if imprinted but a day.

Next morning Joan found that as the wild border lay behind her so did the dark and hateful shadow of gloom. Only the pain remained, and it had softened. She could think now.

Jim Cleve cheered up. Perhaps it was her brightening to which he responded. They began to talk and speech liberated feeling. Miles of that back-trail they rode side by side, holding hands, driving the pack-horse ahead, and beginning to talk of old associations. Again it was sunset when they rode down the hill toward the little village of Hoadley. Joan's heart was full, but Jim was gay.

"Won't I have it on your old fellows!" he teased. But he was grim, too.

"Jim! You—won't tell—just yet!" she faltered.

"I'll introduce you as my wife! They'll all think we eloped."

"No. They'll say I ran after you! . . . Please, Jim! Keep it secret a little. It'll be hard for me. Aunt Jane will never understand."

"Well, I'll keep it secret till you want to tell—for two things," he said.

"What?"

"Meet me to-night, under the spruces where we had that quarrel. Meet just like we did then, but differently. Will you?"

"I'll be—so glad."

"And put on your mask now! . . . You know, Joan, sooner or later your story will be on everybody's tongue. You'll be Dandy Dale as long as you live near this border. Wear the mask, just for fun. Imagine your Aunt Jane—and everybody!"

"Jim! I'd forgotten how I look!" exclaimed Joan in dismay. "I didn't bring your long coat. Oh, I can't face them in this suit!"

"You'll have to. Besides, you look great. It's going to tickle me—the sensation you make. Don't you see, they'll never recognize you till you take the mask off. . . . Please, Joan."

She yielded, and donned the black mask, not without a twinge. And thus they rode across the log bridge over the creek into the village. The few men and women they met stared in wonder, and, recognizing Cleve, they grew excited. They followed, and others joined them.

"Joan, won't it be strange if Uncle Bill really is the Overland of Alder Creek? We've packed out every pound of Overland's gold. Oh! I hope—I believe he's your uncle. . . . Wouldn't it be great, Joan?"

But Joan could not answer. The word gold was a stab.

278

Besides, she saw Aunt Jane and two neighbors standing before a log cabin, beginning to show signs of interest in the approaching procession.

Joan fell back a little, trying to screen herself behind Jim. Then Jim halted with a cheery salute.

"For the land's sake!" ejaculated a sweet-faced, gray-haired woman.

"If it isn't Jim Cleve!" cried another.

Jim jumped off and hugged the first speaker. She seemed overjoyed to see him and then overcome. Her face began to work.

"Jim! We always hoped you'd—you'd fetch Joan back!"

"Sure!" shouted Jim, who had no heart now for even an instant's deception. "There she is!"

"Who? . . . What?"

Joan slipped out of her saddle and, tearing off the mask, she leaped forward with a little sob.

"Auntie! Auntie! . . . It's Joan—alive—well! . . . Oh, so glad to be home! . . . Don't look at my clothes—look at me!"

Aunt Jane evidently sustained a shock of recognition, joy, amaze, consternation, and shame, of which all were subservient to the joy. She cried over Joan and murmured over her. Then, suddenly alive to the curious crowd, she put Joan from her.

"You—you wild thing! You desperado! I always told Bill you'd run wild some day! . . . March in the house and get out of that indecent rig!"

That night under the spruces, with the starlight piercing the lacy shadows, Joan waited for Jim Cleve. It was one of the white, silent, mountain nights. The brook murmured over the stones and the wind rustled the branches.

The wonder of Joan's home-coming was in learning that Uncle Bill Hoadley was indeed Overland, the discoverer of Alder Creek. Years and years of profitless toil had at last been rewarded in this rich gold strike.

Joan hated to think of gold. She had wanted to leave the gold back in Cabin Gulch, and she would have done so had Jim permitted it. And to think that all that gold which was not Jim Cleve's belonged to her uncle! She could not believe it.

Fatal and terrible forever to Joan would be the significance of gold. Did any woman in the world or any man know the meaning of gold as well as she knew it? How strange and enlightening and terrible had been her experience! She had grown now not to blame any man, honest miner or bloody bandit. She blamed only gold. She doubted its value. She could not see it a blessing. She absolutely knew its driving power to change the souls of men. Could she ever forget that vast ant-hill of toiling diggers and washers, blind and deaf and dumb to all save gold?

Always limned in figures of fire against the black memory would be the forms of those wild and violent bandits! Gulden, the monster, the gorilla, the cannibal! Horrible as was the memory of him, there was no horror in thought of his terrible death. That seemed to be the one memory that did not hurt.

But Kells was indestructible—he lived in her mind. Safe out of the border now and at home, she could look back clearly. Still all was not clear and never would be. She saw Kells the ruthless bandit, the organizer, the planner, and the blood-spiller. He ought have no place in a good woman's memory. Yet he had. She never condoned one of his deeds or even his intentions. She knew her intelligence was not broad enough to grasp the vastness of his guilt. She believed he must have been the worst and most terrible character on that wild border. That border had developed him. It had produced the time and the place and the man. And therein lay the mystery. For over against this bandit's weakness and evil she could contrast strength and nobility. She alone had known the real man in all the strange phases of his nature, and the darkness of his crime faded out of her mind. She suffered remorse—almost regret. Yet what could she have done? There had been no help for that impossible situation as, there was now no help for her in a right and just placing of Kells among men. He had stolen her—wantonly murdering for the sake of lonely, fruitless hours with her; he had loved her—and he had changed; he had gambled away her soul and life—a last and terrible proof of the evil power of gold; and in the end he had saved her—he had gone from her white, radiant, cool, with strange, pale eyes and his amiable, mocking smile, and all the ruthless force of his life had expended itself in one last magnificent stand. If only he had known her at the end—when she lifted his head! But no—there had been only the fading light—the strange, weird look of a retreating soul, already alone forever.

A rustling of leaves, a step thrilled Joan out of her meditation.

Suddenly she was seized from behind, and Jim Cleve showed that though he might be a joyous and grateful lover, he certainly would never be an actor. For if he desired to live over again that fatal meeting and quarrel which had sent them out to the border, he failed utterly in his part. There was possession in the gentle grasp of his arms and bliss in the trembling of his lips.

"Jim, you never did it that way!" laughed Joan. "If you had—do you think I could ever have been furious?"

Jim in turn laughed happily. "Joan, that's exactly the way I stole upon you and mauled you!"

"You think so! Well, I happen to remember. Now you sit here and make believe you are Joan. And let *me* be Jim Cleve! . . . I'll show you!"

Joan stole away in the darkness, and noiselessly as a shadow she stole back—to enact that violent scene as it lived in her memory.

Jim was breathless, speechless, choked.

"That's how you treated me," she said.

"I—I don't believe I could have—been such a—a bear!" panted Jim.

"But you were. And consider—I've not half your strength."

"Then all I say is—you did right to drive me off. . . . Only you should never have trailed me out to the border."

"Ah! . . . But, Jim, in my fury I discovered my love!"

LOOK FOR THESE GREAT
POCKET 🦘 BOOK BESTSELLERS
AT YOUR FAVORITE BOOKSTORE

THE TOTAL WOMAN • Marabel Morgan
THE BOTTOM LINE • Fletcher Knebel
THE PIRATE • Harold Robbins
YOU CAN SAY THAT AGAIN, SAM! • Sam Levenson
THE BEST • Peter Passell & Leonard Ross
CROCKERY COOKING • Paula Franklin
SHARP PRACTICE • John Farris
JUDY GARLAND • Anne Edwards
SPY STORY • Len Deighton
HARLEQUIN • Morris West
THE SILVER BEARS • Paul E. Erdman
MURDER ON THE ORIENT EXPRESS • Agatha Christie
THE JOY OF SEX • Alex Comfort
RETURN JOURNEY • R. F. Delderfield
THE TEACHINGS OF DON JUAN • Carlos Castaneda
JOURNEY TO IXTLAN • Carlos Castaneda
A SEPARATE REALITY • Carlos Castaneda
BABY AND CHILD CARE • Dr. Benjamin Spock
BODY LANGUAGE • Julius Fast
THE MERRIAM-WEBSTER DICTIONARY (Newly Revised)